DELIVER ME

ALSO BY MALIN PERSSON GIOLITO

Quicksand

Beyond All Reasonable Doubt

DELIVER ME

MALIN PERSSON GIOLITO

Translated from the Swedish by
Rachel Willson-Broyles

SIMON &
SCHUSTER

London · New York · Sydney · Toronto · New Delhi

Originally published in Sweden as *I dina händer*
by Wahlström & Widstrand, 2022
Published by agreement with Paloma Agency

First published in the United States by Other Press LLC, 2024

First published in Great Britain by Simon & Schuster UK Ltd, 2024

The cost of this translation was supported by a subsidy
from the Swedish Arts Council, gratefully acknowledged.

1 3 5 7 9 10 8 6 4 2

Simon & Schuster UK Ltd
1st Floor
222 Gray's Inn Road
London WC1X 8HB

Simon & Schuster: Celebrating 100 Years of Publishing in 2024

Simon & Schuster Australia, Sydney
Simon & Schuster India, New Delhi

www.simonandschuster.co.uk
www.simonandschuster.com.au
www.simonandschuster.co.in

A CIP catalogue record for this book
is available from the British Library

Hardback ISBN: 978-1-4711-6036-3
Trade Paperback ISBN: 978-1-4711-6037-0
eBook ISBN: 978-1-4711-6038-7
Audio ISBN: 978-1-3985-2885-7

Printed and Bound in the UK using 100% Renewable
Electricity at CPI Group (UK) Ltd

For Dad

My times are in your hands; deliver me

—Psalms 31:15

THE BOYS

They're playing on a hill, wearing nearly identical jeans and short-sleeved shirts, their shoes well worn and their eyes bright. One has blond hair down to his shoulders; the other, dark curls that constantly fall into his eyes. They'll be starting school this autumn, but their legs are chubby and they run so fast down the hill that their feet can't keep up with them. First one child falls, then the other. Maybe he falls on purpose, he always wants to copy his brave friend, climb just as high, jump just as far, run just as fast. They don't cry, not even the one who often bursts into tears at the slightest thing. There are no grown-ups nearby, no one to instruct them to check if they're hurt. Instead, they sit there for a moment, facing each other, breathless, warm, full of laughter. As if on command they get up and keep running. Bruises and scabs won't be discovered until hours later; right now there is too much to do.

The long-haired boy's house is in one direction, while the other boy lives on the other side of the highway with his large family. The sun lingers close by, in a warm clearing. Beyond the hill are magical mounds of rock, desolate buildings, and endless adventures.

The world awaits them both.

THURSDAY 6 DECEMBER

1

The shots were fired, two in quick succession and then another two, at 10:55 p.m. on Thursday 6 December. The first snow of winter had just begun to fall, tentatively at first, but soon the ground was blanketed in white.

Even at this time of night, there was background noise from the eight-lane interchange. Its hum grew quieter for a few hours each night, but it was never fully silent.

On one side of the highway, everything was brown and concrete grey. There you would find the high-rises of Våringe, the skate park, the square, and the eighteenth-century church that had once been the pride of the neighbourhood. The floodlights around the large sports pitches were dark, the alarms on the school armed. Balcony doors were closed, curtains drawn.

On the other side, a tract of green space shielded the residential neighbourhood of Rönnviken from the roar of traffic. In Rönnviken there were four pre-schools, a wooded area with a well-lit jogging track, a grade school, and a private high school with a special programme in international economics. There was also a golf course: eighteen holes with four water hazards; there was a waiting list to become a member. Adjoining the golf course was a playground. Just a mile or so away, on the slope down to the Baltic Sea, were lemon-yellow, turn-of-the-century villas with ocean views. The sea was velvety black, but Advent stars glowed softly through the many mullioned windows.

Under the highway, between Rönnviken and Våringe, ran a poorly lit pedestrian tunnel, built to make it possible to walk from one side to the other. *It's easy to die in Våringe*, said some sloppy graffiti on the wall of the tunnel. Someone had made a half-hearted attempt to clean up the spray paint, but the text was filled back in. *Easy to die, but fucking hard to live*, it said, alongside the original graffiti. The second graffitist had taken their time, filled in all the lines in tidy letters, and painted a speech bubble around the quote, not with spray paint but with what appeared to be a paintbrush and regular paint. A third someone had added a fat, bright-green arrow: *Move to Rönnviken, quit whining!*

Gunfire had become common in a number of Stockholm suburbs, but this was the first time it had occurred in Rönnviken. No one reacted to the sound, not even the teenager who had been forced to take the family dog out for a pee and was no more than a hundred yards away from the playground, and not far from the seventh hole on the golf course.

The shots rang out and faded. A couple of fistfuls of gravel thrown into perfectly still water. And for a minute, or maybe two, it was as though time held its breath.

The silence was broken by a boy running out of Rönnviken in slippery gym shoes. He dashed out of the playground, across the small road, and down to the pedestrian tunnel. There he passed the graffiti, came out on the other side, and passed the lower section of the Våringe playground. It looked like he might be on his way to the square. But all the shops there were closed, even the grocery store that used to be open nights, seven days a week.

A stone's throw from the place where the boy stopped, a man got out of his car and tried to open the door to the private parking ramp at Våringe city centre. There was a light breeze, almost mild, but the air was the sort of cold that made joints creak and pipes explode. The garage door seemed to be frozen shut; the remote wasn't working.

While the driver stood in the falling snow, shaking the remote in annoyance, the boy took a phone from his pocket. Two of the nine streetlights he passed after emerging from the tunnel were working. One of them spread a faint glow over him. Besides his flimsy shoes, the boy was wearing jeans that were frozen stiff, a half-buttoned jacket, and a hood pulled hastily over his head. He was out of breath, his whole body was shaking, and he had trouble making the phone do what he wanted. At last he brought the phone to his ear and began to speak into it. As he spoke, he stamped his feet, making a dark patch in the fresh snow. Now and again he turned around, but there still wasn't anyone there. His voice drifted off on the wind. As he ended the call and wiped the phone against the leg of his pants, he looked around once more. He didn't notice the man by the garage. He started walking toward a bus stop about thirty yards on.

Just a minute or so later, a bus arrived. Right before the boy boarded it, he tossed the contents of his pockets into the trash can next to the bench. As the bus left the stop, the man finally got the garage door open, drove in, and closed it behind him.

The phone the boy had just used was still on, a faint glow filtered up through the trash. Thirty seconds passed before the screen went dark.

2

'Förshla-vägen... Sösh... shit, fuck... I don't know, I... I think it's called... I don't know what this street is called, it's that place where... you have to come.'

The caller was sobbing hysterically. It was a few seconds before he could speak again.

'Sösh... föshl... fuck it, hurry... he's dying.'

'I can't tell what you're saying.'

Salwa was an emergency dispatcher and was sitting at her screen at SOS Alarm communications centre, the unit closest to the cell tower this emergency call originated from. It was eight minutes past eleven, and while the centre had endured high call volumes earlier in the evening, things had just begun to settle down. About an hour ago, Stockholm's home team, AIK, had lost an important hockey game against one of the series leaders, which meant a rowdy night. A bus carrying fans from the opposing team had been

7

vandalized, there had been big brawls at two nearby sports bars and at the subway station by the arena.

'You have to speak more clearly.'

It's chaos here,' she had texted her husband. 'Lots of calls, we'll talk when I get home.' Salwa's husband was more anxious than usual, hadn't wanted her to go to work.

'What could happen to me there?' she had asked. 'I'd take a cable to the head?'

In theory, working at the comms centre was nothing but phones and buttons, speakers, maps and screens. In theory, she was far from the smells, bodily fluids and violence. Still, it was the same story each time she answered an emergency call and heard the panicked voices. There was no way to protect herself. The stink of beer-guzzling drunks, hand-rolled cigarettes and week-old sweat, run-down stairwells, filthy kitchens, bedrooms where the sheets were never changed, children who hid but could never escape – all these images popped up in her head, so fast and so clear. Her husband was well aware; he was the one who lay awake beside her at night.

He's dying.'

It was increasingly hard to hear the caller. The rest of his sentence faded away. Salwa took a deep breath and made her voice steady. It sounded muffled, as if the caller was holding his hand over the speaker. Sometimes people did that when they didn't want anyone to recognize their voice.

'Where are you?'

He was breathing hard. Salwa wanted to let him catch his breath, but he kept talking.

'He's going to die if you don't come. He's dying, do you hear me? He's dying.'

'Take it easy, okay? I'm going to help you. Where are you?'

'Förshle…Föshle…'

She still didn't understand what he was trying to say. From her seat in the call centre, Salwa could see snow falling. It didn't look windy, but it sounded like the caller was outdoors.

'Where is he bleeding from?'

Her calm attitude seemed to help, the caller stopped gasping into the phone. His bright voice was easier to make out. And the crying, it was plain to hear he was still crying. Then she realized. The caller was a child.

'I don't know where…from the head, it's, he's, it's his head. He's been shot and he's dying, you have to come. I…he…he was shot in the head.'

Salwa glanced at her colleague one desk over. He looked back at her and raised his eyebrows. This was no false alarm. She nodded at him to join in the call.

'Listen to me,' she said. 'Just take it easy. We're going to help you. But it's important that you remain calm. Do you hear me? Can you tell me where you are?'

'I'm...' He was crying harder again, but his voice was clearer now. 'He's up at the playground by Rönnviken golf course, I don't know what the street is called, there's a daycare there. Förskolevägen, maybe? He's by the swings near the path, near Vårstigen. He was sitting on the swing, and then – now he's on the ground.'

Salwa's colleague had patched the police into the call. The caller couldn't hear it, but he was bringing them up to speed on what little information they had. The police's regional command centre was in the same building, just two floors down. Salwa had tried to explain to her husband the machinations that were set in motion each time she received a call that put everyone on high alert.

'It's like an anthill. Prosecutors, investigators, teams to be assembled, centres contacted. I'm only speaking to one person, but in the meantime all these cogs begin to turn, one by one, without my doing a thing.'

He had teased her about it.

'Are you part of an anthill or a cog in a clockwork? Because there aren't any cogs in anthills, are there? But, most importantly, are they aware that you're the queen?'

Salwa was very familiar with the Rönnviken playground. It was no more than a mile from the apartment building where she lived with her husband and their two-year-old daughter. She had been there

many times. Salwa cleared her throat; it was important to establish rapport with the caller.

'Listen. I need your help right now. Is the patient
breath—'

'What the fuck, shut the fuck up, how should I
know, you have to go there, you fucking—' He was
shouting again.

'Have you left him? Do you think you could tell
me what happened?'

'None of your fucking business. None of your
fucking...shut up.'

The hysteria was back. Even if the boy was still
on the scene, he couldn't give CPR, not in this state.
Salwa spoke as gently as she could.

'We're going to help you and your friend. Is he
your friend?'

'What? What the fuck did you say? None of
your fucking business. I'm not there. He's lying
there, that's all I'm gonna say. Are you coming, or
what?'

'Do you think you can go back to your friend and
check to see if he's breathing? The ambulance is on
its way, I promise, but I could use your help in the
meantime. Do you think you can—'

The boy hung up. The call ended.

Salwa took a breath, drawing it in as deep as she
could. She closed her eyes, counted silently to four,
and placed her hand on her belly. In one ear she
could hear the comms centre issuing orders. She kept
counting. *Five. Six. Seven. Eight.*

Her belly was growing faster this time. She was wearing her husband's jeans, and when she sat down, she unbuttoned them under her shirt. But if she didn't lean back, her belly pressed against the underwire of her bra. She wished she could go to work in pyjamas. *Nine. Ten.*

She massaged her sternum with one hand to ease the pressure a bit. With the other, she typed on the keyboard to find the number that had called her. It was hidden.

Calls from Rönnviken were out of the ordinary, and when they did come in they were mostly about heart attacks, teenagers on bad trips or with alcohol poisoning, or panic attacks masquerading as heart attacks. She couldn't remember ever getting a call about a gunshot wound from there.

If a kid from Rönnviken has been shot, she thought, *the prime minister will probably show up to light candles and give a speech.*

'On scene at Lilla Gränsgärdet. The ambulance will be here in a minute.'

Salwa listened to the comms centre until they told her she could leave the call. When her headset went silent, she pulled it off her head and placed it on the control panel before her. Her colleague bent toward her and placed a hand on her arm.

'Go have a cup of tea.'

Salwa closed her eyes and nodded with gratitude. She could go to the toilet and take off her bra. Maybe that would make it easier to breathe.

There was half a pot of cold coffee in the staff kitchen. She filled the kettle, then poured the water back out to get rid of the rings of lime build-up, but she didn't have the energy to scrub it out. She took out her mug, put a teabag in it, and leaned against the counter while she waited for the water to boil. On the table were the remains of a marzipan cake; must have been someone's birthday. She swallowed down a wave of nausea.

When the water was ready, Salwa filled her mug. She stood there blowing on it, but didn't take a sip.

Her colleague stepped into the kitchen. There was a grave look on his face.

'They found him face down by the swings.'

Shot while he was swinging?

'How old?'

'In his early teens.'

'Dead?'

'No info on that.'

Her colleague rested his hand on her arm again. He looked sad, as though she needed sympathy.

'It must feel terrible,' he said. 'Just terrible.'

Salwa nodded.

It didn't even happen in Våringe, she wanted to say. *So why would it be any worse for me than for you?*

'Yeah,' she said instead. 'It is terrible.'

THE BOYS

They got to know each other at the playground in Rönnviken, where there were charming swings in every colour of the rainbow, climbing walls and sandboxes, one with silky-white sand you couldn't use for sandcastles. There were playhouses too, a whole row of them, tons of tricycles to borrow, jungle gyms with ropes to hang from and thick steel cables to use as tightropes.

In the daytime, the parking lot behind the tall gates of the golf course was full of shiny cars. Unnaturally perfect lawns spread out in all directions. Thin women with round breasts took walks two by two along the pedestrian paths, with fitness trackers on their wrists and fluffy dogs on leather leashes.

Leila, the mother of one of the boys, came to the playground as often as she could, even though it wasn't in the city where she lived. It took a long time to get there by bus; there was a transfer. Instead she would walk there, coming through the pedestrian tunnel and up the hill along with her friends and their kids, pushchairs loaded with juice and cookies, maybe some grilled chicken and extra wet wipes if it was Sunday. It was like an amusement park, but free.

The other boy lived just a few hundred yards from the park, and his parents, Jill and Teo, frequently let him go there alone even though he was only six years old. They would come get him if he stayed too long, but they would only stand by the edge of the sandbox and call out to him to leave right away. They seldom came down to say hello to the other parents; their friends never took their kids there.

The first time the boys met, one was sitting on a swing and refused to get off when the other thought it was about time for him to have a turn. But instead of arguing, the taller boy stood up on the swing and let the shorter one sit in front of him. They worked together to get moving, and they swung higher than everyone else. This wasn't like either of them; they were both the kind of kid that was prone to fighting.

When they met again a few days later, they played like best friends. After that, they started pestering their parents to visit the Rönnviken playground. It was the last thing they said before they fell asleep, and the first thing when they woke up again.

'You should be really nice to that boy,' Leila joked. 'That way we can visit his house and eat caviar on golden toast, and whatever else millionaires eat.'

Jill and Teo said nothing about their son's new friend. The first time the two mothers met, Leila got the impression that Jill didn't even know their kids knew each other. But when Teo suddenly showed up at the sandbox a few days later, he was the one who came up to Leila and asked for her phone number. He talked fast, and at length, had very white teeth and deep-blue eyes. He was like a salesman, Leila thought. Or someone who wanted to buy something. Friends for his son, maybe.

3

Twenty-nine minutes before Thursday became Friday, the screen of Detective Inspector Farid Ayad's phone lit up. Just a few hours earlier, he had been trying to comfort his daughter Natascha, who was having trouble sleeping.

'Think of your favourite dreams,' he had whispered, kissing her on the forehead, inhaling the scent of his thirteen-year-old. 'Think of those when you're falling asleep, and they will come true.'

He often said this; he wanted his three daughters to feel that for them, anything was possible. On good days, he could almost believe it was true. When he stood on his very own 6,600-square-foot lot, lighting the grill on an early summer day, or when he came home from work and found all three kids lying on the sofa in the living room, each on her own phone and with the TV on too, he was warmed by something that resembled pride.

But once Natascha fell asleep and it was his turn to lie there restless, listening to his wife's gentle snores, it wasn't dreams of a bright future that occupied his mind. It was work. He should change jobs, make a career of something else, get out of Våringe. He had moved away from Våringe over five years ago; it was high time to stop working there too.

Each month, fresh offers came his way.

'You can't stick with the same job all your life. If you want to become chief inspector and lead your own investigations, you need experience beyond Våringe. Don't you want to be done with those kids someday? Come work with us at the National Operations Department, come work with us in violent crimes, come work with us in Umeå, Sundsvall, Nyköping, Laholm.'

These offers always prompted the same thoughts. And once he'd fended those thoughts off, the nightmares arrived, as though they had been lurking just around the corner, and wouldn't be satisfied with merely popping up in his sleep.

The phone was on vibrate and buzzed rhythmically and persistently. Farid's wife Nadja sighed and pulled a pillow over her head.

'Text me,' she mumbled, 'when you know if I can count on you tomorrow.'

It wasn't a payday weekend. The hockey derby had taken place far enough away that it should have

been another department's problem. All signs had indicated it would be a calm night in Våringe. But this
call was coming from a former colleague. These days
he worked for the violent crimes unit, as director of
the task force.

'What the hell does he want?' Farid muttered.
The director would hardly be calling at this hour to
offer him a new job.

He swiped the phone from the nightstand, put in
his earbuds, and went into the bathroom.

'Gunnar,' he said, closing the door behind him.
'Are you having trouble sleeping? Do you want me to
sing you a lullaby?'

His colleague ignored him.

'A call came in from Rönnviken, just the other
side of the pedestrian tunnel between there and
Våringe. A shooting, just a few minutes ago. Seems
to be a minor. Sorry if I woke you up, but can you
head over there? It might be some depressed teenager from Rönnviken who offed himself with daddy's hunting rifle, but that's not what it seemed like
from the call, and if it's one of yours, from Våringe,
I want to know it ASAP, I'm tired of always being
two steps behind.'

'Of course.'

Farid picked up his jeans from the bathroom floor.
He pulled them on as Gunnar explained where to go.
He held off on zipping his fly until he had peed and
rinsed his hands.

'Call me as soon as you find out whether it's someone you know. Hurry up now. They're still there.'

Farid was in the garage before they'd hung up.

When he pulled onto the street, he turned the wind-
shield wipers on high and the heat up to max.
It was snowing – hard, fast. He stuck his removable
blue light on the roof and sped to Rönnviken. It took
him under ten minutes to get there. He parked beside
one of the two ambulances on the scene. Two patrol
cars were nearby. Only once he'd stepped out of the
car did he realize he'd left his coat at home. He cursed
under his breath.

The paramedics were lifting the stretcher into the
ambulance.

'Can I have a look at the victim?' he tried. 'I might
know who it is.'

They ignored him and closed the doors, but he
had already seen all he needed to see.

A couple of curious onlookers had gathered, an older
woman in an ankle-length mink fur and two dog
owners with round puffer jackets and pointy hats. A
colleague from the Våringe police was standing a few
yards off; he raised a hand in greeting and started toward Farid. So far, Farid wasn't feeling the cold; the
adrenaline was keeping him warm.

He stood there as the ambulance drove off. A few seconds passed before they turned on the siren. He'd seen the body and the clothing, both what the victim was still wearing and what the paramedics had cut off him. He really hadn't needed more than a glimpse for his suspicions to be confirmed.

His colleague from Våringe placed a hand on his shoulder. Farid jumped. Rage hit him in the gut with such strength that it knocked the wind out of him. He didn't shout. He didn't start to cry. But his knees wanted to give way. He forced himself to stay put until he could no longer see the flashing blue lights. Then he took his phone from his pocket and texted his wife.

'You'll have to take Ella to school. They need me here.'

4

'Leila?' asked the policewoman when the door opened into an apartment a block away from Våringe city centre. It was quarter to one in the morning; Leila had been awakened by the doorbell. The policewoman acted like they knew each other already, like they were on a first-name basis. But Leila didn't have the energy to make a fuss, not there, not then, not in the middle of the night, when her neighbours might wake up, so she nodded.

'We have to go to Karolinska,' the officer said. She said something after that too, but Leila didn't understand, it had something to do with the Rönnviken playground.

She knew Karolinska was a hospital. It really sounded like a name for a restaurant, but she didn't say so. It was a bad idea to try to joke with the police, or to say anything that wasn't necessary. Not even with officers who tilted their heads kindly like this one did.

The policewoman was talking about Billy.

'Billy is sleeping,' Leila explained, as clearly as she could. All four of her kids were home. It was a small apartment, and she had tucked him in herself, kissed him goodnight, even though he pretended to think such things were dorky.

But the policewoman didn't seem to understand what Leila was saying.

'We have to go to Karolinska,' she repeated. Her shiny, bleached hair was pulled back in a thin ponytail, her uniform was snug. Her dark roots made it look like she was wearing a black headband. As she spoke, she strode into the apartment, planting her feet wide apart, without taking off her shoes and without Leila having invited her in.

'Is my husband at the hospital?' Leila placed her hand on the policewoman's arm. 'Isak isn't my husband anymore.'

They had separated, but Billy's dad was always finding new ways to get into trouble, and she was always getting dragged into it in one way or another.

I never should have asked him for help, she thought.

The policewoman shook her head.

'It's not Isak, it's Billy.'

Leila shrugged in resignation. There was no point. It was always the same story. She and the policewoman didn't understand each other.

'Billy is sleeping.'

'We need to hurry,' said the officer, looking at Leila's nightgown. Leila was losing patience, sick of listening to this. All she could do was ask the officer to follow her to Billy's room. If she couldn't explain, she would just have to show her what she meant. This was her usual tactic when someone didn't understand her.

She knocked on Billy's door before opening it. He was the only one of her kids with his own room. Leila slept in the living room with her oldest daughter, while the other two shared the apartment's only real bedroom. Billy's room was tiny, not much bigger than a closet. The light inside was off, but the light from the room outside filtered through the doorway. They both looked at the bed. Then the officer turned on the light. Leila blinked. She approached the bed and placed her hand on the bedspread. It was clear there was no one there. Yet she let her hand pat the place where Billy should have been. She patted and stroked, harder and faster. Worry swept over her like the cold downdraft through a fireplace. Icy, inconceivable fear.

'I not understand,' she whispered.

'We need to hurry,' the officer said again. 'We have to go.'

Panic spread quickly, Leila's dry tongue thickening in her mouth. She hurled herself from the bedroom, shoved the policewoman aside, yanked open the other doors without knocking, turned on lights without warning. Her youngest daughter began to cry. Her oldest daughter gave a shriek, her other son swore softly and pulled the covers over his head.

Leila called Billy's name over and over. She threw
open the bathroom door.

He wasn't there either. She tore clothes from the
wardrobe that stood in the living room, crammed between the TV and the bed. The policewoman stood
alongside her as she got dressed. She was talking
about the Rönnviken playground again.

'Do you know who Billy might have gone to meet
in the middle of the night?'

Leila shook her head.

'No, no. Not know.'

'We have been told Billy had a very good friend
from—'

'No!' Leila made her voice as firm as she could.
'He is not friend with him anymore. He does not go
to that playground. Never again.'

They went to the front hall. Leila shoved her
feet into her shoes. She tried to smile reassuringly
at the kids. Her oldest daughter, Aisha, was holding
her younger sister Rawdah's hand. Tusane was pressing his blankie to his cheek. He was eleven, but he
still had his blankie. They watched Leila with wide
eyes; Rawdah was twelve, she hadn't wanted to hold
her sister's hand for several years. When the officer
opened the front door, the neighbour was standing
there, had apparently woken up when Leila was calling for Billy. He was wearing nothing but a robe and
slippers, and he nodded gravely as the policewoman
spoke.

'It's no trouble, I'll be here if Aisha needs help, or if…it's no trouble at all.'

Leila was used to people looking at her like she understood nothing, even though she did. But now it seemed that words had become untethered from reality.

'We need to hurry. We have to go. We haven't been able to find an interpreter.' The policewoman looked enquiringly at Leila's oldest daughter.

'No,' Leila said. 'I don't need interpreter. Aisha stays here.'

The policewoman nodded. The neighbour nodded, and the kids too, three baby birds in a row. Leila glanced one last time at the living room, but Billy wasn't there this time either.

Then the officer herded her out of the apartment.

THE BOYS

It was never dusty at Leila's place, but it was always chaotic.

'Welcome,' she said to her son's new friend the first time he came over to play.

'Whoa,' he replied as she opened the front door and he saw the cramped hall. Before Leila could respond, Billy pulled him along to the little nook they'd crammed a bed into so they could call it his room. Little Tusane struggled in her arms, he wanted to dash after his big brother. They were three years apart, but he absolutely idolized Billy.

She wanted to follow them too. She certainly understood what that boy was thinking. *I have no reason to be ashamed*, she wanted to tell him. *Who do you think you are?* But she let him be. *Whoa. All he said was whoa.*

'Sure,' the boy's dad, Teo, had replied, when she texted to ask if his son could come along to their house to play. One word, nothing more. No 'that sounds fun' or 'lovely' or 'next time they can come to our place.' Leila must have spent half an hour considering how to compose her text. She had typed, deleted, started over. She had checked her spelling and showed Aisha the text to have it corrected. Aisha was two years older than Billy, eight years old and top of her class. It had taken the boy's dad, Teo, one second to answer. So casual. But he hadn't mentioned anything about when Dogge needed to be home, or when he planned to come pick up his son.

She took a dummy from her pocket and gave it to Tusane.

'You can play with Mama,' she tried, and put him down. Then she straightened the shoes the boys had kicked off. She hung up the jackets they'd thrown on the floor and picked up her oldest daughter's backpack – it felt almost empty. She placed it on the hat rack. *I have no reason to be ashamed*, she thought again. None at all. Tusane could watch a movie. Maybe she would give him some chocolate cookies so he would let the boys play in peace.

She could hear them through the wall. They were laughing, absorbed in one another. Aisha and Rawdah were at the kitchen table. Aisha had a stack of schoolbooks in front of her. Rawdah was drawing on an ad circular with a crayon.

'We're playing school, Mama,' she said. 'Aisha is teaching me. I can read and write now.'

'No you can't,' said Aisha.

'Can too,' Rawdah said, and went back to drawing.

Tusane had fallen asleep on the sofa with his bottom in the air and his thumb in his mouth. Leila knew she should wake him up. Otherwise it would be impossible to get him to sleep that night.

I'll just start on dinner, she thought. *He had a fever yesterday, so it's good for him to sleep.*

She turned on the radio but kept the volume low so it wouldn't bother Aisha. The voices on the radio were no more than a hum, waves from the country she still called home. The kids didn't want to speak her language, but they understood everything. Leila's dialect got weaker with each passing year. She sang her own mother's songs to them when they couldn't sleep, and whispered the pet names her father had taught her. When they fought, she used words that didn't get caught halfway out, she apologized afterward without an accent. They replied in Swedish.

She'd bought two chickens on sale. She lifted the lid of the pot that was always on the stove because it was too large to fit in any of the cupboards. From the pantry she retrieved the vegetables, crushed four cloves of garlic with the heel of her palm and the flat of a knife blade, picked off the skin, tossed the garlic in the pot. Tonight she could take her time, it was just her and the kids, she had changed the lock on the door, they didn't have to worry.

Billy's new friend ate three helpings; Billy only had two. Tusane hadn't wanted to wake up so she had transferred him to the crib and given him a bottle of warm milk. He hadn't even woken up when she put him in a nighttime diaper. The girls were talking over each other, having a loud argument about something one of them had said but not done, or had done even though she wasn't allowed to. Billy's friend said nothing; he just ate. He chewed with his mouth closed, held the knife tight in his right hand.

'Can you put him in an Uber?' was Teo's response when she texted him to say it was probably time for his son to go home. A long message this time. 'We're at a restaurant, I've had too much to drink to drive to Våringe. The police would stop my car on sight.' He had closed the text with a smiley, the one with squinting eyes and its tongue sticking out.

Am I supposed to think this is funny? Leila thought. *That your fancy car would seem stolen if you drove it in Våringe? Haha, so hilarious.*

'Put him in an Uber?' Leila imagined that this was how they did things in Rönnviken. They paid for each other's taxis. *No big deal, I'll get it next time.* Leila had no intention of paying for an Uber. But she didn't have a car of her own, or even a driver's licence. And she had to get up early for work. The kids had to go to school. She didn't want to walk him over to Rönnviken. She didn't want to leave her kids home alone. So she rang the neighbour's doorbell and handed him the leftover chicken. She had put the food in a plastic container with a lid, it was still warm. Then she asked if he could drive her son's friend home.

'Isak is…well, you know Isak. Not here. And the boy's parents can't pick up. I cannot leave Tusane, I think he is sick.'

The neighbour smiled. He reached for his coat.

'Of course.'

'Goodbye,' Leila said once the boy had dug out his shoes. He ducked his head and muttered something. 'You are always welcome again,' she continued, hesitant. 'You should feel at home with us.'

'Thanks,' the boy whispered.

As he vanished down the stairs she turned the locks, both the upper and lower ones. That should be enough for tonight.

5

As soon as he'd instructed one of his colleagues to go to the home of the victim's mother, Farid called task-force director Gunnar Löfberg. Gunnar answered on the first ring.

'So? Is it one of yours?'

'The victim's name is Billy Ali. I've known him since he was six. He and his best friend were errand boys for a local character called Mehdi Ahmad. Until six weeks ago, when Billy's mother got fed up and convinced him to join a disengagement programme. It seemed to be working, but now I don't know what the hell to think. A couple guys should go talk to Mehdi Ahmad. He's officially listed as living with his mother, but there are a few other addresses in Våringe where he's also known to hang out.'

'Of course.' Gunnar sounded subdued. 'Mehdi Ahmad? Is that a name I should recognize?'

Farid went on: 'Eh. Mehdi's no big shot, but he's been building up a reputation in Våringe for almost a decade. He deals some stuff, unclear where he gets it from. He did some time for possession and assault, but not for very long. He's got ambitions, and he's awfully popular with the kids in Våringe. They think he's *Snabba Cash* and Yasin the rapper rolled into one. But I'd like to go see the victim's best friend, Douglas Arnfeldt. He and the victim have hung around Rönnviken playground together since they were little, and Douglas lives right nearby. The last time I picked them up there and drove them home was less than six months ago, maybe four.' He gazed over at the sandboxes. 'That time they were out of their minds from overheated spliffs. As far as I know, unlike Billy, Douglas never expressed a desire to break ties with Mehdi.' He cleared his throat. 'I would like a warrant to search his best friend's house, can you make it happen?'

'A kid from Rönnviken who started playing gangster? How the hell did that happen?'

'Yeah, well,' said Farid. 'You tell me.'

'I'll try to get you a warrant, but you should get moving. Cross your fingers I don't end up with some persnickety prosecutor who wants us to dot every last *i* and cross every *t* just because it's Rönnviken. Do you have the address?'

'Of course.' He knew it by heart. 'But hang on. Maybe I can pave the way and make the prosecution's decision easier.'

Farid approached the two colleagues who had been first on the scene. They were each sitting on a stretcher in the other ambulance. Both back doors were open. One was a young guy who probably hadn't been on the job more than a few months; he was staring vacantly into space as a paramedic stuck a DNA swab in his mouth. He was bloody up to his shoulders. Farid hadn't met him before, but he knew the older officer well. For the past fifteen years, ever since he'd left a party with the wrong shoes, everyone had called him Sneaks. Sneaks was nowhere near as blood-spattered. Evidently he'd let his younger colleague take responsibility for doing CPR.

Farid nodded at Sneaks, who nodded back. As he held his phone to his chest, he lifted a hand toward the younger guy.

'Hey there. I'm Farid.'

'Gustav,' his colleague responded.

Farid waved his phone.

'I've got Gunnar with the task force on the line, he's going to help us get a warrant for the victim's best friend, who lives right near here. And I was wondering if the two of you...' He trailed off.

Sneaks stood up.

'This friend lives nearby?' he said.

Farid glanced at the far end of the playground. Sneaks nodded enthusiastically.

'Because when we arrived, it looked like someone had walked straight up that way.' A question in his eyes, he pointed at the hill past the crime scene. 'It was awful dark,' he went on. 'It was snowing when we got here, but it had just started.' He hesitated, looking at Farid. 'But, I mean…if you're wondering whether it looked like someone had left the scene of the crime in that exact direction, I have no problem saying, well, I can't rule it out, anyway.'

Gustav too had started nodding. He had more to add.

'It was dark, we had other stuff on our minds, but hell yes, we thought it looked like someone had run up that way. For sure.'

Farid brought the phone up again.

'Did you hear that, Gunnar? The victim's best friend lives a stone's throw from the scene of the crime, which is also their usual meeting spot. The first officers on scene say it looked like someone might have left the playground in the direction of the best friend's home. It's true that this friend is just as young as the victim, but he's already gotten into plenty of trouble. You know how touchy these kids are, a broken nail can lead to shots fired.'

Gunnar's response was a *hmm*.

'What's at this address? A house, is that all?'

'There's some sort of outbuilding as well, I seem to recall. On the lot. Not a shed, but some old play-house or something, huge, with gingerbread and a porch. So I'd prefer the warrant cover the whole property. The suspect lives there with his mother.' Farid gave him the address.

'A kid from Rönnviken offed a kid from Våringe?' Gunnar sounded tired now. 'This is going to be a fucking circus.'

'We don't know that. We don't know anything,' said Farid.

'No, okay. But head over there right away and take someone with you. I'll text you when I've got the warrant, but you don't need to wait. And tomorrow, when we put the investigation team together, I'll ask to have you on loan, okay? I want you to be one of the investigators, you can't be lead investigator, and you have only yourself to blame on that count, but I want you to be involved. Can you help me?'

'Of course,' Farid muttered. 'And if anyone protests, you can tell them no one knows these kids like I do, probably not even their own parents. You'd be idiots to let anyone but me handle this.'

'Exactly.' Gunnar sighed again. He wanted to hang up. 'But, listen...'

'What?'

'Watch out for the chandeliers.'

6

By the time he finally made it through the front door, his teeth were chattering. He was also desperate to take a crap. He kicked off his shoes, clenched his butt cheeks, took shallow breaths, and walked on stiff legs straight to the bathroom. He thudded onto the toilet seat. A split second after he'd pulled down his pants, he had emptied his bowels. He flushed twice.

It hadn't been his plan to go home. The problem was, he had no idea where else to go. So he'd gotten on the bus and now here he was. Mum's pills were in the medicine cabinet, he pressed one out of the foil, then another.

He tossed the pills in his mouth and swallowed them with water straight from the tap. Then he took off all his clothes and sat down in the shower. By now, his whole body was racked with strong convulsions. He felt like he had to throw up, but didn't. The cold-water tap was hard to turn, it had rusted.

Soon the water was way too hot, his skin burning all over, not only where the eczema was. He groaned but stayed under the spray, closed his eyes, dug his fingernails into his palms, squeezing his eyes tight. White spots danced on the insides of his eyelids.

'Fuck, fuck, fuck,' he muttered to himself, tucking his knees to his chest, bringing his arms over his head and ducking his neck, rocking along to his convulsions, letting his hair get wet and fall into his face. The water was still pouring over him. 'Shit, shit, shit, shit.' The words became a sound high in his throat. *Shitshitshitshitshit.*

His skin hurt, his hands ached, he looked at them, they seemed swollen and were faintly purple. He knew he should wash up, use soap, scrub beneath his nails, rinse all traces of what had happened from his body. But he didn't have the strength. His mind was racing. It felt like something was trying to get out of his skull through his forehead. The pain progressed, creeping through his skeleton and making his muscles ache. As soon as his skin got used to the hot water, he lay down and simply stayed there. The tile floor was rough against his cheek, he picked at the crumbling caulk along the wall.

Ten minutes later, he heaved himself up from the shower floor and shut off the water. He had stopped shaking, the bathroom was full of fog, and he swept himself in a towel, then put Mum's robe over it. It didn't smell gross, just a faint whiff of her perfume. Mum still liked perfume and kept eight different kinds of it in the medicine cabinet. But she only used it on the days she managed to take a shower.

He picked up the clothes he'd been wearing from the floor and carried them back out to the hall. The laundry room was just one room over and had its own entrance from the backyard, but that door didn't open; its frame had swollen. They never went that way anymore, so it didn't really matter. He stuffed everything he was carrying into the washing machine. His stained underwear and wet socks were still stuck in his jeans; he added way too much detergent and started a cycle, couldn't see which one. He hadn't turned on the overhead light, but that was for his own sake, he wanted it dark. Doing laundry or turning on a light would never wake Mum.

Once the washing machine was running, he went to his room and got under the covers, still wearing the robe and towel. He felt chills coming over him again when he noticed that the sheets smelled like sweat, but he took short, shallow breaths and it didn't smell like urine, didn't smell like blood. Not that icy stink of death and panic. The chills vanished as quickly as they had come. Then his skin, his head, began to buzz. That was the pills. Soon his pulse would slow, soon it would be quiet inside his head.

One slow wave at a time, the pills washed away the itching. One slow wave at a time, they warmed his blood. He tried to breathe more slowly, do what Mum said she did when she wanted to relax: breathe through your nose, fill your lungs, empty them again. He tentatively closed his eyes, pressed his arms alongside his body, didn't move, didn't let the cold air of the room under the covers, and he thought that if he could just sleep, *just as long as I can sleep tonight*, for a whole night, he would be able to figure out what to do.

He swallowed his fear, yet it rose like bile in his throat; he squeezed his eyes shut harder, it didn't help. The images in his head wouldn't go away.

'The ambulance is on its way,' she had said, the woman who answered his 112 call. 'Help is on the way.'

She didn't mention the police, but he could hear them coming even before he got off the bus. First the cop car, then the ambulance, just a minute or two later. The ambulance siren was different from police sirens, and fire sirens too. He'd been able to tell them apart since he was little. Dad thought it was funny; when Dogge was younger, Dad would joke about it with his friends.

'When my son hears the cops coming, he runs as fast as he can in the other direction, whether or not he's done anything. For my kid, a police car is like the opposite of an ice-cream truck.'

Then he would offer his most charming smile, the one that made him look like a movie star, the one that had made Mum smile. 'It's very strange,' Dad would say. 'Makes you wonder where he got it from, who taught him that. Maybe I should ask Jill?'

That would get a laugh from Dad's friend, without fail. But Dad was right. Dogge hated those cop bastards, he always had, at least ever since he had got to know Billy. You didn't have to flee from ambulances, and when the fire truck came you had to see what was up, but the police were a different story. They were out to get you.

He took a deep breath. Let the air out again, one breath at a time. It was warmer under the covers now. Slowly, slowly his racing thoughts grew calmer.

He flipped onto his belly. His body was getting heavier. He wrangled himself out of the towel and robe and tossed them on the floor. Now he was finally warm, naked under the thick duvet. The blood whooshed in his ears, but the noise in his head was quieter.

It's going to be okay, he thought. *Everything will be fine. I heard the ambulance, it came right away.*

The doorbell blared. The sound cut right through blood and skin and bones, all his muscles. It wasn't some neighbour kid ding-dong-ditching on their way home from an unchaperoned party, it was a long, firm tone. It was followed by loud pounding.

He did his best to get out of bed, pull on the robe, and answer the door as quickly as possible. But he fell, got up again, regained his balance, and limped sideways into the hall. The top lock wasn't engaged, all he had to do was turn the lower one and open the door.

Outside waited two police officers, one in uniform. The other one was wearing only a shirt and sweater, no coat or hat, even though it was freezing out by now. They were standing under the broken cast-iron-and-glass porch light that hung from the ceiling.

The officer without a uniform was called Farid and had been to Dogge's house many times before, although it had been a while since he'd been inside.

The patrol car was parked facing their gate, with its headlights on. It was lighting up the whole yard: the snow-covered patio furniture no one had brought in when summer was over, the playhouse with its door that had come loose from the topmost hinge, the hazelnut bushes that never produced any nuts, the flagpole with its broken line and rotting base, the gnarled trees with apples no one ever picked. A couple of apples had clung to their branches this past autumn; the rest had made a bumpy carpet on the ground beneath. All the fruit had first rotted and then been covered, first by frost and now by snow.

Farid was standing closest to the door. For three seconds, no one said anything. The only sound was the thudding of the washing machine.

'Dammit, Douglas,' Farid said at last. Normally, he never called him Douglas. Never, ever. Not even when he was angry. 'What the hell have you done?'

THE BOYS

The first time Farid saw Billy and Dogge together, they were no older than six. Billy was wearing a Patrick Vieira soccer shirt, the French national team one, and it was so big it fell to his knees. He had a soccer ball in a net bag over his shoulder. Farid knew him already, because Billy's father Isak was one of Våringe's clumsiest petty thieves. But Farid had never seen Dogge and his dad before. It was clear they weren't from Våringe. Dogge's complexion was as pale as Billy's was dark, and he must have been two inches shorter. He was also wearing a national team shirt, Sweden's, of the exact right size, but with no player's name on the back. His father was wearing a wrinkled, snow-white linen shirt, had tanned forearms and pale blue jeans. He wore boat shoes with no socks. Dogge's father wasn't wearing a watch, just a band of braided leather around his wrist.

Are you a finance bro with surfer dreams, Farid wondered, *or is it the other way around?*

It was high summer, Farid's uniform shirt was plastered to his back. His hair was glued to his forehead under his cap. He felt an intense longing for a shower, for shorts and a T-shirt and an ice-cold beer, and yet he stopped to nod at the boys, who nodded back. The father put out his hand, and Farid shook it.

'Teo Arnfeldt,' the father said. 'This is my son, Douglas. Dogge, say hello.'

He seemed hyper, perhaps not entirely sober.

'We're on our way to these guys' football practice, first time for my boy.' Teo tried to tousle his son's hair, but Dogge moved his head away.

'Quit it, Dad. Come on, we have to go.'

They chatted for a moment, although Teo did most of the talking.

Farid spared a thought for Billy's father Isak, with his jouncing gait and nervous hands. Isak wasn't the type to chat, least of all about his son.

'The boys' coach is a legend,' Teo said. 'He should have retired ages ago. But he refuses to give up his boys' team. And if you want your son to train with future national team players, Rönnviken is the last place to be. Here in Våringe, you all live for sports! We Swedes have a lot to learn from you, not least about passion and discipline.'

Farid nodded. He didn't mention that he'd had the same coach himself, as a teenager. Maybe it was Dogge's father's breeziness, his curious gaze. Or the fact that he didn't seem to be nervous in the least, talking to a police officer. Whatever it was, it got on Farid's nerves.

He's on safari, he thought. *The white man visiting the colonies.*

The sun fell on Teo's back as the small group moved off, but he didn't appear to be sweating. It was the time of day and year when all the colours were brightest. Farid saw the way Teo looked at Billy and Dogge. Two boys from different backgrounds who'd become friends. Poster children for the uniting power of sports. This was the sort of thing that should end well. There was nothing fateful about it, not even if you took into account the hot day and the approaching thunderstorm.

7

Astench emanated from the house. The floor of the hall was dark with filth, the wallpaper yellowed by nicotine. The robe Dogge was wearing was dirty and its belt was crooked. He avoided looking at Farid, his eyes roving. It had been over a year since Farid had been inside the house, and he hardly recognized it. He turned to his colleague.

'Be sure to stop that washing machine. The techs will need to empty it when they get here. See if you can find the boy's mother. And secure these shoes here.' He pointed to the floor. 'I want them bagged before anyone can accidentally kick them around.'

Then Farid grabbed Dogge by the arm and pulled him away from the hall. The kitchen was only three doors away, but it smelled rancid in there, so he turned around in the doorway. They went to the living room instead.

The last time he had dropped Dogge off, he'd left him at the gate. Dogge's mother had come down from the house, it was clear she didn't want to let Farid in, that it was worth curious looks from the neighbours as long as she could stop him from coming inside. He hadn't insisted – what he had to say could be said outdoors.

Pick your battles, he'd thought, and let it slide. *I should have asked to come in*, he thought now.

There was a blanket on the sofa; he removed it and let Dogge take a seat. The boy sank deep into one corner and tucked his legs up beneath him, leaning his head against the back of the sofa and closing his eyes. He was pale, his skin almost grey. He'd scratched a zit open on his forehead and there was a sore at the corner of his mouth. He looked sick.

'We need to wait here a few minutes,' Farid said. 'But then we'll go. You'll see a doctor and we'll talk, you and me. What did you take? Is your mom at home?'

He'd heard about the bankruptcy, of course, and the investigation into Teo, which had been closed. But he never would have imagined things were this bad, that you could live like this in Rönnviken.

Dogge didn't respond. He hardly seemed aware of his surroundings.

Why wouldn't you sell this house and move to a smaller place? Farid wondered. *If you needed money? Why wouldn't you ask for help? Aren't there any relatives who could pitch in?*

'What the hell happened?' He was only muttering, he didn't mean for Dogge to hear, but Dogge

startled and awkwardly wiped his lips with the back
of his hand.

'Huh?'

He seemed to have showered very recently, but he
still looked grubby.

'Nothing,' Farid said. 'You just rest for now. We'll
talk later.'

8

At twenty past one, Dogge was led to the patrol car in his mother's robe, with small brown paper bags over his hands and blue plastic shoe protectors on his feet. When he asked to change into something else, Farid said no, he wasn't even allowed to wear the shoes he wanted.

On the way out, Dogge saw one of the police officers talking to his mother. They must have woken her up, she was sitting on a chair in the kitchen with her head in her hands, her hair tangled, in a dirty twist of a bun at her nape. Another officer had opened the washing machine and scooped the soaking-wet clothing into a garbage bag. The door to Dogge's room was open. Two cops wearing rubber gloves were going through his things. The shelf above his bed, the box beneath it, the desk, the dresser, and the very back of the wardrobe.

Dogge caught sight of himself in the hall mirror. His cheeks blazed with shame when he thought of how Mehdi and the other guys would laugh if they could see him. He knew what they would have said.

'Going to a costume party, Lasse? Dressed as some old-ass nursing-home bitch? Where's your nightie and curlers?'

Billy was the one who'd come up with the nickname, and Mehdi and Billy collapsed in heaps of laughter. Such a dorky, ultra-Swedish name. Dogge laughed too, at least for a little while.

'Why,' Billy had asked, 'does Douglas always turn into Dogge, and not, like, Lasse? Shit, you look like a Lasse! In some old movie about someone on the run from an orphanage.'

First they took him to the hospital. There he had to take off his clothes, stand naked on a piece of paper that was spread on the floor, open his mouth and spread his legs. A female doctor took samples and placed them in glass containers with screw-top lids. Her hands were soft and cool, Dogge closed his eyes as she scraped a swab under his nails and gently ran a comb through his hair.

'I'm almost done,' she said in a quiet voice. Dogge held his breath as her cool hand brushed his own.

A man in jeans and black shoes took photographs. When they were finished, Dogge was allowed to put on a set of lightweight pyjamas. They gave him an equally lightweight blanket with the hospital logo on it, and he draped it over his shoulders when they drove him to the station. He was freezing in the car, even though Farid turned the heat up as high as it would go. He was sitting in the back seat with Dogge. He kept his large hand on Dogge's back, and Dogge knew it was to be ready if he tried anything, so he could grab him by the back of the neck like cops do. He knew how they were, the police, how they beat you up and took your shit, that they were thieves and racists, Mehdi was all too familiar, had told him all about it. Billy too. But still, for a little while, it felt nice. Farid's hand reminded him of Dad's, the hand that could do anything.

Hold my hand, calm Mum down, shuffle cards, moor a boat, open a beer without an opener, mix drinks, kill spiders. Count money, tie knots, break and fix.

At the station, he was allowed to put on a pair of pants and a long-sleeved V-neck shirt. The clothes were too big, made from a thick green fabric, and not particularly warm. In the interrogation room he fingered the hem of the shirt. There was a loose thread at the seam, he tugged at it but it didn't come out.

His head was spinning. He tried to organize his thoughts, but it was hard. His head felt like that weird wad of cotton stuffed into Mum's pill bottle – he'd left that bottle in his bed, they must have found it. The pills gave him a dry mouth, and what he'd taken earlier that evening, before he met up with

Billy, always made his heart start pounding a few hours later.

'You've got no fucking proof,' he'd said to Farid in the car. 'No proof.'

It was hard to speak clearly, with his tongue so swollen. But Farid hadn't responded, just stared with that goddamn look on his face and said something to the cop who was driving. It was like he wasn't even listening.

Okay, so he was the one who'd made that call to 112. But he'd done it from a burner phone. No one knew he'd made that call, not even Farid could know, it was impossible. And he'd run all the way to Våringe to ditch everything. There had to be lots of people there who got rid of stuff like that. They should suspect someone from Våringe. Maybe they would let him go soon, once they realized that.

They technically weren't allowed to question him without his mum there. He knew that. But he also knew how Mum got when someone woke her up, how she always was these days if you didn't let her sleep until she woke up on her own. It didn't matter what anyone said, who was saying it, or what Dogge had done, she was always the same. Dead eyes, dead inside, dead in all the ways that mattered.

Five years ago, she would have demanded to be present when he was interrogated, she wouldn't have accepted it any other way. Three years ago, she would have tried to protest. Maybe she still would have said something at the beginning of last year. But last year was a long time ago.

'You've met Vivianne before,' Farid said. 'Since your mother won't be there with you today, she will be looking out for your interests.'

Vivianne from social services had purple glasses and purple fingernails. She looked like she'd just rolled out of bed.

'Mm-hmm,' said Dogge. But he didn't say hello. The first time he'd met Vivianne, she'd even had a purple streak in her hair. It was gone now. She liked clothes that looked like they were made of patchwork quilts, and she wore shawls wound around her neck as though she always had a cold. Mum called her Aunt Lavender. Today Aunt Lavender had red eyes; she looked like she'd been crying, and Dogge wanted to punch her in the face.

'Do you want me to talk to your mum?' she wondered.

Dogge looked at her.

'No.'

She shouldn't pretend like she knew his mum, he thought. She knew nothing about them. Dogge's mum wouldn't want to talk to Aunt Lavender. She wanted to be left alone. She wasn't like Billy's mum, who had her women's group and book club and was part of a parents' group that took turns going out on Friday nights, taking walks wherever they thought they might find kids getting up to stuff they shouldn't. Mum would never have done something

like that, or Dad either. Dogge could hear his father's
voice.

'Walking pup tents wandering the streets, keeping an eye on kids to make sure they don't set the
neighbours' cars on fire – obviously necessary in
Våringe, but in Rönnviken we pay enough taxes to
have that sort of thing dealt with.'

'Do you want me to talk to your mum?' Aunt Lavender asked again. As though she thought he hadn't
heard her the first time.

'Just shut up,' he said. And she actually did.

Farid looked annoyed. 'You have the right to
a lawyer as well,' he said. 'I can't imagine we'll be
able to get hold of anyone at this time of night, but
is there anyone in particular you want? Maybe your
dad knew someone?'

9

Leila didn't have to sign in at the front desk, the policewoman did it for her. They seemed to know who she was, because the officer didn't have to explain why they were there, she just gave Leila's name and a nod. Leila just had time to catch a glimpse of the receptionist's sympathetic gaze before she was shown to the emergency department waiting room. It was the middle of the night, and the room was full of people.

A woman with tired eyes sat two yards away with a sleeping child in her arms. Tears trickled slowly down her cheeks. An older woman whose skin was pale and grey was sitting on the very edge of her chair, holding her wrist, as her husband barked at the woman at registration. Leila found herself standing in the middle of the room. The policewoman brought a chair, set it down behind her, and placed a hand on her shoulder to guide her. Leila sat. Her arm hung down along her side. She looked at it, thinking that she should rest it in her lap, or get out her phone to call Billy's father. But her hand remained still. Her eyes fell on a man pacing back and forth in the corridor, gesticulating as he talked to himself.

My son has been shot, she had the sudden urge to blurt. *The police say that someone shot my child.*

But she'd forgotten how to make her voice work.

Another police officer entered the waiting room; he took her arm, helped her up, and led her out.

A group of people walked past and stopped nearby, one of them laughed loudly. The corridor was chilly, Leila was starting to feel cold, she was trembling. Someone draped a blanket over her shoulders, gave her a mug of something warm to drink, but the mug was too heavy, she handed it back.

'I need to ask you a few questions,' said the officer. 'When did you last see your son?'

'He is at home in his room,' she mumbled. 'He is lying in his bed.'

The officer repeated the question. And she answered it: she had said good night to Billy just after ten, as she always did these days. And she said it again, loudly this time, what she'd already said back when the ponytail officer had claimed what she'd claimed.

'It's not true. What you are saying is a lie.'

Suddenly she wanted to go home, bring this new officer into Billy's room. Billy would be there. She could feel her strength returning, because now she realized that she had forgotten to check the balcony. He had gone out there; what she had seen with the policewoman must have been wrong. Of course it was wrong. Billy had woken up and heard the police coming, slipped out to their balcony, jumped down to the neighbours' balcony and then down to the street and had gone to a friend's house. He must have done it while Leila was getting dressed.

Her voice returned. She explained.

'It's impossible,' she said. 'It isn't him.'

Then the officer asked if Billy often ran off at night.

'Does he do that a lot? Jump off the balcony to the neighbour's and then down to the street?'

'No,' Leila replied, 'no, no, no. I didn't mean.' She raised her voice, but she was having a hard time expressing herself. It was always so hard to find the right Swedish words when she was stressed. The words started to clamber over each other, spilling out in the wrong order. 'You don't understand. He has stopped. All of that. Being with them, doing that you-know-what.' She raised her voice even more. She was almost shouting. 'You know this, he takes tests, he is clean, he quit it all. That was before, not now, now everything fine. Now everything is fine.'

The officer stopped a passing nurse.

'There must be some room we can use,' he said. 'We can't do this here. We need privacy.'

The officer took Leila into a small room where there was still no Billy. They wanted her to sit down, but she stood up and used all of her energy to keep from screaming.

'Where is my son? If you know where he is, why you are not taking me there?'

Now both officers were speaking. They said he had been found up at the Rönnviken playground.

'Who do you think he went there to meet?'

At that, she could no longer stand.

'No. You are lying. He no was there. He no would go there.'

Her muscles were rock-hard, every part of her body strained to breaking point. Yet it couldn't hold her up. She had to grab hold of the chair to keep from falling off.

'You are lying, you are lying, you are lying. Why would you say this?'

She knew what they thought. The playground had been Dogge and Billy's meeting spot. *But it wasn't anymore.*

'You are lying.'

Leila's voice got even louder. She didn't care if the police became angry with her.

'You have to understand. You have made a mistake. Is not Billy, you do not have him, if you have him I would get to see him, it's not my son you have, it is someone else.'

They let her scream. No one got mad, or upset, or even annoyed. Their voices were gentle, far too gentle.

'We need to know as much as possible about your son's life. So we can figure out exactly what happened.'

'No,' said Leila. 'No, no, no. Nothing happened. Everything is fine.'

The police showed her Billy's wallet and passport. They were in a plastic bag and looked dirty. On the back of the passport was a sticker with Billy's name. That was dirty too, but Leila could read what it said. The police said there was a colleague of theirs who knew Billy, that Farid had identified him, and with that, every muscle in Leila's body stopped working. She slid to the floor, they had to catch her, hold her up.

'He has always the passport with him,' she whispered. 'Always, I say to him. It is important, I say.'

Then they took her away from there, went two floors up. The policewoman propped her up. The corridor was long, the room they entered large and quiet. Machines hummed in the background. And there lay Billy. Perfectly still. Beside him stood a doctor and two nurses, waiting.

Leila turned to the doctor; she understood he was the doctor even though he didn't have a stethoscope around his neck. He smelled faintly of sweat and disinfectant.

They had covered Billy's head in dressings, but she could place her palm to his collarbone and she knew the contours of his body. His rib cage moved up and down. Leila cried into her hijab, its edge growing dark with tears.

'He is breathing. Right, he's breathing? He will be fine soon. Of course he will be fine.'

'We've done all we can do,' said the doctor. He tried to catch her eye. 'But there's nothing more to be done.'

Leila forced her voice to remain calm.

'No,' she said. 'No, no.'

She ran both hands down her son's cheeks, over the skin there that had begun to change form. Soon he would be a grown man. Not quite yet, but soon.

'I understand how difficult this is,' said the doctor. 'But these decisions must be made as quickly as possible, and it's important for you to understand.'

Leila looked at the machine. The sound rumbled, crept closer. It lasted a brief minute, an eternity. Time ceased to exist. She turned to the doctor.

'*You* must understand. Not me. Billy cannot donate organs, he needs them, his heart will beat without help, he will wake up, he must wake up. He will be fine soon.'

Each night, Billy washed his face with her bar of black soap. Two days ago, she had asked if he wanted a bar of his own, some soap specially made for teenage skin, and he had been embarrassed and pretended not to understand what she was talking about. She let her thumb brush over her son's face, up to his eyebrows. When he was younger, she would rub between them, massaging his forehead when he had trouble sleeping, after a nightmare, perhaps.

'You see?' Leila whispered. She let go of her son and tugged at the doctor's arm. She had washed both her mother and her sister after they died. She knew what skin looked like when life left a body. She knew how death smelled. 'Feel him,' she begged, but the doctor placed his hand on hers instead and squeezed it.

'It only looks like he's sleeping,' said one of the nurses, 'but he isn't.'

When Billy slept, his upper lip trembled, his jaws worked, his forehead creased and smoothed, his eyes moved beneath closed lids. When he was younger, and still wanted to sleep in Leila's bed, she had had to move to the sofa to get any rest. Leila knew he wasn't sleeping now.

'I'm so sorry.' The doctor didn't want to let go of Leila's hand. 'He will never wake up again. He's only on these machines so we can use his organs, if you and your husband agree. But even that won't help for much longer. There is a limit to how long we can keep his body functioning.'

Leila pulled her hand back.

'I put him in bed. Just a while ago. I said good night. Like a little boy. I sang lullaby for him, he laughed. That was just a while ago. It can't be. He can't be here. It can't be.'

She had exaggerated everything, pulling the covers tight over his body and stuffing them under the mattress. He had laughed at that. *Quit it, Mum.* He had kicked his foot gently to loosen the covers. She had kissed his forehead and cheeks. How many times had he said that to her? A thousand? *Quit it.*

'We went to the police,' Leila continued, looking up at the officer who had brought her here. 'You know Farid? You said he was the one who found my Billy? We went to Farid, we have always known him. Farid helped us.'

The officer nodded. Leila took a breath.

'Billy wanted to quit. Fresh start, he called it. Farid called the person in charge of that, Billy went to all the meetings, he was on time, he did the tests, the drug tests, he didn't want to be... My husband said...' Leila's voice cracked as the words tumbled over one another. 'Tomorrow we were going to...' She turned to the doctor. 'His latest urine test was clean.' Her voice wasn't trembling now. 'He behaves. My son is doing exactly what he promised. Everything is different. He doesn't go to the playground. Doesn't meet with Dogge.'

There was a scab on the inside of Billy's arm.

'You see?' she whispered to the hospital staff, or maybe just to herself. 'We must wash it. Otherwise, infection. He scratches. It will start to bleed.' She was crying now. Silent, fat tears. 'He will be fine...'

The nurse placed a hand on her arm. Leila didn't have the strength to push it away.

One by one, they left the room. The doctor went first. 'We'll be right outside this door if you need us,' they said. And then she was alone.

I will never leave you. Just yesterday, her son was an hour old, with a gaze that contained the world. When they were alone on the maternity ward he lay against her bare chest. And she made him a promise. *I will hold you tight and never, ever, ever let you go.*

She unwound her hijab, dropped it on the floor, and lay down beside her son.

She lay so that Billy's head ended up under her own, the dressings rough against her chin. She worked one arm beneath him and pulled him close. The sound of the machines faded to a light rush, an ear to a shell, water and wind. Leila whispered to him in her own language.

'I washed you when you were small and couldn't do it yourself. I tucked you in each night long after you needed me there to fall asleep. I took you to school on your very first day, I picked you up each time they called to say you were sick. If you need me here so you can leave me, I'm here. I will always be here.'

And then she turned Billy's face toward her neck, took in the scent of his hair, and let him warm her, the woman who had been his mother, one last time.

10

Dogge's eyes drifted toward the door. Above it was a clock, it was two thirty. Beside the door stood a uniformed officer, hands clasped, keeping watch so Dogge wouldn't try to get out.

Dogge turned to Farid instead. Opened his mouth. But he didn't know what to ask, what he was allowed to ask, what he could ask, so he closed it again and tried to breathe slowly.

What little calm had almost been within reach just now was gone, replaced with a rising panic. He couldn't sit still.

'Are you okay?' Farid frowned.

Dogge was sweating. His heart was racing. He was sweating and freezing, freezing and sweating. His thoughts and his fear collapsed on top of each other.

'I gotta get out of here.'

'Sit down,' said Farid.

'You've got nothing. No proof. You can't lock me up on nothing.' Dogge looked at Aunt Lavender, but was only addressing Farid. 'What the fuck are you going to do? Throw me in jail? You can't do anything to me. Nothing. You can't touch me, no one touches me.' His voice broke, but he regained control of it. 'You come to my house and just grab me when I'm sleeping and I don't know where you got all these ideas but I didn't do anything. You can't treat me like a criminal because I'm a kid and I didn't do anything.'

He turned to Farid. 'Where am I going to sleep? I need to sleep.'

Yet it was Aunt Lavender who answered.

'We're looking into where to place you. We'll discuss the matter with your mother and we'll let your lawyer know—'

'Leave my mother the fuck out of it.'

Farid interrupted him.

'First, and most important, we're going to talk about what happened tonight. Then we can discuss what's going to happen.'

Aunt Lavender cleared her throat and licked her lips.

'You'll be informed as soon as we know.'

Dogge's head was pounding. It was against the law to put minors in prison. That was why kids like him and Billy were given important errands, the police couldn't lock them up. Mehdi had told them that. This was such a well-known fact that it was even in the newspaper. Politicians talked about it. But now it seemed like he was going to be locked up after all.

'I want to go home. I want to go home right now.'

'First we're going to talk for a bit,' said Farid. 'And I'll try to find you a lawyer. You won't be allowed to go home.'

He held his phone to his ear, talking fast and sounding annoyed; Dogge couldn't understand what he was saying. Was he talking about him?

'I don't need a lawyer, I'm a minor. I can't go to jail, I don't want one of your fucking buddies.'

Farid scoffed.

'Don't worry, it won't be any friend of mine. They'll assign you someone tomorrow morning. And by all means, don't worry about your rights. We don't want that. We will of course do everything in our power to protect you. No need to worry on that count.'

Farid didn't sound like his usual self. He sounded furious. He kept emphasizing 'you' in an exaggerated way and it sounded like he wanted to spit in Dogge's face. Dogge's heart started pounding again. Panic swelled inside him, coming on fast like a fire in dry grass. He wanted to ask for something to make his heart stop beating so hard. Why hadn't they given him something at the hospital? He'd seen the doctor talking to Farid before they left.

My heart is going to bust, he thought. *A hammer through flimsy paper. Mum's pills aren't helping. I'm going to die.*

Was Farid allowed to interrogate him while his heart was pounding like this? It had to be visible through his skin, through his clothes.

'I don't fucking feel good. My heart – there's something wrong with it. I can't be here.'

'Here's what we're going to do,' Farid said. 'If you want, I'll drive you back to the hospital, but there's nothing wrong with your heart. What you're feeling is not, for once, the absence of all the crap you shove into your body as fast as you can, it's plain old anxiety. I imagine you'd better get used to it. So while we're waiting to find out where you're going to sleep tonight, I want you to tell me what happened. You are going to talk to me, because Billy is dead and I do not fucking think that's just fine, and your father would hit the roof if he knew what you've done. Your father liked Billy. Do you think he would be happy about this?'

Dogge fell silent. All he could hear was his own gasping breaths.

'What did you say?'

'Billy is dead.'

Farid stared at him. Dogge tried to meet his gaze. He didn't want to make eye contact, that could be dangerous. Looking someone straight in the eye was power. But if he averted his gaze, it would mean that Farid had won.

'I don't have fucking anxiety.' His voice hardly worked. 'Anxiety is for fags.'

'Okay.'

74

'And I don't have a lawyer. I don't know any. You'll have to ask my mum.'

'We have asked your mum. She thought it would be best if we found you one.'

When Dogge's breathing got heavier, the social worker placed her hand on his arm and leaned toward him.

'Don't touch me!' he screeched, pushing her away even as he stood up. His chair fell to the floor. His chest ached so badly now, it felt like someone was sitting on him and drawing a belt around his rib cage, tighter and tighter around his lungs. The social worker had recoiled against the back of her seat. She looked afraid, as though he were an animal. Farid got another call, mumbled into his phone for a moment, then hung up and stuck the phone in his pocket.

'We'll figure this out,' he said. 'It's okay. Sit down.'

'Billy's dead?'

'Yes. He died at the hospital.'

'Okay.'

Dogge's leg began to jounce, up and down, up and down, he tried to press it down with his hand but couldn't make it stop. He scratched at the inside of his elbow, the eczema wasn't so bad there, but the scabs were fragile, he could feel through his sleeve that it was starting to bleed. He stopped scratching and rubbed instead.

Once, last year, he had almost hugged Farid when no one was looking. Farid had found him down in

Våringe city centre, alone, without Billy, and he had given him a ride home even though Dogge wasn't even drunk, and he'd followed him to the gate. That's where Farid had left him, but before he took off, he had placed one arm around Dogge's shoulders and his hand over his forehead and angled Dogge's face up to his own and said, *Take care now, try not to do anything stupid.*

Now, Dogge met Farid's gaze. For an instant he thought Farid was going to put his hand on his forehead again, let it rest there for a moment, that he would say, *There, there, kiddo, everything's going to be fine, you'll see.* As if he were Dad. Dogge would have told his father everything, and Dad would have hugged him and said, *Of course it's not your fault.* He would have known that it wasn't Dogge's fault that things had turned out the way they did.

Dad knew things could go to shit. And he'd had big, strong hands that were gentle and firm when they touched Dogge, and made everything better, so he never had to be afraid of anything.

Dogge thought about Farid's hand in the car, against his back. If he would just do that again, if Dogge could just feel the weight of that hand, it would be easier to breathe. But Farid didn't touch him, all he did was stare. Straight into Dogge's eyes, without blinking.

'This isn't a game. It's time to start talking, Dogge. I want to know why Billy had to die, and you're going to tell me.'

'Stop. Shut up.'

'You have to tell me, if I'm going to help you.'

Dogge rested his head on the table and muttered into its surface.

'It wasn't...' he began. 'You can't...I can't...I'm just...'

'I can't hear you. You have to speak up.'

'Mehdi...I didn't want to...it's not my fault.'

'Okay? What do you mean, it's not your fault?'

The little recorder on the table blinked. But Farid wasn't looking at it; he was only looking at Dogge.

'He said Billy had to die...so I did it. I did what he said. I'm only a kid. It's not my fault that Billy...I was only doing what Mehdi wanted.'

THE BOYS

The boys started school. One in Våringe, the other in Rönnviken.

There were seven boys and sixteen girls in Dogge's class. Five of the boys already knew all the letters of the alphabet. Everyone but Dogge could already write their name. In preschool, he'd got into fights almost daily. At school, people left him alone. It was as if no one saw him. Not even in the changing room, where he showered last of all, fastest of all, with his back to the room and his towel on a hook inside the cubicle. His form teacher, a woman with a centre part and flat shoes, asked questions, handed out paper, drew on the board, spoke in a gentle and serious voice. One time Dogge raised his hand, just to see if she would look at him. He didn't know the answer, but it didn't matter, because she didn't call on him.

He biked to school. At the end of the day, he biked home again. Billy didn't have a phone of his own, so Dogge couldn't call him on his phone and ask if Billy wanted to meet up, but he went to the playground almost every day to wait, just in case. During the second week of school, Dogge developed eczema on his neck and the backs of his knees. He scratched it until it started bleeding and formed little round scabs. Now they noticed him, but only in the changing room before gym class. One of his classmates started to call him Salami. *Greasy and spotty.* After a few weeks, they got sick of that too. But no one wanted to shower at the same time as him, they thought he looked gross.

There were thirty-two children in Billy's class. He always sat at the back of the room, and for the first couple of weeks he could sit there and talk pretty loudly, for a pretty long time, before the teacher would say anything. But all the girls except two, and three boys in nice shirts and leather shoes, gazed at the teacher like he was a celebrity or maybe like they had a crush on him. Each time Billy talked in class, they turned around and glared at him.

'Be quiet,' they said to Billy at least four times each class period. 'You have to be quiet.'

When Billy couldn't stop talking, despite being admonished, he had to go to the hallway and wait five minutes to be let in again. One time he didn't wait, he just walked straight out to the playground, through the gate, and home.

'My tummy hurt,' he said to his mother when the school called to say he had been absent that afternoon.

'Go see the school nurse next time,' Leila said.

'Okay.'

'Otherwise I'll have to talk to your father.'

'Okay.'

Billy knew what that meant, what his father would do if he found out Billy wasn't behaving himself. Leila knew too, and would never follow through on her threat, but she said it anyway.

'I'll go see the nurse next time, Mama. I promise.'

Billy made several new friends at school, the girls thought he was funny, even the ones who found him annoying and wished he would be quiet during class. Billy could make everyone laugh, even the teachers.

There were assigned seats for lunchtime at Dogge's school, just like in the classroom. Each class had its own table. The boy who sat next to Dogge had golden-blond hair that he combed straight back, so it looked like he'd just got out of the shower.

'My dad says your dad is a fucking joker,' he said one day, just a few weeks before the boys' first Christmas break. This made Dogge happy. He'd always known his dad was funny, although he wasn't always sure when he was supposed to laugh.

The next day, the boy with the shower hair switched spots. The kids weren't supposed to do that, but no one seemed to care and Dogge didn't say anything. No one moved into the empty spot, but he didn't say anything about that either.

One Monday, after Easter, in the second term of Year 2, Dogge didn't bother to return to class after their lunch break; instead he biked over to Billy's school. He knew where Våringe School was. They hadn't seen each other as often these past few months, only at weekends, and they hadn't hung out at all the most recent weekend. Billy hadn't come to the playground, even though Dogge had seen his mother there with Billy's younger siblings. When he asked, Leila said Billy was at a party at a classmate's house.

No one noticed when Dogge walked into Billy's schoolyard. Lots of kids went to Våringe School, hundreds of them, maybe a thousand, and there was no way to keep track of what they all looked like. No adult stopped him to ask if he actually attended this school. He was able to look around undisturbed.

'Hey,' Billy said when Dogge finally found him. Billy laughed, a strange laugh, and he shot anxious looks at the other boys around. But at least he didn't say Dogge couldn't play with them. He didn't tell him to go away, to find someone else to hang out with. Instead he took his mark and kicked a football at a board so it bounced right back again. Another boy took it and kicked it back to Billy via the board.

'I'm cutting school,' Dogge said. He wanted Billy to know.

'Yeah, I'm not stupid,' Billy said. Now he almost sounded angry, but only almost. He kicked the ball so hard at the board that the boy who was supposed to catch it missed and had to run after it.

When the end-of-break buzzer blared across the playground, the other kids disappeared. Billy lingered, standing in front of Dogge and cradling the ball.

I can wait until you're done with school, Dogge wanted to say, but he couldn't bring himself to. *If you want to go to class I can wait here. Then we can go to the square, I've got money, Dad gave me a whole bunch, we can go to the store and I can buy us both some candy. Or we can go into town and buy a new game, something cool, what do you want?*

He gulped. Maybe Billy didn't like him anymore? He had other friends now.

'Fuck school,' Billy said at last. 'It's boring as hell. Want to do something?'

11

People called him Weed. He didn't remember who had come up with it, but it had stuck. Weed got his nickname just a month or two after he and his wife Sara took over the grocery store in Våringe. He was twenty-three at the time, had come to Sweden two years earlier, and was already a father of two. These days, even Sara used the nickname. They had named the store Weed's Market.

The morning after Billy was murdered, everyone in Våringe was talking about what had happened. Weed found out about it from his eldest son.

His son had heard about the murder from a friend. 'Billy's dead. Dogge killed him.'

Weed met Sara's gaze over the breakfast table. She was thinking the same thing he was. But Weed didn't let her say it.

'That's terrible,' he said instead. And then he rose from his chair, drank the last of his coffee standing, and took the car down to the square. He opened the market as usual. Sara took the kids to school.

'Sup, Weed,' the customers said to him as they came in.

'Hi there,' he replied, because he had never been a fan of slang.

Just a few months after they had bought the store, he had decided to find out who the real Weed was. At first he thought people were messing with him. That it was an insult, and he had to pretend to think it was funny so he wouldn't seem foolish. He was a small man, only five foot four, with dark, curly hair, not only on his head, and he had never weighed an ounce over ten stone. Weed was a hockey player, he read online, maybe the most famous one in Sweden. There were lots of photos. Hockey Weed was the size of a barn door and just as wide. His blue eyes had stubby lashes and his head was shaved clean.

'What on earth do I have in common with that guy?' he'd asked his wife.

'Your smile,' Sara replied, placing her hand on his cheek. 'And your stubbornness. You never give up. Not ever, not until you've won.'

When his wife brought up his stubborn nature, Weed felt happy and proud for reasons he couldn't quite put his finger on. It made him smile, and she smiled back, and when she did that he had everything he needed.

The first time Sara had smiled at him, he was nineteen and she was four months older. They had met at university in Ankara, he was studying agribusiness; she was studying political science. The fact that she wanted to be with him was still the greatest miracle of his life.

But Weed was not a competitive person. His stubbornness was necessary for other reasons.

Weed's Market was on Stora Torget in Våringe. Its name, 'Big Square', was misleading; it was just the central part of a pedestrian mall. But the market itself was almost 6,500 square feet, and in their first few years there they'd put produce stands outside the entrance. At weekends he sold cut flowers, which he bought from a guy he'd met during a course in small-business ownership from the Workers' Educational Association. Weed's Market was not your typical corner store; you could find everything you needed and a little more there.

Still, it had always been a challenge to get people to shop at his store instead of going to one of the big chains, with their car parks the size of eight football pitches and their low prices. For the first few years, Weed had lain awake at night, trying to figure out how to personalize the market's selection, tailor it to the citizens of Våringe. Everyone who came to buy their groceries from him should feel that they could find exactly the products that were important to them. He put up a bulletin board and a suggestion box by the recycling-return station and urged his customers to let him know what they wanted him to bring in. He eavesdropped by the shelves and wrote long lists to remember what he learned about what his customers wanted. Basmati rice, *airan*, apple tea, rosewater, pickled garlic, and za'atar by the jar. Whenever he got the chance he would ask questions, lots of questions, and he learned to interpret the most cryptic responses. People were bad at asking for things, but good at showing when they weren't satisfied. And if you asked a direct question, they seldom dared to do anything but answer. Even if they sometimes lied and said everything was fine, and that they didn't want to ask for anything, it was clear by looking at them what they really thought. It took a little more time and some extra effort to get things right, but it was worth it.

Weed and Sara earned lots of money in those early years. The store became a place you could go not just to do your shopping, but also to chat for a while, be social. The produce was nicer than at any other grocery store, Weed knew what to purchase, and never put out overripe avocados or bruised apples. He sold twenty kinds of nuts and twice as many varieties of bulk dried lentils and beans. There was a gambling corner with a TV that showed harness racing or

Allsvenskan league games, and there were always at least two old men sitting there with well-chewed pencils in their mouths. Sara and Weed worked in shifts, and when both of them had to be there they brought the kids along. The kids would do their homework in the staff room or sit on the floor behind the cash register, drawing or reading.

When Weed arrived at the store the morning after Billy was murdered, the first thing he had to do was clear the snow away from the entrance. The very first customer wanted to talk about what had happened. And all the customers that followed wanted to discuss the same thing. It was a good day for the store. Everyone wanted to linger by the cash register for a while.

'Are they going to keep killing each other until no one's left?'

'I know Billy's mother, she said he quit all that, that he was a good boy now.'

'Billy's mother did everything she could for him. But it didn't help, there must have been something wrong with him.'

'Billy always had issues. When you live the way he did, you die young.'

'It must have been revenge. The police don't care about us, they don't protect our kids.'

They had plenty to say about Dogge too.

'If he'd been the one to die, instead of our Billy, there would be an outcry, and maybe then the police would finally pay attention.'

'It's kids like Dogge who finance the drugs, Rönnviken is where the demand is, if the police would dare to take action there we wouldn't have any problems.'

'It was his initiation into the gang.'

Weed listened to everyone and managed to say the right words.

They're just kids. A mother shouldn't have to bury her child.

He nodded when they said good things about Billy and pretended like he hardly knew who Dogge was.

The first time Billy and Dogge pinched something from Weed's Market, they were only eight years old, hardly old enough to take seriously. They weren't the only ones, so he did what he usually did with young shoplifters. He confiscated what they'd stolen, told them not to do it again, and sent them on their way.

But it escalated quickly. Still, Weed had been convinced a talk with their parents would do the trick. Typically, if he could get the parents' phone numbers out of the kids, he would call, otherwise he would pay them a visit at home; there was always some customer or another who knew where they lived.

The fourth time he caught Dogge, he even went over to Rönnviken and tracked down his house. There he had to stand on the front steps to explain why he was there, and Dogge's father said he would have a serious talk with his son.

Billy's mother invited him into her kitchen, she listened, served him tea. She assured him it would never happen again. But it did. At the height of it, it sometimes happened several times in a single week. Sometimes more than once on the same day. He stopped trying to get hold of Billy's mother, he knew how much she worked, he knew whom she was married to, she was doing the best she could.

When Dogge and Billy turned thirteen and were no longer satisfied with mere shoplifting, he decided to move the produce into the store. Dogge and Billy weren't the only troublemakers, but they were the worst ones. Weed invested in two security cameras. Nothing helped. He started calling the police. They came almost every time, at least at first, but since Dogge and Billy were just kids they couldn't do anything but take down their names, tell them to leave, and contact social services. On rare occasions they offered the boys a ride home. But as soon as the police were gone, the kids were back. And social services held meetings with the parents while the kids kept filling their pockets with bulk candy, breaking the glass front of the cigarette machine, throwing spice bottles at each other and other customers, overturning shelves, breaking bottles, pouring soda into the fish counter, and smearing blue cheese on the recycling-return station. Weed got palpitations just to see them biking by on the street. He had nightmares about them.

Still, it would become far worse.

The library next to their store had to close. Spending cuts was the official explanation. The same reason was given when the social services office moved from Våringe city centre to the next town over. And when the public services vanished, so too did the security guard the council had been forced to post there, and who sometimes, but only sometimes, helped Weed herd the boys away.

For a few weeks, Weed hired his own security guard. But the guard cost more than the store brought in some days, and fewer and fewer customers were braving their way in, so he had to let the guard go. When the kids were hanging around on the square outside his door, the store was deserted. If they ran off somewhere else, he might get a customer or two, but they did their shopping as fast as they could, didn't stop to chat at the register, and skipped the meat counter entirely. Dogge and Billy broke the TV in the gambling corner three times before Weed decided to get rid of it completely. No one sat there anymore anyway, they went to the neighbouring town to turn in their tickets. And after a couple of guys broke into the stockroom and stole a bunch of packages, he lost his authorization to serve as a post office satellite.

One month later, his insurance company sent word that they were electing not to extend his contract.

When Weed decided it couldn't get any worse, he decided to close at seven each evening. But then the council installed a security camera on the square, while the police went on TV and declared that things were about to get serious. They unveiled Operation Snowstorm. The streets would be cleaned up and the trouble would end. He started staying open until midnight again, but only on weekends. He had to. If he didn't bring in more money, he would go bankrupt.

Weed noticed very little of the increased efforts from the police; he only had a perfectly average store, and even flashy operations had to prioritize their time. There were so many places that had to be monitored: the schools and preschools and the community pool and the after-school club that organized dances for teenagers, and the forested park where they went afterward. There were more locales than there were officers. And they couldn't put up security cameras everywhere, who would want to live in that sort of society?

'You of all people should know that,' one of the officers said when he asked why one of the cameras couldn't be installed outside his store. 'You should know what happens when you let the state surveil everything, isn't that what you fled from?'

And Weed had nodded and gone home and down to his basement.

On a shelf, behind the boiler, was a baseball bat. It was made of oak and was thirty-two inches long. He'd had it for years, but it had been lying there unused.

He took it down from the shelf, wiped the dust away with his hand, and went back upstairs, out to the garage, and drove back to work. No one saw him as he placed it under the main register where he sat when he was working alone in the store. You couldn't see it from the outside, but Weed knew where it was. That was enough.

The day after the murder, he listened to every-one who came into the store to talk about the terrible event. He managed to say all the right words. What he was really thinking, he didn't say – not even to Sara.

12

I hear congratulations are in order.'

Farid hadn't even taken his seat at the oval conference table. A medium-blond, middle-aged man with excessive gums and at least two buttons too many undone on his checked shirt extended his hand.

'Not that it'll do much for our deplorable clearance rates, that ship has long since sailed, but still. I'm Bengt, I heard you're going to help us with the interrogations since no one knows these kids better than you. And that certainly does seem to be true.'

Farid shook Bengt's hand and sat down. Bengt went on.

'A fourteen-year-old fingering an older gangster for instigating murder. Good one. I won't ask how you did it. These days you can hardly say "boo" without getting the PC mafia after you. And God help you if you try to violate some kid's human rights by, I don't know, taking away his phone or some other deeply traumatizing shit. Yeah, now that I think about it, those of us who get to work with you are the ones who deserve the congrats.'

'A bit premature for that, I think,' Farid muttered.

He looked around the long, narrow room. At the front of the room hung a large projector screen. Three boxes showed the people who would be attending this meeting virtually. The long walls of the room were covered in a total of six whiteboards. A woman of around twenty-five, with buzzed hair and a Metallica T-shirt that was too small, was writing on one of them.

Across from Farid, on the other side of the table, sat the man in charge of this investigation, Chief Inspector Svante Larsson. Farid had met him before, at a class on witness psychology. Svante's hair had become greyer since last time, but his belly was just as flat, his back just as straight, and his smile just as nonchalant.

'You're here!' Svante pushed his chair back. 'Welcome! Let's get going, then, we were waiting for you. No time to waste.'

'Am I late?'

'Oh, no, don't worry. If all your interrogations are as fruitful as the one you did last night, you can arrive whenever you like. We'll follow your lead. It's not exactly common for us to get a tip on a real-life gang member of actual legal age thanks to another gang member. What was his name again?'

'Mehdi Ahmad.'

'That's it. You'll have to tell us about him – it's a new name, at least for me. Could you recap today's interrogation for us as well, if you don't mind? You talked to the kid again today, right?'

Farid nodded.

'Two hours ago. It didn't go as well this time.'

'I can imagine. But first, let me introduce our gang. I asked Sneaks and Gustav to be here; they're not part of the investigation team but I still wanted them at our first meeting. Good to get a summary of the night's events from the guys who were on the scene. Next we've got Lisa, she's our IT coordinator...'

'Lotta,' muttered the girl in the Metallica shirt. She stopped writing on the whiteboard and turned to face Farid. 'My name is Lotta.'

Svante continued, unfazed.

'Sebastian is our forensic coordinator.'

The man next to Svante raised his hand. He had small hands, a small nose, glasses, and jeans with an ironed crease. No parting in his hair, but he'd used gel to create a just-so tousle. *Civilian*, Farid thought. *Maybe a criminologist. Turned in a thorough CV with no spelling errors or missing punctuation, with a tiny photograph and a section on his hobbies: cycling, playing padel tennis and watching Netflix.*

Svante went on.

'We've got Jonas and Lena here from Våringe, they'll be helping us go through all the material from the security cameras in the area. There's quite a bit of footage, to put it mildly; seems like there's a camera on every driveway in Rönnviken, and in Våringe there are surveillance cameras at every intersection. So we've got our work cut out for us there.' Two trainees Farid had met before raised their hands. 'And then we've got three guys from investigations, they're here over video.' Svante nodded at the screen at the front of the room. Two of the three men waved. The third seemed to have a poor connection: his image had frozen as he stared with his mouth ajar.

'Is that all?' Farid frowned. 'No one else?'

'Welcome to the new Sweden. We're a team of ten, at least for a week. Bengt, by the way, we need someone to serve as registrar for the preliminary investigation, that'll have to be you. Have a chat with…' Svante pointed at Lotta. 'She knows what's up.'

Bengt nodded reluctantly.

'Don't leave here without filling out your contact info on there.' Svante nodded at one of the whiteboards. 'And before we hear about the latest interrogation, let's start with a situation report; we'll go around and tell you what we've been up to while you were reading bedtime stories and having snacks with young master Douglas.'

He nodded at Sebastian, who opened his laptop, but before he could start talking Svante spoke up again.

'And, oh right, Foad, there was something we wanted to ask you. Have you had a chance to listen to the emergency call?'

Farid nodded.

'Dogge was the one who made the call, yes. No doubt about it.'

'Good. Then you can have at it, Sebastian.' Svante leaned back in his chair. Sebastian cleared his throat and adjusted his glasses. He began by reading aloud from the whiteboard, where someone had drawn a timeline.

'The call came in at 23:08, our first car was on scene nine minutes later. The area was secured and the paramedics were let into it at 23:38. The ambulance left just before midnight, the victim was declared dead at the hospital about an hour later. We believe he was shot a few minutes before eleven. We found four empty cartridges at the playground. The doctors at Karolinska pulled two bullets out of Billy, and our techs cut another two out of a tree behind the swings. No weapon, unfortunately, but the cartridges have been sent for analysis. The scent dog couldn't work in the snow, so that was a dead end. Our colleagues stopped two cars around three o'clock on Friday morning; we know they belong to guys Mehdi Ahmad hangs around with, but that didn't turn up anything either.'

Lotta moved to one of the empty whiteboards, wrote *Mehdi Ahmad* at the top, and handed the marker to Bengt.

'Can you write down what we've got on him and his people?' she said quietly.

Bengt accepted the marker with a nod, but didn't get up. Sebastian kept talking.

'The search of Dogge's house didn't turn up any weapons either. We took the usual stuff out of Rönnviken, phones and computers. The half-washed clothes Dogge was wearing have been sent off. We've been told that his shoes, which we found on the floor of the front hall, have visible traces of what might be blood: they're doing a rapid analysis and we can expect an answer tonight or tomorrow at the latest. There are three security cameras at the playground, they were installed about a year ago, after park staff found a used syringe in one of the playhouses and some human waste buried in a sandbox. Two of the cameras still work, and even though they were both aimed at the sandboxes and the rows of benches alongside them, you can see Dogge and Billy in the frame for a few seconds as they walk by on their way to the swings. They're talking. They're not fighting. Neither of them is carrying anything, as far as we can tell. You'll find all the tape we judge as relevant to the investigation in our Dur2 database. By the time they reach the swings they're out of the picture again, so we don't have any material that shows the actual shooting, but no other people turn up in these images. Ten technicians have searched the scene and the area around it. Cartridges, yeah, like I said. Four bullets, I mentioned that too. Blood and litter, check. The samples from Dogge and the clothes he had put in the washing machine have been sent off, and the samples from the shoes, but I already said all that. We're waiting on the results.'

'Did you find anything on Billy?' Farid asked as he took his laptop from his backpack and docked it at the station by his seat. Sebastian answered.

'His phone, that was all. He had a bunch of missed calls from unknown numbers, and a text, you've already seen that. The one that told him to come to the playground.'

'Was there anything at his house?' Farid started his computer.

'Nothing except...well, there was an empty suitcase in the living room. Like it was out because someone was getting ready to pack. The family liaison asked Leila about it, but she had nothing to say. And they're pretty cramped in there, maybe it was just meant to be used as extra storage.'

'How can we find out if they had any trips planned?' Lotta had stopped writing and turned to face the table.

'We've gathered the computers that were in the apartment,' Sebastian said. 'They were school computers, and the family has asked to have them back as soon as possible. They need them for the kids' schoolwork. But maybe on one of those?'

'Their mobile phones?' Farid entered his log-in info.

'We've only got Billy's.' Svante had crossed his arms. 'The prosecutor decided there were not sufficient grounds to seize the others at this juncture.'

'Do we have all the family's email addresses?' Farid looked at Lotta.

'The ones they've given us, yes. But if they've bought plane tickets and don't want us to know, I'm sure they will have used an account they won't tell us about. And anyway, we're not allowed to check those at this point.'

'Okay. The phone Dogge used to call in the shooting?'

'An unregistered pay-as-you-go phone,' Sebastian replied. 'We haven't found that one either. Not at Dogge's house, and not at the playground. We've ordered cell tower dumps to check the traffic in the area. We've confiscated Billy's private phone, like I said, as well as Dogge's.' He looked at Farid, who nodded.

'And Mehdi?'

'Gone but not forgotten,' Bengt said cheerfully. He'd tucked his pen behind his ear. 'We're still looking. He isn't at home with his mother, nor is he at any of the addresses where he tends to spend time, according to our sources. And naturally, no one has any idea where he is, least of all his best friends. He's hiding out.'

'Do we think he's in Sweden?' Svante tucked a portion of *snus* under his upper lip and turned to Farid. 'What do you think? What can you tell us about him?'

'There's no way to be sure, but I'd guess he's still somewhere in the vicinity of Våringe. It's not like Mehdi has a villa in Spain, he's not on that level. It's most likely he's lying low with a new girlfriend or some buddy of his. He'll turn up.'

Svante adjusted his *snus*.

'So, Foad? How did it go, questioning Dogge today?'

'My name is Farid Ayad.' He looked around the table. 'I work as a juvenile investigator in Våringe, as you know, and I'm on loan to help with this investigation, primarily the interviews. As you also already know, Dogge identified Mehdi as the ringleader yesterday, or, you know, this morning, to be precise. We hadn't had time to take him to his accommodation yet, and he took the opportunity to talk. By today he had sobered up, and he'd been able to meet with his lawyer, and now Dogge swears Mehdi is as innocent as a lamb.'

Svante leaned back in his chair, placing his hands behind his head and his feet on the chair in front of him.

'So he retracted his accusation?'

'Yes.'

'Hmm.' Svante closed his eyes as though he were considering what Farid had said. After a few seconds, he looked up. 'Do we really need to attach any weight to that?'

'Well, I don't quite know what else we could do. What do you mean?'

'You reviewed your notes with him and he signed them, right?'

'Yes.'

'Then let's go with that. Did he tell you anything about the weapon? Who gave it to him? Where is it now?'

'He says it was a Glock.'

Svante grinned.

'Guys like Mehdi love Glocks, don't they?' He sounded triumphant. 'Everyone in that line of business loves a Glock.'

Farid cleared his throat.

'Exactly. So we can't draw any conclusions from that. You wanted to know who Mehdi is. If you ask me, he's basically a wannabe. Not a nice guy, awfully violent, but his bark is bigger than his bite, and the only ones who really fall for it are the kids in Våringe. They worship him.'

'Would he be able to get a kid to off someone?'

Farid nodded.

'Definitely.'

'Well, there you go.' Svante clapped his hands together.

'I'd like you all to hear...' Farid hooked up to the room's speaker system. 'I'd like you all to hear how the second interrogation went.'

He pressed play. Dogge's voice filled the room.

'No, no. It wasn't Mehdi. I was wrong. He didn't say anything to me. Nothing. Never.' Dogge's voice was clearly breaking. 'I hardly know Mehdi. He never said nothing.'

'So you decided to kill Billy all on your own?'

'No, no…it wasn't my fault. It was…it was…I don't want to say.'

'Did someone else tell you to kill Billy?'

'I'm not saying.'

'Who gave you the gun?'

'I'm not saying.'

'What kind of gun was it?'

'A Glock.'

'Okay. How did you get hold of it?'

'I don't remember.'

Farid's deep sigh was evident on the tape.

'Did you buy it?'

'No.'

'Did someone give it to you?'

'I don't remember.'

'You don't remember?'

'No.'

'Where is the gun now?'

'I don't know.'

'You don't know?'

'No, I forgot.'

'How do you know it was a Glock?'

'Uh…I just know. Everyone knows! Everyone knows what a Glock looks like.'

'What does it look like? Can you describe it?'

'It's a fucking cop gun, don't you know what a Glock looks like?'

'The Swedish police don't carry Glocks. Can you describe for me what it looks like? Can you explain how it works?'

'If you want, you can give me one and I'll show you. If you don't think I can shoot, I'll show you.'

'Who taught you?'

'Huh? I...uh...' Dogge cleared his throat. 'No one.'

'Maybe you forgot?'

'I don't remember.'

'You don't remember? You remember how to use a Glock, but you don't remember who taught you how? Did the same person who gave you the Glock also teach you how to use it?'

'No...I mean, I don't know.'

'Did you bring the gun to the playground?'

'Mm-hmm.'

'Why did you bring the gun?'

'Because I was...no comment.'

'Who decided you and Billy should meet at the playground yesterday?'

'No comment.'

'Billy got a text that he was supposed to come to the playground, or else someone would come to his house. Are you the one who sent that text?'

'Uh-uh.'

'So, Billy was the one who decided you should meet up?'

'No.'

'So it was you?'

'No fucking comment.'

'But you did meet up there?'

'How the fuck else could I have shot him?'

'How did you know he was going to be there, if you hadn't agreed to meet?'

'Shut up.'

'In the middle of the night, you two decided to meet at the playground. Why?'

'I don't want to answer your fucking questions. I don't have to tell you nothing. Not one fucking stupid-ass question, you can just go to hell.'

'What did you do with the gun after you shot Billy?'

'Go to hell.'

'Where did you toss it?'

'None of your business.'

Farid pressed pause and looked around the crowded room.

'Anyway, it goes on like that for a while.'

Sebastian raised his hand.

Star student, Farid thought.

'Yes?'

'All the surveillance material we've made it through so far shows the same thing. Dogge and Billy were alone at the playground. We haven't looked through all of it yet, but we know one thing for sure, and that's that Dogge didn't go straight home from the playground. He got on the 530 bus bound for Våringe city centre at 23:09, he rode it for some time before getting off and boarding the 501, which goes to Rönnviken. But when I looked at the grounds for the warrant for the Arnfeldts' house, it looks like we thought Dogge went in the exact opposite direction?'

Sebastian looked at Sneaks and Gustav. They, in turn, looked at Farid, who sighed.

'A decision had to be made quickly, and I might have...'

'Forget about that,' Svante rushed to say. 'I saw the warrant too, and I know exactly what you meant. It was dark and nasty outside, and you had to be sure to get into this Dogge's house. Nothing untoward about that, as I see it.' He turned to Sneaks and Gustav. 'But if we ignore what you thought when you were asked yesterday, what did you notice at the scene, really?'

'I guess I was mostly thinking about whether anyone was still there,' Gustav said. 'Whether anyone was armed, and then we saw the kid, and... yeah, by then I wasn't thinking about much of anything besides him.'

Sneaks nodded.

'You've seen the pictures I took on my phone while Gustav was performing CPR. They look like the ultrasound pictures my daughter showed me when she was expecting twins. It's too dark to see a damn thing. He could have gone in any direction at all. It probably didn't start snowing until right after Billy was shot. Even if it had been the middle of the day, there wouldn't have been any tracks to find.'

'Okay,' Sebastian said. 'Then I suggest we make a new note of that, for you to enter into the log.'

Svante sat up straighter in his chair.

'We've got Billy's phone too. And Billy got a bunch of calls that night from the phone Dogge used to call 112, but he didn't answer a single one. Then he got a text message. "Come down to the playground right now or else" – that was more or less it, right?'

Sebastian looked down at his computer. He seemed to be searching for something.

'But did Dogge talk to anyone besides Billy?' Svante went on. 'Did he talk to Mehdi? Before the shooting? Or to debrief? Like I said, we've asked for the tower dumps to get a handle on what was going on nearby, but it would be best if we could get hold of the actual phone. If Dogge's going to keep sounding like a member of parliament getting slapped with a DUI in all his interrogations from now on, we need more on Mehdi. Can we get a couple of warrants on him? A wiretap, maybe? Better intel on his gang?' He turned to Farid. 'What are they called? What's their name?'

Farid shrugged.

'They don't have one, as far as I know.'

'Let's call them…' The corners of Svante's mouth turned down. 'Call them…X-Boys, that's good. Uh—' He waved at Lotta. 'Will you make a note of that?'

Lotta went over to the whiteboard that had *Mehdi Ahmad* on it and wrote *X-Boys* under his name. Svante nodded, pleased.

'Good…and I want us to put out a national alert on that bastard Mehdi. Give the people of Våringe some peace and quiet, put this gangster behind bars. Won't that be a nice Christmas present for our dear citizens?'

THE BOYS

During their very first summer holiday, Dogge and Billy attended a day camp at the Rönnviken sports centre. It lasted two weeks, and Dogge's father paid for it. The staff loved Billy.

'What a charmer, quite the little guy you've got here, so full of energy,' they said when Leila came to pick him up. They smiled, but she still felt nervous.

'You're behaving yourself, right?' she asked as they walked to the bus.

'Of course,' Billy said.

'Billy likes to test boundaries,' they said the next time she came to the sports centre. They were still smiling, but perhaps a bit more hesitantly. Even so, they seemed to think his antics were amusing. When they were going to be outside, Billy would hide indoors, inside the drying cabinet or in the staff room. Once they found him in the pantry, where he'd climbed the shelves and emptied the big cookie jar, the one only the staff were allowed to eat from.

When the camp director came in, Billy lay down in a flash, still with two cookies in one hand, and pretended to be asleep. The director thought he was so adorable that he took him in his arms and carried him to the break room sofa and let him keep sleeping there.

'It was like Emil and the sausage,' he said to Leila.

Leila didn't understand the reference, but she laughed hesitantly.

'Billy is irresistible,' the director went on.

Leila nodded. Billy put his arms around her and pulled her close.

'Never forget that, Mama,' he said proudly. 'I'm ear-zestable.'

But there was a lot Leila didn't know about, of course. Things only Dogge knew.

Sometimes Billy brought Dogge along when he wanted to do things he wasn't allowed to do, and Dogge was always terrified and loved every second. Dogge never said no, never protested. If they were discovered, he always took the blame, even when Billy didn't try to pin responsibility on him. All Billy had to do was smile.

'I'm soooorry, I knooooow, it was stupid, I'll never do it again, I sweeeear.'

When the summer holidays were over, Billy and Dogge kept playing football together. Billy gave the coaches high fives and leaned in close to them, joking softly to make them think it was all for them.

In school, he cheated on every test, as he told Dogge. He never went to the bathroom when he asked to leave class to pee, yet they let him go every time. And then there were all the things he didn't have to say aloud, but that Dogge knew anyway. When there was a fire in the football club's office storage area, the police came, but Billy wasn't even called in by the coach to answer questions about his whereabouts at the time. One day, when the players from the girls' team went to their changing room after practice, all their clothes, every last garment, were in the showers, each of which were turned on full. One of the girls pointed out to the coach that Billy had left ten minutes before everyone else and hadn't returned. To that, the coach gravely declared that this was a serious accusation and she should let the adults handle it.

When they were twelve, and Billy began to blow off practices, the coach still let him play in the first team for every match, and when he walked them through tactics and formations, Billy was the one he looked at, even though the bench was full of boys who had attended the practices Billy had skipped.

'Billy's got an eye for the game,' said the coach. 'Pass to Billy, keep Billy clear, make space for Billy.'

Billy just smiled, and at half-time he dragged Dogge off the substitute bench and disappeared. They smoked in secret, since it was absolutely forbidden. The coach never noticed how Billy smelled, but he searched Dogge's bag at every practice to make sure he hadn't brought any contraband.

The adults let Billy do whatever he liked and never asked questions they didn't want to know the answers to.

We believe you, Billy. You could go so far. You just need to focus, Billy. You've got the power, you can do anything.

They said nothing about Dogge, but at least they left him alone – after all, he was Billy's friend.

Now and then, some grown-up would talk to Teo about Dogge. He always nodded solemnly and listened to what they had to say.

'You have to stop being such a fuck-up,' he would say as soon as they were alone. And Dogge nodded and promised he would. He wanted to be more like Billy. Billy was his very best friend in the whole world. They didn't go to the same school, but Dogge went to Billy's house almost every day, and when he got there Billy wanted to spend time with him. He had almost disappeared, but Dogge had managed to get Billy back. And he wasn't about to let him disappear again.

13

It was nearly ten o'clock by the time Farid left the station on the night after the murder. He'd stuck around a while to help go through surveillance footage. It was a never-ending task. They didn't even know what they were looking for, aside from pictures of Dogge and Billy. A car coming by to deliver the murder weapon to Dogge? A person stopping to pick up the used gun? A third or maybe even fourth perpetrator or accomplice?

On the way home, he stopped at Rönnviken playground. It was just as dark now as when Billy had been taken away by ambulance the night before. Yet everything looked different. Blue-and-white police tape cordoned off the area around the swings. About thirty yards away, the traditional candles were lined up. They flickered in the light breeze. Earlier that day, a dozen or so teenagers had gathered here, Farid had learned when he read the news at lunch, but they seemed to have moved along by now. The police spokesperson had confirmed it: Billy was 'previously known to the police'; it 'couldn't be ruled out' that his death was 'gang-related'. The general public wouldn't grieve for him for long, no big evening marches or petitions would be organized for his sake.

But a few photographs of him had been put up, along with handwritten notes, frozen flowers, and a toy or two, and the streetlights down by the pedestrian tunnel seemed to be working now.

Farid wanted to make a few passes of the scene, see with his own eyes that the gun wasn't just lying around waiting to be found by a child at play – in the bushes right next to the swings, for instance. It wouldn't be the first time for such a serious mistake. He parked in the same spot he had the night before. A colleague approached him, but when he saw it was Farid he raised a hand in greeting and returned to his post a bit further up, near the golf course's car park. He or another colleague would stand there for another day or so. Until the police tape was removed, the candles fizzled out, and everything went back to normal.

The playground was in an odd location, with the road that formed the border of the district on one side and the recreation area and artificial golf course slopes on the other. But within the police tape was a first-rate play area with several slides, two enormous climbing structures, a climbing wall, three large sandboxes with different kinds of sand, and a long row of swings of various sizes and models.

A man with a dog on a lead and two kids of around ten were approaching the cordons. Farid stood a few yards away from them, held his phone at hip height, and took a photo, even though one of his colleagues had a night-vision camera in a car a little further down the street. Altogether there were four officers on the scene, two in plainclothes and two in uniform.

When the little family came up alongside Farid, one of the kids set a candle on the ground and lit it. Farid crouched down and picked up a stiff, frozen teddy bear that was hugging a school picture between its plush arms. In the picture, Billy was wearing a white shirt and a narrow black tie and had nothing in common with the boy who had been loaded into the ambulance the night before. Nor did he look like the Billy Farid had known.

The first time Farid had discovered him high on something, Billy was ten and with his father. Isak was too drunk to notice what was wrong with his son. Or maybe he did notice, but was too drunk to do anything about it. Farid performed a rapid test that came up positive for marijuana, and took Billy to Leila and Isak to jail. That same day, he wrote a memo of concern to social services; two days later he and two colleagues went to Billy's school and spoke with the staff there. One week later, they took a drug-sniffing dog through the school. The dog indicated four student lockers and one teacher's coat. The school put the teacher on sick leave and organized learning days to inform the students of the dangers of using narcotics. Farid came back to the school to hand out brochures that the students threw out the moment they thought he wasn't looking.

Three weeks later, he found Billy unconscious, in a wooded area just outside Våringe. In the ditch next to him was one of the brochures, now soaking wet. That time, Billy ended up in Accident & Emergency with alcohol poisoning. His stomach was pumped and he was sent home the next day. It was his eleventh birthday, and social services booked a new appointment with the family, and Farid went home to Nadja and said, for the umpteenth time, that the only person who could make sense of this world was Aunt Fatima.

Farid's aunt Fatima, his father's sister, had come to Sweden the last of everyone in the family, once her children were grown and her husband had been dead for many years. She saw signs of the end of the world everywhere. Low-flying swallows were an omen not only of rain, but of death. The fox who took the neighbour's cat was a sure sign that someone close to her had been struck by a fatal disease. And if the wheat lay down after a July thunderstorm and didn't want to stand up again, she knew a relative would soon meet a violent end.

That first summer, when there were over twenty shootings in Stockholm, Aunt Fatima moved in with Farid's parents. It was the same summer as all the forest fires in Hälsingland. The next summer, a woman was killed just outside Malmö as she held her six-month-old daughter in her arms. The year after that, two kids on their way to preschool were hit in the legs by stray bullets and injured, and when Fatima and Farid's parents were driving home from a party in Västerås one pitch-black night in September, they were forced off the road, right into the ditch, to keep from hitting a moose that seemed to have run straight into traffic. They were unhurt, but it wasn't as if that fact made Fatima any less morose.

Her examples just kept coming. The 2004 tsunami, the mass murder at Utøya, any time terrorism struck a place Fatima could locate on a map, the floods in Belgium, the heat waves in Canada. The roses in Farid's garden blooming in December and the pine trees outside his parents' house getting a fungal infection that turned their needles yellow. The melting ice and the Australian drought. All of these were signs of the impending apocalypse. And Fatima mumbled to herself, chanting things no one understood.

'Don't look away!' she would cry when Farid came into his parents' den, where she was always sitting in the same deep chair. 'Dare to see the truth, don't shy away, no one can save us.'

If he tried to cheer his aunt up, or kiss her cheek more times than usual, she would wave him off as if he were contagious somehow. Sometimes she sang in a creaky voice a song no one understood or could sing along to. When she was finished she would translate the lyrics word for word. If there was anything she loved more than talking about judgment day, it was a truly tragic song.

'All my life I've laughed at Fatima behind her back,' Farid said to his wife. 'But she's right, and I'm an idiot.'

When Farid had had a look, first at his watch and then over by the highway, he took out his phone and typed a long message to Svante.

'Did your search extend all the way to Våringe? If Dogge got on the bus in Våringe city centre, we have to check that whole path as well, all the places he might have ditched the weapon. Rubbish bins and so forth must have been emptied by now, but tell me you checked them yesterday?'

He looked at his watch again. It was high time for him to make his way out of here and head home to his family for a few hours. He needed to grab his jacket, the one he'd borrowed at the station was too small. Maybe he would also be able to get a few hours of sleep.

The father at the memorial had crouched down to comfort one of his kids, who was now sobbing loudly. The other kid was holding on to the dog, who was blithely peeing on a giant bouquet of flowers. Farid's phone buzzed. It was a news flash. The photo that had been disseminated to all law enforcement units last night popped up on his screen. A national alert had gone out, Svante had got his wish. The headline read, 'Leader of X-Boys Sought in Murder of 14-Year-Old.'

Farid turned on his phone flashlight. Bent double, he slowly followed the hedge all the way around the playground. When he got back down to the other side, the father by the newly lit candle had grown weary.

'Come on,' he said to the kids.

They seemed ready to go too. The younger one reached his arms up in the air. His father lifted him up and, with some effort, set him on his shoulders. He nodded at Farid, who nodded back. The other kid fished a half-chewed drawing out of the dog's mouth and tossed it back into the sea of flowers. Then they walked off. Farid's phone buzzed again. It was a reply from Svante.

'We searched exactly as far as we needed to search. Thanks for your concern, but I'm no idiot, Foad.'

14

S he's waiting for you in the meeting room.'

The lawyer's name was Charlotte, and she had the same old-guy briefcase and ugly, un-parted hairstyle as when he first met her yesterday morning.

Dogge had only vague memories of being driven to a house in the early morning hours after the shoot-ing, a big house in a neighbourhood he didn't rec-ognize, and of someone asking if he wanted to eat, brush his teeth, change into something to sleep in. He'd shaken his head and fallen dead asleep on top of a narrow but surprisingly soft bed. An armed police officer had stood outside his room all night. The cop woke him up the next morning to say that his lawyer had come to meet with him. It was several merciful seconds before he understood why.

———

The lawyer didn't say flat out that it had been a stupid idea to talk to the police without her, but Dogge could tell that's what she was thinking.

'You have to tell them that,' he said at first. 'You have to say I was snowed when they questioned me yesterday because Mehdi is going to fucking kill me, understand?'

The lawyer nodded, but protested anyway.

'There's no need to retract your witness statement. The police have to make sure you are protected. Don't worry.'

She clearly did not understand. So he did the best he could during his next interrogation, without her help. It didn't work very well. Farid got angry and asked a million annoying questions, and it was obvious he didn't believe a word Dogge was saying. Farid asked the same questions over and over again, until Dogge's head was spinning and he forgot what he'd said in the first place.

'I'd rather not say' was an answer that worked pretty well. But it was boring, saying the same thing all the time.

'I can't say', 'I don't know', 'I forgot' were other statements he tried. But Farid never seemed satisfied.

'They're going to kill me, understand?' was the most effective reply. It slipped out of him once, and then even Farid seemed to believe he was right, that on that particular point he wasn't lying.

Mostly Farid kept harping on the gun. Where had he got it and where had it gone? After a while, all of his questions revolved around it.

When he could no longer bring himself to say 'I don't know, I forgot,' Dogge stopped responding entirely. That turned out to be the best tactic of all. After fifteen minutes of sitting slumped in his chair, his arms crossed, Farid ended the interrogation.

'I guess we'll pick this up again tomorrow.'

'Sounds good,' said Charlotte. 'We're not getting very far like this.'

Now it was time for a third interrogation. Charlotte and Farid were sitting in the same places as last time.

'Did you sleep well?'

'No.'

'Do you feel like talking about what you did with the weapon?'

'No.'

'You're aware we found the cartridges?'

'Yes.'

'You're aware we will be checking to see if there are any fingerprints on them?'

'Fucking CSI, sure.'

'Were you the one who loaded the weapon?'

'Uh...'

'Are we going to find your fingerprints on the cartridges, Dogge?'

'How the fuck should I know?'

'What do you *think*?'

'None of your business.'

Aunt Lavender came into the interrogation room just as Farid turned off the recorder and Charlotte stood up. She smiled as though she had good news.

'We've secured a spot for you in a home, a state facility not far from here. To be sure, it is a home for guys a little older than you, but we had to find a place where we can be sure you won't run into anyone from Våringe. And the security there is very tight. Our top priority is making sure you feel safe. We can take you there right now.'

'Now?'

'Yes.'

'Like right away?'

'Yes.'

'I don't want to go to some fucking facility. I want to go home.'

'You can't go home.'

'But I can't live there. I can't live in a state home, you don't get it. I can't.'

'Goodbye, Douglas,' said the lawyer. 'We'll talk soon.'

He had to ride the elevator with Farid all the way down to the garage.

'We've got a car waiting,' said Farid.

'It wasn't my fault,' Dogge muttered. 'It wasn't my fault.'

But Farid didn't seem to be listening anymore.

THE BOYS

Dogge started showing up at Billy's house without
notice. He had a bike, which he would lock up inside
the stairwell, winding a chain around the railing. He
never took the lift, because Leila had once told him
that one of their neighbours had got stuck between
two floors and wound up in there for four hours before someone came to let him out. After that, Dogge
always ran up the stairs.

He would sit down on a step and listen to music so
loudly that it crackled out from his headphones. He
waited for Billy to come home from school, killing
time by pulling up the legs of his pants and scratching the backs of his knees. When Billy arrived he
turned off the music, adjusted his pants, and wiped
his hands on his back pockets.

One day, Isak let him in.

'Dad only lives here sometimes,' Billy liked to
say. 'Mum wants him to move out forever. But he
keeps coming back anyway.'

Isak had got a key from Aisha, he told Dogge. He needed to come in to grab something.

'You can come inside with me.'

Later that night, Dogge heard an encounter between Aisha and her mother in the hall.

'What was I supposed to say, Mum?' she cried. 'I couldn't tell him I didn't have a key. He knows I do.'

If Isak was home, the boys never stuck around in the apartment. The tiniest thing could set him off, Billy had said.

'He doesn't hit us, mostly just Mum. And then she gets really mad and changes the locks. If she can afford it.'

So when Isak was in the apartment, they went down to the square. There wasn't much to do there, but sometimes a group of older guys would be hanging around the patio seating at the pizza place, drinking from cans and smoking even though it wasn't allowed there, and even though some of them weren't eighteen yet. Dogge and Billy liked sitting on the other side of the square to watch them. When the waiters came out, the guys would flick their cigarettes into the bike path, sometimes only half smoked. Billy would run over, pick them up, and wrap them in a paper towel so they wouldn't fall apart.

'I'll teach you to smoke,' he promised Dogge. 'I know how to do it.'

'So do I,' Dogge muttered. But not too loudly; he still wanted Billy to show him.

Sometimes, too, they would go to Dogge's house. Billy loved spending time in Rönnviken. There, they were free from Billy's siblings – his little brother could be such a pain. Teo liked to show Billy any new fancy gadget he'd bought, speakers for the stereo system or Japanese knives that had the sharpest blades in the world. Once he let Billy ride along in a car he'd borrowed from a friend, a Bugatti Veyron.

'It's the world's fastest car,' Teo said. 'It costs twenty million kronor.'

Billy got to sit in front, next to Teo. There was no back seat, so Dogge stayed behind as they drove off.

'We'll go for a ride tomorrow, you and me,' Teo said when they got back. Billy's cheeks were flushed.

'So fucking cool,' he said.

'Yeah, it's sick,' said Dogge.

The next day, the car was gone.

'Next time,' Teo said when Dogge asked about the ride. 'I have to work right now.'

The boys had started Year 3 when one of the guys who hung around the outdoor seating at the Våringe pizzeria leaned over the patio fence and snagged Billy by the shirt. He was the one the other older guys looked at the moment he spoke, the one who never bothered to toss his cigarette when the staff came out. The badass one.

'My girl wants a chocolate bar,' he said. 'You on it?'

Billy nodded. 'For sure.'

They went to Weed's Market. Dogge had money, but it was more fun to lift candy. Billy asked Weed where the yeast was while Dogge stuffed three chocolate bars under his shirt. As he approached the exit, he heard Billy.

'Oh no, I forgot Mum's purse. I'll have to come back later.'

'Go ahead and take the yeast,' Weed said. 'Your mum can pay me next time she comes in.'

Dogge waited on the other side of the square. The blood was rushing through his veins; it felt like he'd just ridden a rollercoaster but without feeling the least bit sick. Billy took the chocolate and tossed the yeast into some bushes.

'Did you hear what Weed said? "Your mum can pay later." What a fucking idiot.'

They laughed until they couldn't breathe and their bellies ached.

When they got back to the pizzeria, Billy handed over the chocolate. The older guys were still sitting there, drinking Cokes.

'Thanks, kid,' said the most badass one, stuffing the chocolate bar into his pocket.

'Who is that?' Dogge asked as they walked off.

'Mehdi,' Billy replied, in the voice he used when he thought Dogge was being a dork. 'I mean, everyone knows who Mehdi is. Fucking everyone in Våringe. Seriously, how stupid can you get?'

15

They drove through the woods for over an hour. With walls of evergreens and snow on either side of the police car, it felt like driving through a tunnel. Dogge had been staring at the wall of trees for so long that his vision was flickering.

'What the hell are you even doing here?' he said to Farid, who was sitting beside him in the back seat and staring out the other window. 'Don't you have your own kids to drive places? Like picking them up from belly dancing or Koran lessons or something?'

Farid ignored him.

'You think I'm stupid?' Dogge went on. 'You think we're going to do some bonding, just you and me, no lawyers? And I'll tell you even more about Mehdi. There's no point, I'm not high anymore, you can't trick me into saying things that aren't true.'

A train with seemingly endless carriages thundered by.

'Calm down. We've known each other long enough to be able to chat about whatever. Do you like spending time in the woods?'

'Sure,' Dogge scoffed. 'Best shit ever. I'm a Scout leader, didn't you know? I love picking mushrooms and baking cookies out of bark and all that shit.'

'I'm not trying to trick you. I was just curious.'

Dogge groaned.

'Well, I'm not some fucking Syrian anyway. Who never gets more than three blocks from their satellite dish. You're the only *blatte* in this car,' he said, hoping the slur would get a reaction.

'Hardly,' came a voice from the driver's seat. 'There are at least two *blattar* in this car. Possibly three, I don't remember if I emptied the trunk before we left the station.'

Farid smiled. Dogge slumped down in his seat.

'Are we almost there? Or are you driving me to fucking Norway?'

By the time they slowed down in front of the gate to the youth home, it was getting dark. There were spotlights mounted above the fence. They came on as the car approached. Before they could drive in to park, they had to announce themselves via an intercom.

On the other side of the gate, they were met by two men, a younger guy of around twenty-five and a man who appeared closer to sixty.

'My name is Josef,' said the older man, shaking Dogge's hand and holding it until Dogge looked at him and said his own name. He seemed strong. The younger guy just nodded and kept his distance.

'That's Momi,' said Josef.

'This is where I leave you,' Farid said, handing over a small paper bag. 'This is a prescription for Dogge, to help him sleep.'

'Is there anything else we need to know?' Josef wondered.

'Nothing besides what we discussed on the phone,' Farid said. He turned to Dogge. 'We'll be in touch.'

Josef took Dogge by the arm, not very firmly, and headed for the entrance.

'It's going to be okay, Dogge,' said Josef. 'You don't need to worry.'

16

The part of the youth home where he would stay was a squat, one-storey building with two wings, enclosed by a twenty-foot perimeter fence. The wings were angled toward a yard that was divided into two mirror-image sides, each with a round table and snow-covered basketball court. These outdoor areas were separated by a path that led up to the centre of the building and the main entrance. The path was also surrounded by a fence, not as high as the perimeter fence but still impossible to climb over.

As Dogge, Josef and Momi approached the building, the area was lit up by four bright spotlights. It had been shovelled, but it was clear the ground was frozen.

They entered through the big door in the middle. Josef led Dogge down a narrow corridor and into an oblong room. On one side of the room was a low bench; on the other side were two doors with barred windows at the top. Both doors were ajar. In each room there was a plastic mattress next to a floor drain. The rooms were otherwise empty.

'I have to sleep there?' Dogge whispered. He didn't want to sound scared but didn't manage to keep the fear from his voice.

Momi took him gently by the arm, placed his other hand on his back, and caught his eye.

'No, Dogge. Don't worry. This is the check-in area. You'll have a real room. With a real bed, of course. You'll have your own bathroom, with a toilet. These rooms are for those who need a few minutes to calm down. We're just going to get you checked in. You seem calm to me. Are you? How are you feeling?'

Dogge cleared his throat.

'Good. Good, I'm okay.'

'We're here to help you.' This time, it was Josef speaking. His voice was deeper, but just as soft as Momi's. 'You'll start by giving us a urine sample. Then you can have a shower.' He nodded at a bathroom with an adjoining shower that didn't have a door. 'And a change of clothes.'

Josef pointed at two stacks of clothing that lay on the bench. It looked like a regular old tracksuit; Momi was wearing a similar one. And two plain T-shirts, four pairs of briefs, towels, socks, and a pair of gym shoes with no laces. On top of the clothing were toiletries: a bar of soap, a toothbrush, a tiny tube of toothpaste.

He peed naked while Josef and Momi watched. They took turns speaking, explaining everything that was going to happen, what they expected of him. He didn't listen very carefully. Once he had showered, he pulled on the tracksuit.

They went back out into the corridor. He'd already forgotten where they'd come in. His head was spinning. As they walked through the building, Josef pointed out the different rooms.

'There's the kitchen. You aren't allowed in there.'

'There's the staff room. You aren't allowed in there.'

'There's the visiting room. We haven't received a list of your visitors yet, but once we do you can meet with them in there.'

'Who the fuck do you think is going to visit me?' Dogge muttered.

But it didn't seem like Josef heard him.

'Here's the common showers. You won't need to use these because you can shower in your room. We have two units, with eight boys in each module, and you'll be staying in the south one. Momi and I work forty-eight-hour shifts, along with four other people. There are always at least six adults with you around the clock. And then there are the teachers and some other staff, of course.

'Down this corridor is the workshop. Let us know if there's anything you'd like to try out in there.

'We have four classrooms, they're not in this building, I thought we would go through your schedule tomorrow.

'If you want to use the gym it's best to say so the day before so we can book a time slot for you.

'This is where our psychologist usually is. Some-times the police conduct interviews in this room, if the visiting room is in use.

'If you'd like to meet with a pastor we can try to bring one in. They usually come if we call and ask. Or, maybe you're Muslim?'

Dogge shook his head.

'Do I look like a Muslim to you?'

'What would you say a Muslim looks like?'

They entered a room that was divided in two. One side was furnished with a sofa, two easy chairs and a large TV. Two guys were on the sofa. Four oth-ers stood around a larger table, looking at a computer screen. On the other side was a dining table.

'This is where you'll eat all your meals, along with the other boys in your module. You just missed dinner. But there's an evening snack at nine. We'll come get you then.'

There was something about their body language, the looks they gave him, how they held their arms as they stood up, how their hands were slightly curled into fists even though they weren't about to fight. No one looked like that in Rönnviken. But lots of people in Våringe did. Sometimes Dogge felt like he knew people he'd never met before, just because they reminded him of folks in Våringe. Once or twice he had almost said hello, but stopped himself at the last second. You had to be careful not to say hi to people you didn't actually know. There was no way to predict how they might react.

He would never be able to look like that. When he did his first couple of errands, Mehdi had said it was an advantage, he liked that Dogge looked different from everyone else. It was *fucking practical* and *we can make good use of that*. Billy said he didn't care; the main thing was that at least Dogge didn't look like a fucking snob.

You can meet the guys later, in peace and quiet when we eat. But first you'll be able to spend some time in your room. Get some rest.'

Dogge nodded and turned around to follow Josef. One of the guys on the sofa laughed loudly at something. Dogge startled. He turned his head and saw a glimpse of the guy before Josef came up alongside him and his view was blocked.

There was something about that laugh – he'd heard it before.

When they arrived at his room, the door was locked. Josef opened it with a key attached to his belt.

'I made the bed for you,' he said. 'You're actually supposed to make it yourself. From now on, you'll have to do it. But I figured you would be tired. That you would need to get some rest.'

'Thanks,' Dogge muttered.

'I won't lock the door when I leave,' Josef continued. 'But you can lock it from the inside if you'd like. We can always open it, and we can see you if you open the door and leave, because there are cameras and sensors. But it's up to you whether you want to keep it locked.'

When Josef left the room, Dogge turned the lock until it would turn no farther. Then he lay down on the bed, tucked his knees to his chest, and closed his eyes.

It's just my imagination, he thought. *All those guys just look the same. No one knows me here, no one knows who I am. We're a hell of a long way from Våringe.*

Then he fell asleep.

THE BOYS

The first time the boys got picked up by Farid was the hottest day of the summer holiday, the year they both turned nine.

They had biked up to the shuttered chicken factory, and Dogge was already thirsty as they ditched their bikes on the gravel lot in front of the driveway that led to the abandoned building. Neither of them had brought anything to drink. They ran over to the gravel pile, filled their pockets and a plastic bag with rocks, and then broke every window in the building. It took over an hour. They had to go back for more rocks four times. The best part was inside the factory-floor section, where shards of glass from the windows up by the roofline rained down on the floor and made down, dust and old feathers rise like mushroom clouds from the firm-packed floor. Billy laughed like a fool. The loud sound, the space in the vast room, the feeling of being alone in the world, just the two of them, fizzed inside Dogge. No one worked up there anymore, the factory had been deserted for fifteen years. The smell of dead birds was the only clue to what had once been here.

Farid and a colleague stopped them as they were biking home; someone had seen what they'd done and called in to report them.

'They're always after us,' Billy liked to say. 'They hate us, they don't want us to exist. Cops are so fucking prejudiced. They always go for the same people, it's discrimination. You're lucky, Dogge, it's a good thing to look like you do, you get to escape the pigs.'

But Billy was wrong. Farid scooped up both of them. They had to put their bikes in the trunk, and then they were driven home.

Farid offered Dogge a bottle of water, but he said no. You should always say no to the police, Billy had taught him that.

'Yes please,' said Billy.

And then he smiled his big smile, with all his teeth, as though Farid had picked them up as a favour, as though he were their friend. Farid, who was sitting in the back seat between them, smiled back.

They dropped Billy off first. His mother came dashing out to the street, shouting and waving her arms. Billy was clearly ashamed. His mother was always so loud and never seemed to care if anyone heard her chewing him out.

Dogge's parents were the opposite. No one was allowed to hear when they were angry. They waited until they were alone.

As Farid explained what the boys had done, Teo nodded gravely. A wrinkle appeared on his forehead.

'That's absolutely unacceptable. I don't know what got into him. I will have a serious talk with Douglas.'

But once the police had left, he came into the kitchen where Dogge was eating cereal, he was on his third bowl, and looked at him. He shook his head slightly but didn't say anything. Dogge could tell he was smiling when he walked off.

When his mum got home from work, she asked what had happened. The neighbour had told her the police had brought Dogge home.

'It was no big deal,' said Teo. 'Nothing to worry about, you'd think the police had better things to do than chase after little kids for throwing rocks at an abandoned building. Can't they just let the boys play in peace? Who could they hurt up there? A homeless magpie? A runaway rat?'

Dogge's mum agreed.

'They should use their resources to fight actual crime. The Lindgrens had a break-in last week, and it took the police two days to show up. The burglars took their Liljefors painting and broke a whole collection of numbered Orrefors pieces, but it's like the police don't even care.'

17

Josef opened the door slowly. Dogge was lying on top of the covers in the clothes he had been given at check-in. Hardly an hour had passed since Josef had left the boy in this room. If he were to guess, Dogge had fallen asleep about a minute after the door closed.

That was typically what happened. The boys who came to them were usually stressed to breaking point; some of them hadn't slept in days. They had frequently self-medicated against the worst of their anxiety, and might show up with withdrawal symptoms, especially the ones who were addicted to benzos.

It sometimes took the benzo kids weeks before they could sit down for a whole meal, even if they'd been weaned off them at the hospital first. But when they were allowed to lock the door, when they were alone, with bars on the windows and security cameras watching, with a perimeter fence and six grown men right outside, always there to protect them, from themselves and others, they could fall asleep at last.

Only here, behind lock and key, could they feel safe, far from their own homes, the street, the people who claimed to be their parents, their best friends, their family.

Josef had kids who begged to come to the isolation room, to solitary, just because they *wanted it quiet in their heads*. And when he explained that they couldn't be there, not without an order from the director of the facility, and never for more than four hours at a time, they began to cry.

He cleared his throat softly. He wanted to wake the boy as gently as possible, avoid touching him. Lots of them had a hard time being touched. Dogge startled.

'We're about to have evening snack. I figured you must be hungry, and once we've put it away there won't be more to eat.'

'I'll come. For sure.'

Dogge looked bleary. He wiped his mouth and ran a hand through his hair.

'You can go straight to bed again afterwards, if you want.'

Josef stood near the door and waited as Dogge put on the plastic sandals he'd been given at check-in.

'If you need to pee, I can wait outside.'

'I don't.'

'Okay.'

D ogge didn't say anything as they walked down the short hallway to the dining area. The door to the gym was open; one of the guys was working out. Josef stuck his head in to see which staff member was there with him.

'Are you coming for a snack?' he asked his colleague.

'We're on our way. Emil wanted a couple more minutes to finish his routine.'

'See you there,' said Josef, turning around to continue on.

Dogge stood before the open gym door and stared into the room. His gaze seemed to have frozen on Emil Pavic, who was sitting on one of the benches and doing bicep curls with an 11-kilogram weight. Emil stared back and smiled as he lifted the barbell up and down, up and down. Josef sighed, stepped back, and pulled the door closed.

We'll have to keep an eye on that, he thought. Emil wasn't typically a fighter; they'd placed Dogge in their quietest unit, but there was no reason to take unnecessary risks.

'You can't go to the gym while someone else is there, Dogge,' he said. 'You can only work out one at a time, with supervision, and only if there's time. You have to let us know ahead of time. Okay? And I think we should hold off on the gym for a few days.

All these new routines will be enough for you to get used to.'

Dogge was still standing frozen at the door, so Josef took him firmly by the upper arm and pulled him along to the dining area.

'Wake up, kiddo. Let's go eat. Soon you'll be back in your room so you can sleep. There's usually nice sandwich fixings and good yogurt for our nighttime snack. Do you like yogurt?'

'I'm not hungry,' said Dogge.

'Let's go,' said Josef. 'It's time to get some food in you.'

18

Salmon was the only fresh fish Weed sold in his shop. But there was plenty of it. If you didn't want it fresh, you could buy it frozen, smoked or salt-brined; thinly sliced or in balls; marinated, portioned or whole. Sometimes he brought in an order of shrimp; that usually sold well. There was also lots of herring, but all of it was pickled. Weed didn't like herring. Nor did he understand the point of lutefisk, and he'd only ordered *surströmming* one year, and then he stopped. No one in Våringe ate rotten fish from a can, especially not Weed's customers.

At home he strove for more variation. Everyone in the family – even Eva, his youngest, who periodically claimed to be vegan – ate smoked mackerel and salt-brined salmon. But if it was up to Weed, he preferred the fresh fish recommended by his wholesaler: monkfish, sole or turbot. Today he had brought home two sea bass that weighed over two kilos each. It would be a lot of food, but he'd got one for free, and his sons were incredible eaters. He was cleaning the fish when his oldest son, Jacob, came into the kitchen.

'Please set the table,' said Weed. His hands glittered with fish scales.

'Dogge got sent to a home,' said Jacob. 'It's really far away.'

Weed turned on the tap and let the water flow over his wrists. It quickly grew ice-cold.

'Please set the table,' he said again, nodding at the stack of plates he'd placed on the counter. His son picked up the plates and began to arrange them on the table.

'How do you know he was sent to a home?' he asked. 'Did you read it online?'

'I just know. It's really far away, Dad. Really far. This isn't gossip, it's totally true, I know it for a fact.'

'Does Eva know? Did you tell Eva?'

Jacob nodded and took five glasses from the cupboard above the dishwasher. Weed chopped tarragon and dill, scooped a big chunk of butter from the tub, and massaged the herbs into it before dividing up the mixture, tucking it along with a quartered lemon into the bellies of the fish. The oven was already hot; he moved the potatoes to the lowest rack and put the fish in to bake.

'Will you light the candles?'

Jacob nodded again.

———

It had been just over a year since it happened. *Four hundred and twenty days.* He had found her in the stockroom. She was there because that was where Dogge and Billy had left her.

As they sat down to eat, Weed glanced at his youngest daughter, tried to catch her eye, tried to sense what she was thinking. She was thirteen now and had started wearing make-up. Thick black lines around her eyes.

'She's too young for make-up,' Weed had said to Sara.

'She'll never be old enough, not for you. Let her be,' Sara had replied. 'Make-up never killed anyone. It's a good sign that she wants to look nice. And it's perfectly normal that she wants to look older. All girls her age do.'

But the make-up didn't make his daughter seem older. It only made her look unhappy. The blacker the eyeliner, the sadder she seemed. Her clothing didn't help. She bought tights and ripped them up, she cut the fingertips off gloves, she wore holey jeans.

She's putting on a costume, Weed thought. *Because she doesn't want to be herself anymore.* He could hardly say so, not even to Sara.

'We don't control how our children want to dress,' Sara said when she saw Weed's reaction. 'That's not the kind of parents we are.'

So he said nothing about her clothes either. And he couldn't ask his daughter how she was doing because the simplest questions would make her furious and he would never get an honest answer anyway.

But now, despite that, he tried. At the dinner table, where she wasn't usually too dramatic. He blurted out the question and immediately took another bite of fish, peering at her as discreetly as he could.

'So what do you think?' he wondered. 'Does it feel better, knowing that Dogge is gone?'

She nodded, doing that Swedish thing of saying 'yes' on an inhalation, so it sounded like a sob.

Sara repeated what her son had so recently said.

'He's really far away.'

Eva didn't have anything to say about that.

'I'm not very hungry' was all she said. And then she left the table.

THE BOYS

The first time Dogge heard Mehdi laugh the way only Mehdi could laugh, they were in Year 4. This was one year after he asked them to get him the Kexchoklad bar. Mehdi hadn't talked to them even once since, he'd hardly even looked their way. Still, Billy always seemed to know right where he was.

'We have to show Mehdi we can do anything, that he can trust us,' he told Dogge at least once a week. And they tried to stick close by without seeming pushy. Yet Mehdi hadn't asked for more favours, he didn't even seem to recognize them.

'The first errand,' Billy declared. 'I mean, a real one, not some dumb thing like pinching chocolate, you can't ask for it, you just get it. It's your first medal, your first sign of respect, and no fucking little brat around here would be stupid enough to talk to Mehdi without being spoken to first.'

And yet that was exactly what Billy did. Without being contacted, without knowing beforehand if it was okay. Dogge knew that Billy was a daredevil, but this was his craziest move so far.

They had decided to meet in the tunnel one sunny September day. Billy's school was on a field trip, but he'd told his mum his foot hurt after their most recent football practice. Dogge was cutting school. From the tunnel they biked to a building on the outskirts of Våringe; Billy had heard it was Mehdi's new place. But the building seemed to be undergoing renovations, although there weren't any workers there, just empty scaffolding, fluttering plastic sheeting, and buckets with the dried remains of cement. The door into the apartment had been removed, and it smelled like fresh paint. They went into the living room. There stood two big L-shaped sofas in front of a TV. Mehdi was sitting on one. A guy he called Blue-Boy was showing him something on a phone. Blue-Boy had a shaved head, ice-blue eyes, and a blotchy neck. They'd seen him with Mehdi many times before but had never heard his name. Two other people were playing *FIFA* on the TV. Dogge and Billy stood in the living room doorway. There wasn't any room for them, nowhere to sit down, nothing to do. But before Dogge could make Billy see that they should leave, Billy started talking.

'This one dude comes to my school every fucking lunch period to sell pot and oxy,' he said. 'It's not yours. You want us to take care of it, or what?'

Mehdi turned around, looked up from the phone, and stared at Billy without saying a word. He took a few drags from his vape pen. The bright-blue liquid bubbled.

Dogge thought, *Shit, shit, he's going to throw us out, stupid fucking Billy, what is wrong with you?* But before anyone could say anything, Billy tap-danced across the floor, like in an old black-and-white movie, and stopped with his hand pointed in the air like a pistol, pretending to fire it two feet from Mehdi.

'You think we should take care of it?' he said again. And then he swept out his gun hand and bowed.

Mehdi blew a narrow stream of smoke from the corner of his mouth. Dogge couldn't breathe. All the doors in the apartment had been removed, you could see into every other room from the living room. They were all empty but one, where a mattress with wrinkled sheets and a duvet with no cover lay on the floor.

That was when Mehdi started laughing. He had a wonderful laugh, it came from his belly and sounded like a song. He laughed for so long that it turned into a brief coughing fit, and then everyone around him started laughing too. Everyone but Dogge, who still didn't dare.

The Monday after Billy did his dance number, Mehdi drove to his school. Billy called Dogge an hour later.

'We have to go back to see Mehdi,' he said, breathless with excitement. And then he told him what had happened.

Mehdi had parked his car in the disabled spot outside the teachers' entrance. He waited there until the guy who sold oxy showed up, as he did every lunch break. The dealer was maybe seventeen, not so old that he couldn't be mistaken for a pupil at the school. He must have recognized Mehdi, because he stopped short and hesitantly walked over to the parked car. Billy and four other guys were standing four floors up, watching as Mehdi shoved open the passenger door from the inside and the guy got in. They stared at the roof of the car for a few minutes, maybe three, and then the guy got out again and ran for the subway. Once he was out of sight, the car drove off.

Billy was waiting for Dogge outside the building they'd visited less than a week ago. They went up the stairs. There was an apartment door now, but no doorbell. They knocked, and Blue-Boy opened. When he saw it was them, he just nodded.

'I'm so fucking hungry,' Mehdi said as they came into the living room. He was standing up, with a gaming controller aimed at the TV.

'You'll handle it, boys? Right? And get me some *snus* while you're at it.'

———

They lifted a rotisserie chicken down at Weed's Market. Dogge stuck it inside his shirt, and it was so hot it burned him. Billy scored a carton of *snus* from the stockroom. Dogge heard him say to one of the neatly combed idiots who worked back there that it was for Mehdi. They gave it to him without further ado.

'What are you up to?' Weed called when Dogge pulled his jacket closed and headed for the exit. 'I see what you're doing.' Dogge started running. 'Stop him!' Weed shouted, but everyone Dogge passed backed away.

When he got home later that night, he put his shirt in the washing machine, but the grease stains wouldn't come out. It didn't matter to him. He would keep that shirt anyway.

19

Dogge was holding his cock. He wanted to call it that, *cock*, even though he didn't think it felt like a cock. Especially not right now. It was small and soft, as if you could squash it. He tried to get it to wake up, he wanted to jerk off, thought it might calm him down. But it wasn't working. He would have liked to watch some porn, that usually made it happen without his thinking about it, or because he could stop thinking, but he still hadn't gotten his phone back.

When Josef had shown him to this room a few hours ago, he'd hardly made it out again before Dogge was asleep. But now it felt like he would never sleep again.

Earlier, he had hardly registered what this room was like. The windowpanes were frosted, it wouldn't be possible to see out, not even when the sun came up. There was a bed – it was bolted to the wall; a desk, also bolted; and a chair. Two shelves, but nothing to put on them. He hadn't been allowed to bring anything. Not even his underwear was his own.

Yet he had liked the room, even the bed. When had he last fallen asleep so quickly? He couldn't recall. Josef had pointed at a button by the door. Dogge could press it whenever he liked, Josef had explained. His voice was kind but firm, as though he was the type that brooked no arguments, as though he wanted Dogge to understand that he was in charge.

At the hospital where Dad had spent his last few weeks, dinner was served at an hour when normal people, or at least children, had a snack. Dad said they made them eat so early so the staff could go home and spend time with their kids.

Dogge wondered what kind of breakfast they served at this state home. Porridge, maybe? He hated porridge.

Billy always laughed at Dad's preferred breakfast of hard-boiled eggs with caviar from a tube. *Svenne* food, white people food, he called it. And he laughed at how Teo always wanted to go to the sea.

'The archipelago...you white people are obsessed. You love life jackets and boats and canoes. And the seeeeea! Life is not worth living if you've never seen the seeeea. Isn't that right, Teo?' Dad had laughed. He never took offence when Billy said that Svennes were idiots. Svennes were average white Swedes, they weren't rich, weren't fancy, didn't

live in Rönnviken. Teo didn't feel like the target of
Svenne jokes, for the simple reason that he wasn't
one – not even when he was eating that Svenne clas-
sic, caviar from a tube.

Dogge could have eaten anything for breakfast,
would have accepted anything, if it hadn't been
for what happened when Josef took him to evening snack. It had ruined everything. His heart
felt weird too. It was beating kind of irregularly.
He'd said so to the doctor he saw just before he
was brought to the state home, but she said there
was nothing wrong with him, it just felt that way.
If it feels weird, then it must fucking *be* weird, he
wanted to reply. She told him it was because he no
longer had access to drugs. As if he were some fucking junkie, one of the ones lying under the overpass
and shaking and whining at him to give them something, that they would blow him if he wanted. Two
of them were older than his mum. Yet they spoke
to him as though he were the adult, they respected
him, they were afraid.

You could get those junkies to do anything if you
had something good to offer. Once he had almost
fucked one of them, one of the youngest ones, but
she smelled bad and had a sore right below her collarbone. It was weeping and looked nasty. He had
simply walked away. At first she was furious, but she
calmed down when Billy gave her four grams, free
of charge. Dogge knew he did it because he felt sorry
for her, but he was also a little scared and wanted her

to leave them alone. Dogge totally understood. They had never talked about it afterwards.

The doctor who didn't think there was anything wrong with his heart did at least give him some pills to help him sleep. He'd got one from Momi just now, he swallowed it right away, but his heart was still beating super strangely. This bed felt rock-hard now, not at all like before. A rubber mattress atop unyielding wooden slats, it was like lying on the floor.

How long ago had he met Billy at the playground? He didn't want to think about it. It would invite those other thoughts in. But had he only been here a few hours? What had he done this morning? Had he got any food then?

They'd set a tray of breakfast on the desk while he talked to Charlotte the lawyer, but he couldn't remember what was on it. He must have had lunch, at least? But he'd forgotten what that was too. Something with potatoes? Or pasta? It was impossible to remember.

He was hungry when Josef came to get him. He thought a sandwich would taste good.

But then Josef stopped in front of an open door. He said something to the guard inside. The other guy in the room had short hair and the same kind of grey T-shirt and navy-blue track pants Dogge had been given when he arrived. This was another inmate, but Dogge realized straight off he was older, at least seventeen, maybe eighteen or nineteen, he looked like an adult. He was leaning forward and holding a gigantic hand weight, which he curled like it was light as a feather. Then Dogge saw the back of his neck. He had a tattoo of a bird with spread wings that curved around his neck. He recognized that tattoo. The fear made his blood curdle, his heart began to beat so sluggishly that he thought it was going to stop.

'There's no need to worry.' That was the last thing Farid said before he left Dogge at the home just a few hours ago. Josef and Momi had said the same thing. He'd believed them, despite what Billy had taught him, told him so many times that he knew it by heart.

'If the cops say "trust me", they're already fucking you in the ass.'

The Italian. That's what Mehdi called him. Not because he was Italian. Mehdi had told them that this guy once ate so much spaghetti while on a bender that he started puking, and when he stopped throwing up there were strands of spaghetti coming out his nose. People had called him 'the Italian' ever since. Dogge had forgotten what his real name was.

When the Italian saw Dogge, it was like something rattled in his head. He smiled, a big smile, his teeth so white it looked like he had a lamp in his jaws and one of his eyebrows looked thicker than the other. As Josef closed the door, Dogge heard the Italian drop the weight he'd been holding. The thud was so loud that Dogge jumped.

He had killed someone, hadn't he, the Italian had killed someone?

———

With a deep sigh, Dogge let go of his penis and pulled up his track pants. There was no point.

He tried to breathe normally. Just because he'd met him once with Mehdi didn't mean the Italian knew what he'd done, or what he'd said about Mehdi in that first interrogation. *He's just some guy Mehdi knows. He's not even from Våringe, he doesn't know anything. He's locked up. He doesn't know what I did.*

He looked at the digital clock on the bedside table. Twelve hours until breakfast. Outside his window, the sky was pitch-black.

20

't's possible that Rönnviken is heaven on earth.'
Farid closed the dishwasher with a bang and went
back to the kitchen table, where Nadja was picking
at a bowl of ice cream. 'But it's a shitty place.'

He'd had one beer, and then another. Felicia was
'out'. When he asked what time she was planning
to be home, she explained that she was going to 'lie
around all day' tomorrow. Natascha was in her room,
killing cops on her computer, and Ella had fallen
asleep in Farid and Nadja's bed.

He was tired, his eyes were stinging. He had got
maybe four hours of sleep since the murder, five if
he counted the hour he'd spent dozing in front of his
computer while he was trying to help read through the
phone records. But at least this evening he had made
it home for dinner. They'd run with lights on all the
way back from the children's home where they'd left
Dogge. Farid had asked his colleague to drop him off
at home. His car could stay at the station. Tomorrow

was Sunday, and no one would make a fuss if he left it there.

'Okay.' Nadja licked her spoon. 'Let's hear it.'

'The calls that come in from Rönnviken, what are they about? Unchaperoned parties at 400-square-metre houses. When we arrive, what are we supposed to do? Hold back the hair of sixteen-year-olds who are puking all over their 20,000-kronor jackets and still insisting, *Yeah, I can drive myself home, I've got a car*? They aren't cars, goddammit. And those kids don't have licences. If they did, I could confiscate them. Do you know what all those quadricycles cost?'

'No.'

'More than the down payment on our house. They go twenty miles per hour and cost a quarter million kronor. And when their daddies panic after the stock market takes a dive, they call an ambulance because they think they're dying. When they can't manage to properly tie up their boat at their own dock, and it comes loose and floats off, they report it stolen and get reimbursed by insurance. Sure, the men hit their wives out there too, and sometimes we have to break into a locked garage because someone is trying to gas themselves with the exhaust of the latest sports car, but the fact remains. Nothing fucking happens in Rönnviken that they shouldn't be able to handle on their own, with hired security guards. Why should we waste resources on them? We could use those funds where they're truly needed.'

'Is this about Dogge and Billy?' Nadja reached across the table, grabbed the bottle of beer from Farid, and took a sip. 'Or are you going into politics?'

'No, I'm not going into fucking politics. Up until the day before yesterday...or, hold on. Right, two days ago. Up until when Billy was shot, Dogge didn't even get up to his goddamn tricks in his home territory, he always went to Våringe for that. And sure, a shooting in Rönnviken, boo-hoo, now violence has permeated every segment of our society or whatever they're saying on the news...but no one from Rönnviken was actually affected. The opposite, in fact. It's still just the kids from Våringe and places like it that are dying. While Dogge gets patched up and taken care of and fussed over and coddled and—› He took a deep breath. ‹And it's still Rönnviken that gets all the resources they ask for and will gladly take a little more, just to be safe. We don't want the millionaires to risk anyone stepping funny on their lawns.'

'Millionaires are a vulnerable group,' Nadja nodded. 'Leaking breast implants, the roofs of their cabriolets that have to be manually closed, and those K-Cups that always seem to run out. They've got it tough.'

'In Rönnviken all it takes is a resident seeing a car with Polish plates go by for the national police commissioner to hold a press conference and the minister of justice to send out a convoy of officers to make sure it's not a band of thieves out doing recon. Do you want me to explain why we were on the scene so fast when the call came in about Billy? Because we had a preventive patrol there. In fucking Rönnviken? Why?'

'How is the investigation going?' Nadja handed the bottle back to Farid. She, too, was a trained police officer. Sure, she had quit back when they were expecting Felicia, at only twenty-three, and these days she worked as a lawyer for the police union, but she understood Farid's work. Despite the law school education she had completed during maternity leaves, she thought like a cop, and Farid had always spoken openly with her. 'Any progress?'

'Yeah, we've helped Mehdi strengthen his brand. A national alert went out on him today, did you hear that? Overnight we made sure he went from being an unimportant, small-time gangster from Våringe to being a national celebrity who hires little kids to murder other little kids. And then there are those who think a national alert has no practical significance. Excuse me?' He tried to suck the last few drops from the empty beer bottle before slamming it on the table. 'But maybe that's not what you meant by progress.'

'It wasn't. Have you talked to Billy's mum?'

'Not yet. She's been interviewed, but not by me. She had nothing to say, but we've increased security around her and the kids. I'm going to try to meet with her next week, we'll see.'

'What else?'

'On the investigation? It's moving forward. Dogge had Billy's blood on his shoes. And gunshot residue. He was captured on a security camera from the playground along with Billy, right before the shots were fired. And he called 112 from Våringe before he took the bus home to Rönnviken, where I picked him up. So that particular part of his story appears to be trustworthy.'

'Sounds like a strange detour.'

'He probably went to Våringe to dump the weapon. Along with the phone he used to call 112.'

'Have you found them?'

'No. They waited over twenty-four hours to check over that way.'

'Why?'

Farid took a breath.

'I...I was convinced he had run straight home and I was so dead set on getting a warrant for his house, I didn't feel like having a debate with some bleary-eyed prosecutor, so...there's almost no way we'll find anything now.'

'Why do you have such trouble trusting the system? You would have got your warrant in the end. I'm starting to think you have a grudge against lawyers.'

'Not true. I sleep with one on the regular. I don't have a grudge against her.'

'Not as regularly as she would like. Were you the one responsible for the investigation at the scene? And the search?'

'No. But I should have told them—'

'Let it go. You don't have to take credit for everything, do you? No matter what you said at the scene, they're supposed to have checked the nearest bus stops in every direction, right?'

'I should have told them to. And what's more, Dogge was high the first time I interrogated him. At three in the fucking morning. He's fourteen. I should have waited, but I didn't bother. It was just too much. That Billy...that Dogge...that he...'

'How high was Dogge? What did the doctor say?'

Farid waved his hand dismissively.

'Nothing like that. The doctor said he was under the influence, but it wasn't the sort of...he didn't need to be admitted. But I could have let him sleep off the worst of it. There was no need to rush. I could have gone back to help out with the search instead.'

Nadja nodded. She stood up and took her empty bowl to the dishwasher.

'Sure. You could have. But do you think what he said is true? Did Mehdi tell Dogge to kill Billy?'

'How should I know?'

'I think it sounds exactly like something Mehdi would do. Tell him to off Billy. Why not? Billy disengaged, right? Maybe Dogge had to prove he was worthy of staying?'

'I don't know.'

'Why else would he kill Billy? Wasn't Billy his only friend in the world?'

'Yeah.'

Nadja pressed two buttons and closed the door of the dishwasher. It turned on with a faint hum.

'Want some tea?'

'No, thanks. I'd be up to pee all night long. I have to go to bed before I fall asleep right here. I have to work tomorrow.'

Nadja opened a cupboard and took out a mug. She started the kettle.

'I don't believe for a second that Dogge was making that up. Especially not if he was high. From what you've told me about him, he doesn't seem that sophisticated. I think Dogge told you exactly what was up with Mehdi. Dogge's not from Våringe. He's not as shaped by the culture of silence. I think he decided to tell the truth, or just did it because he couldn't come up with anything else. Or because he regretted his actions. It's one thing to accept an assignment, Dogge would hardly be the first to do that, but when he saw Billy, saw what he'd done, maybe it clicked for him that that life isn't so gangsta after all? And just because he took it all back the next day doesn't mean that he wasn't telling the truth the first time. Billy disengaged. You say he didn't mean anything to the gang, but since when does someone like Mehdi need a good reason to off someone? And besides, with Dogge's help, he wasn't taking any sort of risk.'

She filled her mug and came back to the table.

'Sure, that's true,' said Farid. 'But if I want to get him convicted for instigating the murder I have to show that Dogge wouldn't have killed Billy if it weren't for Mehdi. And that Mehdi had intent. Or else I'll try to get him on aiding and abetting. But how can I do that if I don't even have a weapon to trace back to Mehdi? Or at least something to show he's been in contact with Dogge. Preferably a phone, a phone would be great.'

Nadja took a sip of the hot beverage.

'Have you got any physical evidence?'

'I just told you. Gunshot residue and Billy's blood on his shoes.'

'That's good, right?'

'Sure. But the fact that I can prove Dogge did it doesn't make anyone happy.'

'Didn't you say you had the cartridges too? Have you found anything on those?'

'Mm-hmm.'

'Anything usable?'

'Mm-hmm.'

'What? Come on, Farid, just tell me.'

'Two sets of fingerprints on the cartridges. And traces of some fucking mixed DNA, whatever that is.'

'What did you say?' Nadja put down her mug. 'Two sets? But that's huge.'

Farid nodded.

'We got the results back on the fingerprints about an hour ago.'

'Do you know whose they are?'

'Yes. Dogge's and Billy's.'

'Excuse me?'

'I know.'

'What does that mean?'

'That Billy had touched the ammunition that killed him.'

'Wasn't he shot in the back of the head?'

'Yes, the back of his neck and his back. At close range. But the weapon wasn't touching him.'

'Are you planning to argue that he shot himself?'

'I seriously doubt he did.' Farid stood up. 'The techs are also suitably hesitant on that point. They can't even analyze that trace of mixed DNA, they don't have the necessary equipment, so they sent it to Holland.'

'But?'

'No buts. I'm dead on my feet, honey. I'm not going to be able to sleep with the sexiest lawyer in the world tonight. We'll talk more when I know more.' Farid leaned over and kissed her lips.

'Hold on a sec, though. There is a but. *But* it's Mehdi's fault. No matter what he's said or done, he's the one who makes sure kids in Våringe can get all the drugs they could possibly want, and then some. What's more, he's their idol, and he's the one who taught them that if you get mad at someone you just kill them. I know that's not enough to put him away for Billy's murder, but it should be. Because if it wasn't for that fucking Mehdi, Billy would be alive today, and if I don't manage to get him locked up he's going to kill more kids, one way or another. And if he's the one who told Dogge to kill Billy, what's to say he'll stop there? We've got Billy's family under police protection now, but for how long? If we can't prove there's a threat to their safety, we won't be allowed to devote resources to it.'

He sighed. 'And that's it for my "buts". I have to be alert when I decide how and when to confront supervillain Douglas Arnfeldt with my ideas about right and wrong. Because if I can't get him talking again, it won't matter what the technical investigation turns up. Mehdi will be able to keep doing what he's doing, whatever that is, totally undisturbed. Good night.'

THE BOYS

At Billy's house, every room was full of his siblings and their clothes and schoolbooks and voices that never stopped talking. Billy's little brother was the most annoying of all. He would do anything to be included; Dogge and Billy did their best to avoid him.

When they were about to turn ten, they had stopped caring about swings and sandboxes, slides and hide-and-seek, yet they met up at the playground more and more often, sometimes hanging out there for a whole evening. Once it got dark, they no longer had to worry about the little kids and mums and park patrol.

Sometimes, too, they would go to Rönnviken city centre. But it was hard to have a good time there. It was more fun in Våringe. Every time Mehdi saw them, he said hi. Sometimes he'd give them a cigarette, and a few times they came along to his mum's apartment to play *FIFA*. They even had dinner there once. After the meal, Mehdi played music, not the kind Dogge's dad played, but music that was about Mehdi's own life. He explained that these were things that had happened to him, or could happen to him, but he didn't seem afraid. His buddy Stein Q had written the songs. Stein Q was from Våringe too, had been in Mehdi's class at school. Dogge learned all the lyrics by heart, Billy already knew them.

When they were at Mehdi's place, Billy told his mum they were hanging at Dogge's. Dogge didn't have to tell anyone anything, his parents never asked where he was going.

No one drank at Billy's house, Leila threw Isak out if he came home drunk, made him go to the home of another guy who drank and had also been thrown out by his wife. The neighbours helped her. Sometimes she asked the imam to talk to him, Isak respected him.

There had never been a party at Billy's – there simply wasn't enough space. He had too many siblings and not enough rooms. Smoking wasn't allowed, not even on the balcony, and the bathroom lock was broken so you couldn't even be sure you'd be left in peace when you were on the toilet.

At Dogge's however, there was a party every weekend, sometimes on both Friday and Saturday, and many Wednesdays as well, because Wednesday was called 'Little Saturday', so you were allowed to drink without some cunt bitching at you, as his dad liked to say.

Dogge and Billy liked Teo's parties; they would go through the coats to see if any of the guests had some money they could take, no one would notice anyway. Sometimes they walked around the house emptying the half-full glasses that had been abandoned on every table and on all the windowsills, on the bathroom counter, the kitchen counter, the floor of the guest bathroom, shoved under the sofa. They would get drunk and throw up in the bathroom, Billy in the toilet and Dogge in the sink. They found half-smoked cigarettes, and, if they were lucky, an open pack of cigs. But the guests used up all the cocaine themselves, they weren't careless with that.

Dogge's dad had any number of friends. Always new people, always strangely similar to each other. They were nice to the boys, wanted them to dance with them, or sit at the table during dinner. They loved Dogge's dad, how he could open bottles of champagne with a sabre and oysters with a regular knife, how he laughed, the stories he told, the jokes he made, how he always had new projects in the works and old classics blasting from the stereo. They like Dogge's beautiful mother too, even though she was strange and quiet, ate so little and slept so much. They laughed when Dogge's dad pulled her off the sofa or out of the bedroom and sang favourite pop songs, changing the lyrics so they were about Jill, so loudly the glasses clinked.

'This is Billy,' Dogge's dad would say, 'my son's best friend.' He seemed proud, as though Billy were a trophy he'd won. He seldom introduced Dogge.

They already know who I am, Dogge tried to tell himself. *I'm his son, and in the end that's more important.*

It was hard to know what Billy thought of spending time at Dogge's house. Most of the time it seemed like he loved it. But once, when he was drunk and splayed on Dogge's bed, looking up at the large plaster ceiling rose, he said he thought it was a weird house.

'It's huge, it's in fucking Rönnviken, but it's not like you expect it to be. It's a house for rich people, but it kind of feels poor, the furniture is too old. Expensive, but like stuff in a museum, ugly as hell and smelling like it's been in a basement for too long.'

Dogge had laughed. But he was annoyed too. *So don't hang out with me if you think my house is so ugly.* But of course he didn't say anything. He didn't want Billy to stop hanging out with him.

One time, Leila came to pick Billy up, even though he had his bike and Leila didn't have a car. When Billy heard the doorbell ringing, he ran downstairs, taking the steps two at a time. As soon as Jill opened the door, he squeezed by her and vanished out.

'Come on, Mom,' he said. 'We'll miss the bus.'

He's ashamed, Dogge thought. *He doesn't want his mom to see what it looks like in my house.*

21

Farid was sitting at the station. *Aktuellt* had done a special report on gang violence during its Saturday-night news programme. It had taken as its starting point the murder of Billy Ali and the search for Mehdi Ahmad. The report included a panel discussion about the escalating levels of deadly violence and the culture of silence, and a hotline had been set up where anyone could call and speak directly to the police.

Many viewers had felt the urge to declare that immigration must be halted, the national police commissioner removed from his position, public service shuttered, the editor in chief of *Dagens Nyheter* locked up, and the government replaced. Some wanted to share their opinions about the host's weight and hair colour; some wanted to know where she had bought her blazer, and of course there were those who wanted to kick out all the fucking Somalis, they stink and do drugs and rape our beautiful blonde women.

But there was a dearth of callers who actually wanted to talk about Billy's murder. A couple of anonymous tipsters said that Billy and Dogge had been best friends 'because it said so on Flashback', and most wanted to point out that 'obviously it was a hit job, anyone can see that'. One person claimed that 'this kid was nuts, he always has been', but only a single person claimed to have actually seen someone running away from the scene at the time of the murder. Farid had asked Lotta to send him the audio file of that call.

'There's so much shit going on in Våringe, I didn't think there was much point in mentioning it to anyone but the wife. And she hardly bothered to listen when I tried. But there's all this talk on your show about how society needs to take responsibility for organized crime, what a load of horseshit, why would I be responsible if parents can't keep their children under control and the police can't do their job?'

'But you had something you wanted to tell us?'

The trainee who had taken the call spoke in a Skåne dialect.

'Yeah, and that circus director going on about all the boundaries parents are supposed to set this way and that...I'll tell you where that line should be drawn, and it's a whole different kind of border and it's a hell of a long way from Våringe.'

'I'm sorry?'

'The national police commissioner. Just because you put a uniform and epaulets on an outhouse doesn't make what he says anything but a load of shit. If Sweden had been protected from this kind of scum, he would be out of a job, because there wouldn't be anything for old Mr Barnum and Bailey to do.'

'Okay...the national police commissioner, sure... was there anything else you wanted to share with us?'

'I was there. I saw him.'

'Where? Who did you see? The national police commissioner?'

'Does the national police commissioner go strolling around Våringe at night? Give me a break. Last Thursday night I was standing there freezing my balls off when he came running by. Up from the pedestrian tunnel, it was a few minutes past eleven, right after that darky got popped, but I didn't know it at the time. I just thought he had been burgling houses in Rönnviken. He was coming from that direction, and no one would be stupid enough to break in anywhere in Våringe, hey? Can't warm yourself by stealing the fur off a naked mole rat. I figured it had gone south. Someone had caught him in the act, so to speak. One of those private security firms who keep an eye out in Rönnviken, maybe? Why else would he be pelting down the hill like a shit-faced ostrich? He had it coming, I thought, hell yes, beat the crap right out of him, I thought, yeah, I'll own that. I'm only saying what everyone is thinking. And then he stopped to chat on his phone like nothing had happened. And then he went down to the bus station and tossed something into the trash can. But no, I didn't see anyone come after him. No, I didn't think about going over there. Why would I? Did they just let you out of your padded cell? Not a chance. It wasn't like he had stolen my stuff. And what the hell was I supposed to do, with these knees? I could run like a goddamn gazelle when I was his age, but that was before the arthritis. Both knees, one hip, my lower back, even my fucking thumb crackles like a scratched record. I'm as rusty as a fistful of damp nails, I sure am. But whatever. Hold that little brat for me and I'll give him a taste of my right hand, because I can still use that sucker. For one thing or another.'

Farid listened to the recording twice. Then he reached for his phone and called up the caller. His name was Ulf Pettersson, and was called Uffe for short.

Of course you are, Farid thought wearily. *Of course you are.*

22

When Weed was little, a man without hands would often sit by the market where he went with his parents to shop. On a twined cord around his neck, the beggar wore a basket for people to drop coins into. Weed's dad said the military had chopped off his hands because he was a thief. Still, it was important to always give him something. Dad gave him money, Mum gave him food or something to drink in the heat. Let others judge, they said to Weed. Kindness makes a good pillow.

The thief sat in the same spot every day year-round, his back crooked, his head lowered, and his short arms resting in his lap. One time Weed asked his mother how he wiped his behind, and she slapped him. She typically only slapped him when he did something truly stupid or dangerous, but this time it was like the slap came out of nowhere, and she didn't even know why. She hugged him afterwards, hard. But she didn't answer him, he never found out how the man dealt with his hygiene, or even how he could eat and drink what Weed's mother put before him.

Outside Weed's Market sat a woman on a scrap of carpet. She was there seven days a week, even Sundays, with a shawl around her head and fingerless gloves on her hands. She always stayed until Weed closed up shop for the day. He never gave her money, but she could have any ready-made sandwiches that weren't sold that day.

She always bowed her head and brought her hands together before her chest to thank him.

'Thank you, thank you, so kind, thank you, thank you.'

And Weed felt ashamed.

Sit up straight, he wanted to say. Make something of your life. But he said nothing, and just thought of his parents.

The fact that he had been hit as a child wasn't something he felt was formative. His dad only hit his kids when they disobeyed. Not hard, but often. When Weed grew big enough to object, these punishments came to an end without anyone making a big deal about it. He often imagined that his dad meant well and didn't know how else to be.

It was quick work, to slap a hand that was approaching a stove, much quicker than explaining the danger of fire. A boxed ear didn't result in burns.

One teacher at the school Weed attended in his very first years was fired for punching one of the mouthy children so hard he broke a tooth. According to the school rules, teachers were only allowed to spank them with a belt or hit their knuckles with a ruler. Using fists was strictly prohibited. The kid with the broken tooth was the son of the pharmacist.

But Weed didn't hit his kids. Sure, he sometimes got angry. One early morning he had thrown half a glass of water in the face of his oldest son when he came home five hours late from a party and then laughed when Weed scolded him. But he never hit them. It would have felt like a betrayal of everything he believed in.

If anyone asked, he would say it was a matter of respect. He didn't ever want his own kids to experience the shame he felt when his father hit him. When he didn't know what to do to make them listen, he talked to Sara. Sometimes they would laugh at how their kids spoke to them, how they said things they never would have dared to say to their own parents. But they were always on the same page. Corporal punishment was not an option.

The sandwiches had sold out today. But as early as two o'clock, Weed had set aside a rotisserie chicken thigh. It was cold now. He gave that and a litre of milk that was past its sell-by date to the woman on the carpet.

'Thank you, thank you, so kind, thank you,' she said, bowing her head so deeply that he could see the back of her shawl.

'It's nothing,' Weed mumbled. 'It's nothing to thank me for.' And he hurried off.

In the car, he turned on the radio. The man who was wanted in connection with the murder of the fourteen-year-old in Våringe had been found. He was in custody, under reasonable suspicion of involvement in the shooting. The detention hearing was scheduled for Wednesday, December 12. Weed turned off the radio.

THE BOYS

'*As long as you're home before dinner*' was Leila's typical response when Billy asked if he could go over to Dogge's house. He was only ten, but he wasn't a little kid anymore, she couldn't keep him at home all the time. 'Six o'clock at the latest, I need help. There's no reason your sisters should have to do it all.'

He promised, almost always, to do as she asked. But most of the time, it was past eight before he showed up. Sometimes he would send a text to say he was on his way. Leila would stand on the balcony and wait until she saw him coming out of the tunnel. Then she would go inside and turn on the radio.

He's home now, she thought, *it's not the end of the world. Dogge's parents smoke, that's why he smells. He's probably already eaten, that's why he goes straight to his room, that's why he's never hungry anymore.*

Sometimes, when Billy was late, she would text Teo to ask him to send Billy home, but Teo hardly ever replied. She didn't like him. She didn't have Jill's number, and Jill didn't seem especially dependable either. But who was Leila to judge other people for the men they lived with?

I've got enough going on with my own, Leila thought. *I can't spend my time worrying about rich people's kids too.*

Sometimes Billy biked over to the playground to meet up with Dogge. Sometimes they ran to the woods, sometimes they went down to the city centre. But Billy was never allowed to be out after dark. Leila told him so frequently. Don't talk to strangers, don't go too far.

'Always tell me where you are. If I'm working, tell me anyway.'

You're too strict, she thought when he didn't do as she said. *If only Isak could help me*, she thought too. He needed a father who would give him a stern talking-to.

Before Billy started school, he helped out a lot, especially with his little brother Tusane. He liked it, picking up his little brother and resting his chin against the baby's gossamer curls, comforting him when he cried. He stopped once he got to know Dogge.

Instead it was Aisha who helped Leila keep an eye on him. When she turned eleven they had a party at McDonald's, twelve girls were invited, Isak didn't show up, but Billy was there. He sat at the end of the oblong table.

'Chew with your mouth closed,' Leila heard Aisha hiss at her brother. That brought a smile to her face and an ache to her heart.

Leila knew that the boys admired Mehdi, the troublemaker who wore a bulletproof vest and sunglasses in the middle of winter. She had met his mother a number of times at the town hall. Mehdi's mother wasn't a big talker, but they exchanged smiles.

'I don't want you spending time with him,' Leila had said to Billy more times than she could recall.

'He's nice, Mum,' Billy said. 'Don't worry. He's nice.'

Leila had tried talking to her husband.

'Mehdi's just a boy himself,' said Isak. 'He's not a man. He's no boss, that's all just rumours. People love to run their mouths about things they don't understand. Don't worry.'

What could happen, really? Leila said to herself as she lay awake in bed, staring into the darkness. *They're only ten years old.*

Dogge and Billy always kept close by, in Våringe or in Rönnviken. They always stuck together. If an older boy was letting them play video games at his house, it was nothing to get worked up about. Mehdi lived with his mother too. Leila wasn't worried. She trusted the boys. Or at least Billy – she trusted Billy.

23

In Tusse's new room, which had so recently been Billy's, there were no windows. But the darkness was right outside. He knew that. Pitch-black and unforgiving. If he fell asleep, the dream from yesterday would return. The bird spreading its wings, extending its claws, and landing on his body to rip his heart out with its beak.

He had no intention of mentioning his nightmares to Mum. He wouldn't say a word. But he did his utmost to keep from falling asleep.

On the first and second nights, they had got to stay at a hotel while the police went through the apartment. Mum came straight there from the hospital, there wasn't much left of the night by then, but it was still dark out. They'd been given two adjoining rooms with identical shiny floors, hard beds, showers and toilets that floated in the air. The doors could be unlocked with white cards the size of credit cards. If you stuck them in the same pocket as your cell phone they wouldn't work anymore. Then you had to go down to the lobby and ask for a new one.

But they had only used one of the hotel rooms; he and Aisha had dragged their pillows and blankets into the other room. They curled up close to Mum and Rawdah in the bed.

No one could sleep. If Mum wasn't crying, Rawdah would begin to sob. Aisha waited until she was alone in the bathroom. She locked the door and turned on the shower and thought no one could hear. The staff brought breakfast on a tray, but no one was hungry.

Dad didn't have to stay at a hotel, he was staying with Uncle Malik.

They saw him for a little bit on Friday, but he was so drunk that one eyelid was drooping.

Mum hadn't even taken off her coat before she told Isak it was time to leave.

A policeman was on a chair outside their hotel room. Once, when Tusse opened the door, the policeman startled like he had just woken up. But Tusse didn't mention this to Mum, she had other things to worry about.

They were questioned one by one, even Rawdah.

'I don't know,' Tusse had replied to each question. 'I don't know anything.'

———

By Saturday morning, they were back in the apartment. Tusse had to move into Billy's room.

'I don't want to,' he told Aisha.

'You have to,' she replied.

So he did. He did everything, just as he was told.

'You can't go out.'

'You can't see your friends.'

'We have food at home, you don't need to go shopping for Mum.'

All day Saturday and Sunday, people stopped by to visit. Friends of Leila's, colleagues, neighbours, parents of the kids' friends. Parents of children they hardly knew. Everyone brought food. Casseroles and Crockpot dishes. Moussaka, lasagna, grilled chicken, *sambusas*, mac and cheese, *cambuulo*. One person, who'd brought a spinach lasagna on Saturday, came back late Sunday evening.

'Did you hear? They got Mehdi. He's in jail. He's behind bars now.'

He said it like it was information they'd been waiting for, news that would make them happy, or at least relieved.

'I see,' Mum had said, handing over a plastic container full of meatballs the size of tennis balls. A bit of tomato sauce had ended up outside the lid; she wiped it away with her thumb.

Whatever food didn't fit in the fridge she gave to neighbours, to the police, to the imam, to anyone who came to visit and wasn't already holding something. She also filled plate after plate and gave them to Tusse and his siblings. Shoved a fork into it and forced them to accept the food.

'Thanks,' Tusse said, and put the plate down when she wasn't looking. He wasn't hungry. He couldn't eat real food, he only wanted biscuits and sweets, all the time, until he felt so sick that he could throw them back up again.

Now the last guest had left. Only Mum and his sisters were left here at home, and Tusse had closed the door to what would be his room from now on.

The sheets didn't smell like Billy, only like detergent. Mum had put everything that had been in Billy's room into boxes. When they'd arrived home, all his stuff was out, on the bed, because the police had gone through it. The sight made Leila cry. But she quickly got control of herself, fetched three empty boxes from the storage area in the cellar, and started packing.

Leila didn't sleep, didn't eat, never sat down. She just occupied herself with Billy's things, putting them into boxes, taking them out again. One of the boxes was next to her bed, two others were in the kitchen. The shelves behind Billy's bed were empty, his wardrobe was empty, his dresser was empty. Tusse could have decided to get his things and put them there. *Do something.* But he couldn't. Instead he put his blankie into one of the boxes of Billy's belongings. He shoved it deep inside, where it couldn't be seen.

I don't want to.

They'd started planning the funeral. The police had said they couldn't come and get Billy's body yet, but it was like Mum didn't understand.

'I need it,' she said, and Tusse didn't know if she meant Billy's body or the funeral, or if they were the same thing.

Mum had asked for help at the mosque.

'It's important,' she said. Again and again. She sounded very angry.

'We'll work it out,' said the imam, putting his hands around Mum's. Then she cried for a while, instead of being angry. But they still didn't know when they could bury Billy. And no one had said a word about that other thing, what the imam had promised Mum before Billy was shot.

The police officer on the chair outside the hotel hadn't accompanied them home. The policewoman who called herself their family liaison had asked if they felt safe going back to their building. For a brief moment Leila had looked like she was going to get mad again, but then she said, 'Of course.' Then the policewoman gave Leila a business card and said she could call day or night, all she had to do was drop a line if they had any questions at all. 'Thanks,' Leila said, placing the business card in the kitchen. One minute later, she had placed a warm potato gratin from the neighbour two floors up on top of the card.

It was Sunday. Billy had been dead for nearly three days, and Tusse was going to do all he could not to fall asleep. Because if he fell asleep the nightmares would come, the truth would come, everything Tusse knew, the stuff he would never forget.

If only I hadn't said a word to Mum. If only I had done nothing. If only I hadn't betrayed Billy. Then Billy would still be alive.

It's all my fault.

THE BOYS

'*What does your dad actually do?*' one of Dogge's classmates asked at the beginning of Year 5. It wasn't the first time someone had asked him that, and he gave his usual response.

'He's got a project.'

His dad always had a project in the works. But this time, his classmate wouldn't let it go.

'Your dad's project is in the paper. My mum says he should be in prison.'

Dogge knew what the newspapers said. His parents had talked about those articles. They'd said his dad wasn't mentioned by name, but everyone still knew it was Teo they were talking about. What his classmate didn't know, though, was the part about the idiots. The ones who had tricked Teo. It was their fault everything was going sideways. But Dogge couldn't say so.

'It's the idiots who should be in prison,' he managed to say at last.

'Your dad is an idiot?' his classmate said, delighted. The girl next to him laughed. 'Is that what you're saying?'

At that point, Dogge stopped trying to explain. He used his fists instead. Only once, but the guy got a bloody nose and a toothache, his whole shirt turned dark red, and Dogge had to wait in the principal's office while they called both of his parents. Neither picked up. Dogge wasn't allowed to leave. The secretary called again after lunch. When Teo finally showed up, he was so angry there was no point in trying to explain.

Teo dropped Dogge off in front of the house. He had to go inside by himself.

'I have to go into the city,' his dad said curtly. He didn't ask if Dogge had his keys.

Jill had a migraine and didn't wake up when Dogge rang the doorbell. She had put in earplugs and taken a pill. But he got in through the back door, which was seldom locked. When Teo got home again, he lay on the sofa drinking dark-brown whiskey. They didn't talk about school. They hardly ever did.

Dogge had a difficult time with the theoretical subjects. But his woodshop teacher had once said he was 'pretty good'. Dogge told his father so.

'Congratulations. Maybe you can become a plumber,' was his response.

Dogge looked up a plumber's salary online. Then he realized what his father meant. Only a dope would be satisfied with making that much. Dogge knew his father thought he was a dope, that wasn't news.

No one asked Billy what his dad did. No one at Billy's school thought it was strange to have a dad who sat around at cafés playing cards with his friends every day, all week. Still, Isak had had a number of jobs, just never for very long. It was hard for him, he would say. And when he lost his driver's licence, it got even harder.

'No one cares that I'm a better driver than all the other idiots. They still don't want to let me drive. I'd be happy to work, but what am I supposed to do? Tell me that.'

Leila didn't say it was hard for Isak; she had stopped talking about him entirely.

But Billy didn't need his father. Billy was smart. Everything was easy for him. He could speak English and sound like they did in the Harry Potter movies, or else he could switch into a nearly perfect imitation of Dr Dre. When Dogge tried to say something in English, it was like his tongue swelled in his mouth. It took him a long time to find the words. But Billy understood everything, even maths. Once when he was at Dogge's house he found Dogge's maths book and did all the problems in the first three chapters simply because he was bored. The only problem was that he was also always the first one to get bored with new things, and with teachers' explanations. He had told Dogge all about it.

'I can't keep listening, it's totally fucking impossible, I have to think about everything else that pops into my head. If a car drives by on the street, where's it going? Who's inside it? What are they up to, and is someone going to die?'

One night, when Teo was on a business trip to try to fix the problems the idiots had caused him, Dogge and Billy took Jill's car. It was parked on the street, and they hauled a wheelie bin over so no one could take their spot while they were gone. They had driven before, with Teo. But they'd never driven alone, and Billy drove all the way out through Rönnviken, and onto the highway, and didn't turn around until they were three exits away.

They rolled down the windows and let the winter air fill the car.

'We fucking rule, Dogge!' Billy shouted, putting the pedal to the metal. They turned the volume up as high as it would go.

I don't need my dad either, Dogge thought. *Billy and I will make it on our own. We don't need anyone else.*

When they got back to Rönnviken, someone had moved the garbage can back and parked a different car there. They had to park thirty metres down the street. But Jill never noticed, or at least she didn't say anything.

Dogge fell asleep with music in his headphones that night, the same song they'd been listening to as they drove the car. It was all about what they would do when they got money, money of their own. Sick boats and cars, pools, trips, chicks. Dogge and Billy weren't like their dads. They were better, a thousand times better.

Billy probably would have been the best student in his whole school if only he'd been able to concentrate. Dogge wasn't the best at anything, no matter how hard he tried. Saying he was good at the kind of thing that would let him fix toilets, that was basically like saying he was stupid.

But he didn't need some useless education. He wasn't going to become a plumber, that was obviously a joke, it would never happen. He was going to rule.

With Billy, he was untouchable, better than everyone else.

24

'Has the county council's baked-goods budget been slashed?' asked Uffe, the man who'd seen Dogge fleeing the scene of the crime, as he emptied four triangle Tetra Paks of milk into his lukewarm coffee.

Farid had been hoping to clear his mind with a harmless witness interview before going to the jail to talk to Mehdi. He was regretting his choices already. Mehdi's lawyer was on the warpath, absolutely furious about all the alleged violations his client had been subjected to since he was picked up. But hopefully this interview would be over quickly, at least. Uffe was anything but taciturn.

'It was cold, it was dark, and it was snowing like hell. Or, well, it was just snowing. Not like back in the fifties, when we had to shovel our way out of our houses and stay home from school for weeks at a time. No, it wasn't falling so hard I couldn't see him, why would I lie about that? Are you calling me a liar?'

'You said you thought he'd been burgling homes?'

'It looked like he was in a hurry. If I'd been sure he was up to some thuggery I would have called the police. But you don't call the police just because you see someone running, do you? Don't you cops have more important things to worry about? Hell, I have no goddamn clue what he was doing out and what he had been up to and why he was running. He must have been freezing his dick off in those ugly jeans, and wanted to make it home as fast as he could. Maybe that's why he was running.'

'You called—'

'Yeah, thanks, Sherlock, you said on *Aktuellt* that folks should call in if they saw something. And I was reading *Stop the Press* online and they had a picture of the kid who got shot. And they all look the same, oh yes they do. All those thugs and their thuggish ways, is it that hard to get to grips with? Anyway, when I saw that little bastard out jogging last Thursday, I had two thoughts. For one, that's a little thug there. And two, he's not exactly blond, is he. Blonds have more fun, don't they, right? Anyway, this one wasn't having fun, I know that much.'

'The person you saw running had dark hair? Is that what you're saying?'

'I didn't need to see his fucking hair, I know who runs around Våringe in the middle of the night. He had one of those sweatshirts over his head, like some goddamn E.T. phone home. One of those hood-whatevers?'

'Oh. A hoodie? Then how could you tell what colour his hair was?'

'All this talk about his hair, maybe I didn't see his hair. No, I didn't. But I know how they usually look. Why would he have been some brand-new sort of species? Yeah, I heard the shooting was actually down in Rönnviken, but I know what—'

'Is there anything else you can tell me?'

'He stopped running down by the bus station and stopped to talk on his phone instead. No, I didn't overhear any of that conversation. Then he dumped the damn phone and a handful of trash in the bin and got on the bus.'

'Did you see what he was throwing away?'

'Do I look like a goddamn birdwatcher? With binoculars in my pocket in case some heron or barn owl shows up behind the recycling station? I just wanted to get my goddamn garage door open and be home. I wouldn't have anything against going home right now either, in fact. What the hell do you want me to say? There's a hell of a lot of kids running around nights in those neighbourhoods, why do you think I pay a fortune so I can park my car in a garage? Do you know how many damn cars burn up every year out by us? No, you don't. Because I guess you have more important things to do. Like singing in the police choir, maybe. Or baking buns for afternoon coffee time. Buns you eat up all by yourself when you're on break from all this whining about how society needs to take responsibility. But there's one thing even you know, and that's that these damn kids running around all night aren't exactly selling Christmas calendars door-to-door.'

'Did you see someone else?'

'Shit, no. No one was chasing this kid, or he wouldn't have stopped to wait for the bus, would he? And he was all alone, I can swear to that.'

'And you didn't see anyone but him?'

'What are you, a broken record? How many times do you want me to say it? Ask me something else. You don't have to be a rocket scientist to figure out what you want me to say.'

'What is it you think I want you to say?'

'You're hoping I saw that fellow whose picture all the papers and news reports have plastered around like he's one of the princesses' goddamn kids. That he came running after the kid? Is that why you forced me to come here?'

'Did you?' Farid wondered. 'Did you see him?'

'Was there a rush on the drug factory outside my garage, but I just forgot to mention it? No sir. I have never seen that ugly piece of shit you're look-ing for in all my life. By the way, I heard you found him, is that true? Just think, huh? Even a blind squirrel, and so forth. The fellow I saw was a lit-tle fucker who came running from Rönnviken and then took the bus back the same way he'd come. Can I go now? Do you think maybe you and your colleagues can manage without me? That you will be able to solve one of the hundreds of shootings where the solution is actually as simple as a jar of mayonnaise? Because I would really like to get back to my own life here.'

'Then I'll thank you for your time,' Farid said. 'It's much appreciated.'

He followed Uffe out. He lingered by the door for a moment, watching the stiff-legged man through the glass doors as he headed for a car that was parked in a reserved spot.

He listened to his messages while he waited for the lift.

Mehdi's lawyer had confirmed that he was available.

'No rush,' said the investigation team's forensic coordinator Sebastian over voice mail.

Sebastian had apparently been assigned more tasks than he was actually paid to handle, because he then declared that he'd booked the interrogation room for eleven o'clock, would that work? It was twenty minutes to eleven. Farid ditched the lift and jogged up the stairs, had to get his coat and car keys.

He called Sebastian.

'After the murder, Dogge ran away from the playground and through the tunnel up to Våringe, to ditch the gun and his phone,' he said. 'We've got a witness who can place him at the bus stop past the pedestrian tunnel on the Våringe side, and who saw him dump his things there, into a trash can at the bus stop. Not just the phone, something else too – I'd wager it was the weapon. I assume someone has already checked the rubbish bins?'

'I think so.'

'I know there's not much point double-checking with whoever collects the rubbish there, but can we do it anyway?'

'Of course,' said Sebastian. 'I'll make some calls. Isn't that bus stop near the square? Sometimes people hand in lost items at nearby shops and restaurants. If they don't feel like bringing them to the police.'

'Surely no one would turn in a Glock at the local pizzeria. Not even in Våringe.'

'No, but they might with the phone. It could be worth a try.'

'Definitely. Where did they find Mehdi?'

'In a hunting cabin outside Mariefred. He had broken in and was in the process of emptying the pantry. Someone from the local hunting league there saw the lights on and called us.'

'Good. Does one of you all want to come with me to interrogate him?'

'I think Svante's already counting on keeping you company.'

Farid cursed softly.

'I'm sure he doesn't want to miss it. Mehdi's interrogation is liable to be awfully important.'

'Sure, of course,' Farid said. 'I'm guessing we'll be able to pack up and head home to celebrate solving the whole case by this evening. Especially if we've got Svante's help. What could go wrong?'

Sebastian was still laughing when he hung up.

25

They wanted Dogge to 'get started with school right away'. It sounded like a joke, but no one laughed. Momi dropped him off in a classroom with a man who looked like a bodybuilder. It was just going to be the two of them.

'All instruction is individually tailored,' Momi explained before he left.

The bodybuilder began to explain a maths problem that seemed designed for someone who hadn't yet learned to count to ten.

Dogge hated school, he always had. He hated the teachers with their lesson plans, educational goals, and email threads, teachers who went back and forth between complaining about his poor attendance and looking so concerned when he was actually present.

Year 3 was when he began seriously skipping school. He had always known the code to his mum's phone, so he copied a text she'd sent once when he was sick for real, and another from when Jill and Teo had pretended he was sick so they could spend a long weekend in London. He sent variations on these two messages from his mum's phone to the school whenever he wanted to be absent for days at a time. Jill seldom read anything the school sent, so it didn't matter if they responded. Besides, Dogge had marked the school's email address as spam.

His mum slept a lot. And Dogge imagined his teachers were relieved when he wasn't there, because then they could concentrate on looking concerned because one of the guys in a polo shirt had shared a video on Instagram of a girl in their class showing her arse as she drove a moped in a short skirt, instead of trying to explain stuff to Dogge, who didn't want to learn it anyway.

He knew Billy didn't bother to send any explanations for being absent. If the school called the phone number on file for him, they would reach his big sister Aisha, because that was who Leila had used for Billy's contact info. Leila hated talking on the phone, especially in Swedish. Most of the time, Aisha ignored whatever the school said when they called. She would chew Billy out, but neither of them wanted to upset their mother, who had enough problems as it was.

It was going to be harder to skip school at the state home. Class with the bodybuilder was just as boring as regular class, although it was easier. Dogge had never done maths homework in his life, but even he could do this.

He managed to stand it for twenty minutes before getting up and declaring that he had to use the bathroom. The bodybuilder looked at him with that sceptical face all teachers got when Dogge asked for something.

'Would you rather I go in the bin?'

The bodybuilder followed him to the common bathrooms near the classrooms. Momi had searched him after breakfast, just like that, had gone through all his pockets and run a metal detector over his back and between his legs. Dogge hadn't even had the strength to protest. When he got to the bathroom, Momi was standing there waiting.

'You can go,' Momi said to the bodybuilder. 'I'll take these guys to lunch when they're done.' Then he turned to Dogge. 'You can go in by yourself. I just need to make a call, but I'll be here outside if you need me.'

'Like if I want help wiping my ass?' Dogge asked, pulling open the door to the toilets. 'Is that what you mean?'

The door closed behind him.

The Italian was standing at the urinals. He turned around and smiled. Dogge stopped short.

'Come here,' said the Italian. 'Why not have a little chat?'

Dogge went up to the urinal trough and opened his fly.

The Italian moved closer. Dogge could feel the Italian's urine splashing up onto the leg of his pants. But he didn't dare move, not even an inch.

'Aren't you wondering, where's Mehdi? Are you thinking about that?' the Italian said, facing the tile.

Dogge tried to control his breathing.

'No. Or yes? Is everything okay?'

The Italian scoffed.

'The pigs grabbed Mehdi yesterday. Did you know that? You didn't know that. You know where he is now? He's in jail now.'

He remembered this about the Italian. He always spoke in questions and answers. First he would ask a question, and then he would answer it himself.

'Why did they take him in? Why would they do that, you're wondering?' The Italian paused. 'Because you talked, man. The snitching came straight out of your ugly bill. Quack, quack, quack.'

Dogge held his breath. The pipes gurgled softly, but there was no other sound. The Italian went on, unconcerned.

'How do I know the cops tossed Mehdi in jail? I know that stuff, that's the kind of stuff I know. How do I know it was Dogge's mouth that put him there? Everyone knows. Not exactly hard to figure out. Isn't Mehdi barred from contacting anyone? He sure as fuck is. Didn't they take his phone? Of course they did. Have the cops been able to keep Mehdi from finding out every little thing he wants to know? Never. He knows I'm here chilling with you, for instance, and what does he think of that? He thinks it's great. The cops don't know the Italian is Mehdi's brother. They think the Italian isn't from Våringe, they think, so that's fine. They haven't got a clue. The cops know fuck all. Mehdi isn't worried about the cops. So what is Mehdi worried about? What do you think? You, man. Mehdi is worried about you.'

Dogge swallowed. The Italian smacked his lips.

'Is Mehdi just one step ahead of the cops? No, and not a yard either, not a fucking mile, maybe a hundred miles. But he doesn't like jail. Jail is bad business. Is he supposed to play Yahtzee with himself? Solitaire? No. How long is he going to be twiddling his thumbs in there? Until Dogge takes responsibility. All the other stuff the police have on Mehdi is bullshit. What Lasse said, though, is not bullshit. Without Lasse, there never would have been a fucking national alert. Murdering a fucking nobody of a fourteen-year-old is not minor shit for Uncle Blue. Even if you, Lasse, are the biggest loser piece of shit of all. And shit gets flushed, you know that.' The Italian pressed the flush button and went on. 'Lasse's lips have got to stop flapping. One way or another.' He shook his head sadly. 'Do you feel sorry for Mehdi?

I do. Poor bastard, that Mehdi,' he said, stuffing his cock back in his pants.

'I didn't—' Dogge attempted. 'I told them—'

The Italian interrupted him.

'First, you have to listen. Just listen, okay?'

Dogge nodded.

The Italian went to stand by the sink.

Dogge tried to pull up his own pants as fast as he could.

'Mehdi is not happy, not happy at all. Did he think he could trust you? He did. He didn't think you were a snot-nosed little brat who would piss himself the very first time he was questioned. Disappointed is what he was when he heard, Little Lasse. Mehdi was disappointed.'

The Italian went to the hand dryer. The jet of hot air roared.

'I already said it wasn't Mehdi,' Dogge managed to say when the dryer stopped. 'I mean, I'll talk to the cops again, explain better, I swear.'

The Italian turned to the mirror, pouted his lips, clicked his tongue, and shook his head slowly. After examining himself in the mirror for a moment, he placed one hand on Dogge's shoulder.

'I'll make everything okay again,' Dogge repeated, his eyes on the mirror. He was struggling to keep his voice under control.

'Believe me, trust me, I'll fix it.'

'Sure, sure,' mumbled the Italian, patting him distractedly on the shoulder. 'Of course you will...'

In a more cheerful voice, he said: 'Mehdi wants me to keep an eye on you. Because we don't want anything scary to happen to Little Lasse. No one wants Lasse to get hurt. Isn't that right?'

Dogge shook his head.

'We don't want anything nasty to happen because that would make Lasse super scared and we don't want Lasse to be scared.' The Italian transformed his voice at the end of his sentence, pouting his lips out even more into a big, wet kissy-mouth. He was talking as if to a baby or maybe a puppy. 'Lasse Lasse-little. Don't be scared. We're going to take care of you.'

26

I t had been Farid's turn to do the grocery shopping for two weeks. Nadja had texted him a list.

'If you come home without all this you might as well just stay at work.'

Yet it wasn't until he drove up to Våringe Square that he remembered.

He was heading home after two very drawn-out and pointless interrogations with Mehdi and an equally pointless update session with the investigation team. He would have liked to stop by the parking garage where Uffe kept his car, to get an idea of what could be seen from there. But as he drove past Weed's Market, he stopped. It must have been a month since he'd last been there; he could have a look around and get the shopping done while he was at it.

Weed looked tired.

'How are you doing?' Farid asked as he came into the store.

Weed didn't respond. Instead he forced himself to smile.

'How's Nadja?'

'She's getting after me, says I've got my priorities all wrong. Working too much, not helping out enough at home.'

'And she's right, I'm hearing?'

'Always. Unfortunately, Nadja is always right.'

Back when they lived in Våringe, Farid's oldest daughter, Felicia, had loved coming to Weed's Market. She wasn't the only child who did, in those days. Farid had seen how Weed was with the kids, the ones who came in to read comics in secret or look to see if any bulk candy had fallen on the floor.

'You have a question, you just ask,' he would say to the ones who had nowhere to be after the library closed. He treated them like important customers with specific desires. Not once did he tell them they had to buy something if they wanted to stick around. What's more, he would let them do 'quality control' on the sweets before filling the bins, and he always told them they could read any comic book they liked, as long as they handled it carefully.

'I can sell anyway,' he would whisper in his funny accent, if he saw a kid standing there paging through a *Bamse* comic. Sometimes he would give away old issues that were a little the worse for wear.

'Take home, if you want? I can't sell, better some-one get to read than just throw away.'

Weed's Market was more of a boys and girls club than the actual Boys and Girls Club. But that was years ago now. Today, the Boys and Girls Club was closed, and the kids who read comic books at Weed's Market without paying their way had been replaced by a whole different kind of kid.

'Have things calmed down now?' Farid asked.

Weed shrugged.

'Calmer, yeah. Always after a shooting, a few weeks. But also calmer, everything else...' He swept his arm toward the empty store. 'Not many custom-ers left. Not good times. Not even murder is good for business.'

He tried to laugh. It caught in his throat.

'You'll see, it will...' Farid began, but he changed his mind.

'How is the investigation going?'

'Moving forward.'

Mehdi had not said a word, of course. Two days until the detention hearing. They would have to re-lease him if the investigation didn't turn up some-thing new.

He clapped Weed on the arm. There was nothing more to say. He pulled out a trolley and began to fill it with goods. When he had gone through the list, he moved on to the meat counter. *Always good to have something in the freezer*, he thought. At the register he selected a few bulk packets of sweets and four bags of crisps, a glossy magazine each for the girls and both evening papers.

Nadja would say he had a guilty conscience. That he was trying to buy his way out of it. She would, of course, be right.

THE BOYS

When they were ten years old, the boys became spies.
It wasn't some dorky game, it was for real. Mehdi
explained what it involved, sounding extra serious.

'In case we need someone to keep a lookout, warn
us when the cops are coming. Stuff like that. This
is the first position on the way to becoming a full-
fledged member of my organization.'

Billy and Dogge didn't ask what came next, or
who had been spies before them. You weren't supposed to ask Mehdi about things if you didn't have to.
They would learn as they went along.

Being a spy wasn't hard, but it was exciting.

The first time, at the end of March during Year
5, they were directed to stand by one of the main
roads into Våringe while Mehdi 'had a chat' with the
owner of the pizzeria. Billy and Dogge didn't know
what the talk was about, nor did they need to.

'It's not like he's ordering a Hawaiian, probably,'
Billy said. They laughed.

The second time they were given a spying assignment they had to stand down on the street by an apartment building on the south side of Våringe while Mehdi changed the locks on the basement storage units. He needed them.

'I can't keep the stuff at my house, obviously,' he said.

Billy and Dogge nodded. Mehdi talked to them as if they were nearly grown, which meant they shouldn't ask stupid questions. So Dogge asked Billy once they were alone.

'What kind of stuff did he mean?'

Billy was annoyed.

'How should I know? Drugs, maybe? At my school they say Mehdi works for someone in the city, that Våringe is his turf.'

'What about the people who live there, though? Don't they want to use their storage units?'

'Are you stupid or something?' Billy said. He didn't elaborate.

Still, there didn't seem to be all that many people in Mehdi's organization. Nor did they ever meet any big drug lord from the city. But Mehdi had lots of friends, and a constant stream of new chicks, and they always got paid.

Once, when they were twelve and had been spies for almost two years, they got to come along when Mehdi and two of his buddies were going to beat up some other guy. When they arrived at the industrial area where it was going to happen, they saw the guy. He had a wet spot on the front of his jeans, like he'd pissed himself.

'Shit, he's been asking for this for-fucking-ever,' Mehdi said before he got out of the car.

Dogge and Billy didn't hear any of the actual assault – there were a number of closed doors between where they stood keeping a lookout for cars and where Mehdi and the other two had gone. After half an hour they came back out. The guy was no longer with them. Mehdi's buddies took one car, and Dogge and Billy got to sit in Mehdi's back seat. As Mehdi entered the highway, he called the emergency number and asked for an ambulance. Once he'd explained where it should go, he tossed the phone out the window. Then he turned up the volume on the stereo. But they could hear him mumbling through the music.

'Shit, he's been asking for that for-fucking-ever.'

That time, Dogge and Billy each got a 1,000-kronor bill.

But the best thing about being spies was the stuff they got. They hardly ever had to pay. Mehdi was always good to them. Billy could ask for extra too.

'You're a walking party, huh? You've already started in on girls, kid?' Mehdi laughed. 'What a fucking Casanova.'

And Billy laughed back, it was true that he loved girls. He always wanted to bring them home, but only to Dogge's. There weren't as many parties at Dogge's place these days because the idiots were still causing trouble for Teo and that gave him headaches, weird ones, throbbing that wouldn't go away even with a double dose of painkillers. But even so, Billy wanted to go to Dogge's house whenever there was some girl he couldn't make out with outdoors.

'You get why.'

And Billy would lie on Dogge's bed with his girl, trying to get her clothes off, while the girl's friend sat next to Dogge and played with her phone.

'Don't you like chicks?' Billy would ask Dogge. 'Why don't you do anything? Are you a fag or something?'

That made Dogge want to hit Billy, but Billy laughed to show him it was just a joke. Dogge figured he should get a girl too, a really hot one, and show Billy he wasn't a fag. But it wasn't that easy, he didn't know any girls who looked at him the way they looked at Billy.

27

Farid lingered in the car for a moment before getting out. Not to catch his breath, more to collect himself. The last time he'd seen Leila was seven weeks ago, when she and Billy had come to his office.

Leila was the one who'd called him, saying that she and her son needed to talk to him. He had been surprised. Leila was never rude to him, but this was the first time she'd asked for his help.

They'd hardly made it into his office before Billy started talking. He wanted to know how it worked, what he should do to 'start over'. He'd used those words, 'I want to start over, a restart, back to factory settings, know what I'm saying?'

Farid himself made the call to the disengagement team, the one that got the best results. Billy and Leila stayed put as he dialled, and he put it on speakerphone so they could ask questions. Leila had kept her tears at bay initially, being practical and matter-of-fact, demanding that the representative of the programme immediately set a time and place to meet in person and continue the conversation. When they hung up, Farid told her it was important to make sure Billy visited the station once a week to submit to a drug test, because that would make it possible to access more help.

'If you're serious, we're here for you,' he'd told Billy. 'I promise we'll give you all the assistance you need. But you have to do the work too, you have to want this, or else it will all go to hell.'

And Billy had taken his mother's hand as she cried into her hijab.

One week later, he had his first meeting with the disengagement team. Farid talked to them afterwards and found that they were cautiously optimistic; Billy was young, which meant the chances of success were significantly better.

Together they had discussed the security situation. An evaluation was done.

'Get in touch if you receive any threats,' Farid had said to Leila. 'You have to promise me you'll call if you feel the least bit frightened.'

What had she said? Had she promised she would? Farid didn't remember.

A colleague had questioned her after the murder, but nothing came of it. An hour ago, the family's liaison had called Farid to say that Leila had asked to meet with him instead of with her.

'Of course,' he'd said. 'I'll head over right away. I have a few questions I need to ask her anyway.'

He made sure his parking permit was easily visible in the windscreen and got out of the car.

Billy's big sister Aisha answered the door. The front hall was full of shoes – all different sizes of trainers, a pair of bootees, two pairs of lined children's boots. Farid brought a hand to his chest and lowered his head. Aisha shook her head in annoyance and moved aside so he could pass. He toed out of his shoes and managed to find a hook on which to hang his jacket.

'Mum is in the kitchen.'

Leila was standing with her back to the door. She was wearing a long, colourful dress and a bright-blue hijab loosely swept over her head. She turned around when Farid stepped in. She smiled wanly. Her shoulders slumped.

Grief shrinks people, Farid thought.

'Tea?'

'Yes, please.'

She picked up a tray with four teacups and a plate of biscuits. Beneath her stood a child of around three, clutching her skirt tightly.

'She's not mine,' she said. 'I'm watching my niece today, she has a cold and my sister needs to work.'

A girl of about twelve sat at the kitchen table, reading. She had dark circles under her eyes.

'This is Rawdah, she's got homework to do. We'll sit in the living room. I've asked Aisha and Tusane to join us. The kids are home from school, I thought it was best...' She swallowed. 'But back tomorrow, no point in trudging around here at home.'

In the living room, Billy's little brother got up from the sofa. Farid hadn't seen him in over a year. He bore a remarkable likeness to Billy, the same crooked smile and skinny neck. But he looked tired, with the same dark circles under his eyes his sister had, and even skinnier. He offered his hand.

'Everyone calls me Tusse. I'm the youngest. I'm eleven, but I'm the man of the house now.'

Leila let out a tired snort.

Tusse sat down on a neatly made camp bed that stood next to the sofa. Besides the sofa and the bed, the room had a wardrobe, a bookcase, a TV stand with a TV on top, and three chairs. Tusse gestured to show Farid where to sit. He sat down beside Aisha on the sofa. Leila sat across from them in a deep easy chair of green leather. She held her niece on her lap.

'Thanks for asking me here,' Farid said, accepting the teacup Aisha handed him. 'You'll all want to know how the investigation is going, of course. I'm sure you'll understand that I can't tell you everything, but I'll try to explain what I can. I also understand that you want to bury Billy, and I promise we're working as fast as possible. But it's best if you talk to your liaison officer about that.'

'Dogge shot him, from behind because he's such a damn coward, and you think Mehdi told him to do it as some sort of punishment because Billy wanted to quit. But you're the only ones who think that; everyone here knows that snobby bastard did it.' Tusse, furious, stuffed two biscuits into his mouth and chewed. His voice was trembling.

'Don't swear.' Leila reached out to take the plate away and held it toward Farid. Her hand was shaking, but not much. Farid took a biscuit.

'Thanks.'

Rawdah was standing in the doorway. Her voice was soft, but Farid could still hear her.

'Dogge's dad had a lot of guns.'

Tusse stood up from the camp bed and nabbed two more biscuits. He tossed one into his mouth.

'Yeah. Exactly!' He nodded eagerly. 'He did!'

'Dogge's dad had guns?' Farid asked. 'Where'd you hear that?'

'He was a hunter. Rich guys like that go hunting every weekend. He had a whole cabinet full. Billy said he got to look at them and hold them, he told me so.' Tusse was speaking with his mouth full. 'Dogge's dad did lots of things with Billy, he liked Billy. Like, more than his dorky son.'

Leila grabbed his wrist and retrieved the second biscuit.

'Calm down. Quiet. Don't talk nonsense.' She turned to Farid. 'He knows nothing about guns. Nothing.'

Rawdah, in the doorway, spoke up louder this time. She sounded near tears.

'It's not nonsense, Mama, it's true.'

Farid tried to catch Leila's eye. But she stood up to hand her niece to her daughter. The child began to cry right away. Leila herded them out of the room and shut the door. Yet the loud shrieks were still audible.

Back in her chair, Leila looked at Farid.

'My children hear a lot of rumours. They like reading online. Everyone in Våringe talks, everyone saying different things. Almost different. But no one saying it was Mehdi. Everyone says it was Dogge, alone, no one else. Only Dogge. Maybe his dad had a pistol. I don't know, maybe true. But my children know nothing about guns.'

Farid nodded. He tried to ignore the crying child he could still hear from the kitchen. He wanted to talk to Leila alone, maybe talk to the kids too, one at a time. He would have liked to have peace and quiet when he met with Leila, to help her understand that he wasn't trying to catch her children out in any way. She didn't much like the authorities, he was well aware.

When she came to him with Billy to get him into the disengagement programme, it was clear that she saw this as a safeguard against pressure from social services. Billy had seemed motivated, or else Farid couldn't have helped them, but Leila had also demanded assurance from Farid that they wouldn't take Billy away from her, as long as he completed the programme. That he wouldn't be placed in foster care. Farid had tried, as best he could, to make it clear that he couldn't make any such promise.

But this wasn't a calm moment during which he could gain her trust. It felt more like a chaotic charter flight where everyone had stood up early to be first off the plane.

The information that there had been guns at Dogge's house was new. He would have to write a memo about it, it was pertinent to the investigation, even if it did seem to be about hunting rifles. It would have been better if he'd learned this information during a formal interrogation. But Leila hadn't wanted to come to the station, and he didn't want to force her to. So here he was.

'We're not sure yet about what happened,' he said. 'We know Dogge was there when Billy died, and we know he was the one who called 112 and reported that Billy had been shot.'

'Don't give us that bullshit. He shot him.' Tusse bounced on the camp bed. He seemed to have as much trouble sitting still as Billy had at his age. 'Everyone knows he shot him. Are you saying the cops don't know that? That's a lie! Why else would you send him to a state home if he didn't do anything? For rest? Why not rest up at some fancy hotel? Like in Spain maybe? Like the fucking snob-ass Svenne he is? Why are you lying? Dogge's the one who shot him, can't you just say so?'

Farid turned to Leila.

'I've got a question for you, may I ask it?'

Leila nodded.

'You know we've got Billy's phone.'

She nodded again.

'Billy received a text from the phone Dogge used to call 112. And it said, "If you don't come to the playground in twenty minutes and bring the stuff, he'll come to your house. You know what I mean."' Farid looked at Leila. 'Do you understand what that means?'

'No.' She was whispering now. Tusse had stood up.

'Mum doesn't know,' he said firmly.

'None of you know what sort of stuff he was supposed to bring?'

'I said no.' Tusse's voice was higher now. He was talking fast. 'Mum doesn't know, how would she know?'

'Okay,' Farid said. The baby's screams had grown louder. He heard Rawdah pacing back and forth outside the living room, singing a song with no melody. 'Maybe we can talk about it later. I heard you wanted me to explain what they found when they performed Billy's autopsy.'

'Yes, I don't understand it all. Want to be sure.'

'Do you want to go through it right now? With the kids here?'

Leila nodded.

'Now.'

Farid picked up the bag he had set in front of himself, took out the autopsy report, and placed it upside down on the table between them so Leila could read it while he pointed.

'Here's where it says Billy died of gunshot wounds. This means he was hit by two bullets, but both were fatal, each on its own. It also says that he was otherwise in good health and there were no signs of drugs or alcohol in his system when he died.'

Leila began to cry.

'Was it the drugs you were worried about?' Farid handed her a paper napkin from the gold holder next to the plate of biscuits. She crumpled it in her hand.

Tusse stuck out an arm and managed to grab four biscuits. He got all of them into his mouth. Crumbs flew as he spoke.

'Mehdi had nothing to do with this, you all should leave him alone. And Mum knows nothing. How could she know what that stuff was, obviously she doesn't. Don't you get it? Focus on Rönnviken for once. It was Dogge, I swear.'

'Why?' Leila ignored Tusse.

'I don't know, Leila. And you're sure you don't know what kind of stuff Billy was supposed to bring to the playground?'

Leila was squeezing the napkin so hard her knuckles turned white.

'Dogge called the emergency number from an unregistered phone, one of the kind—'

Tusse cut him off.

'A burner.'

'Yes,' Farid said. 'Dogge used this burner phone to contact Billy, Leila. Do you know—'

'I don't know. Not Billy. I know nothing.'

Rawdah was standing in the doorway again. The little girl was wriggling in her arms, and managed to get down to the floor.

'Mama? She's so annoying, I can't take care of her anymore. I have homework to do.'

Leila stood up, blew her nose with the napkin she was still holding.

'We must stop talking. Thank you for explaining autopsy. I need to go now. Another day, maybe? But we have nothing to tell. We know nothing.'

She patted Farid's arm a few times, then let her hand rest on his forearm. For an instant, Farid thought she was going to hug him.

'Nothing to tell,' she whispered again. 'I cannot... I'm sorry.'

Then she left the room, taking the child with her. The little girl stopped crying as soon as she was in Leila's arms.

'She needs sleep. I must put her to bed. Goodbye, Farid.'

Aisha followed him into the hall. Tusse went into the room that had previously been Billy's and closed the door. Farid didn't see Rawdah. Once he had his jacket on and was bending down to put on his shoes, Aisha leaned down and whispered to him.

'Mum wants us to say Mehdi wasn't involved. That we're not afraid of him. That he doesn't have anything to do with this. She told you Mehdi didn't threaten us, but he did. More than once. He wanted money when Billy was going to disengage. Lots of money. And Mum paid, she thought it would be enough, he said it would be enough, but then ... who knows what Mehdi might do. Mum is afraid that if we talk to the police, he's going to get out of jail and say Billy had unpaid debts when he died and Mum has to pay them. Mum doesn't have any money, she can't pay more. She will never tell what Billy did for Mehdi and what Mehdi did to him. But we're scared.'

'How much did you pay?'

'I don't know, Mum doesn't want to say. But a lot. You can't tell her I told you. She would hit the roof.'

'And the stuff Billy was supposed to bring to the playground, do you know what it was?'

Aisha shook her head slowly.

'I can't ... You can't ... Mum ...' A muscle in her jaw tensed. 'We're scared, don't you get it?'

Farid took Aisha by the arm, gently but firmly.

'There's something you need to understand as well. I can't put Mehdi away if no one talks. I can't protect you if you don't tell us you're being threatened, I can't get Mehdi off the streets if you don't tell me what he does. I'm not a magician. You have to tell me. You have to talk, or there's nothing I can do.'

The door to Billy's room opened. Aisha gave a start and yanked open the front door.

'You have to go now.' She shoved Farid out. 'Bye. Don't say anything to Mum. Not a thing.'

As soon as he was outside the door, she closed it behind him.

Farid walked slowly down the stairs. Just as he reached his car, he felt his phone buzz. It was a WhatsApp message from a strange-looking number, a video file. He stopped on the street and downloaded the clip. It was twenty-two seconds long. It had been taken from an odd angle, as if someone had been filming looking up from the floor.

Two of the four people in the image were clearly visible. Billy and Dogge. Both boys had their hands bound in front of them and their jeans and underwear pulled down to their ankles. They were on their knees, facing each other. A man was standing on a chair between them. He was urinating. The image didn't show his face, but it was clear to see that he was letting the stream of urine move from Billy's face to Dogge's and back again. Dogge was crying loudly. When the stream hit Billy's cheek, he had a coughing fit. It looked like he was about to throw up.

Another man stood with his back to the camera. He was moving back and forth, into and out of the frame. He was laughing, loud and drawn out. In his hand he held a Glock. The man turned around. His face was covered by a balaclava; he disengaged the safety on the pistol, leaned forward, and whispered something into Dogge's ear.

Farid couldn't hear what he said, and he still couldn't see the man's face, but he knew who it was. He would recognize Mehdi even with a sack over his head. Then the clip ended.

28

'Today we actually have some good news, for a change.'

Svante was standing at the front of the investigation room, by the screen. He held a half-eaten saffron bun in his hand, his third one. 'Really good news. Sebastian is currently my favourite officer, and that's not just because he brought these.' He raised the bun. 'But first I just want to say, because I know you're all wondering, that we've put Leila and her kids under heightened security. The kids are back in school, and, well, you know how that goes...but in any case we've got someone in plain clothes following them there and back home. And while he can't be in three different classrooms at the same time, it's better than nothing.'

'They couldn't have one each?' Farid wondered.

'Request denied, I'm afraid. So we'll have to work fast. Mehdi's detention hearing is this evening. As for the WhatsApp number that sent you that video,

Farid, it seems the word is—' He looked at Lotta. 'The number doesn't exist? Is that what you're saying?'

Lotta nodded.

'Yes. It's possible to open a WhatsApp account with a fake phone number. We could try to find out the IP address it was sent from.'

Farid interrupted.

'Forget it. I know who sent it. She'll never speak to me again if I try to pin this on her and she finds out I traced her message.'

Svante nodded and swallowed the last of his saffron bun. He eyed the untouched one in front of Farid.

'And when it comes to the men in the video, we won't have time to get the analysis of that material in before Mehdi's detention hearing. So, Farid, we'll have to settle for your opinion for now. Who do you think they are?'

'I don't *think*. I don't have to guess, I *know*. Mehdi's on the right, in the video, with a balaclava on his head and a Glock in his hand. The fellow with the huge bladder is Roger Mäkele, also known as Blue-Boy.'

'Have we talked to this Blue-Boy?'

'Of course.'

'And he was chatty, I assume?'

'He won't make a peep. He's the type that doesn't even want to confirm his name.'

'A real tough guy.' Lotta smirked.

'We'll bring him in too, I think,' said Svante. 'Blue-Boy can celebrate Saint Lucia Day in lock-up. On suspicion of the kidnapping of Billy and Dogge, based on that video. I'll talk to the prosecutor. Bengt, you take someone along and go bring him in. You, Farid, you can go to the detention hearing and tell the judge what you saw in the video. There's no one else who'd be willing to back you up? None of the family members, I take it?'

Farid shook his head. Svante sighed.

'Well, it'll just have to do. And then we've got the story about Dogge's dad and the guns, how are we doing there?'

Lotta looked up.

'We added a note in the investigation material. But there's no gun of that type registered to Teo Arnfeldt. We've spoken with Jill Arnfeldt and she firmly denies it; he only had old hunting rifles, and the Enforcement Authority seized them when he declared bankruptcy. Teo Arnfeldt was also a member of a rod and gun club. I called them and it seems like he'd been there a few times to shoot, but they weren't aware of his having had a Glock.'

'So he could have borrowed a pistol from a friend?'

'Sure. Or he could have bought one illegally.'

'Are we going to get any further than that?'

'No. I don't see how.'

'Well, anyway, we haven't found a Glock at Dogge's house, and that's something, right?'

'Can we get a judge to go along with saying Dogge received a gun from Mehdi, if there are witnesses saying Dogge had access to guns at home?'

'We can try.'

'Let's talk about something more pleasant.' Svante reached across the table and swiped Farid's bun. 'Sebastian? Can you bring us up to speed?'

Sebastian lit up.

'Yeah, so the phone showed up. Farid thought we should find out how we checked the rubbish bins by the bus stop where Dogge boarded the bus, so I made a few calls. And it turned out some lady found the phone just a few hours after the shooting. She fished it out of the bin when she tossed a banana peel; thought it was kind of weird for it to be in there with the rubbish, because if you lose a phone you drop it on the ground or it falls out of your pocket when you sit down, but you don't drop it right into a rubbish bin. And she also thought it was weird for someone to throw away their phone. It wasn't broken, she could tell. Anyway, maybe this isn't important, but the lady turned it in nine hours later in the lobby of the police station in the city, and I've talked to her, so I know all about how it went down.'

'Nine hours?' Lotta shook her head. 'In the city?'

'Yeah, that station is right next to where she works, and the city police are open late Fridays. She didn't think it would matter where she turned it in, that the police must have some centralized database for lost and found items they could check in case someone walked in asking about a phone.'

'A centralized database would have been nice,' Bengt muttered.

'For sure,' said Sebastian. 'Even better if she'd found the gun too.'

'But she didn't.' Svante swallowed the last of Farid's bun.

'No. The park patrol emptied the bin at eleven o'clock Friday morning. If there was anything else in there that would have been of value in the investigation, it vanished right around the time Farid began the second interrogation with Dogge.'

'Mm-hmm,' Svante nodded.

'But the message we found on Billy's phone is still there, on this phone. It's also possible to see that a few calls were made from it forty minutes before the shooting, beyond the unanswered calls that were made to Billy's phone. We've matched them to the tower dumps. These calls went to another prepaid number without any known owner. They were brief calls, the longest lasted four minutes. And then, two minutes after the last call to this other burner ended, the message was sent to Billy.'

Farid jumped in: ' "If you don't come to the playground in twenty minutes and bring the stuff, he'll come to your house. You know what I mean." '

'Exactly.'

Svante cleared his throat.

'So what do we think?'

'That Dogge talked to Mehdi right before he texted Billy.'

Lotta stood up and went to one of the whiteboards.

'Yes,' Sebastian nodded. 'Exactly.'

'Which would indicate that Mehdi did in fact give Dogge this assignment?'

Lotta wrote the unknown telephone number on the board and ended it with a question mark.

'Yes.' Sebastian leaned back in his chair.

'But the number he called, we can't link that to Mehdi?'

'No.'

'And the damn pistol belonged to Dogge's father?' Svante asked.

'No,' Farid was quick to say. 'There's nothing that actually suggests that. Billy wasn't shot with a hunting rifle.'

'But what's this stuff he was supposed to bring to the playground? And where is it now?' Svante muttered.

'Everyone in Billy's family knows, I can say that much for sure,' said Farid.

'Even Leila?'

'Even Leila.'

THE BOYS

In the four weeks before he died, Dogge's father used a wheelchair. In the final two, he couldn't even get out of bed, and had to move into a special hospital located in a four-storey mansion by the sea, which was more like a hotel than a hospital. Dogge's mother explained that it was called a hospice, and everyone who was admitted there was going to die soon. This was how Dogge came to realize that his father would never recover, that he was going to be a guy with a dead dad.

A yellow Lab lived at the hospice, a fat old boy with arthritis and rotten teeth. It liked to lie near the humming aquarium in one of the empty common rooms, snoring. Sometimes Dogge went out and sat beside the dog and petted it behind its ears. Then it would give a satisfied sigh, and once it rested its head in his lap.

His father never rolled out of his room to pet the dog. He just lay in bed, his watery eyes staring at nothing in particular. But one time he turned to Jill, and after staring at her for a few minutes, he said, 'Damn, when did you get so ugly?' Normally this sort of comment would infuriate her, prompt weeks of sulking. She would shout and rage, *How do you think I'm handling things?* But this time, she didn't get mad. She didn't even respond. Even though she could have said, *Have you looked in the mirror lately?*

In the four months between Teo finding out that he was sick and his ending up in the hospice where he would die, he lost nearly three stone, and his muscles melted away like candle wax. Dark-blue spots appeared on his face; they looked like bruises, as if someone had been beating him. His lips were so dry they turned white. Even though he never went through chemotherapy, because it wouldn't have helped make him better, he had lost most of his hair. Even so, it wasn't his appearance Dogge found most frightening, but how weird his dad had become. He sometimes woke up in the afternoon, slurring his speech like he was drunk and angry, even though he wasn't drinking at all – not even water. And in the midst of his slurring he might stop speaking and start making loud, sobbing moans, as though he were throwing up waves of undigested food, but all that landed in the steel basin he kept in a cabinet on wheels next to his bed were small, neon-yellow globs of mucus. And when he was finished, he would grab Dogge's hand, without wiping his mouth first, and say, 'Listen, you have to listen,' and then he would launch into long sentences that didn't mean anything, where the first part of the sentence didn't match the end, and using words that were super complicated, words he never used before he got sick. As he rambled, Dogge would stare at the slimy, yellow traces around Dad's mouth as though transfixed. Why didn't he wipe them away? He didn't dare to ask.

During the last week, Dogge was allowed to miss school, and he and Mum were each given a bed in Dad's room. But Dad slept almost all the time, not just at night. Dogge lay on his bed, playing on his phone, and wanted to leave. Mum paced back and forth, sat down, got up. Went into the hall to see if she could find anyone on staff to ask the same questions she'd asked before.

'Is he in pain? How much longer? How will I know when he dies?'

A few times each hour, Dogge's father would crack his eyes open and look out at the room like a drowsy snake. But he didn't seem to recognize Dogge, and if it had been more than an hour since his last dose of morphine, he would mumble long harangues full of slurring curse words that sounded like he'd made them up.

The process of dying didn't make Teo sentimental or extra loving or even meaner, he simply became a completely different person, someone who had nothing in common with the father he had been.

29

Farid waited in the hallway, there was no reason to interrupt the class. He'd peered through the glass pane in the door and spotted him there, in the second row, next to the window. Tusse hadn't noticed him; he was gazing out at the playground.

The teacher had a rope of tinsel in her hair, apparently already warming up for tomorrow's Lucia celebrations. *7:30 at Ella's school; 10:00 in the auditorium at Natascha's school.* Nadja had sent this message by email, text and WhatsApp, even though she knew he'd already entered all the important times into his calendar. Natascha was going to be her school's Lucia. He heard Nadja's voice in his head.

'She was chosen by her classmates, don't you get it? That's a huge deal when you're fourteen. If you don't make it, don't bother coming home.'

When the bell rang, he backed up against the wall across from the door. Tusse was one of the last to leave and was walking by himself. When he caught sight of Farid, he stopped short. His panic was plain to see.

'No,' Farid said quickly, raising his hands. 'Nothing like that. Your family is fine. I just thought it would be a good idea for us to have a talk in peace and quiet.'

'Not here,' said Tusse. 'I don't want to talk here.'

Eleven years old, Farid thought. *And already worried about being seen with a police officer.*

'If you want, we can go to the station. I can make it look like I'm forcing you to come. I can't put you in handcuffs because I'm not allowed, but you can shout and yell as much as you want.'

Tusse smiled slightly.

'That's okay.'

They got into Farid's car, and he drove them away from the school and onto the highway. Less than a minute passed before Tusse started talking.

'I can't say anything about Mehdi. Or Mum, I can't say anything about Mum, I need you to understand that.'

'Okay.'

'But if I tell you something you can check up on, no one must know you heard it from me. Do you promise not to tell anyone I told you?'

'What's that?'

'Billy was supposed to go away. He was going to leave Sweden. Mum had set it up with our uncle, I've never met him, but Billy was going to live with him.

We were waiting for the visa, it hadn't come yet, but
you can check with the visa people.'

'Why was Billy going to move away?'

'Why the hell do you think? I can't say what, but
he was supposed to do something for Mehdi, as payment for... I can't tell you... and then he couldn't do
that thing anymore, because he... I can't tell you that
either. But the stuff he was supposed to... Billy had
to leave Sweden because... I can't tell you.'

'But what am I supposed to check up on, Tusse?'
Farid let go of the wheel with one hand and placed it
on the boy's shoulder. 'What do you want me to do
here?'

'The Glock wasn't Dogge's dad's, it was Mehdi's.
And you can ask the imam, the one called Hassan,
because he knows everything. Imams aren't allowed
to lie about this stuff. Ask Hassan, do it. He has to
tell you. He has to help us, because he promised to
but then he didn't because he didn't have time, but
now he has to because Billy is dead.'

'Okay,' Farid said hesitantly. 'I'll talk to Hassan.
But how did you know it was a Glock? I didn't tell
you that. It wasn't in the papers. So how did you
know your brother was killed by a Glock?'

Tusse bowed his head. His tears fell onto his
jeans.

'I know,' he said. His voice was so faint it was
almost inaudible. 'I know because I was there when
Mehdi taught Dogge and Billy to shoot it.'

THE BOYS

Tusse got to come along with Billy and Dogge when they went with Mehdi and Blue-Boy to the old chicken factory for target practice. The plan was for them to help create the shooting range. It was a sunny October day, the sky deep blue, the trees behind the industrial area a thousand different colours.

The roof on one side of the factory had caved in since the days when Dogge and Billy used to come here to play, and one of the walls was leaning considerably. Someone from the council, or maybe the police, had been there to cordon off the area. The plastic tape fluttered in the breeze, and there were four warning signs around the building.

HAZARDOUS AREA. PRIVATE PROPERTY. DANGER OF COLLAPSE. NO TRESPASSING, VIOLATORS WILL BE PROSECUTED.

They went behind the building and paced out three ranges: one ten yards long, one twenty, and the last thirty, or perhaps a bit shorter; Dogge lost count toward the end and Tusse ran off to pee, but neither Blue-Boy nor Mehdi seemed to care. The back window of the car they'd driven over in was full of glass bottles and empty cans. They lined them up along the side of the building. Dogge took off his sweater, his T-shirt felt damp in the autumn air but he wasn't cold. After about an hour, Mehdi asked if they wanted to try. Not Tusse, he was too little, but Dogge and Billy were old enough.

'Then again, the cartridges are pretty damn expensive,' he added. 'Maybe you don't got the *floos*.' He laughed loudly when he saw their disappointed faces. 'Don't you know a joke when you hear one? Ammo's on me.'

Blue-Boy got out four boxes.

They put up a fresh row of bottles and cans. Mehdi handed them each a Glock and showed them how to load them and switch off the safety, then he backed off and lit a joint.

'Go hard.'

They shot the guns tentatively at first, to keep from wasting ammunition. Mehdi was annoyed.

'Go hard, I said. I don't fucking have time to hang out here all day. Are you afraid you're going to hit this shit, or something?'

He went up to Billy, took the Glock from him, and loaded it with a fresh batch of ammunition, emptied his own pocket of even more bullets, placed them in Billy's hand.

Billy planted his feet wide, turned the pistol on its side, and squeezed the trigger as hard as he could, like Tupac and Snoop, like Abidaz and Yasin. Dogge did the same. He thrust his hips and chin out. *Fuck you*, he wanted to shout, and he bit his lower lip. But he ran out of ammunition before Billy. When his gun clicked, Billy pulled out the loose bullets he'd got from Mehdi and gave them to Dogge.

'I've got tons. Take these. Finish that shit. Prove you've got the balls.'

Everyone laughed, even Billy's little brother. Tusse was lying on his belly behind them, his chin resting in his hands. He was too little to shoot, but not too little to be part of this.

The most fun was hitting an empty can, it made a cool sound and you could go pick it up and see clearly where the bullet had gone in. The glass bottles just shattered, and it was impossible to tell if you'd hit it square on or just grazed it, the bottle flew into a thousand pieces either way. The wall of the factory behind the bottles was dotted with more and more bullet holes. In a few places there were big holes, smoke twining up along the wall. It was hard to hit their targets even from ten yards off, but they tried twenty too. They didn't bother with the longest range.

Near the end, Billy emptied his magazine straight into the air, laughing wildly. It had been ages since Dogge had seen him so happy. While Billy danced around and around, Dogge felt the last four bullets he'd been given. They were still in his pocket.

Then he handed the gun back to Mehdi, who made sure the magazines and barrels were empty before handing them over to Blue-Boy, who placed them in a large shoulder bag.

The bullets in Dogge's pocket felt cool and smooth against his skin, and he rolled them in his hand the way Dad used to do with the stress balls Jill gave him when he was still working on his projects. Now Dad was sick, had a constant headache, nothing helped, and sometimes it hurt so bad he screamed.

He took the bullets out and looked at them again. Four of them – they looked like they were made of gold. He would keep them forever. Billy had given them to him. One day, he would get a gun of his very own, and he would use them.

They climbed into the back seat of Mehdi's car. Billy and Dogge on either side, Tusse in the middle.

'Well done, boys,' Mehdi said before dropping them off at the square in Våringe. 'Soon you can start doing real stuff. Soon I'll be able to make real use of you two. Well done.'

30

Dogge watched through the glass pane into the kitchen as Momi took the prepackaged dinners out of the food trolley. Before each meal, this trolley was rolled into their unit. Someone different brought it almost every time, but all of them wore a shower cap and a disposable apron, as though the food were hazardous waste and must be handled carefully.

When Momi was done taking the meals from the trolley, he opened them and poured their contents into larger tubs, which he placed on the table where they would eat. Dogge assumed this was to make it feel like a regular meal, but it didn't work.

It was a quarter past four, and they were going to have lentil stew for dinner. The only people who voluntarily ate vegetarian, as far as he knew, were Rönnviken girls who actually didn't want to eat at all and the folks in Våringe who were active in the Muslim Association and wore tube socks and sandals year-round. Dogge never would have eaten this at home. It smelled like farts and there was no way it wouldn't taste disgusting. He had, however, frequently eaten prepackaged food because Jill didn't like to cook, and if they didn't go to a restaurant they would usually order in. Even though Teo wasn't much interested in eating at all, especially not towards the end.

Sometimes, when Dogge was having a meal on his own, he would cook – he knew how to make spaghetti and rice, and you could get good sauces in jars. Once he'd even boiled a potato, but since he hadn't felt like peeling it he never ate it.

Once Momi had placed the bowls of food on the table, he called everyone over for dinner.

'Look at this shit,' said one of the guys. He was wearing a bright-yellow hoodie with no string in the hood and jeans with no belt; he had a scar on one cheek. Dogge didn't know his name. 'Not even pigs would eat this.'

'You haven't tasted it yet,' said Momi.

'What's in it? I'm allergic.'

'To what?' Momi went to the kitchen and took the empty packaging from the trash. 'Tell me what you're allergic to, and I can tell you if there's any in here.'

'Lentils,' said the guy with the scar.

'You're not allergic to lentils. According to your records, the only thing you don't eat is hazelnuts.' Momi tossed the packaging to Dogge. 'Please read the contents to us. There aren't any hazelnuts, are there? Read it out loud.'

'What, can't you fucking read?' Dogge threw the packaging down. He hated reading aloud. 'Do I look like a fucking story-time lady or something?'

Momi didn't respond. He just picked up the packaging from the floor and looked at Dogge, as if to check whether he was planning to throw anything else. After a brief silence, he stuffed the packaging into the rubbish bin next to the kitchen entrance.

'Maybe the story-time lady would consider taking a seat? It's time to eat.'

Dogge didn't have the strength to protest. He sat down next to the guy with the scar.

'They give us this shitty food so we'll turn into primo members of society and go to school and raise our hands and get ourselves some shit job and a wife who gets fat as soon as the first baby comes, but we'll still screw her so she has a second kid and gets even fatter.'

Dogge laughed. The guy kept talking.

'We're supposed to act right so we can have salaries and conferences and courses and copy machines.'

'And fat wives.'

Momi smiled.

'Start by eating your dinner. We can talk about the future later.'

He scooped food onto Dogge's plate. It smelled just as nasty as he'd known it would.

Then the Italian came in, along with Josef. Both of them sat down.

No one dared to stare, but the whole room turned toward the Italian, he was magnetic. He didn't say a word, not even about the lentil stew. He seemed distracted, as though he'd been interrupted while doing something important, or needed to ponder a thorny problem. When Momi asked if he wanted some stew, he shook his head and reached for the breadbasket. He took six slices and spread a thick layer of butter on each. Momi didn't protest, even though he'd just said they were only allowed to have four slices each. Then the Italian turned his bread into sandwiches. He still didn't say a word. He just chewed.

'Did you see the game?'

Everyone but Dogge had seen it. It had been shown in the big common room the night before. Momi was asking everyone around the table, but his eyes were on the Italian.

'Hell of a sweet goal in the eighty-eighth.'

The Italian didn't respond.

Momi let his eyes wander to the next person. He didn't respond either.

'Silence is the mark of a good meal, eh?' Momi gave a wry smile, but he didn't ask any more questions.

Whatever it was the Italian was preoccupied with, it didn't seem to have anything to do with Dogge; he hardly even glanced in his direction. But when everyone was sick of shoving the lentil stew from one side of their plate to the other, and Momi finally told them they could be excused, it was as though the Italian suddenly noticed Dogge was there. Instead of heading straight out of the room, he slid up beside Dogge, and when Momi wasn't looking, he made his move, whispering close to Dogge's ear.

'Don't take no fucking sleeping pills tonight. You got that? You have to stay awake, be ready, no dozing off.'

Then he was gone. When Dogge got to the common room, the Italian wasn't there.

He went to his own room. When he got his pill, he put it in his mouth but didn't swallow; instead, he stuck it in the pocket of his jeans as soon as he was alone. It felt like in a movie, he'd seen people pretend to take pills tons of times in movies about innocent people who ended up in the nuthouse, or who were held prisoner by some madman.

And then he just lay there. The ants in his feet woke up and crawled up and down his legs. He scratched his calves and the backs of his knees so hard that he ended up with blood under his nails. But he still didn't take the pill. He did what the Italian said, because if the Italian said something it was just like if Mehdi had said it.

Ten o'clock came and went, and eleven, and midnight, but nothing happened. And his legs were still itching. When Dogge turned out the lights, the room went pitch-black, almost as dark as it was outside the window. He stood on the bed and tried to see out the milky windowpane. He fingered the pill in his pocket.

Am I allowed to lie down? He lay down. *Am I allowed to close my eyes?* He closed his eyes, but he still couldn't sleep. *Am I allowed to get under the covers?*

How was he supposed to know what he was or wasn't allowed to do? There was no one to ask. He got under the covers, but now he was wide-awake. It was quiet in the hallway. Not a sound anywhere, not even from the room next door.

Wouldn't it be best to kill me in my sleep? Wouldn't it be better for everyone if I fell asleep and never woke up again?

31

As soon as Farid dropped Tusse off at home, he called Svante.

'We need to send a tech to a shuttered chicken factory a few miles from Våringe, I'll text you the coordinates.'

Farid briefly recounted what Tusse had told him.

'It's been more than a year since they did target practice up there, and I can't be totally sure it was our gun they were playing with, but with a little luck we might find some bullets to compare with the ones we took out of Billy.'

Svante interrupted him enthusiastically.

'Did you get this kid's statement on tape? We need a proper witness statement to tie Mehdi to the chicken factory and the weapons that were fired there.'

'If we get a match, I'll see what I can do. But let's start by sending some techs up there. They might not even find anything we can use. I don't want to sabotage my relationship with Billy's little brother if I don't have to.'

'Of course, of course!' Svante sounded incredibly pleased. 'For sure. Well done!'

After they hung up, Farid called Hassan the imam. They were already acquainted. Hassan was the goalie on the council's football team, and they'd played friendly matches against the Våringe police a few times.

'Drop by anytime,' said Hassan. 'We're open around the clock. If I'm not there, you can just give me a call and I can be there in under fifteen minutes.'

'Not quite the same hours as us,' Farid declared. 'The station is only open to the public between four and six p.m., Mondays and Thursdays.'

Hassan laughed, but not in a mean way.

Four palm trees were planted outside the mosque. They reminded Farid of the moth-eaten animals in the Norrland forest exhibit at the Biological Museum, which he'd liked so much when he was little. His mother had had to take him there many times, and he would lie on the floor and stare through the glass, preferably at the bear, which he found the most fascinating. Its fur was patchy, bare in several places. Once, when he was there, a capercaillie lost an eye.

The palms outside the Våringe mosque were not stuffed, but they were dead – treated with a substance that was meant to keep them in good shape. Yet they weren't all that nice, despite the strings of lights that had been wound around their trunks to light up the main entrance.

Hassan wasn't up in the prayer hall; he was one floor down. There were two changing rooms there, as well as a gym and a half dozen smaller rooms.

'We're having a homework session,' Hassan explained when he stepped out of one of the rooms. 'But they'll be fine on their own for a bit. What did you want to talk about?'

Farid hesitated. They sat down in the room next door to where the children were doing their homework.

'Do you want something to drink?'

Farid shook his head.

'I need to talk to you about the Ali family, Leila Khalid's kids.'

'I had an inkling.'

'What can you tell me about them?'

'That you don't already know? That Leila and Ali haven't lived together for many years, that Leila has had to raise her kids on her own, without any help from her husband, financial or otherwise. Billy was a good kid, if you ask me. He loved his mother, but, well, he had some problems too.'

'In what ways have you provided assistance to the family?'

Hassan frowned.

'Why don't you just ask me what you want to know, straightforwardly, and I'll answer if I can?'

'Was Billy going to leave Sweden?'

'Yes. He was going to go stay with Leila's family. Live there for six months, was the plan. He'd applied for a visa but didn't have time to get it approved.'

'Why not?'

'Have you talked to Leila?'

'She won't tell me anything of importance.'

'And I can't get into what she's told me, because I'm bound by confidentiality.'

'Confidentiality?'

'Don't play dumb. You know very well that I can't share anything she's told me in confidence. The trip was no secret, the congregation had collected money for the family so Billy could get away. We thought it would help him complete the disengage-ment programme.'

'Was that the only reason?'

'Talk to Leila.'

'I have talked to...' Farid hesitated, 'some of the other members of the family as well. Have you had much contact with the rest of the family?'

'Just Isak, really.' Now it was Hassan's turn to hesitate. 'But Isak and I have talked quite a bit.'

The door opened, and a girl of about nine stuck her head in.

'We need help. We don't get what to do for cir-cumference and all that.'

'I'm coming.' Hassan stood.

'Should I talk to Isak? Is that what you're saying?' Farid asked. 'We've interviewed him, the family liaison has questioned him twice, but he didn't have much to say. As far as I understand, he doesn't have a lot of contact with his kids. And as you said yourself, hasn't Leila taken care of most of that on her own?'

Hassan stopped in the doorway and turned to face him.

'Unfortunately I'm not able to get into what sort of conversations I've had with Isak, either. I take my duty of confidentiality very seriously. And I think it will be hard for you to talk to him. Because he's not in Våringe anymore. His phone contract seems to have ended. No one has seen him since two days after Billy's death. From what I understand, he took off with the money we collected for Billy's travels. He got it from Leila. We haven't decided what to do about that, probably nothing. We had already given the money to the family. The fact that it wasn't meant to go to Isak is beside the point. But I have to go now, the kids need to finish their homework and then I have to walk them home. After all, we don't want anything to happen to them.'

THE BOYS

The first time they saw each other after Dogge's
father died was outside Weed's Market. They had arranged to meet up there.

Dogge had zero intention of going along to the
funeral home and listening as some dusty dude with
an ugly tie asked what kind of music Teo had liked,
and what they should write in the obituary.

Jill kept bothering him about it. 'A cross for the
graphic on top, or maybe an anchor? Should we in-
clude Teo's parents' names, since they're paying?
"Sleep well"? "Rest in peace"? "Please consider a do-
nation to the Cancer Fund?"'

Mum could take care of that herself. Even though
she had already overslept for two meetings and still
hadn't called Teo's parents to tell them he'd said he
didn't want them at the funeral.

When Billy approached Dogge, he looked sad,
like he'd been crying.

'I'm so...' he began. 'Your dad was...'

Suddenly Dogge got the feeling Billy was about to hug him. To keep that from happening, he took a half step back, turned around, and walked through the doors, into the store, straight to the shelf of sodas, where he grabbed a bottle of Coke and shook it hard before putting it back and starting on the next one.

'Wipe that sad look off your face,' he muttered. 'It wasn't your fucking dad who died.'

He shook the bottles of soda one by one. Billy stood next to him without doing or saying a thing. Weed was nowhere to be seen. The employees who filled in when he couldn't be at the store never dared to confront Billy or Dogge. They might be standing just a foot or two away when the boys picked things up, filling their pockets with the most expensive items from the meat counter, taking fistfuls of candy from the bulk bins. They wouldn't say a word. The boys always threw away everything they'd taken as soon as they left the store. Most of the time they didn't even eat the candy.

'Come on,' said Billy. 'Let's go to my house instead.' He sounded like a grown-up trying to get Dogge to calm down. 'We can watch a movie, just chill a little.'

But Dogge didn't feel like watching a movie. He couldn't stand Billy's annoying siblings. All he wanted was for it to be quiet inside his head. If they went to Billy's they couldn't smoke up, couldn't do oxy, and there wasn't any alcohol to sneak. Dogge didn't have any money, and Mehdi had stopped giving them drugs for free. He had to get his hands on some cash, and he had to talk to Mehdi. He dropped a two-litre bottle on the floor, the Coke inside foamed, the bottle rolled off.

'*You* go home and chill if you're so fucking tired.'

That was when he saw her. She was standing by the sweet packets. It was Weed's daughter, he knew that much. How old could she be? Almost their age. At least twelve. She wasn't all that cute, but she wasn't ugly either. He started for the confectionery aisle.

I'm not a fucking fag.

Billy watched for a moment before following him. Now he was annoyed.

'Where the hell are you going, Dogge? Let her be. She's just a kid. What has she done to you?'

'Lay off me. I'm not going to hit her, I'm just going to see if she has tits yet.'

32

We prioritize all types of crime.'

Those were the words of the officer who was being given screen time to talk about the escalating, deadly violence among children and teenagers. Farid erupted in a scornful laugh and turned to Nadja, seeking her agreement. But she had dozed off, with her mouth half open and her thumb on the screen of her phone. At least she had put down her glass of wine. Farid reached for it; his own had long been empty. He grabbed the bowl of crisps while he was at it. He'd bought the crisps for the kids, but they weren't here. Felicia had had to catch a bus, she was going to 'practice for the Lucia procession, Dad, everyone's there, I'll be home before midnight'. She was 'in a hurry', and now she was 'out' and had promised to come home 'on time'.

He'd asked what kind of Lucia procession this was, could he and her mother come watch?

'Come on, Dad,' she'd said. 'None of the parents are coming, it's just for school. And aren't you going to Natascha's and Ella's ones anyway?'

'Did you make the bus?' he'd texted her half an hour after she left. She hadn't responded.

Natascha was so nervous about her Lucia procession that she had cried herself to sleep. Her Lucia gown was ugly, or too short, or too wrinkly, Farid couldn't remember which. Her Lucia crown would be borrowed from the school. *What if it doesn't fit?* she had sobbed. And when she finally calmed down, Ella started crying. She didn't want to be one of Lucia's handmaidens anymore, she wanted to be Santa instead. They didn't have an elf costume in her size. This was 'no fair.' Ella said that she had 'the meanest parents in the whole world, you just don't get it'.

When their two youngest were finally asleep, Nadja had opened a bottle of wine, and one glass later she, too, was asleep.

He looked at his phone. The techs up at the chicken factory had pulled tons of bullets out of the wall and cartridges from the ground. It was going to take time to sort through this material, Lotta had written. But they'd been given approval to keep Mehdi in custody. Svante had sent four happy emoji. But Farid was still waiting on some reaction from Felicia. How many times had he asked her to turn on her location so he could see where she was? Just as many times as she'd promised to do it: 'Later, Dad, I'll do it later.'

He took a handful of crisps, placed them on his chest, and began to eat them one by one. Nadja suddenly snorted and dropped her phone. She pulled up her feet, placed them in his lap, and nestled into the back of the sofa. Farid rested a hand on her hip.

Why wasn't Felicia responding? She'd said they were meeting up at a friend's house. *Most violent crimes take place in the home*, he thought. Lucia practice? They were probably hiding out somewhere where they could drink in peace, without risking discovery by her dad's colleagues. He could hear his daughter's voice in his head.

'We don't drink! Only the humanities kids drink, not us.'

Farid sighed. The other day, as he was driving to work, he'd seen Natascha in the distance, coming the other way on her bike. She wasn't wearing a helmet. She had been when she left the house, but by the time she got a quarter mile down the road it was carefully tucked into her bag. He had texted her, *You have to wear a helmet!* She had replied two hours later. Thumbs-up. He couldn't even do anything about that.

On TV, the officer continued to rattle off clichés.

'I think about how behind every murder there is a victim, there are family members, there are people suffering. I think about how we have to consider the victim, we have to consider the family members, we have to consider those who are suffering. Because they suffer terribly and have been subjected to so much.'

Nadja snored. The officer on TV was really on a roll now.

'The measures we're currently taking are not sufficient. Gang-related crime is out of control. We've got more shootings than ever. Children shooting children. The system is broken, society is in pieces, we have to fix it, we have to fix all of it.'

Farid emptied the glass of wine and looked at the remote control. It was too far away. He couldn't change the channel. If he got up, he would wake Nadja.

He'd met the officer on-screen a few times. He popped up whenever there was a camera nearby. Felicia had shown him his Instagram account. If its contents were to be believed, his colleague's workdays were filled to the brim with heroic deeds performed at the fringes of society, while his weekends were spent as an extra in various TV shows.

'All crimes are a threat to democracy,' the officer now declared. His voice was deep and grave. 'Democracy is the most important asset we have. Incredibly important. We must set the bar at ground level, we won't accept anything less, nothing will evade our radar.'

Farid shook his head in disbelief and fired off another text to Felicia.

'All good?'

Still no response.

'Just answer. I'm worried.'

Six years ago, he had been a speaker at parent-teacher night at the kids' school. One of the parents had asked him what he thought a fifteen-year-old's curfew should be.

'Ten o'clock,' he'd said.

Two of the parents had laughed out loud. They thought he was joking. Only now did he understand why. Felicia would be seventeen in two months. If he'd told her to be home at ten, she wouldn't even have dignified him with an answer. He wasn't even sure Natascha would have.

'We each have to take responsibility. Parents and teachers, all the adults, we all need to set boundaries. My colleagues and I are sick to death of this,' said the officer on TV. 'Everyone needs to pitch in. We police officers, we don't let go even for a second,' he went on. 'The thin blue line. We are unflagging, we stand stronger than ever in this ill wind, and we are used to storms.'

'You are unflagging,' Farid muttered to himself, taking a few more crisps. 'What luck.'

'It's for the sake of public safety, and for democracy, that we prioritize criminality. Every type of crime, everywhere.'

Not a single twitch of the eye – could this guy *hear* himself? In any case, the host of the programme was losing patience.

'You're saying you prioritize all crime?'

'Absolutely. That is of the utmost importance.'

'So you prioritize bike theft, sexual assaults, violence in the home, minor drug offences, criminal damage, murder and runaway cats?'

'Runaway cats are not a crime.'

'Still, I see on your Instagram account that last week you took the time to rescue a cat from a tree.'

'I do what I can to be helpful.' The police officer did a Scout's honour sign and chuckled.

The host didn't laugh.

'Do you know approximately how much it would cost to realize your ambitions for Swedish law enforcement?'

'I'm no politician, that's not for me to figure out. But security cameras don't cost that much.'

'All the studies show that cracking down with heavy surveillance in one area only causes crime to move a few blocks away.'

'Then we'll put cameras up there too.'

'Oh?'

'There will be cameras everywhere we need to make sure that the general public feels safe.'

'Everywhere?'

'Yes.'

'You don't see any issues with this?'

'Why would I? If you don't do anything stupid, you have nothing to be ashamed of. Want to avoid the police? Okay, then don't commit any crimes. And we'll leave you alone. Don't act like an ass, and it will all work out.'

Farid shook his head again and looked at his phone. Still no response. He checked Snapchat, Instagram, and TikTok to see if she had posted any updates, maybe even her location. But he couldn't find any evidence that she had been online. *She blocked* me. *She doesn't want me to know.* He sent a question mark, nothing more. He imagined her glancing at her screen when her phone buzzed, but ignoring it. *Just Dad. I'll answer later.*

He lifted his wife's feet out of the way, got up off the sofa, grabbed the remote, and turned off the TV. He'd heard enough.

Then he picked up the phone again. He composed another text and sent it to the family's group chat on WhatsApp too. 'Is it too much to ask for you to respond? How much time could it take?'

Worry. Always this worry. It lived in his stomach, awakened in the wee hours, woke him up, wouldn't let him get back to sleep. It drew its energy from any number of things – if it wasn't one of the kids coming home late, it was a vague pain in his back that might be metastases from some undiscovered cancer, or some matter that had to be dealt with, finished, prepared. On Fridays, the ones he didn't have to work, he drank half a bottle of wine or three beers or maybe a little more, and for a little while the worry would loosen its grip, like the split second before a swing changes directions in midair and starts back down again. But before he could relax, that relief would be switched out for sleeplessness and tangled sheets.

———

Felicia came home at four minutes past midnight. When she opened the door to their bedroom and whispered *Good night*, he pretended to be asleep. Five minutes later, he was. When his phone woke him up, it was almost five in the morning. He answered, stumbling out of bed and dashing from the bedroom.

She snuck out again, he had time to think as he threw open the door to Felicia's room. His oldest daughter was sound asleep.

'Thank God.' The words slipped out of him.

'Huh?' The duty officer was waiting on the line.

'Oh, sorry. I thought something had happened to the kids.' Farid regretted his words again. 'My kids, that is.'

'Hmm.' The duty officer sounded curious.

'I'm sorry,' Farid said again, heading down the stairs. 'I'm listening. What did you say? What happened at the state home? I don't understand. What did you just say they did?'

As the duty officer spoke, Farid sank onto the sofa.

'How the hell did that happen?'

'I don't know much more, this is all the information I have for the time being. It happened a few hours ago, we sent a car.'

'Okay. Thanks.' He heard his own breathing echo on the line.

'Are you coming in? Or will you be heading there?'

'No, they'll have to handle it without me. There's no point in my going. I'll be at the station around lunch. I have two Lucia celebrations to go to first. My middle daughter is Lucia. I can't miss it, she would never forgive me.'

33

'Your father has moved away.'

Mum told them over breakfast three days after the murder. Tusse hardly reacted.

'Where to?' Aisha wondered. But Mum didn't know, just that he'd gone somewhere far away and wouldn't be back.

'Isn't he going to say goodbye?' asked Rawdah. 'Isn't he going to say goodbye to us one last time?' But before Leila could respond, Rawdah started to cry.

Tusse didn't. He wouldn't miss his father – or at least he didn't think he would. There was no more space inside him to miss people; Billy's death was taking up all that room.

Tusse didn't know how old he'd been when he realized Billy was the best person in the whole world. But his mother often teased him about it.

'If only I had someone to look at me the way you look at your brother,' she laughed.

But it had been the other way around with his sister Rawdah. Even before she learned to talk, she would stare at Billy like she was wondering who he was. Leila often joked about that too, how for a while she was sure Rawdah thought Billy's name was 'No', because that was the only thing she said when he got close. *No.* Not angrily, not with fear in her voice, more like a stern statement: No. Not him. Anything, anyone, but him. 'Between the two of you, it was hate at first sight,' Leila laughed. 'And it was the opposite with Tusse.'

The first time Tusse spent a whole day alone with his brother, Billy was seven and he was four. Leila had taken the girls to visit relatives in Gothenburg. Isak was home, but got drunk and fell asleep fifteen minutes in. But it didn't matter. Leila had bought crisps *and* sweets, and Tusse could sit there watching Billy play video games for hours. He loved it. When Leila had to work, Billy sometimes took Tusse to daycare before walking to school himself. If Tusse cried when Billy had to leave, Billy would simply comfort him. It brought him lots of praise from the daycare teachers.

'Where's Mum?' the teachers would ask. 'In the car,' said Billy. That was good enough for them. Leila had never had a car. She didn't even have a driver's licence.

Billy was the one who taught Tusse all the things a dad should teach his son. He taught him about respect and chastised him when he was rude to their mother, because even if Billy himself sometimes shouted at Leila, it made him furious when Tusse did.

He told Tusse to be nice to their sisters, even though he liked to tease them until they were screeching in anger. And Billy was cool. He always had the best clothes, listened to awesome music. For a long time, Tusse thought his brother had all it took, that he would succeed in everything.

But then Billy started having nightmares. He was big then, thirteen, almost fourteen. The nightmares happened often, several times a week, and they got worse and worse. Sometimes he would come and get Tusse from the room where he slept with Rawdah and carry him to his bed so they could sleep head to toe.

'I don't want to sleep by myself,' he said to Tusse. Like he was a little kid. If he did fall back to sleep, he would sweat and make noises. He always locked the door when he got home and didn't like being near windows. And he often looked like he'd been crying, sometimes even in the afternoon.

Billy stopped taking Tusse along to see Mehdi. Once he smacked him when Tusse followed him anyway.

'Go home, you fucking brat,' he shouted. But Tusse had understood. Billy wasn't shouting because he was angry, he was shouting because he was scared. Because he didn't know how to stop being scared.

So Tusse had asked for help. That's what grown-ups said you were supposed to do. And now Billy was dead. Billy had always been there, and he was always supposed to be there, and now he was gone. He hadn't said goodbye either.

THE BOYS

One month after Teo died, Dogge and Billy went to
the Rönnviken school dance. Dogge had stolen two
tickets from a bag that was just sitting there in the
hallway one day when he was at school. The party
was primarily for the students in Year 11 – the oldest
students – and the girls were wearing gowns, while
almost all the guys had suits and ties. When Billy
showed his ticket at the entrance, they eyed him for a
few seconds before letting him in. But they didn't say
anything about how he and Dogge were too young.
The tickets were enough.

Outside the dance, a girl was smoking. She glanced
at Dogge and then at her friend, and they laughed
the way cute girls do when they see guys they like.
Dogge's face went hot; this was the first time a girl
had looked at him like that. She was laughing a lot,
but not necessarily in a mean way, and maybe she
had been drinking, but only a little. Her boyfriend
was there too. He was in Year 11 but was shorter than

Dogge, and he was definitely drunk. Billy caught on right away to what Dogge was thinking.

'He's probably stronger than he looks,' he said.

'I don't give a shit,' Dogge replied.

He'd got pretty good at fighting. First it was the idiots and the Enforcement Authority that made him brave. The Enforcement Authority had come to seize the stereo, the crystal stemware, the dining room table, and both the new and inherited lamps. They had emptied the house of everything that was fun to own. It felt like all they left were the light bulbs, one TV and the sofa with cigarette burns in its upholstery. That was the end of the parties. Dogge's dad would have liked to keep having them: 'I don't need a stereo system to have a good time.' But after the newspaper articles, no one accepted his invitations. And then he got sick. After that, even he didn't want to party; he was too tired.

When the Enforcement Authority cleared out Dogge's house, it got quiet at home. When his dad died, it got quiet at school too.

He had stopped being afraid when Teo died. And when he was fighting, it was quiet inside his head, at least for a little bit. You could always find some reason to fight. Now, no one would ever even think of teasing him for his eczema again, or about his dad – they stopped talking to him. But sometimes they looked at him for a little too long, and that was how they learned that Dogge liked to fight.

This girl's boyfriend was very easily provoked. All Dogge had to do was stand a little too close, and he told them to get out of his face quick as fuck or else they'd regret it, but before the words were out of his mouth Dogge had kicked him in the crotch, and when he fell forward, Dogge pulled him up by the hair and kneed him in the face.

That made Billy laugh. But when the police arrived, Dogge had no one to laugh with, because Billy had vanished. Dogge was the only one they grabbed.

'Ask Billy,' he told the cops. 'He knows what happened. He saw the whole thing.'

A thousand times, he thought. *A thousand times I've taken the blame so Billy doesn't have to. But he can't even be here to tell them what a punk that guy was.*

The police called his mother and drove him to the station, even though he told them he hadn't started it, it was that girl's fucking boyfriend. Besides, the boyfriend wasn't the only one bleeding, Dogge's knee was bleeding, that guy's teeth must have ripped his jeans when he kneed him. But no one cared. The boyfriend didn't even have to come with the police, he got to go to the hospital and get pictures taken of his 'wounds'. No one took a picture of Dogge's knee.

At the station, they asked questions about the fight. Even though Dogge couldn't be charged with assault, they wanted to know what had happened.

His mother was there when he was interrogated. But she cut off every question and wouldn't let him respond.

'The other guy started it,' Dogge tried to explain. Jill cried and sniffled that 'it was an accident'.

'Knocking out someone's front teeth is no accident,' said the social worker, with pursed lips and a pompous expression.

Dogge couldn't bring himself to care, all he could think about was how Billy had bolted. And of the girl who looked at Dogge like she liked him. Turned out she hadn't cared about him at all. When her short, ugly, drunk boyfriend hit the ground, she came rushing over, totally beside herself. She cried and sat on the ground and put his head in her lap, shouting that Dogge was fucking crazy.

'Do you like that girl?' Farid asked when he questioned Dogge. 'Was that why you beat up her boyfriend?'

'She's a fucking whore,' Dogge replied. 'I don't give a shit about her. That ugly fucking dude is the one who started it.'

'Did you think she would like you more if you beat up her boyfriend?' Farid asked again.

'I don't give a shit about her,' Dogge repeated. 'It's not my fault.'

'It was an accident,' Jill insisted.

34

Dogge's head thumped against the van's interior, over and over, there was no way he could stop it. At first he had been able to dampen the thuds, but he no longer had the strength. They'd told him to lie still inside the vehicle, that he had to lie *in that exact spot*, his back right up close against the side, pressed against the icy tyre. He wasn't allowed to sit up, not even a little. Could they see him from the front seat? Were they looking? He wasn't about to chance it.

The floor of the van smelled sour – fish, maybe? Or rubbish. He tried to wriggle closer to the wall for better support, but it didn't work; instead his head thudded against the floor again. *Don't even fucking try to sit up, and for Christ's sake don't stare out the window. This ain't no fucking charter flight.* They'd been so angry. He'd never seen them before, yet it was like they hated him.

Mehdi would never get in a van. He liked fast cars, expensive cars, cars that belonged in music videos, with convertible tops and hot girls in the back seat. He seldom actually had any cars like that, but he was the one who decided where they would stop, how fast to drive, and whether they could play music on the stereo.

Dogge tried to bring his hands closer to his head to soften the thumping, but there was nothing to hold on to, and the car seemed to be moving at top speed through overgrown forest: stumps, branches, rocks, ditches. Terrain neither the tyres nor the shocks were made for.

Someone in the front seat put on some music. The bass throbbed in Dogge's chest. Mehdi always played music, he never sang along, yet you knew it was all about him. The fact that Mehdi wasn't here, in this particular car, didn't mean anything, he was still the one in charge of it all. The fact that Dogge was lying here, that was his decision. That they'd broken him out, that was his decision. What happened next would also depend on what Mehdi wanted.

He looked at the plastic cowling that covered the back wheels. He could cling to that. But they'd told him to lie still and if they stopped the car, opened the back, and saw him sitting up, what would they do? Kill him? Or were they going to kill him anyway, no matter what he did?

———

When they entered his room, he was asleep. Somehow he had dozed off even though he didn't think he could, and he was deep inside a dream about a house with long hallways and doors that led nowhere. The dream lingered when they woke him up. One of them was wearing a police uniform. They didn't turn on the lights, instead one of them shone his phone flashlight straight into Dogge's eyes, and the other grabbed his shoulder and shook. Then they pulled off his blanket, the ugly, flat blanket that smelled like dust and institutions. And there he lay, blinking, with both hands over his crotch.

One of them was holding Momi's keys. Another was holding a gun, the same model Dogge had used to shoot Billy. For an instant he thought it was the same gun, that he was about to be shot with his own weapon.

'Christ, would you wake up!? Are you slow or something? We have to go!'

Dogge managed to tear his eyes from the gun and sit up in bed. He had fallen asleep with his track pants on, but under them he was naked, and he pressed his hand to his crotch again. He used his other hand to grab the hoodie he'd wiggled out of sometime during the night.

It only took a few seconds to realize that the guys in his room weren't the cops. They didn't have cop voices. Besides, they were speaking softly, like they didn't want anyone to hear. The police always wanted to be heard.

'I'm coming, I'm coming,' he managed to say, pulling on his trainers as fast as he could.

'Bring real clothes,' hissed the fake cop. Dogge shoved underwear, socks, jeans, and another hoodie, one he thought was clean, into a bag. All the clothes he had here were things he'd gotten from the staff. *Charity clothes*, Billy would have called them. Clothes no one wanted to be seen in. He hated them.

Then they took him by the arm and dragged him into the corridor. The Italian was waiting for them there. He smiled his strange smile, the one that made him look like a rock star standing onstage, thanking the crowd for their applause. He held a thick down jacket Dogge had never seen before.

The gates were wide open. The van was parked just outside. Yet another guy was waiting there, holding a handgun to Momi's temple. Momi looked scared and much smaller than usual, it was like he had shrunk. They'd stripped him of most of his clothes, and his hands were bound behind his back. Then they forced him and Dogge into the back of the van, on its floor. But Momi only got to stay there for a little bit.

Now it must have been an hour since they had thrown Momi out after having stripped off the last of his clothes, even his underwear. Dogge didn't think they'd done anything more after that, because they drove off so fast and he hadn't heard any weird sounds. No shouting, no shots, no blows. But he didn't know for sure, because he hadn't looked. He didn't want to see, didn't want to hear. He definitely didn't want to know.

I don't give a shit about Momi. He doesn't mean anything to me. I don't know him.

They hadn't let him change clothes. The bag of his belongings had rolled to the other end of the van, and there it remained. Even if he wanted to, had dared to, he couldn't get changed now, it was too bumpy. But he was freezing in his thin track pants and drenched in sweat beneath his hoodie.

The van screeched to a stop. Dogge slammed into one side of the vehicle. The flash of pain in his head was so bad that his vision flickered. The doors flew open, and outside stood the guy who had been wearing a cop uniform. He'd changed clothes. Before Dogge could get up, the guy grabbed his arm and hauled him out of the van. If he started to hit him, Dogge wouldn't have a chance.

Mehdi was tall too, and he was strong. Mehdi was so strong he didn't even have to make any effort to get respect. It was enough for him to look you in the eye or place a hand on your shoulder. And you knew. He wouldn't take any shit; Mehdi would never let anyone push him around or tell him what to do or not to do. But Dogge would never dream of trying to pull away. He wasn't that dumb. He didn't say anything, just tried to remain upright.

The fake cop tossed the bag of clothes at him. He caught it.

'You've got thirty seconds.'

Dogge didn't hesitate. He started by pulling off his T-shirt and putting on the hoodie he'd brought. Then he stepped out of his shoes and bottoms, pulled on his jeans and coat, an ugly anorak Momi had forced him to take from the charity box, but at least it was black. He would have liked to put on the underwear too, but he was afraid it would take too long so he didn't bother. He shoved the clothes he'd taken off into the bag. As he was putting his trainers back on, three other cars swung in and parked next to the van. The Italian stepped out of the car that had followed them through the woods, and approached one of the two new cars, a Volvo station wagon.

Now that no one was dragging him around, he had to manage on his own. But when he approached the Volvo, the fake cop took his bag from him, opened the back hatch, and tossed it in. Then he nodded and gestured at Dogge, as if to say *No, you're not sitting in the back, what are you, stupid?* The Italian got in the front seat, Dogge had to crawl into a dog kennel in the hatch. It was large, but not large enough; he had to sit bent double, with his knees up to his chest. He had to keep his head down, his neck bent, and his chin tucked to his throat. After they closed the kennel door, they tossed a blanket over it. He couldn't see out. Panic crept up his spine.

I can't breathe. It's too cramped. I'm going to die here.

He knew three guys who had died. And that wasn't even counting Billy. The oldest was twenty-seven years old and called Stamps because he liked to kick when he fought. Stamps was a dad, Billy had said he had two kids he saw most weekends. Dogge couldn't call Stamps a friend, it wasn't like he could call him up, or like he'd shared things about his life with him, but he liked Stamps. He offered Dogge smokes without Dogge even having to ask. Once Stamps gave him 200 kronor out of nowhere, and he hadn't had to do anything for it.

'Go buy a soda, you look thirsty.'

When Stamps got shot, he was at a pizzeria outside of town with his family. At that point, Dogge hadn't seen him for months. He never found out why Stamps got shot, but it didn't surprise him.

The youngest person he knew who'd died, not counting Billy, was nineteen, and Dogge had met him while they were on a job. He was called Blondie. Maybe it was because he bleached his hair white, maybe it was for some other reason, Dogge never asked. Blondie wasn't the type of person you asked questions of. But Dogge liked him too.

Billy and Dogge had been told to keep a lookout on one of the entrance ramps to the highway where Mehdi was planning to rob an armoured truck, and Blondie laughed at one of Dogge's jokes when they met up afterward: he laughed for a long time, even though the joke wasn't all that funny. He didn't think Blondie had been high at the time, but he couldn't know for sure. It was always hard to tell. Four weeks after the truck robbery, a jogger found Blondie's body under one of the bridges in central Stockholm. He'd drowned, and his head was so thoroughly caved in that it took several days for them to identify him.

At school they said he'd killed himself, that he'd jumped. But Mehdi said that was bullshit. Someone had kicked his head to mush, then shoved or thrown him into the water to be absolutely certain he was dead. Mehdi liked Blondie. The only time Dogge saw him almost cry was when he learned that Blondie was dead.

The third dead guy, Billy said Mehdi had made happen.

'Blue-Boy told me.'

Dogge couldn't remember having met him, but Billy said he for sure had.

'He tried to cheat Mehdi out of some money and that made it personal,' said Billy.

Mehdi had arranged to meet this dude up by the lake where people went swimming in the summertime. Dogge wondered if the guy knew what was going to happen. He must have, but that meant he also knew it didn't matter, that there was no avoiding it. No one could refuse to meet up with Mehdi. Just like Dogge couldn't refuse to go with them when they came to the state home to rescue him, or take him away from there to kill him, he didn't know which it was. In any case, he had no choice but to do exactly what they said.

The second leg of the journey started out almost as
fast and bumpy as the first leg had. The sounds he
was making sounded like they came from an animal.
But after only a minute or two they must have emerged
onto a larger road. Now he wasn't banging his head as
the car lurched; the drive was much smoother. And
he closed his eyes, he tried to breathe calmly, and gingerly stretched his legs out as best he could. His neck
and back ached from his position, and with the tiniest
movement his knees bounced into his chin and pain
shot into his forehead. His mouth tasted like iron. He
could tell he was crying, but he was doing it quietly so
they couldn't hear him – he was sure of it.

'You shouldn't cry,' his dad had always said. 'If
you do, no one will take you seriously.'

But if he cried anyway, Dad wouldn't say more
about it, he would take him into his arms, pull him
close until the tears stopped. He did this even when
Dogge was big, and even though he hated it when
Dogge cried. And Dogge could turn his face towards
his chest and breathe in his scent, which belonged
to Dad alone. The memory of how it felt when Dad
hugged him stayed with him, he would never forget it.

The car sped up. It must be on the highway now.
Where were they going? If Dogge had been braver,
he would have asked. He was sure they would hear

him if he shouted loud enough. But he said nothing. He didn't want to remind them he was there. Besides, he knew they could take him anywhere.

The Italian was talking to the guy who was driving. They'd put music on again. Same as in the van, except louder now. It meant he could no longer make out their words, only their voices. They sounded hyped up, happy, maybe. He could hear them laughing a lot.

It was warmer here than it had been in the van, much warmer. He wished he hadn't put on his jacket. He tried to change position, find one that would allow him to breathe without making his neck hurt so much.

The car stereo turned off. Aside from the engine and the studded tyres against the smooth asphalt, it was quiet. Someone rolled down a window; Dogge felt the cold draught and had time to take a deep breath before the air filled with the sweet scent of weed. It made him feel nauseous, but he could not throw up, not in here, there was no room. *I'll suffocate.*

'What the hell are you doing?' Dogge heard the fake cop's irritated voice. 'You can't fucking smoke in the car. You know how he feels about that.'

'Is this his car?' The Italian suddenly sounded uncertain.

'Well, it's not your fucking car.'

The odour of marijuana went away. The windows went up again. The silence returned. Dogge tried once more to find a more tolerable position, but it didn't work. He couldn't cry now; they would hear him. Under no circumstances could he cry.

Don't fucking start crying.

'Dad…' he whispered, as softly as he could. 'I don't want to die, Daddy. I don't want to die.'

THE BOYS

The next time they met up, the day after the school dance, Billy tried to apologize.

'You know how my mum can be,' he said. 'She would have lost her mind. I had to take off. Jill is cool, though. A guy from Våringe can't fight in Rönnviken, I'd go down for everything from raping Princess Victoria to murdering, like, the president.'

'Sure,' Dogge said. And soon after that he was sent to a group home. Aunt Lavender explained that his mother needed relief, that she had asked for help.

'This isn't the first time, Douglas,' said Aunt Lavender. 'First there was the terrible incident with the girl at the grocery store, and now this. I think you understand why we can't let this go on. It seems like you need some help to get things under control. What do you say, Douglas?'

Dogge knew his mother wanted to get rid of him, she wanted to be left alone.

Everyone at the home was stronger than him, bigger, angrier, more dangerous. Maybe he was pretty decent at winning fights in Rönnviken, but here he had no chance. On the first day he was kicked in the crotch by a guy who thought he'd looked at him funny. The next day, another guy forced him to eat a sandwich he'd spit three globs of coughed-up mucus onto. He couldn't sleep in the room they gave him, the radiator hummed so loud it gave him a headache, but they just laughed at him when he said he wanted to switch rooms.

'Would you like to check into a hotel, maybe? Where the room service is better?'

He hated that place so much he asked to talk to one of the therapists they wanted to foist on him. He cried for a long time, and talked about 'how everything had affected' him. It wasn't hard to play the part of the kid they wanted him to be.

'I just want my mum,' he said. 'I was so angry, I've been so angry ever since Dad got sick. And now he's dead. He's never coming back. But I get that I don't... I just want to go home, I'm sorry, it will never happen again.'

That helped. Someone convinced his mum to let him move home again.

He waited a week to tell Billy he was back. But then he called. Who else could he call?

'You sound awful weird. Am I bothering you or something?'

'Don't be silly,' said Billy. 'Of course not. It's just...oh, nothing.'

'Wanna meet up, or what?'

'Sure.'

'At Weed's?'

'You think we should? Dogge, I really think—'

'That stupid fucking Turk, I hate that bastard. We can—'

'Let's meet up in the tunnel instead, Dogge, that'll be better. Jesus, chill out. You have to chill out.'

35

The car stopped. The engine turned off and they opened the dog kennel. But by then, he couldn't get out. His legs wouldn't cooperate, and Dogge had to grab them with both hands and lift them out one by one as the Italian laughed at him. By so doing he was finally able to shuffle his way to the open back hatch. But when he tried to stand up, his legs fell out from under him and he collapsed to the ground. By this point, the Italian was laughing so hard he was gasping for breath. The guy who'd shoved Dogge into the kennel wasn't laughing. He was furious.

'Christ, pull yourself together. This pussy-ass rescue mission ends now. I'm not carrying you, if that's what you were thinking.' Then he walked off. The Italian stayed behind.

Dogge punched his own thighs to get the blood moving. He wasn't crying now; he'd stopped over an hour ago. He breathed as calmly as he could. Deep breaths. The Italian got tired of laughing and shook his head.

'How the fuck do you look?' he muttered, mostly to himself. 'You look fucking ridiculous.'

Then he offered Dogge his hand and pulled him up. Dogge was still trembling all over, but he managed to stand. With tiny, cautious steps, he followed the Italian over to an apartment building. Dogge didn't recognize it. In the dark it looked like a grungy-white building with a black roof. On either side of it were three identical buildings. The top three floors had larger windows and bigger balconies. There were electric Christmas lights or stars or thin strings of lights in a few windows. Dogge counted twelve storeys. In front of each building was a playground with swings, a slide, a jungle gym and a frozen sandbox surrounded by low hedges, grassy areas with patches of snow and lone, naked trees. Had he been here before? It looked like a thousand other apartment complexes.

In a half-renovated building where Mehdi'd had one of his apartments, Dogge and Billy had found an open basement storage unit and furnished it with a mattress, candles and an old cooler full of sweets and crisps. Everything in that space, except the food, had come from apartments in the same building. It wasn't hard to get into them at all, and there was almost always at least a few things left behind. They selected only the best stuff: four soft blankets that appeared clean, and two large pillows that only

smelled a little musty. They even managed to haul
an old easy chair down from the seventh floor. They
had been able to spend nine months down there before getting kicked out, and Dogge had loved it. In
the summer it was as hot as a sauna and smelled
rotten. But as winter approached, the air grew drier,
and as long as they wore enough layers they hardly
ever felt cold. Just before the sun went down, rays of
sunlight would filter through a narrow window up
by the ceiling. Minutes later, it would be as dark as
at the bottom of a bottle.

'It's like a fucking coffin in here,' Billy would
say. 'I feel like a fucking corpse. Why are we sitting
in here when we could be in one of the apartments?
We're such stupid idiots.'

But Dogge felt safe there. No demons could find
him underground.

'We're visible from the outside in the apartments,
and Mehdi doesn't want to attract unnecessary attention,' he said, and that put a stop to Billy's whining.

Sometimes they slept there. Billy would tell his
mum he was sleeping over at Dogge's, and Dogge
didn't have to say anything. They smoked spice and
drank cans of Monster Energy, watched porn on their
phones and talked about nothing.

This street was as deserted as those outside the abandoned apartment building. But it wasn't deserted
in the same way, people lived here, even if there was

no one around right now, and he could have tried to escape. But he didn't. Instead he tried to walk as close to the Italian as he could, as though he had Dogge on a leash. It was early morning, but still pitch-black. Just before they reached the front door, the Italian turned around. Dogge stopped short to keep from running into him.

'Do you want to hold hands or something? What the fuck are you doing?'

'Where are we?'

'None of your business.'

'Thanks,' Dogge said as the Italian held the door for him so he could enter the apartment building. He still didn't know where he was or what was about to happen, but he would never ask again.

'You happy not to be locked up anymore?' the Italian smiled. His eyes gleamed in the darkness.

Dogge waited, but the Italian didn't say more. When he was inside the building, the Italian followed. Dogge let him by.

'You're welcome,' the Italian mumbled, his back to Dogge. 'It was nothing. Nothing the fuck at all.'

The lift didn't work. Either it was broken, or else someone on an upper floor had forgotten to close the lift door behind them – whatever the reason, it didn't come when the Italian pushed the button. So they walked upstairs. The Italian was more out of breath than Dogge when they reached their destination six floors later. The door was open. The Italian walked into the apartment and threw himself onto a white sofa that was in the centre of a gigantic living room, in front of a TV that was on. The room had a massive picture window all along one side, from floor to ceiling. Dogge found himself standing by the sofa.

The guy who'd driven them there was slumped in one of the four easy chairs. On his lap was a girl with a cropped T-shirt and very long, loose, wavy golden-blonde hair, and also a pair of baggy grey tracksuit bottoms. Her bare feet had bright-pink toenails. They were paying close attention to a football match on the enormous TV.

Dogge looked out the window wall. The sky was no longer totally black, the snow gave a faint glow, but everything was fuzzy and shadowy. In the distance he could see a church all lit up, it could be Våringe Church, the one by the square. He still didn't know where they were, but if that was Våringe they must be near one of Mehdi's old hangouts. He'd had to leave that place, but maybe this was his new one? When he turned to look back around the room, he noticed that the girl in the easy chair was looking at him. She flashed him a quick smile, as though she felt sorry for him.

After his dad died, there had been a few weeks where everyone stared at Dogge with their heads tilted to the side. As soon as he left home they were there, giving him that sad look, especially at school, the teachers with their gentle pats and prying questions that meant nothing.

After a month or so they got tired of all this and went back to shaking their heads and letting out sighs of accusation. All the calls home to Mum started the same way: 'We know Dogge is going through a tough time, but…' 'We know things are hard right now, but…'

The truth was, they had no idea what it was like.

Mum hated this fake sympathy too, almost as much as she hated when people called her up to talk about Dogge and what she ought to do about him.

'I don't want their flowers and their stupid questions. I'm drowning in flowers, they sit there in their ugly vases smelling like ass. I just want them to leave us alone.'

Billy, at least, had not tilted his head to the side. He had left Dogge alone, let him party, seriously, more than before, as much as he needed. After the funeral, he'd dropped acid four days in a row, and Billy had let him sleep over so he didn't have to go home. When Billy's mum tried to snoop, Billy protected him.

'Lay off, Mum. He's sad, he just feels kind of sick, let him be.'

But even so, Dogge didn't want to stay at Billy's anymore. He stopped sleeping there, because even if Billy didn't interfere in what he did, Dogge could see the way Billy looked at him when he thought he wasn't paying attention, and he hated that crap.

Here, people could look at him as much as they wanted. He sure wasn't about to hit anyone. So he said nothing to the girl in the easy chair. He let her stare without so much as sending an angry glare back. When she finally stopped looking at him, he took a step to the side.

'I'm going to the bathroom,' he mumbled. No one responded.

The Italian had fallen asleep with his mouth open and his legs spread wide. He must have been exhausted. Or else he could fall asleep anywhere, and fast. Billy had been the same. Sometimes, he'd told Dogge, he fell asleep in class, at the very front of the room, while the teacher was talking to him.

'I'm going to the bathroom,' Dogge tried again.

He didn't want to go if it would make them mad. But they didn't even look at him. The guy in the easy chair stuck his hand under the girl's shirt and grabbed her breast. She gave a low laugh and bent down so he could reach better. Dogge backed out of the room and found the bathroom almost right away, it was the second door he opened. He went in and locked the door behind him. He sat down on the toilet and peed, and he tried to poop too, but it didn't work. Then he just sat there. He wondered how long he could stay there without making them mad. He pulled a towel down from the rack beside the bathtub and balled it up, then pressed it to his face. He wanted to scream, but he was afraid to. He wanted to cry, but he was afraid to do that too. Instead he breathed, faster and faster, a few tiny sounds escaped him and he pressed the towel harder against his mouth.

He couldn't let them hear him. He couldn't let on how scared he was.

He absolutely couldn't let on how scared he was.

THE BOYS

Two weeks after Dogge got out of the group home, the boys were given their most important job to date. That's what Blue-Boy said.

'This is serious, got it?'

They got it. They were supposed to stand at an intersection and pick up a bag that Mehdi and two of his friends had to get rid of as soon as they were done with 'a thing'. Dogge and Billy would hold on to the stuff inside until they received further instructions. Billy got to borrow a moped so they could get out of there quickly. It wasn't the first time he was allowed to use it. At night, when they got to borrow it, it was locked up outside his apartment. Dogge had to keep the helmets at his house, both of them, so Leila wouldn't start asking a bunch of questions.

It all started off just fine. Mehdi drove by the meet-up spot, rolled down a window, and tossed a bag out without slowing down. It landed in the bushes next to Dogge, but it was so heavy it crashed right through them and onto the ground. Dogge scooped it up and held it tight as Billy drove. He opened the zipper an inch or two so he could look in the bag.

'I can't take this home,' he said. 'Mum asked my grandma and grandpa to come to the house to see how shitty it is. We can't put a bag full of guns there, not if they're going to walk around with a real estate agent and snoop through every single cupboard to figure out how much they can sell it for.'

Billy didn't say anything. But they drove to Våringe and went down to Billy's basement. Dogge had to wait while Billy went up to the apartment to get the key to the storage unit. They put the bag in the very back; it wasn't visible from the outside because the unit was full of furniture. To notice it, someone would have to first walk behind three chairs that were stacked on top of each other.

When Billy took the moped to school the next day, without a helmet on, he got stopped by the police. It wasn't just the helmet he was missing – Billy didn't have a moped licence, and the moped was registered to a person who no longer lived in Sweden. The police seized the moped and took Billy to the station. Social services was waiting for him there, along with Leila. She didn't yell this time; instead, she didn't say a word. Billy knew that was worse. She'd repeated it so many times already.

'If the social worker says they're going to take you away from me, I will send you away. No one is going to take you, I will never let that happen.'

Three hours later, when he was allowed to go home again, the bag was missing from the storage unit. No one had busted the lock, he asked his mum, but she didn't know what he was talking about. When he called Dogge to tell him what had happened, there was panic in his voice.

'Mum is so mad at me right now. She would have told me if she took it,' said Billy. 'If she'd found that bag she would have reported me to the cops, she's that mad. It must have been Mehdi. They must have come to get it, it couldn't be anyone else.'

Neither of them pointed out the obvious. Mehdi couldn't have got into the unit without breaking the lock. Both of them were thinking the same thing.

It had to be Leila. There was no other explanation.

The next day, Billy got a message from Blue-Boy saying that they were supposed to come to Mehdi's apartment and bring the bag.

They went together.

'There's no point in putting it off,' Dogge said as they rode up in the elevator. 'The most important thing is for you to tell him yourself, that no one else says it first.'

'I'll handle it, no problem,' said Billy. He was so tense that his body was bouncing – up and down, up and down. He rubbed his palms on his thighs as if he were a sprinter at the starting block, waiting for the race to begin.

As soon as they entered the living room, he told the truth, straight out: the police had the moped and he'd lost the bag. There was no way he could blame anyone else, everyone knew the police had caught him. But no one knew about the bag.

'Some bastard pinched it. Mehdi, I don't know how, but someone pinched it.'

Mehdi was half reclining on the sofa, pizza on the table in front of him. With him were two girls Dogge had never seen before. One of them had rubbed her nose when Billy started talking. And at first Mehdi didn't do anything. He took a slice of pizza from the table, eating it slowly. Then he wiped his mouth with a napkin.

'Sure,' he said. 'I hear what you're saying. You just had some real bad luck, is all.'

Billy's sigh of relief was so loud that everyone could hear it. But Mehdi didn't smile. Billy and Dogge sat down on the other end of the sofa. There were more pizza boxes there, enough for them too.

They didn't notice as Mehdi leaned back further on the sofa and pulled a pistol from his waistband. But they did see him rise from the sofa so slowly that it seemed to happen in slow motion. They looked up at him as he moved to stand in front of them. He leaned forward, removed the safety, put his hand around Billy's throat, and pressed the gun to his temple so hard that Dogge could see the skin around the barrel creasing.

'Let me tell you something, Billy Boy.' Mehdi's voice was drawling. His tone didn't match the tense muscles in his arm, his crazy eyes, the black metal. 'If I ask you to do something, you do it. If you fuck it up, I'm not interested in hearing about how someone was mean to you and it's not your fault and you have no idea what happened, because I don't have time for excuses. And when people try to waste my time, it makes me angry.'

He pulled the trigger. When the click echoed out, Billy made a bizarre sound. Mehdi let go of his throat. 'You don't want me to be angry. You don't want me to load this for real, because you really don't want to make me angry.'

Then he stuck the pistol back in his waistband. Sat back down on the sofa, took another piece of pizza from the box. One of the girls laughed absently, as if she'd just seen all of this happen in a movie.

'Run along now,' Mehdi said, his mouth full of pizza. 'There you go. Bye-bye. Home to Mummy. And ask her if maybe she can tell me where my guns are. I'd appreciate that. Otherwise I'll have a chat with her myself when I get the chance.'

Dogge and Billy backed out of the apartment and ran down the stairs as fast as they could. Billy in the lead, Dogge close behind.

Billy didn't cry. Not in the apartment, not even when they got to Dogge's house and went to his room and closed the door. But a strange look had come over him, he was looking around anxiously like he was on a bad trip. Now and then he'd rub his throat, as if to reassure himself that Mehdi's hand was no longer there. A few times he made a fist and thumped himself in the forehead on the spot where Mehdi had pressed the barrel of the gun. His jaw was clenched so hard that the muscles of his neck stood out. Dogge tried to calm him down.

'He didn't mean it, obviously he wouldn't shoot you, he was just a little mad, we'll fix this, it's no big deal. If we can't find the bag we'll ask how much we owe, we can work for it, we can do that, and the moped, we'll just steal another one, we can go over to the high school in Rönnviken, get an upgrade, take a better one, it's going to be okay. No problem.'

Three days later, Billy told Dogge he was going to disengage. Social services was threatening to remove him from his home, and to avoid that fate he had promised his mother and the social worker he would follow the disengagement programme. He'd agreed to submit to regular drug testing.

'If I get caught, they'll send me away on the spot. Mum wouldn't be able to handle it.'

Dogge went to see Mehdi to explain. He said it was only to get Billy's mum and social services to calm down, that Dogge would handle their jobs on his own for now, but that Billy was still around, he would start working again soon. Mehdi seemed to understand, or at least he didn't seem to care all that much. The only thing he was concerned about was what they owed him.

That's how he put it, that 'they' owed him, even though Billy was the one who'd messed up. And Dogge didn't protest.

'We'll pay you back, honest. I've got money coming in, Dad died a few...my father died and my mother's going to try to sell the house because...then I'll have some money.'

Mehdi cut him off, he wasn't interested in Dogge's explanations.

'If Billy is serious about quitting,' he said, 'he'll have to pay severance. Everyone knows that. I don't give a shit if he wants to stay, he's a fucking loser, but it costs money to quit. I've invested in you two, you fucked up, you have to pay.'

Dogge tried to call Billy. They needed to talk. They needed a plan, a strategy.

We'll keep running errands for Mehdi, keep climbing up the ladder, he would say to Billy. We'll go from soldiers to generals, colonels, he would explain. Just like we said. This is just a minor setback, nothing serious, we'll come back. Or we'll quit. If you want to disengage, we'll do it. We'll have to pay extra, but I might inherit some money from Dad if they sell the house and then I can pay for everything. We can do whatever you want. *It'll all work out.*

He called Billy to talk about how they would manage all of this. He called and called, multiple times an hour. But Billy didn't pick up. He never called back. He didn't even answer Dogge's texts, he stopped coming to the playground after school. Once Dogge went up to his school to talk to him, but he wasn't there either. When he went to Billy's house and rang the doorbell, Leila answered.

'Sorry, Billy can't see you,' she said. 'I'm sorry, but I don't want you to come to our house again.'

But she didn't look sorry.

It's your fault, Dogge wanted to say. *You ruined everything,* he wanted to say. *How the hell could you be so stupid that you stole Mehdi's stuff?* But instead he sent more texts to Billy.

'We have to talk. Call me.'

But it didn't help. It was like Billy had been swallowed up by the earth. Gone, quiet, buried.

36

When Weed heard that Dogge had escaped from the youth home, he asked one of his colleagues to stay at the store and take over for the day. Then he went home and straight to bed.

It had been just over a year since it happened, but not a day went by that Weed didn't think about it. His twelve-year-old daughter Eva had come to the store after school, just like always. But Weed wasn't there, so she decided to visit the sweets section, even though she knew she wasn't allowed.

That's where Dogge and Billy found her, her mouth full of coconut buttons and liquorice boats, her favourites.

When Weed got back, she was sitting on the loading dock with her tights in a tidy bow under her chin and her shirt pressed to her bare chest. When he asked what had happened, she started crying, her eyes downcast and her knuckles white.

'They didn't do anything, nothing happened, it's no big deal.'

He pulled her close, carefully untied her tights, and wrapped her in his coat. Then he hugged her, rocked her gently, whispered her name. He let her cry for a long time. Then she told him.

Dogge had dragged her into the stockroom; the three people who worked at the store hadn't seen a thing. Behind the pallets of dairy products they pulled off her shirt. Dogge touched her chest while Billy watched. She hadn't grown breasts yet, but Billy held her still while Dogge pinched her small, flat nipples. Then they stripped off her tights and tied them around her neck.

She had only mentioned Dogge by name; she didn't want to say Billy's aloud.

'He didn't...he told him to stop, Dad,' she said. 'He told Dogge, "Stop it, that's enough", and finally he did.'

Weed didn't bother to push her on it, but he told the police what they all knew: Dogge hadn't acted alone, and he only had one friend. They should have been able to figure this out on their own.

'They're thirteen years old,' said the police.

'My daughter is twelve,' said Weed.

He showed the police Dogge's Instagram account, he told them where he lived, explained exactly where his parents' house was located.

'Can you find your way to Rönnviken? Do you want me to come along and show you the way?' he'd asked, but they didn't respond.

A female officer with braces had taken down his report, and four days later they were informed by mail that the investigation had been closed. The suspect was below the age of criminal responsibility and there were no grounds for bringing charges.

Social services called a meeting, Weed was invited to a 'conversation'. He went, but he refused to bring his daughter.

'Eva will not be required to answer a single question,' was all he said. No one protested.

During that conversation, which was a perfectly ordinary meeting where they served coffee from a pump dispenser, Dogge's mother had cried. The tears hadn't done a thing to her face. Her discreet make-up seemed to be rock-solid. Her unnaturally dark eyelashes glittered, and her blonde fringe fell to the wrong side of her parting, but that was all.

'My son would never do such a thing,' she said more than once.

The social worker had nodded, she seemed to think it was important to keep Dogge's mother calm. Weed had to clench his fists under the table and force himself to take slow and even breaths. Dogge himself said nothing.

'But you did it anyway,' Weed said at last. 'Whatever your mother believes, you did it.'

He had looked Dogge straight in the eye at that point. And Dogge looked back and flashed him a quick grin while his mother took a crumpled tissue from her purse. He smiled as if this were all a joke to him.

'I can't take any more of this. His father just died,' the mother said, dabbing under her eyes. 'He was sick, terribly sick.'

Weed knew this was true. Before the meeting, the social worker had told him that Dogge's father had recently died of cancer.

'They're going through a tough time,' the social worker had said. 'It's not easy for them.'

And Weed had kept himself under control.

But when Dogge took his phone from his pocket and started typing something, with another little grin pasted on his face, Weed stood up and walked out. At that point, he was the one who couldn't take any more of this.

He was never summoned to any sort of meeting with Billy. He called the social worker a number of times and explained that Dogge and Billy had humiliated his daughter together. He said he had all the information they needed, he could come down and explain more thoroughly. Maybe Dogge was to blame for the worst of it, he said, but the other boy was far from innocent. And Billy went to the same school as his daughter. Every day when she went to school, she was afraid he would be there.

The social worker replied that both boys were under investigation, but unfortunately it was confidential and she couldn't discuss what measures might come into play, and then she changed the subject.

'Maybe it would be a good idea for your daughter to talk to someone? It's normal for her to feel upset. Would you like me to get her a referral to a child psychiatrist?'

'Maybe it would be better if we found out what was wrong in the heads of two boys who would do such a thing to a little girl? Maybe those boys should seek care, the ones who are actually sick in the head, instead of my daughter?' said Weed.

When Sara brought Eva home from school the day Dogge escaped from the group home, Weed was already asleep, fully dressed under both the blanket and the duvet. He woke to find them standing in the door to their bedroom. Eva had her Lucia nightgown on, but also the same sooty make-up she usually wore. She'd shaved a line into one eyebrow. *What does that mean?* Weed thought. *Why do you want to ruin your appearance?* Tiny silver skull earrings hung from both ears.

'Are you sick?' Eva asked.

'I'll be better soon,' he said.

She went to the kitchen. Sara placed a hand on his cool, dry forehead but said nothing.

She let Weed go back to sleep. She left him alone until the kids were all in bed, and then she brought him a cup of tea and two sandwiches. He ate them and gulped the tea down so fast he burned the roof of his mouth, and then he finally took off his clothes. He didn't have the strength to brush his teeth or find his pyjamas. Within minutes, he was asleep again.

37

No one had hit Dogge, at least not yet. They hadn't threatened him or forced him to take off all his clothes and pissed on him. The guy who'd driven Dogge and the Italian to the apartment had opened the door to a room with a bed inside.

'You can sleep here,' he'd said. He never introduced himself, but the girl with the golden-blonde hair called him Erik. Her name was Tova. She'd told Dogge so when he came back to the living room after spending way too long in the bathroom. Tova showed him the kitchen too, and said he could take whatever he wanted from the freezer. There was pizza, lasagna, and other ready-made meals. He had heated one of the pizzas in the microwave, filled a glass with water, and gone into the room they'd showed him, where he lay down on the bed. That's where he was now. He'd eaten the pizza cold, a few hours ago. But he hadn't slept at all.

He was hungry again. It sounded like the others were awake. There were so many things he wanted to ask. What was he supposed to wear? Could he shower? Could he use one of the toothbrushes in the bathroom? Were they going to kill him? Was he allowed to go out and sit in the room with the TV or did they want him to leave them alone? But he didn't know who to ask. Who was in charge, Erik or the Italian? Did Tova handle all the practical stuff? They might get mad if he asked things they didn't think were important.

Probably the best idea was to say nothing at all to anyone. To do as little as possible. But he had to go to the bathroom again.

When he stepped out of the room, he heard the Italian call out to him from the living room.

'Little Lasse! Come in here, for fuck's sake!'

Little Lasse. Was that his nickname from now on? Little Lasse was a zero, a nobody, a squealer.

The Italian wasn't alone in the living room. Besides Erik and Tova, he was in the company of two more girls. One was lying on her back on the floor, smoking spice; the other was sitting beside the Italian and playing on her phone. The TV was on, showing a football match, but the volume was down. When he came in, the Italian scooted over on the sofa and patted the spot beside him encouragingly.

'Sit down, for fuck's sake. Come sit down so we can talk. Have you had anything to eat? Did you get some sleep? Little Lasse, Sweden's most wanted, he needs his meals and his rest.' He laughed.

Dogge felt uncertain. It sounded like the Italian was trying to give him a compliment.

'Yeah, thank you, I had a pizza. I hope that was okay.'

'Damn, you have to quit saying thanks all the time.' Now he sounded peeved. 'It's funny as hell, this well-brought-up-snob shtick, but you know your ass-kissing days are way behind you. Sit down, I said.'

Dogge tried to keep his breathing under control. He sat down beside the Italian. It was cramped on the sofa.

'Have you talked to Mehdi?'

'Have I talked to Mehdi?' the Italian scoffed. 'I have not talked to Mehdi. Thanks to you, thank you thank you, Mehdi is still in jail, with full fucking restrictions. Mehdi is not even allowed to talk to his own goddamn mother. So no, we have not talked. But we have communicated in other ways. What have we said? We have communicated about you, Lasse. About what the fuck we're going to do with you. What the hell are we going to do with you? Stockholm's ugliest snitch. The cop-lover.'

He paused, reaching for the coffee table to grab a bag of crisps. He shoved a fistful into his mouth, and while he chewed, crumbs flying every which way, he stared at Dogge. Then he threw down the bag; it landed on the table.

'Lying Lasse. Maybe that's what we should call you? Lying Lasse.'

Dogge's heart skipped a beat.

'What do you think, Lying Lasse? What should we do with a moron like you? There's only one thing we can do, right?'

He put one arm around Dogge and pulled him close. Dogge almost ended up in his lap; he could feel the Italian's thigh against his hips.

'Just one tiny thing,' whispered the Italian, raising his other hand, the one that wasn't pressed close to Dogge's pounding heart. He slowly made a pistol shape with his fingers. He turned his hand just a few inches before Dogge's eyes, then gently pressed his pistol finger to Dogge's temple. With his arm still around Dogge's rib cage, he breathed into his ear.

'Everyone knows what to do with guys like you. Right? What do you say? Do you have a better idea, Lasse? Any other suggestions?'

THE BOYS

Mehdi calculated how much they owed him. He never said how much they had to pay for the missing bag or how much Billy's disengagement would cost; he just gave them a total sum. But there was nothing to discuss – it was an awful lot of money.

There was nothing to sell at Dogge's. He tried to look in places the Enforcement Authority hadn't cleared out, but he didn't find anything of value. There were four lounge chairs in an outbuilding, along with a rusty gas grill on wheels. The chairs must have cost a whole lot, because his father had said *There's no better chairs to be had*, but they no longer looked very swanky, and Dogge didn't know how he would sell them even if he tried. Take photos and list them on eBay like some old lady?

He still hadn't got hold of Billy. But there was no chance Billy would find something at his house. Leila only had things you could buy at the Salvation Army's Christmas market from boxes marked BUY TWO

GET THREE. And robbing an elementary-school dork, that was the kind of thing they had to do together. *Why wasn't Billy picking up? Didn't he get that they had to help each other out?* Dogge would be recognized in Rönnviken; in Våringe he didn't know who he could rob and who he had to avoid, and he had no desire to go all the way into the city by himself.

They were late with the payments. Of course they were late – he couldn't do any jobs as long as Billy refused to talk to him.

Dogge started going to school. Not to go to class – most of the time, he just sat in a hallway, or in one of the lockable bathroom cubicles, but he didn't want to be at home. It wasn't safe there, it was almost impossible to see all the way down to the road from his house, and his mum always forgot to lock the door. Anyone could get in.

At night he would go down and sleep in the living room. He never turned on the TV or the lights. Only in the dark could he see the headlights of passing cars. As soon as it was light out, he would get dressed and leave, before Jill woke up. If he managed to sneak into the school at the same time as the cleaning staff, he could lie down on the sofa in the cafeteria and sleep there until one of the staff, or maybe another student, woke him up and he would have to pretend to go to class. When the school day was over, the janitor always managed to find him and make him leave.

'Your choice,' he would say. 'Either scram right now, or you can come with me to the principal's office and they can call your parents.'

He didn't bike to and from school anymore. Once he'd managed to find an electric scooter that was still logged in, but he almost always had to walk.

On the afternoon when they showed up, he was on his way home, on foot. They drove up alongside him. Two little girls were walking along across the street from him, laughing at something. On Dogge's other side was a seven-foot wooden fence. He couldn't climb over it or run away. Blue-Boy was in the front seat next to Mehdi. Billy was in the back seat. All of Billy's usual energy seemed to have curled up inside his body. The whites of his eyes were double their usual size. Dogge could feel his heart hammering the inside of his rib cage as he climbed into the car. He didn't notice until he'd sat down that Billy's hands were bound with a cable tie. Blue-Boy cleared his throat. He was holding another cable tie. Dogge put out his hands.

Mehdi was driving. There was no music playing. No one spoke. The trip took under an hour. They stopped outside a building that looked like a barn, but Dogge couldn't see any animals. Billy climbed out of the car first; Dogge followed. There was a sharp smell of manure. As the car door closed behind them, an icy wind blew across the yard. Dogge's mouth tasted like rust and it felt like his stomach had been scooped out with a spoon. No one had yet said a word.

Can I trust you two now?' Mehdi asked when he dropped them off at the Våringe woods about two hours later.

'Yes,' they replied. Billy was still crying. Dogge was bleeding from the mouth, one of his teeth felt loose.

'Do you want us to send you a link to our little movie?' Blue-Boy asked with a smile. 'So you won't forget how much fun we had today?'

After Mehdi and Blue-Boy took them to the barn without animals, Billy answered when Dogge called. Almost every time.

There was one last job they had to do, a hundred-pointer, and then it would be over. Once it was done, they'd be off the hook. They would receive further instructions soon.

38

Dogge started to cry – of course he did. In front of the Italian and Erik and Tova and the other chicks, they all saw him cry, panic-stricken, howling, his nose running. The Italian let him go on like that for some time, maybe an hour, but then he got sick of it.

'Take a fucking break, kid. How long do you expect us to put up with this racket?'

But he couldn't. He tried his utmost to stop, but it didn't work, he just cried more. It felt like his lungs were going to burst, the evil had to come out, and when the Italian hauled him into the room they'd said would be his, his sobs turned to shrieks. But then the Italian slapped him in the face three times.

'Shut up. Just shut up. You have no respect. You have no respect for Mehdi, and Mehdi will not accept that.'

Dogge bit the inside of his cheek so hard he tasted blood. When he had his sobs under control, he whispered: 'I do respect him, I do. I respect him.'

When the Italian let go of him, Dogge tried again.

'I said the wrong thing, I know I should have kept my mouth shut,' he said, as calmly as he could. 'If the police bring me in I'll explain better, or, I swear, I won't say anything more.'

'It'd take a hell of a lot for our neighbours here to call the police on us, but you damn well better turn down the volume. Or else I'll go get a real gun. That ought to shut you up. You hear me? Be quiet. If that's what you're going to do instead of running your mouth to the cops, you might as well start practising now.'

Dogge shut his mouth and nodded.

The Italian nodded back. He didn't look as angry anymore. That was the kind of guy he was, you could never be sure how long he'd be angry or happy or when his mood would change. He might be laughing out loud one second, and strangling you the next. There was no way to predict it. And right now, suddenly, he looked like he was about to tell Dogge he'd won the lottery.

'You know what Mehdi decided? He decided Lasse would get a second chance. Not that you fucking deserve it, Mehdi should fucking kill you, but we're not going to kill you, at least not right now.'

Dogge buried his face in his hands. The tears came back, but quieter now, he cried as quietly as if his mother were there. Once again, the Italian was annoyed.

'What the hell? Quit your fucking blubbering, or I'll change my mind and beat you to death right now. I can't listen to this shit anymore. You sound like a fucking dog. And if you're worried Mehdi's gone soft, forget it. You're gonna fucking pay for what you've done. You can bet on that.'

The Italian took a wrinkled piece of paper from his pocket.

'This note says how much you owe, and you're going to sign it. You'll do jobs for us until your debt is paid off. Got that? Yeah, about time you understood. It's pretty fucking late in coming, if you ask me. How many chances are you going to get? How many "one-last-jobs" will you swear you'll do? Are you the fucking Rolling Stones? Out on a farewell tour every fucking year? No, you're not, because this is your last chance. It's a hell of a huge debt, do you understand? Yes, you understand. You're going to do exactly what we tell you to, everything we tell you to, until this debt is paid. Not that hard to understand, right? Not hard at all.'

Dogge nodded again.

'Of course. Thank you. Thank you so much, thank you. I'll do anything. Thank you. Thank you.'

He wanted to sign it right away, he didn't need to read the agreement first, it wasn't like anything in it was up for discussion. But neither of them had anything to write with. The Italian put down the paper and went to the living room. Tova had a pen in her purse. It had purple ink, and Dogge had to shake it to get it to work. He tried to produce something like a signature, but he hadn't written out his whole name all that many times, and he wasn't any good at cursive. Had he ever even signed anything before? Maybe for the school principal, or when he got a new passport.

When he was finished, he ran his thumb over the ink – it made a faint blotch, but it would have to do. The Italian took the contract without looking at it and shoved it back in his pocket.

'Congratulations,' he said. 'Maybe you won't die today.'

And then he left the room and closed the door behind him.

Just ten minutes later, Dogge heard the Italian in the next room, one of the girls was in there with him, maybe Tova, or maybe the one with the bleached-blonde hair and the biggest breasts Dogge had ever seen in real life.

Thud thud thud.

The headboard of the Italian's bed was hitting Dogge's wall.

He could hear the Italian as clearly as if they were in the same room. He figured the Italian must know he could hear everything. That this must be the point.

'Are you a little cunt? Are you? So fucking tight. Haven't you ever been fucked before, or what?'

The girl only moaned in response. It sounded like the porn Dogge sometimes watched.

'You want me to fuck your mouth? You want that?'

Dogge could picture it. Big, round breasts with rock-hard nipples. The Italian sucking them, biting them, pushing into the girl, further than she could take, but she still wanted it. The girls always wanted it, even if it didn't seem that way. It almost sounded like she was crying. But it was probably just for pretend. Dogge squeezed his eyes shut to make the sounds go away.

He woke up a few hours later. The apartment was quiet, and he snuck to the bathroom, locked the door behind him, and took a long shower, washed his hair and his feet and all the places where he smelled bad, and once he'd rinsed off he started over again. He soaped himself up three times, then rubbed himself dry and went to the kitchen and took another pizza from the freezer. He guzzled a Coke as he warmed up the pizza in the microwave. He ate in bed and wiped his greasy fingers on the covers. Then he fell asleep again, in the clean T-shirt and underwear he'd brought from the group home.

39

Farid wanted to work out. He needed to work out. He just had to drop off Felicia at handball, Ella at dance class, and Natascha at a first aid course she was supposed to attend along with her best friend.

'I need to do the Christmas shopping,' Nadja had explained to him.

'Can you drop Ella and Natascha off on the way?' he pleaded. 'I'll pick them up, I promise. You can stay in the city as long as you want.'

If he could convince Felicia to take the bus, that would free up two hours before he had to pick up Ella, assuming he left home by eight o'clock at the latest.

The gym was in the basement of the police station, just four floors beneath his own office. He pictured how he would start with some lighter weights, maybe even run a mile or two on the noisy treadmill, wake his muscles up nice and easy and then work his way to some bench presses, the taste of blood in his mouth, and a body so tired he wouldn't have the energy to be angry. Afterwards he would shower without three daughters and a wife right outside the door, maybe he'd even have time for a few minutes in the sauna if it was on. Not that he loved to sauna, he thought it was pretty pointless, but a few minutes there would usually ease the worst of his sore muscles and it really had been too long since last time.

As he was in the front hall, pulling on his shoes, Felicia came out of the bathroom in tears. She had missed the bus.

'It's a super-important match, Dad. How come everyone gets a ride but me? It's not fair. I'm doing the best I can.'

'Don't worry, sweetie,' Farid heard himself saying. 'Of course I'll drive you.'

Before he had finished his sentence, Felicia had vanished back into the bathroom.

'Love you, Dad, you're the best, I'll be there in thirty seconds, just have to pee.'

Fifteen minutes later, Farid was still standing in the front hall with his car keys in hand.

'I'm leaving now,' he called for the third time.

'I'm coming,' his daughter responded.

Five minutes later, he banged his fist on the bathroom door. It was eight thirty now.

'What is wrong with you? Chill out, I'm doing my make-up, I'm coming, oh my God, I *said* I'm coming!'

Nadja came out of the kitchen with a cup of coffee and a scornful smile on her lips.

'Amateur,' she hissed, and went into the bathroom. Thirty seconds later, she came out, accompanied by Felicia.

'Dad, I'm in such a rush,' said Felicia, putting on her shoes. 'Hurry up.'

When he finally got to the gym, it was quarter past nine and all the stations and free weights he wanted to use were occupied. Next to him, also waiting for her turn, was Lotta, just as visibly irritated as he was that there would be no working out in peace and quiet. In exactly one hour, he had to pick up Ella.

'Any news?' he forced himself to ask.

'Mehdi's being released today.' Rather than look at him, Lotta was eyeing the man who was using the stair machine she was waiting for.

'Excuse me?'

Although the only people in the room were other cops, Farid moved closer to make sure he could hear what she was saying and so she wouldn't have to raise her voice over the deafening music.

'Yeah. His lawyer provided a photo from Dogge's dad's Facebook page. He still has the damn account, like all dead people. Soon dead people will be the only ones left on Facebook. Anyway, eighteen months before Teo died, he was messing around with some buddies at the shooting range. He posted a photo of himself and tagged all his rad buddies and there he was, Glock in hand, very gangsta. The lawyer managed to get a new detention hearing and now the judge doesn't consider there to be sufficient grounds to detain Mehdi. The prosecutor called, he's being released after lunch.'

The music continued. An American woman rattling off words for private parts. Whenever she took a break from listing them, she filled the empty space with moans.

'How's it going for the techs at the chicken factory?'

'Nothing new. They've got their hands full sorting anything that might fit in. And I'm sure they're working on other stuff too. We're not their only investigation; I get a thorough report on their terribly unreasonable workload every time I call.'

'How about the videos?'

'Don't play dumb.' Lotta took a sip from her water bottle.

'What did the techs say?'

'Blah, blah, blah, can't be ruled out, blah, blah, margin of error, video quality, voice, blah, blah. It would have been great if you'd gotten the imam to say something we could use.'

'Yeah,' Farid muttered. 'Sure would've been.'

After that evening in the mosque, Farid had brought Hassan in for a formal interview. He had arrived at the police station with his lawyer. Hassan had repeated what he'd said at the mosque nearly word for word.

Farid showed him the video clip of Billy and Dogge being humiliated.

'Horrific,' Hassan declared. But he wouldn't say who he thought the masked men were. 'I'm sorry,' he said. 'Unfortunately, there are a number of young men in Våringe who like to deal with conflict this way. You know I do everything in my power to put the brakes on it, to interrupt this sort of violence.'

When Farid said, without naming Tusse, that information had come to light that Hassan might have information about Mehdi's access to guns, and a Glock in particular, he was visibly annoyed. The lawyer got to his feet. Standing, he stated that his client had another meeting and then they left.

So now Mehdi will be released and can get rid of the guy who identified him as an accessory to murder in peace and quiet?'

'Yup.' Lotta bounced on her heels and kept glaring at the occupied stair machine.

'I am so tired. If we do our jobs, can't the courts just for once pretend that we're on the same side and do theirs?'

'It's not their job to be on our side.'

The man on the stair machine was tired of being glared at. Lotta climbed on and kept talking as she poked at the buttons on the control panel.

'Don't get worked up. We've got Leila and the kids under protection. Hopefully we'll get our hands on Dogge soon, so we can talk to him again. Maybe he'll give us something we can use. If you could get him to talk, and really tell us something, then we can check up on it and as soon as we've got something to check up on, things will move forward.'

She put on a pair of headphones and pressed a button on her phone. She was done talking to him.

'Sure,' Farid muttered. He tossed his unused towel in the laundry basket by the treadmill. It was too late to start his workout now anyway. He had to pick up Ella. 'I'll do that. I'll bring Dogge home, that's a great idea, can't believe I didn't think of it earlier. And then I'll invite him to my place and we'll eat Christmas cake and drink *julmust*, and as we wait for our saviour Jesus Christ we'll solve this riddle and lock Mehdi up for good. That's what we'll do. What a relief that we've got that all straightened out now. Merry Christmas.'

40

The Italian tossed him a factory-fresh phone, it landed on his bed.

'Christmas has come early this year, Lasse.' He pulled Dogge out of bed and showed him to a bedroom no one was using. He swept his hand around the space. 'Welcome to Mehdi's very own superstore. Take whatever you need. Shit, take what you don't need too. There's plenty more where this came from.'

The room was full of precarious piles of brand-new T-shirts, pants, shirts. Three clothes racks were crammed so tightly with hangers that you could hardly tell what was on them. Nice clothes, some still in their packaging – they must have been stolen off a truck. Dogge began to browse. First he took a down jacket. Billy had stolen a very similar one two winters ago, from a guy riding in the same carriage on the underground. Dogge had been forced to throw it out when Jill asked where he'd gotten it and blew her top when he said he'd borrowed it from Billy. She had threatened to call Leila.

'That is not Billy's jacket. I am so tired of this, I can't deal with it.'

Teo came into his room later that night and told him he had to get rid of the jacket.

'I mean, there's no point in...your mother isn't...get rid of that jacket, just do it, like, I don't have the energy to argue with her about a jacket, okay? I'll get you another one, I'll make it happen. I just have to take care of something else first, and then you can have ten jackets that cost twice as much as that one.'

There were shoes too, must have been fifty boxes. On the outside of each box was a little picture so you could see what shoes were inside without having to take them out. There were almost all trainers. But there were none in Dogge's size, so he selected a pair that were a little too big and put on two pairs of socks. It was plenty warm in the apartment, but it had snowed all night and the snow had stuck; everything outside was covered in white. If they made him go outside, it would be helpful to have warm clothes. The jacket was perfect. It had a huge hood. He would hardly be recognized by any security cameras with that hood up.

He didn't have to worry about what Mum thought of the jacket. They weren't exactly going to be celebrating Christmas together. But maybe he could get her a Christmas present anyway. There were girl clothes in this room too.

If you asked Mehdi who his role models were, he would always put his mother in first place. Dogge's greatest role model had been Teo, until it was Billy. But the Italian didn't know that, he would appreciate that Dogge wanted to give his mum a present.

Of course, Mum wasn't all that big a fan of Christmas. Jill and Teo had never put up decorations or made any special foods. But they'd always given Dogge presents – really nice ones, some years. The last year before the idiots and the bankruptcy, Teo gave him the latest PlayStation, which he got to keep for almost six months before the Enforcement Authority took it away.

Billy's family didn't celebrate Christmas either. But Leila did put up decorations, which Dogge's dad thought was extremely amusing. He had told his friends about it.

'Muslims love anything that glitters or flashes, don't they? I'm mostly just surprised they don't have Christmas decorations up all year-round.'

Dogge and Billy always exchanged presents. One year, when Teo had 'a good deal in the works', he brought Dogge along to buy a present for Jill. That time, Dogge got to buy Billy a shirt that cost almost three thousand kronor. Billy was overjoyed. He loved nice clothes.

Once they were with Mehdi when he robbed a shipment of clothing. A truck was coming from Malmö, full of designer clothes and shoes, it was super undramatic. The truck driver was a buddy of

Mehdi's, he was the one who'd tipped him off about the shipment. They met up at a rest stop on the E4 highway. They'd made sure to disable the security cameras beforehand, both the ones inside the cab of the truck and the ones at the rest stop. Blue-Boy tied the driver up with duct tape, but not very tightly, and not before they were done transferring the goods to the car they'd brought. They also let the driver keep his phone. He was supposed to wait one hour, maybe one and a half, and then pretend to wriggle out of the tape around his wrists and call the police.

After that robbery, Billy and Dogge were given three shirts and a pair of trainers each. Billy kept all the stolen clothes in his locker at school. If Jill noticed Dogge's new clothes, she didn't mention it. After Teo died, she never noticed what he was wearing.

Mehdi often gave clothes away, he'd once pulled off the T-shirt he was wearing and given it to an elementary-school boy. It was clear the little kid wanted to hang out with Mehdi, he even tried to make friends with Billy and Dogge. Sometimes it felt like he showed up every time they left Billy's house, even if they were only headed to the rink or down to the square, as if he had been waiting for them outside. He was even clingier than Billy's little brother Tusse. Sometimes he showed up at Mehdi's, although it was never quite clear how he got in, who let him inside. He had been sitting on Mehdi's living room floor when he got the T-shirt. He'd been so happy that Dogge thought he was going to start crying.

'Chill,' Mehdi had laughed. 'Stop staring at me like you wanna fuck me.'

But Dogge had never been given so many things all at the same time, not even before the idiots, when Dad still liked taking Dogge out shopping.

What clothes he didn't put on he folded and placed on the floor next to his bed. He left the underwear in their boxes. But he took out one pair and threw away the ones he'd slept in. As he brushed his teeth with a brand-new toothbrush he'd found in one of the bathroom drawers, the Italian came in.

'Got any plans today? I don't think you do. But you won't have to spend another day lying around jerking off, we're gonna go out for a bit, you and me, see if maybe we can find something fun to do. Huh? Doesn't that sound fun? Yes, super fun.'

The Italian was on something, he was amped. His eyes danced around the bathroom. He tossed Dogge some car keys. Dogge managed to catch them with one finger.

'You're driving.'

'I don't have a lic—'

'You're driving. If you've got a problem with that I suggest you take it up with the police.' He guffawed, bouncing on his toes. 'Want the number? You can call them on your new phone. Mistew Powiceman, come wescue me, the kids hewe are weal meanies. Come quick.'

Today, the lift worked. The Italian laughed all the way down to the ground floor.

THE BOYS

The woods behind the Våringe sports complex were big enough to get lost in. One summer, when the boys were nine, a child had disappeared and Missing People had organized a search, one with a K-9 team. Dogge and Billy helped out. A woman in a hand-knitted sweater and knee-high rubber boots found the kid sleeping under a tree. He had peed himself, the front of his pants was dark and he smelled. It cracked Dogge and Billy up – he'd pissed himself even though there were a million trees to go on.

The child was found a few hundred yards from the abandoned tent encampment. There was an old caravan there that smelled like shit and acetone. A few weeks after the lost boy was found, Billy's dad Isak moved into the caravan. He had lived there all summer, until autumn came, and then he moved out.

That same summer, Dogge's father rented a motorboat with sleeping berths. Dogge and Billy were supposed to come along for a three-day trip. But

Dogge got seasick on the very first night and they had to come home again.

'At least you're not a weak-stomached landlubber like Dogge,' Teo said to Billy. But he left them both on the pier and went back out again on his own. He was gone for a week. Jill wasn't home either, so Billy and Dogge stayed at Dogge's house on their own, they didn't tell Leila, who thought they were out in the archipelago. When Teo got back, he was very tanned and his hair was sun-bleached, and he gave off a sharp smell of sweat and salt. He lay in bed for a few days until his sea legs went away.

'When I buy a boat of my own I'll take you out,' he told Billy. 'Dogge can stay home.'

Billy laughed as though this were a joke.

Sometimes they took the underground into the city, where there was water everywhere. Old men fished by the parliament building, blond tourists bought tickets to the archipelago ferries down below Grand Hôtel, families with strollers headed 'out to the countryside' with babies in sun hats that were tied under their chins so they wouldn't blow off. But Billy didn't like the city. He thought it felt like being in another country, he told Dogge, but not a cool one.

When they were in Year 8, right after Teo got sick, Billy brought a stained mattress to their basement hangout. He liked to convince chicks to give him blow jobs on it, and one time Dogge walked in just as a Year 8 blonde was pulling her index finger out of Billy's arse; they laughed about it for a long time after.

One day, during their very last summer, they went to Långholmen to go swimming, and one of Billy's school friends had brought a paddleboard, which they took turns going out on. Dogge wanted to try it, it looked fun, but his turn never came. He hadn't even got in the water when they had to head home again. The others had swum out to a floating dock fifty yards offshore, and dived from it, and Dogge could swim, of course he could, but he could only do the breaststroke and everyone else did the crawl there, even the girls, and he had no desire to look like some fucking old bitch who was afraid to get water in her eyes.

41

Pulling off four home burglaries in under two hours was not as difficult as it might sound. The most time-consuming part was getting from one house to the next, not the break-ins themselves.

They were working in Rönnviken. Dogge would suggest where to go, and they would park outside and check to see if anyone was home. He didn't actually know anything about the different houses, but he avoided the embassies, the ones with flags outside, and the ones with overcomplicated gates. The best targets were medium-sized houses without security cameras, a few blocks from the sea. Even though they often had security doors with the most intricate locks and alarm systems on the market, and a direct link to a private security company that would be on the scene five minutes after you'd entered the front hall, it was enough to walk around the house, step onto the terrace, and break a window. Then they could work in peace.

That kind of security system was as illogical as investing in a safe but leaving it on the floor in the middle of your basement. They found just that in the second house. It was heavy, but not so heavy that Dogge and the Italian couldn't haul it to the car. They would open it at their leisure once they got home again. They also grabbed three computers, a few handfuls of jewellery and watches, two paintings the Italian liked and 16,900 kronor in cash. The money was a surprise. Only handymen and drug dealers carried cash, Teo always said, and Dogge hadn't known there were any of those in Rönnviken.

The Italian was so pumped that he gave a few bills to Dogge. He kept most of it for himself, but Dogge stuffed 1,700 kronor in the back pocket of his jeans. He liked cash too. It reminded him of Dad.

The third house was practically next door to Dogge's. He wondered if his mother was home, what she would say if he showed up, walked inside, and said hi. Hardly anything ever made Jill happy, especially not seeing him.

One time Leila had found a joint in Billy's room. It was in a jacket he'd stolen in Rönnviken. Another time, she found a phone in his schoolbag, one with a foldable screen and a camera that could take night-time shots, he had taken it off a middle-school kid. Leila was always snooping around Billy's room, looking through his things. But in the end he always got away with it. He would blame Dogge, and his mum believed everything he said.

'She always says you don't have it easy, so she doesn't say anything. She'd never stop nagging me if she knew. I would never be allowed out again, we'd never be able to do anything together. You get it, right, it's okay, we're cool?'

Dogge had let him continue the charade. But sometimes, when he saw Billy's mum, he wanted to say something. *I could tell you a thing or two,* he had thought. *You think Billy's as perfect as Jesus or Moham-mad or whatever his name is, that Billy's as innocent as a little puppy. You have no idea who he really is. What he can do, what he wants to do. You don't know him.*

Dogge tried to take a TV too, from the third house, but he dropped it. So the Italian kicked it to pieces. They laughed hysterically. When they got to the last house, Dogge kicked apart their TV too, just to make the Italian laugh. But this time he didn't react. The bathroom in that house contained a small pharmacy: medical marijuana, Prozac, four blister packs of tramadol. When they got back to the car, the Italian gave Dogge one of the joints and a near beer. He wanted to drive now. Dogge had to sit in the passenger seat. The joint was weak, but Dogge got to have a tramadol too, and he swallowed it down with the beer and at last the knots in his stomach began to loosen.

That was when the Italian got the phone call. He answered but didn't say much, mostly listened. When he put down the phone, he turned to Dogge and flashed him a big smile.

'Mehdi's free. That fucker is out. He's been out since two.' He laughed hysterically and punched Dogge in the shoulder. 'Who can keep Mehdi down? Not a single bastard can keep Mehdi down. And now we're going to party. Shit, are we gonna party! Mehdi's in charge of the chicks, we'll pick up some other stuff. You like chicks, right, Lasse?'

Dogge nodded and took two deep drags, one right after the other. Then he held his breath. As he exhaled, he replied.

'Yeah, shit, of course.'

His blood was flowing now, hot in his veins.

Mehdi often asked Dogge if he'd gotten laid. It was one of his very favourite questions. *Little baby Lasse, tasted any pussy yet?* It didn't matter what Dogge said, Mehdi always laughed. He could have any girl he saw. No one else had a chance with a girl Mehdi wanted. Even Billy was jealous of him. And Billy had been able to get girls who were ten years older than him, even though he had zits on his face. His oldest sister didn't even want to bring friends home because she thought they acted so ridiculous when he was around.

Dogge took another hit of the joint and burned his fingers.

'Shit, man.' The Italian waved his hand so Dogge would hand over what was left of the weed. 'You suck like a real slut. If you just take it down a few notches, you'll get everything you want. And not just this eco-friendly shit, Mehdi's got the real stuff.'

Dogge opened the glove box. Inside were two spice cigs and four tablets of morphine. When Dogge looked at the Italian, he simply nodded.

'Someone's hot to trot. Sure. Have at it. Just don't take it all. I might want some too.'

Dogge gave one joint to the Italian and took the other for himself. Once he'd taken two hits, he placed half a pill on his tongue, closed his eyes, and waited.

The first time he drank so much he puked, he had been with Billy. His first break-in, the first time he punched someone. The only time he'd tried heroin was with Billy. It was a white powder, Blue-Boy melted it in a spoon and helped them inject it. His hands were so soft as he gently tied up Dogge's arm and found the vein, the needle so thin it was nearly invisible. Afterward Dogge thought that what was in the syringe felt like love, the best kind. It had made him like himself for a whole night.

Sometimes it felt like Billy had been there for all his firsts. He was even there when Dogge almost got to have sex the first time. Billy probably thought Dogge had actually done it, he congratulated him after, even though she was so ugly. Billy had been busy, it was clear from the noises, but Dogge hadn't looked. The girl Dogge ended up with was so drunk she passed out. He had pulled up her shirt and played with her breasts, which were different sizes and just as ugly as the rest of her body. And then he humped against her so her breasts bounced while he held one hand around her throat. He used the other hand to film it all, and you couldn't tell, watching the video, that he was never inside her because he couldn't get hard. The important part was that the video showed everyone he had got laid. Everyone believed it. The girl too, because she texted him the next day to ask if they could meet up for coffee or something. Dogge told her to go to hell. He didn't want to be with an uggo.

But when he got high, it didn't matter that he was a virgin, that he'd never had any pussy for real. Because everything went soft as down, hard as steel, he relaxed, one thousand per cent on, it was the best music turned all the way up.

The Italian drove just over twenty miles per hour most of the way out of Rönnviken. He let the joint hang from his lower lip, he wasn't smoking it. He didn't light it until they were on the highway, and then he took a deep hit. Dogge watched the glow creep down toward his fingers. The Italian turned the car radio all the way up and forced the car to speed faster, the tyres squealing, they exchanged a quick glance. The car was full of smoke. The Italian was sweating.

'Who the fuck needs God?' said Dogge. 'Or heaven, or life or death, when there's this?'

The ash fell onto his shirt. The Italian laughed out loud.

'You're a fucking poet, Lasse. Lasse the Poet.'

Only when the song on the stereo was over did the Italian exit the highway and turn back. He could have taken the first exit to get to Våringe, but then he would have had to turn off the music and drive slowly. It was important not to get pulled over by the police.

'But I can't fucking drive like a mother of three all the time, it would shrivel my dick.'

Dogge laughed. The morphine turned all his worries to cotton candy, each beat of the stereo kept time with his heart.

When they passed Våringe School and were three blocks from Weed's Market, the Italian pulled to the side of the road, turned off the stereo, and rolled down all the windows. He held his palm out to Dogge, who gave him two pills. While the Italian put one on his tongue and the other in his pocket, he reclined the seat until he was lying down. Dogge followed suit, closed his eyes when he saw the Italian's were shut. Nothing could beat this, nothing. The blood was surging through his body, he heard the Italian sigh with pleasure, or maybe that was him? They were sharing this, the Italian was his friend, he wanted good things for him.

A winter chill blew through the open windows. But Dogge wasn't cold. He could fall asleep. But the Italian didn't want to keep lying there. He rolled the window up again, put his seat back up, and opened the door.

'There's a few things we need to handle real quick. Mehdi doesn't like to be kept waiting. There's a grocery store around here, right?'

Dogge nodded.

'Weed's Market.'

'Is it far?'

Dogge shook his head.

'Good. We'll leave the car here, I need some exercise.'

'Sure.'

They hadn't gone a hundred yards when the Italian turned to him.

'There's something I was thinking about.' He was still amped, Dogge had to jog to keep up. 'Something I don't get. Why did Mehdi tell you to off Billy?'

'I mean...' Dogge hesitated. 'Billy was a fucking traitor. We were supposed to, Billy was supposed to do this thing...he'd promised he would...and Mehdi—'

The Italian cut him off.

'And that's what you said, when you got to the police? Just straight out? That Mehdi had told you to off him?'

'I mean—'

The Italian didn't wait to hear the rest.

'You know Mehdi will never forgive you, right?' He laughed. 'He will never, ever, in all his life, forgive that, whatever he's made you think. Because that's the worst thing anyone can do, is snitch. You're dead, man. You know that, right? Mehdi's gonna beat the shit out of you, and if you survive that he's going to kill you. Everyone knows that, everyone knows what's gonna happen.'

Dogge had to catch his breath, look away to keep from crying.

'But...' He felt the panic climbing back up his spine. 'But you said...I signed it, I signed the paper, I'll do anything you want.'

But the Italian was no longer listening. He seemed to have forgotten his own question. He took out the pill he'd just put in his pocket and handed it to Dogge.

'Come on, Lasse. Chop-chop, now. There's a party tonight. You can chat with Mehdi then. Now it's shopping time.'

THE BOYS

One day, when Dogge was twelve, Leila called Jill.

'Dogge has a bag. He packed. He says he is living here.'

Dogge heard Leila on the phone, and then he pictured Jill driving through Våringe with all the car doors locked, parking her car on the pavement right outside the apartment building, and taking the lift with her scarf over her mouth, crowding her way through the breezeway that was crammed with bicycles, broken grills and folding chairs, and ringing the doorbell so briefly you would hardly notice it.

When she stepped into the apartment, she didn't take off her shoes.

'Hi, honey, Mummy is here now. Everything's going to be okay.' She said it so fast it sounded like a line she was reciting.

What had she told Leila? Dogge couldn't remember after the fact. That he'd had a fight with his father? That things had been a little rough at home, but it was fine now?

But he remembered the shame. Hers, not his. To think that her son wanted to run away to this cramped, mouldy-smelling one-bedroom apartment where Billy lived with his mother and all his siblings. To think that he would rather be there than in the house where he'd grown up, the beautiful turn-of-the-century villa that had been handed down through the family. The shame was so great that Dogge could feel it creeping in under his own skin.

Teo was drunk when they got home. The headache that never went away wouldn't even ease when he had been drinking.

'What the fuck is wrong with you?' he'd asked Dogge. 'How fucking stupid do you have to be, to run away from Rönnviken to Våringe?'

He laughed as though this were a joke, and turned to Jill, seeking her agreement. And he got it. She seldom disagreed with Teo, especially not when he was talking about Dogge.

Teo fell asleep on the sofa in the living room. It had been almost a week since the Enforcement Authority had been there, but the sofa remained. Jill locked herself in the bathroom. It sounded like she was going to take a bath.

Hi, honey, Mummy is here now. Mummy loves you. Everything's going to be okay.

Dogge knew she'd only said it so Billy's mum would hear. It was a string of words none of them believed, it was a show for those who were listening, not for him.

Besides, he knew it was a lie. He'd tried to flee, and failed. There was no way anything could be okay now – it could only get worse.

42

I don't think I can take any more of this.'

Farid was halfway through his beer. His mother was watching the kids while he and Nadja were in the city. *Underground in, taxi home. We need alone time without the kids.* A new restaurant at Stureplan, he'd made the reservation over three weeks ago, and regretted it even before he hung up the phone.

'You don't have to finish it if you don't want to.' Nadja patted his hand. 'No one's going to make you.'

'You know what I mean.'

They were still waiting for the appetizer and were supposed to go to the movies after this; Farid had forgotten which film Nadja wanted to see. Since he knew he would fall asleep before ten minutes had passed, he'd agreed to it without listening very carefully.

'It's such a shitty fucking job.'

'You'll find Dogge. It's only a matter of time.'

'And what do you think I should do with him when I see him? Ask him to tell me who's pissing in his face in that video the judge didn't think was worth taking into consideration when she decided that obviously Mehdi had to go free?'

'You told me it wasn't Mehdi peeing on them. That it was the other guy, Mehdi's friend, but you weren't sure because you can only see the lower half of his body.'

'You sound just like that fucking judge.'

'There's no need to take it out on me.' Nadja's tone sharpened. 'I didn't do anything.'

'How could anyone watch that video and then let Mehdi go, can you answer me that?'

'You don't want me to explain anything.' Nadja was still irritated. 'How did the judge account for it?'

'By saying that it couldn't be determined with any certainty that it's really Mehdi in the clip.'

'Is that true?'

'I'd say it's clear as fucking day that it's Mehdi.'

'Have you been able to get anyone to say it's him? Someone other than you?'

'No. And you know why.' He poured the rest of his beer into the glass. 'Because no one wants to get pissed on. Where the hell is our food? What do we have to do around here to eat before the chef goes home for the night?'

'Calm down, Farid. The techs couldn't establish it was Mehdi either.'

'Don't fucking tell me to calm down. I'm hungry. The techs are idiots. What the hell kind of restaurant is this?'

'Seriously, Farid, take it down a notch. You know the drill. When you find Dogge, you confront him with the video. You've made him talk before, and now you have something concrete to back up his story with. Isn't that actually a step in the right direction?'

'You know what, Nadja. I don't feel like backing up Dogge's story. I'm sick of listening to these idiotic little brats make up stories, one after another, and the only thing you can be sure of is that nothing, not a damn thing, is their fault.'

'Okay.' Nadja took the last piece of bread from his hand and popped it in her mouth. 'Was what the techs had to say about the video the only reason the judge released Mehdi?'

Farid muttered something and drained his glass of beer.

'What was that?'

'The judge thinks Dogge shot Billy with his dad's gun.'

'Dogge's dad's? Isn't he dead?'

'When I was talking to Billy's mum at her place, one of his siblings said Dogge had got the gun from his own father, not from Mehdi. I had to enter a note into the investigation material to that effect. And then Mehdi's lawyer dug up a picture of Dogge's dad holding a Glock and, well, that was that.'

'Was it Dogge's dad's gun?'

'Not a chance. But it's hard to link Mehdi to a Glock we can't find if Dogge could have taken it from his own house. Tusse and his sister want to remove Mehdi from the equation. They're lying. All these fucking kids are lying. And I'm gonna toss them in the nearest goddamn jail cell, dammit, and throw away the key.'

'Locking children up in jail won't make anything better.'

'No?' Farid pulled over Nadja's glass of beer and poured half of it into his own. 'Dogge executed Billy. No matter why he did it, no matter if Mehdi told him to or not, the fact is he flipped the safety on a Glock and fired four shots at the back of his best friend's head from less than a yard away. Who does that? He missed twice, however that's even possible at such close range, but the other two bullets hit him in the back of the head and the back of the neck. He wanted to kill him, how can a fourteen-year-old want to do that? Dogge isn't a war survivor, he isn't homeless or orphaned. He is fourteen, almost fifteen, and executed his best friend with premeditation.'

'Children don't have the same ability to consider consequences as we do, their brains aren't fully developed, they—'

'They're going to close the investigation.'

'What? Has it been decided?'

'Not yet. But we know who fired the gun, we aren't going to be able to pin it on Mehdi. Not with the information that Dogge might have taken the gun from his own father. Not a chance. You know how difficult it is to get anyone for instigation. We'd have to prove, beyond reasonable doubt, to bastard judges who believe they get paid to doubt everything, that Dogge never would have murdered Billy if it weren't for the fact that Mehdi wanted him to do it. We'd need to give them a weapon that Mehdi gave to Dogge, proof that Mehdi told him to do it, and preferably two or three reliable witnesses to the whole thing.'

'Maybe you can get him for aiding and abetting?'

'For sure. Or the court could free him even if we hand them a weapon Mehdi carved his name into, and even if the imam testifies that Mehdi said he'd assigned Dogge the task of killing Billy, and we show a video of him actually doing so. Because the judge might think it could be some other fucking idiot in the goddamn video. Anything could happen. But by far the likeliest scenario is that we close the investigation without saying so outright, and then we'll get to go investigate something else where we know exactly what happened but can't prove it.'

'Do you know exactly what happened?'

'That's not the point, Nadja.' Farid raised his voice. The diners at the next table were looking at him. 'I'll give it a week, two at most. We investigate fatal shooting after fatal shooting and no one is convicted. It's been nine days since Billy was shot, and there've already been six more shootings, just in the

Stockholm metro area. Two dead, neither of them even twenty-five years old. You say kids don't have the same understanding of consequences that adults do. Sorry, I don't buy that. They know exactly what they're doing. I could have ended up in one of those fucking gangs, but I didn't. Because I got my shit together. Our kids wouldn't kill anyone, because they know it's wrong. They understand the consequences of firing a loaded weapon less than a metre from someone's head. They get it.'

He was out of breath. Nadja shook her head, annoyed.

'Farid. When you talk about what a rough time you had as a kid, you're referring to the way your mother smeared white ointment around your lips because you had cold sores and how kids at school called you a clown. Or how your father called up one of your teachers to let him know he made a mistake when correcting your history test. You did not have a rough childhood the way these kids have a rough childhood.'

'Dogge's mother is no...well, okay, she is a fucking bitch.' Farid drank up the last of the beer he'd stolen from Nadja. 'But Billy's mother would do anything for her kids. She's like – she's basically the nun in *The Sound of Music*.'

'The nun in *The Sound of Music* isn't the kids' mother. The mother in *The Sound of Music* is dead.'

'Come on, you know what I mean. Everything I've seen from Billy's mother indicates that she's a fucking...who's a good example of a mum, then?'

'All the good mums in literature are dead. Pippi's mum. Dead. Harry Potter's mum. Dead. Anne of Green Gables'? Dead. It's dangerous being a mother. And thankless.'

'Whatever.' Farid brought up his hand and lowered it again, fast. The man at the next table shifted uncomfortably. 'Christ, is it possible to get something to eat or drink in this goddamn place? Dogge doesn't have the right to murder anyone. Besides, we have to fucking lock him up to keep someone from killing him. I can say I'm putting him behind bars for his own safety if you prefer, is that better?'

Nadja leaned over the table and lowered her voice.

'I'm not trying to make excuses for what he did, I'm only trying to understand. It is our duty to understand children, so we can help them. And you need to calm down.'

'There's no understanding them, Nadja. Believe me. I've been trying to understand these kids for almost a decade, and it's no use. They lie about things they don't need to lie about, and they tell the truth when you least expect it. They commit murder because someone laughed at the wrong joke or liked the wrong photo on Instagram, they get a girl drunk and have sex with her while she's unconscious, and film the whole thing. Stop trying to understand them, there's nothing to understand. They're monsters.'

'Hold on. Children who do terrible things – we don't call them monsters. They're children.'

'But when do they stop being children?' The diners at the next table were looking around anxiously now, also trying to get the maître d's attention. Farid didn't notice. 'When can you start demanding that they take some fucking responsibility for their own goddamn actions? When they're ten? Twelve? When their voices start breaking? Or not until they turn eighteen? I can't just keep coddling them anymore, I want—'

'Calm down, Farid, or we're going to get kicked out of here. You can make demands of them. No one is saying you can't. But there's no point in punishing them for the sake of punishment. And in order to give them the proper punishment, we have to understand them. We have to understand why they do what they do, and you need to eat, Farid. You need to get some sleep and you need to be quiet, and you might need to take a little vacation, because you're saying things you don't really mean.'

'I've never been more serious in my whole life. I do mean what I'm saying, one hundred per cent.'

Farid's voice sank to a whisper. He bent his head to the table. The diners around them looked away.

'You don't.' Nadja took his hand. 'You've devoted your entire working life—'

'I've *wasted* my entire life, you mean.'

'You have devoted your life to saving these children, giving them a second chance, because you believe they deserve it.'

'I don't think they deserve it.'

'Of course you do.'

He blinked to keep from crying. Nadja squeezed his hand harder. He swallowed.

'You make a difference every day, my love,' she whispered. 'You know one tiny detail can mean the world. You're just having a bad week, that's all.' She turned to the next table and raised her voice. 'Bad week at work.' They gave hesitant nods.

'They're going to close this investigation.'

'You don't know that.'

'Yes, I do.'

'Okay. But Mehdi will go down for something else... and there are others who need you too, other boys. Things'll turn around soon, *habib*.'

'Sure.' Farid brought Nadja's hand to his lips. He gave a tentative smile. 'But I still want to know if there's any food around here.'

43

Dogge and the Italian had to pry open the sliding doors at Weed's Market to get in. It only took a few seconds to pop them open a few feet so they could squeeze their way through. Dogge cracked up when the Italian's jacket got caught in the opening. But his laughter soon passed, and dizziness took over.

Hungry, Dogge thought, *I'm hungry.* He needed to eat. His skin was crawling. His legs felt like they had gone to sleep, like they were covered in ants. They crawled all over him, he was all itchy, not only from the eczema but inside his body, his blood, everywhere.

There were no customers in the store, and Weed seemed to have sent all the staff home. He was sitting at one of the cash registers, but he stood up.

'We're closed,' he called. Weed was holding the cash tray, had taken it out of the register.

'Good day to you, sir!'

The Italian pretended to bow; Dogge stood beside him. He planted his legs wide to stay steady.

Weed looked tired – not scared, just tired.

The Italian pulled over a trolley that had been left by the exit.

'We thought we'd do some shopping, you don't have a problem with that, do you? We're allowed to get groceries just like anyone else, aren't we? We promise to be quick about it, so you can go home. If the wife is still up, maybe you'll get some pussy? Does she like to fuck?'

Weed didn't say anything.

Dogge caught up with the Italian. They pushed the trolley through the aisles, filling it with items. They'd each taken a paper bag, the big grocery bag kind they sold at the register, and they emptied the sweet containers into them. Right into the bags, one by one. Raspberry boats, chocolate coins, tutti frutti, fruit dummies, raspberry drops, Dumle toffees and cola bottles. The salty-sour balls were all stuck to-gether and landed with a hard thunk. The Italian blew up.

'No fucking salt liquorice, I hate salt liquorice. Leave my fucking bag alone, I don't want your nasty-ass sweets.'

Crisps, meat, soda. Dogge tossed things into the trolley without paying any attention to what they were. They would never be able to carry all of this to the car, they'd have to bring the whole trolley. A frozen cheesecake. Hot dogs, jumbo pack. Six or-ganic cucumbers. Four packets of *knäckebröd*. Twenty packages of extra-absorbent overnight pads. When the Italian noticed the period stuff, he blew up again.

'What am I, some kind of fucking whore? Are you saying I'm a bitch-ass whore? Or is Little Lasse on the rag? Bleeding in your panties, are you?'

He threw the pads out, and two of the packages ended up in the cheese cooler. One he ripped open, and pads fell onto the floor. Dogge kicked one of them, it flew like a projectile and landed on the other side of the meat counter.

'Gooooal!' shouted the Italian. His rage was gone in a flash.

When they reached the checkout counter, they asked for six packs of cigarettes.

'You have to pay,' said Weed. 'If you want me to let you shop, you also have to pay.' He still didn't sound angry. Just tired. 'You don't have a problem with that, do you?'

Dogge was annoyed. He wanted Weed to talk back, it was more fun when he didn't just go along with whatever they did. But he didn't even seem scared. Dogge wanted him to be scared. Surely all he would have to do was shout really loud. Or aim a punch right next to his face. Or kick over the tall stack of shopping baskets. But instead he took one of the 500-kronor bills from the break-in from his pocket.

'You want money? I'll give you money.'

He made a show of smoothing the bill out before placing it on his palm, sticking his hand down his pants, and, with half his arm inside his clothes, hunching and carefully wiping between his cheeks. Then he removed his hand and placed the bill in front of Weed. The Italian was screeching with laughter.

'I'd like my change, please,' said Dogge. 'Everything in the cash register will do, for starters.'

THE BOYS

When Billy and Dogge were assigned their final job together, they were sitting at Våringe Pizzeria. They each had a *margherita* with extra cheese; Dogge had his back to the door and Billy was across from him. Although he couldn't see him, Dogge could sense the exact second Mehdi walked in. It was in the air, you could tell to look at everyone in the restaurant; they didn't turn around to stare, but they were suddenly forcing themselves not to, were actively pretending that everything was exactly the same, as if he weren't there at all.

Because the first thing you noticed about Mehdi was not that he was attractive, it wasn't the car he drove or the clothes he wore. He didn't shave his hair into unusual patterns, like many of his friends did, he didn't sport clothes with big, flashy brand logos, didn't roll down the car windows while blasting music. He didn't even have any large tattoos. His voice was gravelly and calm but not piercing, he wasn't particularly fat or tall, but he wasn't small either.

You noticed Mehdi because of the way others behaved when he walked into a room. The women around him – there were always several of them – spoke about his energy with shivers of excitement, how magical it was. When he smiled his crooked smile, they smiled in return, even the bitchy old ones.

Men, too, fell under his influence, but they called it respect and were satisfied to back off if he got too close, wait until he raised a hand in greeting, stiffen if he touched them, and threaten violence if someone got too close without Mehdi's okay.

People told lots of stories about Mehdi. One rumour said he had played football on the Bromma boys' team but got sick of it, even though he'd been selected for the youth division of the national team. Another said he used to live in New York, where he had worked for a big-time gangster, as his second-in-command. In Berlin he had supposedly invested in a brothel he brought Swedish business leaders to, and in Majorca he'd killed a guy. Billy had told Dogge all of this. He thought the part with the brothel was especially exciting.

'Do you think he has to pay when he goes there? Or does he get to do whatever he wants for free?'

Blue-Boy was the one who explained their task. It wasn't complicated, but it was important for them to do as they were told. They had to arrive on time, throw the grenades through the correct window and that window only. The guy Mehdi wanted to take care of was supposed to be there, but only at that particular moment. They would throw one grenade at a time: first one, to break the window, then the other, as far into the apartment as they could.

'Whoever's got the best arm can do the second one,' said Blue-Boy. 'But it's important for the first one to hit the mark too.' Dogge thought it sounded difficult. But Blue-Boy said a number of times that it would be simple, and Billy nodded.

Billy remembers what we have to do, Dogge thought. *Billy's good at instructions.*

This could be considered arson, Blue-Boy explained. That came with a life sentence, but not if you were fourteen – they wouldn't have to do any time at all if they were caught.

When he was done talking, he leaned over the table and pulled over Billy's backpack, the one he used as a schoolbag. He unzipped it, took the grenades from his pocket, and stuck them inside. It happened fast, no one besides Dogge and Billy saw him do it.

Mehdi sat at another table as Blue-Boy explained. He ended by saying this would be the last thing Billy had to do, there was nothing more. As long as they did what they'd promised to do.

What Billy promised to do, Dogge thought. But he didn't say anything. He stayed perfectly silent, as though the job was just as much about him as about Billy, and *Maybe*, he'd thought, *maybe that's true. If we do this, maybe both of us can quit? Mehdi has never seen me as anything but Billy's friend, I'm not important. He knows I'm not even rich, he doesn't need me. I'll talk to Billy*, he thought. *We're brothers, we're in this together.*

'I'm depending on you,' Mehdi had said before he left. He had come over to their table to stand beside Billy.

Singular you. He was only talking to Billy. Blue-Boy had given the grenades to Billy, even though Dogge was right there too, right next to him.

'I'm going to disengage too,' Dogge said when Mehdi and Blue-Boy had gone.

'Sure,' said Billy. 'Whatever.'

44

Weed's ears were buzzing. A dull sound.

As soon as the two boys had left him alone at the cash register, he called 112.

'We don't have any units in the vicinity, I'm afraid. We'll send someone as soon as we can. We understand. We're doing our best. We will help you, but there are a lot of people who need us right now.'

Weed explained that one of the people who had just vandalized his store was a boy who had run away from a state home and shot a boy in Rönnviken.

'He's high. He doesn't care that I know who he is. They don't care about anything, you have to send someone.'

'Are they armed?' the woman asked.

'No,' he replied. 'Not that I could see. But there are two of them, I'm alone and one of them,' he repeated, 'killed another boy less than two weeks ago. Don't you get what I'm saying? He's wanted. You all are looking for him.'

'We're working as fast as we can, I promise we will help you. But right now I have no units in the area.'

So he called the security firm instead. He no longer had a contract with them, but he wanted to give it a shot anyway. A computer-generated voice answered the phone.

'Enter your customer number followed by the pound sign. Press one for break-in. Press two for assault. Press three for ... Would you prefer to speak to an operator? Press star. We are experiencing a high volume of calls, you are number eight in line. If this is an emergency, please call 112.'

He called 112 again. It felt like an eternity passed between each unanswered ring. When Dogge and his friend had finished their rounds of the store and returned to the register, he had to put down the phone. He didn't want to provoke them needlessly. Maybe they would let him keep his phone if they didn't see it. When they were gone he could call Sara, she could come down and help him clean up. They would leave soon. This wasn't the first time. It wouldn't be the last either. They always left eventually. They always did – once they got sick of it they would go, this time they were being unusually awful, but they would go, they wouldn't stay. The most important thing was to stay calm. His children weren't here, Eva was at home, they couldn't do anything to her.

But then Dogge handed him a 500-kronor bill he'd just used to wipe his behind. He dropped it on the counter and to Weed it looked like there was faeces on it.

So he bent down. He didn't have to reach very far. It was right behind the register.

Once it was in his hand, everything happened fast.

45

Sturegatan was aglitter with Christmas decorations as they came out of the cinema. Nadja shivered. Farid pulled off his hat and put it on her head. She smiled and brushed her fringe aside.

'What did you think of the movie?'

'It was good,' said Farid.

She smiled.

'Good to get some sleep?'

'Yes.'

A group of teenagers came their way from Humlegården, all wearing identical oversized coats and ribbed hats. Two of them were singing.

'We wish you a Merry Christmas!'

Farid stepped aside to let them pass.

They buy the same brands as my gangster kids wear, he thought. *And we still call these ones 'the beautiful people'.*

Down by Stureplan, the snow in the street had melted away, leaving the asphalt black and wet. There was a long line of taxis outside Sturecompagniet, and they had to walk in the street to reach one, since the queue to enter the nightclub was also very long. Farid opened the back door of the taxi at the front of the line and let Nadja hop in, then got in beside her.

The driver had the radio on; a rosary dangled from the rear-view mirror. Farid asked him to turn down the volume and moved closer to Nadja. She leaned into him; he smoothed the hat off her head, stuffed it into his pocket, and took in the scent of her hair.

They were nearly home, but still on the highway, when they saw an emergency vehicle approaching, then another. Both were running with lights but no sirens. They were moving along as silently as their taxi, but in the opposite direction. The beams of blue light swept over the road, into the taxi, and across their bodies as the cars met.

Nadja looked at him as they realized the emergency vehicles were taking the Våringe exit.

Just a few hundred yards from their own exit, a vehicle came up behind them, on its way from Våringe, an ambulance this time. It was using its siren. The taxi slowed down and let it pass.

'I don't need to know,' Farid said, squeezing Nadja's hand. 'They'll call if they need me.'

His phone was in his pocket; he'd put it on silent. But the dull buzz of the incoming call was perfectly audible.

46

Dogge laughed, but then he wasn't laughing anymore.

Weed only took one swing. He had played tennis when he was younger, and at the city's *brännboll* tournament in the park last year he'd hit the ball further than anyone else. He had got three home runs in as many tries. His hands gripped the shaft – just right. The top fingers of one hand overlapped the little and ring fingers of the other. The sound of a perfect hit was the same as ever. It made everything stop.

The other boy backed up, and for an instant he met Weed's gaze. It looked like he was angry, like he might become aggressive. But when he looked down and saw what lay between them, when he saw what had happened to Dogge, he turned around and ran. He slipped in the puddle of *filmjölk* they'd poured onto the floor, but regained his balance and dashed all the way out of the store and vanished.

W eed called the emergency dispatcher a third time.

'Send an ambulance,' he said. 'Come fast, you need to hurry.'

He explained what he'd done. And now there were units available.

As he waited, he sat on the floor and held Dogge's head in his lap. To move him closer, he cupped his hand under the boy's neck, carefully, as he had done with his own babies when they were newborns. Weed's lap grew warm, and as the blood left the boy's body he sang a song his mother used to sing for him when he had trouble sleeping.

Lorî, lorî kurém lorî. My son is hurt, he is sick. My son's wound is a burden to bear. Sleep, sleep my lamb. Sleep, sleep my son. Lorî, lorî.

T he ambulance arrived six minutes later. The police were there soon after, in two cars. He and Dogge were still alone in the store when they arrived, and Weed kept singing, rocking his torso in time with the melody. But when the paramedics came running in with the stretcher, he had to let go. They took the boy. Weed remained on the floor.

The police waited until the paramedics had made sure Weed wasn't hurt. Then they put him in handcuffs. He didn't resist, but he asked to be allowed to lock up the store before he went. One of the officers said no and tried to make him stand up, he wanted to haul him to the car. Once Weed had heaved himself to standing, he looked at the cash register, which was still open. He needed to place the removable cash drawer in the safe. The police didn't have the code. They wouldn't know how to open it. They didn't even know where it was.

'I can call my wife. She can come close up. She can clean up the worst of this.'

Then the other officer turned to him. He had a soft, kind voice and spoke slowly, as though Weed were a little dim.

'We will make sure to inform your wife. You may not lock up, you may not clean or do anything else here. The technicians will take over now. We're going to cordon off the area. We are going to cordon off the store, do you understand? This is a crime scene, and you need to come with us.'

THE BOYS

Dogge's first psychologist was called Helena. He was in Year 3, and Jill's friend had recommended her, she had been there with her own son who had 'some minor ADHD', and she'd said Helena 'was good at helping kids come up with tools'.

Dogge, Jill and Teo took Teo's car into the city. Helena had an office with white walls and white furniture, was wearing a white shirt and bright-red lipstick. She wanted Dogge to draw. *You draw*, he retorted, *if you think it's so much fun.*

Jill only came along the first time. The second time, Dogge had to go in by himself, while Teo said he would wait in the car. Helena had a questionnaire, she asked him questions, he answered almost all of them. When he came out again, Teo was gone. Dogge had to sit and wait on the stairs. It was dark before his dad returned. They never went back to Helena.

The second time Dogge saw a psychologist, it was the school that wanted him to go. The school psychologist in Rönnviken had a beard, trousers that were too large and dirty nails he picked at while Jill talked non-stop because silence made her nervous. They met with him three times, each with all three of them together. Dogge didn't say a word. Later, Teo threatened to take him out of school if this didn't end, and after that they didn't have to go back.

'My son isn't crazy, the school just wants to slap a diagnosis on him so they can get more money, and they needed something to blame since the teachers there are idiots.'

When Dogge was thirteen, he had to see a psychologist who worked with social services. And social services were the ones who said 'it was probably for the best' that Dogge start going there. Teo was bankrupt by then and couldn't pay for private psychologists anymore. When Dogge met with this one, neither Jill nor Teo was allowed to be there. Her name was Jennie, and she wore jeans, black boots and a long-sleeved top, and had four piercings in each ear. She started by telling him that everything he said was confidential and she wanted him to feel that he could tell her anything, anything he wanted to. And then she added, quickly, as though she hoped he wouldn't hear, that he needed to understand that even so there were some things she would be duty-bound to report to the police, or possibly to his parents.

'So,' said Dogge. 'If I tell you boring stuff you won't do anything, but if I tell you something important you'll squeal to the cops?'

Jennie paged through the folder in front of her for a moment.

'Let's say this,' she said. 'If you start to tell me something I think might be the sort of thing I can't keep to myself, I'll tell you right away so you can stop talking if you want to.'

'Well, what am I supposed to talk about, then?' he'd asked. 'My childhood or something?'

'Do you want to talk about your childhood?' Jennie crossed one leg over the other and leaned back.

'Do you think I sucked my thumb till I was ten or peed the bed until I was in middle school or that I want to marry my mum?'

'If you want to talk about that, I'd be happy to listen. You can talk about whatever you want.'

'Why would I talk about my childhood? I'm still a child.'

'Yes, you are.'

'So come up with something else then. For me to talk about.'

'How do you think things are going at school? Do you like it there?'

Dogge had liked preschool, especially when Mum dropped him off early in the morning, when only one staff member was working and Dogge was almost always the only kid there. He got to come to the kitchen and make a sandwich and have a glass of milk. Then they would go to the pillow room and listen to a fairy tale on tape and the teacher would drink a cup of coffee while he ate his sandwich. It was actually against the rules to eat in the pillow room, it was *strictly forbidden*.

'But,' said the teacher, 'it's our little secret, we won't tell anyone.'

When the other kids arrived, he got to play whatever he wanted until it was time for morning assembly. When Dad had to drop him off, they were almost always late – Teo didn't want Dogge to go to preschool at all. The staff would get annoyed. But Dad didn't seem to care, and Dogge didn't like assembly anyway – it went on for so long, and you had to sit down the whole time. If he was late, he didn't have to sit still as long. The preschool had its own playground, where they spent a few hours each day. There were two forts, a huge sandbox, and wheelbarrows you could use to cart the wounded to the hospital when you were playing war. The other boys liked playing war best, but Dogge always had to be dead. He didn't like lying still and not doing anything while the others were shooting stick guns and running as fast as they could, but if he didn't agree to play dead they wouldn't let him play at all.

That was forever ago. He was a different person now.

'I hate school,' he said instead.

'Tell me something about yourself, then,' said Jennie. 'What do you like to do?'

'I don't think I can say,' Dogge said. 'Because you'd have to tell the police.'

She laughed at that. As though he'd said something funny.

When Billy was eight, Våringe School thought he should undergo an evaluation.

'The best thing would be,' said his teacher, 'if we could have some help with helping Billy. Someone who can get him to focus. But that takes an evaluation; without it we can't ask for an extra aide.'

A school nurse helped Leila write an application. Two months later, Billy got to visit the children's clinic for an assessment and was wait-listed for an evaluation.

'Demand is high in our region,' the doctor explained. 'But you have the right to be seen for an initial meeting within ninety days. That is the standard for guaranteed access. Call the clinic if it takes any longer.'

When Billy got an appointment for his evaluation at the children's mental health clinic, Leila came along. She had to answer questions about Billy. Had it been a difficult pregnancy? When did he learn to speak? Walk? When did he stop wearing diapers? Did he still suck his thumb?

'He's growing just fine,' she replied. 'My children are not problems.'

'Unfortunately we don't have the resources he needs,' the school told Leila when the evaluation was over. 'But there are other schools, not in our district, and there are other routes one can take. Maybe you should look into those options?'

When he started Year 7, he had to start going to the mental health clinic again. There would be another evaluation; they called it a follow-up.

'You know what,' Billy said to the psychologist. 'You think I can tell you like a story with a beginning and end and middle and a whole lot of exciting stuff that happens, and once you hear it you can say, Aha, I get it. But I don't have any stories like that.'

The psychologist had been staring vacantly at nothing. When she took a breath, it sounded like she was stifling a yawn.

'I don't mean to say you need to tell me a story,' she said. 'You can tell me whatever you want.'

But Billy didn't think that sounded like a good idea. So he said nothing.

47

The drive from Weed's Market to Karolinska Hospital was under seven miles, four of them on the highway. Weed was taken there in an ambulance, straight from the scene of the crime. There was no emergency, no lights or sirens, and he was allowed to sit up for the trip.

'There's nothing wrong with me,' he said.

Next to Weed sat one of the paramedics and a police officer. Someone had taken his work smock and put it in an evidence bag. His jeans, vest, hands and arms were bloody too, but it wasn't that bad. His work smock had protected most of it. When they arrived at the hospital they had to enter through the main lobby, which was the only entrance besides the emergency department and maternity ward that was still open twenty-four hours.

A Christmas tree glittered next to the check-in desk. The Pressbyrån convenience store was still open, with some plastic-wrapped hyacinths next to a tall rack of get-well cards. A cleaner listlessly pushed his cart through the lobby; there was a drooping Santa hat hanging from the handle of one bucket. The cleaner nodded at Weed as they passed each other, as though he knew him. Weed nodded back. Only then did he realize his hands were bound. In addition, the policeman was holding him gently by the arm, as though they were two ladies out for a stroll, minus their parasols.

'There's nothing wrong with me,' he said again to the officer. 'I'm not hurt. I'm not sick.'

The policeman squeezed his elbow slightly and they kept walking.

'Tomorrow the kids and I are buying a tree,' Weed said. 'Or today? It's today. I guess I might have to call my wife? And tell her we'll have to postpone?'

In the corridor outside the room where they brought him stood four night-shift nurses, each sipping from a cup. Their chitchat continued as Weed walked by; they were laughing as one nurse said that her relatives wanted her to bring homemade cured salmon or home-pickled herring to their Christmas smorgasbord.

'I offered to stop for some barbecue-flavoured crisps,' she said. 'That's as close as I get to homemade.'

That made Weed smile. But as he was guided into an examination room, and the door closed, he could no longer hear what they were saying. A forensic examiner came in. She took a blood sample. He was given a cup to pee in. The doctor and the officer watched. The cup was warm when Weed handed it to the doctor.

'Sorry,' he said.

Then he had to take off the rest of his clothes. The doctor's gloved finger lingered for a second at the mole on the inside of Weed's wrist. Sara had told him to get it checked out, but he hadn't had time. The doctor didn't comment on it; she just continued her silent mapping of his body.

When the forensic examination was over, they sent him back out to the corridor. He was led out of the hospital almost the same way he'd come in, but instead of driving back to Weed's Market they went to the holding area at Våringe police station. No one had put up any Christmas decorations there.

Weed had to wait in one of the drunk tanks, the only one that wasn't already occupied. A faint odour of vomit and unwashed genitals emanated from the plastic mattress on the floor. Weed didn't sit down; he wanted to do his waiting on his feet. He placed his hands on his knees to keep them from shaking. For a little while he crouched, but then he forced himself to get up.

'I'm not sick,' he muttered. 'There's nothing wrong with me. I'm not sick.'

After about forty minutes, he was brought to the interrogation room. His lawyer was waiting there. He had come straight from a dinner with friends, and his forehead and eyes were both shiny. They had twenty minutes alone. Weed asked the lawyer his name three times, he said it and pushed a business card across the table. Weed listened, read the card, and still didn't remember the name when the interrogation began.

The interview was conducted by a woman with a low voice and a shiny pageboy with a long fringe that she kept trying in vain to tuck behind her ear.

'Can you tell us what happened?' she asked. 'Start from the beginning.'

From the beginning? Weed thought.

'How did things end up like this?' she wondered.

His answers weren't satisfactory. Weed could see it in their expressions.

He told them how his store had been vandalized again and again, month after month. He didn't want to talk about what Dogge had done to his daughter, but the police already knew.

'You must have been very angry at that boy,' said the female officer, fiddling with her fringe.

Angry? Weed thought.

'I've tried everything,' he replied. 'No one listened, no one has helped me.'

He thought it looked as though the woman questioning him nodded, but that could have been his imagination.

'How is he, the boy?' he asked the police. But there was no response. 'He's going to be okay, right?' he asked his lawyer. 'He'll be okay again?'

The policewoman looked down at the table.

48

The Italian left the car where he and Dogge had parked it. He didn't hide away, he didn't lie low. He went straight to Mehdi's party.

The party was at an address he'd never been to before, in a different district, close to seven miles from Våringe. The Italian took an Uber, ordering it with his own phone. He could hear the music all the way down on the street, even though the apartment was on the sixth floor. He took the stairs two at a time, and got so out of breath that he could taste iron and had to wait a few seconds before entering the living room where Mehdi was sitting with four girls and six guys. There was cocaine and a bag of cheese curls on the table. Mehdi wasn't high, but he blew up.

'What the fuck did you do with that *blatte-wannabe* wuss? Didn't I tell you to bring him here in one piece so I could have the pleasure of ripping him apart with my own two hands? Didn't I ask you, in my very nicest voice, to make sure to bring him here so I could kill that fucker? Was that too difficult to understand? Were the instructions too complicated? Are you stupid? Where is he?'

The Italian brought Mehdi up to speed. As he spoke, he gazed down at his jacket. He had thought he'd got blood on himself, but he didn't see anything. He ran his hand over his face, once, twice, rubbing his forehead. He looked at his hand, but there was nothing there either. Each time he closed his eyes, he saw flickering.

The last thing he'd seen before he hauled ass out of Weed's Market was that something was running out of the back of Dogge's head, something with the consistency of a slimy snail. He forced the image out of his mind so he could recount the tale while keeping his voice under control. But when he heard himself telling Mehdi what Weed had done, he felt like the stuff that had come out of Dogge's head had got on his jacket, and he began tugging at the right sleeve to get it off.

'He smashed his head in. He broke his skull. I heard the sound.'

The Italian was losing control of his voice.

They're going to kill me now, he had time to think, *they want to kill me themselves, they're going to kill me instead,* and then he heard Mehdi start to laugh. At first he giggled uncontrollably, like a teenage girl, so much that tears came from his eyes. Someone turned off the music. More people came into the living room, all of them smiling, they wanted to hear what had happened, why Mehdi was so happy. The Italian wrenched his other sleeve off, pulled off the jacket, and threw it as far away as he could. Mehdi's laughter got even louder.

'Weed?' he managed to say at last. 'Are you telling me that the bazaar Turk down on the square beat that useless fucking wuss-ass snob to death for me? And here I didn't even think he could fire a staple into a bulletin board. What a joke. Remind me to send flowers or something and thank that import Kurd for his help.'

Then, wiping tears of laughter from his face with his shirtsleeve, he bent down and snorted two lines into the same nostril. He waved at one of the guys to turn up the music.

'Sit down, Spag. Sit down and catch your breath, you look like you just ran a fucking marathon. This is a party, for fuck's sake. We've got so much to celebrate.'

49

Jill's doorbell rang. When she answered it, the uniformed officer outside didn't say a word. Another man, one wearing hair gel and lapels the size of a table runner, stepped forward. He had been waiting behind the police officer and smelled like he'd just shaved, although it was the middle of the night. When he and his aftershave stepped into her front hall, Jill thought he was going to say Dogge had been shot. That would have been the logical option. Instead, he said he was a chaplain.

'Dogge is in the ICU,' the chaplain explained. 'He's going to have an operation,' he added.

'I'm not religious,' Jill replied. 'I don't believe in that stuff.'

When Jill got pregnant, her best friend had given her a necklace: a jingly, egg-shaped pendant with a long chain that was meant to hang down over her belly, so when the baby came out it would recognize the sound and by extension, her.

When Dogge was born, it was snowing, and Teo drove Jill to the hospital in a car he'd borrowed from a friend, even though it didn't have snow tyres. He hardly drove over ten miles an hour the whole way, and by the end Jill was screaming because she thought she was going to have to deliver her baby there in the front seat, with her feet braced against the glove compartment. But when they arrived at the hospital and rang the bell for someone to come let them in, it was as though that button also turned off her labour. Her waters had broken and there were traces of me-conium in them, so she wasn't allowed to go home. The father-to-be, though, vanished as soon as she was assigned a room.

'My mother,' Teo had explained back when Jill was seven months along, 'she says a woman wants to be with other women when she's giving birth,' and although he had never been interested in what his mother had had to say before, and although Jill hadn't had time to think about whether she wanted to be alone or not, she knew she definitely didn't want to have a baby with Teo in the room if he didn't want to be there.

'Call me when you're done,' he said as he left.

He told the midwives he would be back as soon as he could, but that he had to return the car. They'd protested less than Jill had expected. Presumably they, too, thought it was best if he wasn't there, even though he was actually sober.

But the contractions hadn't progressed as they should. After seven hours of waiting, a doctor was called in; if they couldn't get the kid out right away it would mean an emergency C-section. The doctor forced Jill to lie down in the hospital bed even though she was screaming that she wanted to stand. Then he ordered her to push when she just wanted to sleep, because the epidural had finally kicked in. Also, she didn't really know how to push like the doctor wanted. But she couldn't even imagine asking about something like that. Obviously, she thought, women who are giving birth should understand exactly what pushing entails. Or else they shouldn't be mothers.

The midwife held her legs while the doctor attached the vacuum extractor to Dogge's head and pulled him out. The vacuum left a red bulge at the top of his head, and when he was out and Jill got to see him, she thought at first that he was malformed, and that he would always look like that, and it was her fault because she hadn't been able to get him out of her body the way she was meant to.

When they placed the baby on her breast, and he just lay there like a knocked-out jellyfish, she looked up at the doctor. She was still loopy from the epidural and the gas and air.

'Is that him? Is that my baby?'

It was impossible to conceive of the fact that this was her child; he didn't look like any baby she'd ever seen.

The doctor chuckled dismissively, maybe he thought she was joking. The midwife smiled and rubbed her arm.

'He's beautiful,' was all she said. 'Everything looks fine.'

But Jill had thought there must be something wrong. He was all sticky, and his skin was blue.

'He's perfect,' the midwife said when she asked again. A little more sharply this time.

Before the delivery, she'd never considered how babies wave their hands in front of themselves like blind zombies, and that they open and close their toothless mouths like pulsating protozoa. She had thought they were cute, like kittens. She spent hours lying awake on the maternity ward, staring at the baby she had just birthed. He was ugly and slept on his back, with his hands in a pose of surrender over his head. His face was covered in tiny red spots, his hair was dark, almost black, even though she and Teo were both blonde. The same black hair grew on his arms and legs too, he was practically furry.

Jill had fingered the pendant of her necklace and stared at her child. The midwife had placed him on his back in a transparent plastic box on wheels that was made up with the county-stamped hospital sheets. He was snoring – he'd just been born and was snoring already, a grown-up sound.

No one had given Jill anything that could help her recognize Dogge. Nothing that would help her say *Hi there, little one*, in a gentle mum voice that would, in some magical way, make him feel perfectly calm and safe.

Who are you? she had thought, time and again. *Who are you?*

We'd better get to the hospital,' said the chaplain. 'We'll give you a ride,' said the police officer. 'I'm not feeling very well,' said Jill.

50

Weed's wife Sara found out what had happened from a nervous rookie who rang her doorbell an hour after Weed was taken to the hospital. He didn't wait for them to sit down before he began to speak; he started in the front hall.

It took a moment for Sara to understand that it wasn't her husband who had been struck in the head, that no one had hurt him, but that he was being detained at the police station just half a mile away. Then the rookie left her, advising that Weed was not allowed to have visitors or speak to anyone on the phone.

'Unfortunately, I can't say more,' he said.

'Would you like something to drink?' Sara had asked. 'A cup of coffee, perhaps?'

He wouldn't. He had to go, there was a lot to do.

By ten in the morning, three photographers were leaning against the fence outside Sara and Weed's

419

terraced house. One of them was eating a banana.
When he had finished, Sara watched as he lifted the
lid of their wheelie bin and dropped the peel inside.
She wanted to go out and shout at him until he left,
but instead she brought an empty cardboard box up
from the basement. She unfolded it and pressed it
against the kitchen window so they couldn't see inside. Then she sat down at the table. Before her was
a cup of tea. She couldn't remember preparing it, and
stared at the mug as the beverage cooled.

The children came in one by one; Eva climbed
into her lap, and even though her thirteen-year-old
body hardly fit, Sara pulled her close, pressed her
cheek to Eva's. Sam stood beside them, and Sara took
his hand.

Jacob, their oldest son, went down to the store.
But he stopped before he reached it. A TV station
was filming the cordons and interviewing passersby.
Jacob didn't want to risk being recognized.

'What should I say if someone asks?' he asked his
mother when he came home. He sounded angry at
first, and then he started to cry. 'Should I say Dad
murdered a kid? That he killed someone? Did he,
Mum? Did Dad kill Dogge?'

'I have to call the lawyer,' said Sara. 'I have to ask
him what's going to happen to the store.'

'The store?' Jacob shook his head. 'Forget about
the store. Ask him if Dad is a murderer, can you ask
him that? Stop talking about that fucking store. I
hate it.'

Sara let her son go. But she didn't have the energy to make any calls. *I'll do it later*, she thought, and pushed her cup of cold tea away. *If that boy dies... They'll have to tell us if he does, right? They'll call us, won't they?*

Two hours later, Weed's lawyer called. He wondered if she wanted to pack a bag for Weed, so he didn't have to wear jail clothes. Maybe she could send something for Weed to wear during the detention hearing?

'How long will he have to stay there?' Sara asked. 'When can he come home?'

'The detention hearing will take place within the next three days,' said the lawyer. 'We'll know more after that.'

Sara chose a small bag. She brought it to the lawyer's office. He wasn't there, so she left it at the reception desk, with a young woman who had a shrill voice and pouty lips. She was on the phone as Sara explained why she was there; she raised her eyebrows to show she was listening, nodded, and lifted the bag over the counter. Sara went home again. The journalists were gone.

Did Dogge die? she thought as she opened the garage door and drove the car inside. *Should I have asked the receptionist about that?*

Just after three o'clock on Sunday afternoon, Weed was moved to the jail. It was much shorter than the trip from Weed's Market to Karolinska Hospital, because the jail was in the building next door to the station. He and the police officer walked there by way of an underground tunnel made of concrete, with flickering fluorescent lights on the ceiling. Weed hit his head on the elevator door as they rode up to the intake area.

'Are you okay?' asked the officer who was escorting him.

'I'm fine,' Weed replied. But he had to stop and hold his head before they could go on. 'No worries,' he added. 'No worries at all.'

That evening, after he'd eaten his dinner, a flat meat loaf cut into squares along with pickles, cold potatoes, and an ice-cold sauce, he was allowed to call Sara. They weren't allowed to talk about the incident. A guard stood next to him the entire time he was on the phone.

'I'm fine,' he said when Sara answered the phone. She was crying. 'Did you talk to my lawyer?' he wondered. 'You have to ask what we're supposed to do with the store. And the tree. Can you go buy the Christmas tree?'

51

When they called from the reception desk to say he had visitors, Farid was surprised. Although Leila had been summoned to the local Våringe station for a formal interview, Farid had expected that the incident with Dogge would prompt her to stay home, maybe even make her think the investigation was on hold. But now, here she was – and she was even on time. The receptionist wondered if he wanted them to come up to his office.

'Lots of folks running around here today. And these two in particular seem a little on edge.'

Two? Farid thought. *Did Leila get herself counsel?*

'Okay,' he said. 'Please go ahead and send them up in the lift, I'll meet them there.'

But Leila didn't have a lawyer with her; Tusse was accompanying her. He was leaning against the wall of the lift when the door opened. For an instant, before his reason caught up with his thoughts, Farid thought it was Billy. It had been two months since

Billy rode up in the same lift, along with his mother, to join the disengagement programme.

Farid nodded at Tusse and rubbed Leila's arm.

'Do you know how Dogge is doing?' she asked.

'No,' he replied. 'It's serious. But that's all the information I have.'

They walked down the corridor and into Farid's office. He took a seat at his desk chair, while Tusse and Leila took the two chairs he'd brought in.

'Do you like coffee?' he asked. He turned to Tusse and nodded at the Thermos on his desk. He'd brought three mugs in from the staff room. 'It's all I've got, I'm afraid.'

'Sure, guess that's fine,' said Tusse.

He accepted the mug Farid handed him, but set it on the table without tasting it.

'We need to talk,' he said.

'Yes,' said Farid. 'I think that's an excellent idea. I'll record our conversation, is that okay with the two of you?'

Leila cleared her throat.

'Can we wait a moment? I would first like to say a few words that are not recorded.'

'Sure. No problem.'

She picked up her cup of coffee, turned it a few times in her hands, and cleared her throat.

'When I came to Sweden, I got to know a woman with the Church of Sweden. Her name was Silke. She was from Germany and married to a Swede. We were pregnant. I was expecting Billy, she was expecting her little girl. She was a Christian. We didn't talk much religion, only sometimes. But she told me about a psalm. She sang it for me. *You cannot fall farther...* I don't remember exact words... *You cannot fall farther than God's hand. He protects me, he catches me.* Do you know that psalm?'

Farid shook his head.

'I don't believe in God.'

'No. But do you believe that we must protect... if someone falls, is it our duty to catch? That God's duty is our duty? That we must try our best to do as He would?'

'Yes, I suppose I do.'

'Then we believe the same.'

Tusse was unusually still. Not as nervous as he usually was. He glanced at his mother as if to assure himself she was okay. Leila went on.

'I also believe that God catches those who fall. But we have to be there to do the same. When God doesn't...' She held Farid's gaze. 'We have to catch the children who fall. That is our duty.'

'Yes.' Farid didn't know what to say, but before he could say anything Leila raised her voice.

'Billy was my responsibility. I did not save him. I will never forgive myself.' She cleared her throat. 'I must live with that. To keep going... I must save my other children. There is nothing else I can do. And you must help me. That is your responsibility.

God doesn't take away our responsibility. He makes it easier to see. He explains what we must do. We catch the children for God.'

'I want to help you, Leila. I do. But you're going to have to—'

She cut him off.

'Tusane told me about when Mehdi taught Billy and Dogge to shoot. He told me what he told you. Tusane said, we have to tell. Mehdi cannot go on. He is the children's hero, but dangerous man. More dangerous than I thought, more dangerous than you think too. And every year, every day, it gets worse. He brought guns into my son's life. If Mehdi hadn't done that, Billy would still be here. My son would be alive. That is the truth. If Mehdi didn't exist, my son would be alive. God will punish him. And I know you want to punish Mehdi. I know you want to save the children, you tried to save Billy. You want to save Tusane.'

Farid nodded.

'Yes, I do.'

'I want that too. Tusane wants that too. But there are problems.' Leila picked up her mug again. She looked down at the coffee but still didn't drink it. 'There are things you don't know.'

'That is a problem,' said Farid. 'I'd really like for you to tell me as much as you can.'

'You think that. You think that will help you. But it's not true. Because if we tell the truth, everything we know, then you cannot get Mehdi. What we know is the opposite. It helps Mehdi. I don't want to help Mehdi. But the truth will help him. The courts don't listen to what the heart knows, what God knows, the courts only listen to evidence. So I think the best thing is if we only tell you. No one else. No recording. Because I have to save my other children from Mehdi, from guns, from Våringe. And you have to help me, that is your duty. So I will tell you everything. Then you can decide what we should do.'

52

You can come say hello to Douglas.'

That was what they said, that Jill could go in and say hello to him. What they didn't say was that Dogge couldn't say hello back. No one explained what his injuries would look like.

The chaplain who had come to get her followed her in.

'He's unconscious,' he said when he saw Dogge.

'We've sedated him,' said the doctor.

If they hadn't insisted it was Dogge under the sheets on the narrow hospital bed, Jill never would have believed it. The creature they showed her was pale and grey and tiny; not even Teo had changed that much when he was sick. And there were tubes and wires everywhere. Dogge on one end and machines on the other. One tube snaked in under the covers to what she assumed was a catheter, there were electrical leads running under the bandage that went around his head and down over his face.

In his throat was a thick plastic hose. Around the bed, everywhere, were screens blinking with numbers and graphs.

Jill didn't understand what they wanted her to do. Should she touch him? But where? What would happen if she accidentally pulled out a tube or blocked an entrance? Was she supposed to understand the information on the screens? Ask questions about them? Sound the alarm, maybe press a button if anything happened?

She stopped about a yard away from the bed. Why had they said she should say hello to him?

The nurse who'd shown her into the room looked at her with her bright-blue eyes. She pointed at a chair that was far too close to the bed.

'Go ahead, sit down and talk to him,' she insisted. 'Even if he's not conscious that doesn't mean he can't take in his surroundings.'

Jill nodded. *But what does that mean?* she thought. *Why is it called being unconscious if you're still conscious of things?*

Her head was spinning, she thought she was going to lose her balance, so she sat gingerly on the chair. Mums in hospital dramas visited sons in comas. Jill started talking, loudly and clearly enough so the nurse would hear.

'Hi, honey. Mummy is here now. Mummy loves you. Everything will be fine.'

———

The first time Jill got pregnant, she was only sixteen. She had a second abortion before she turned
twenty, but after that she'd had enough. She refused
to keep bopping along to the weary song that was
her life, just singing the refrain on repeat until she
reached the stage of saggy boobs and broken dreams.
Instead she left her boyfriend and her part-time job at
the petrol station and moved to Stockholm.

'It's the best decision I ever made,' she liked to
say. She started working at the front desk of a bank
and shared an apartment in Huddinge with a girl she
found in the classifieds.

On her first summer holiday, she and four girlfriends went interrailing. She met Teo on a local
train between Morlaix and Paris. Jill and her friends
stepped into a compartment where a guy was sleeping, slouched in one of the window seats. His longish
hair was wavy and medium blond; he was wearing
ripped jeans and a snow-white T-shirt with the cuffs
rolled up.

'I'll take that one, with a cherry on top,' she'd
joked to her friends. And then she talked at length
about everything she wanted to do with him, detailed
explanations of the positions they'd try, and how he
was welcome to take her as rough as he wanted. Her
friends laughed, softly so as not to wake the French
stranger who simply oozed southern Europe and ad-
venture. Teo waited until they were nearly to Paris
before he turned to her, put on his most confident
smile, and said, in Swedish: 'When do we start?

Would you like to make out for a while first, or are we just going straight for it?' And then he bent forward, cupped the back of her neck, and kissed her. One of her friends wolf-whistled. Never had Jill experienced anything so romantic.

She had waved goodbye to her friends as they boarded a train for Germany the next day. Instead she went with Teo and his money to Saint-Tropez, Monte Carlo, Elba and Capri. She sent an email to her boss and quit her job when they made it to Florence, and three months later, after they returned to Stockholm, they moved in together. Teo had a house his parents had given him. It had high ceilings, plasterwork and wainscoting in every room. The parquet floors creaked and the pipes gurgled every time you turned on one of the rusty taps. From one of the upstairs windows you could see the sea. Teo hated the house, he said, but Jill was sure it had to be a lie; the house looked like something straight out of a movie. The peeling paint on the gables, the cracked flagstones in the garden – it was the shabby parts that made it truly refined, she thought. That was how you knew it was special, more valuable than what you'd find in a regular house.

The fact that Teo drank too much and did cocaine every single day of their trip didn't seem that remarkable to Jill – they were young, they were living life, burning the candle at both ends since it was more fun that way. And in those early days, he had always wanted her. They slept naked, and she would wake up to his erection against her butt. As soon as he noticed her shifting toward him, if only just a millimetre, he would push inside her. He was never too drunk to fuck; no matter how high he got, it never made him less horny.

When they got back to Stockholm, it was different. Teo had things he needed to do, deals to sew up, guys he had to meet, and he needed something to get himself through his meetings and other stuff to give him the energy to party at night. On the few days he didn't have meetings, and no parties were planned, he had to take yet other drugs so he could sleep. And that stuff knocked him out entirely, sometimes for days at a time. At first she tried to get him to sleep with her, but more and more often he passed out on the sofa or on the floor of his office. Once he ended up lying on the kitchen floor for almost twenty-four hours. She let him be, but put a blanket over him so he wouldn't freeze.

Jill took it easier than Teo, and she thought life was pretty decent. Her anxiety was milder, the evenings almost always smooth and breezy. It didn't matter so much that mornings were tougher and she had to sleep alone and Teo's friends didn't seem all that interested in her. He gave her a credit card, and one time, when he'd struck a good deal with an old classmate, they went to Las Vegas for the weekend and got married. When they came home, her old girlfriends took her out for a night and threw her a belated hen party. Teo didn't like them, but he didn't say anything when she got home. Not even about the fact that they'd dressed her up as a bride and hung a 'kiss me' sign around her neck.

'Where did you go?' he asked. 'Good,' he said when she answered. 'No chance anyone I know would have seen you there.'

They'd been together for almost two years when Jill got pregnant. She was on the pill, but they had been in an intense partying period and maybe she had been a little forgetful sometimes. They'd spent almost four months in Los Angeles with a man Teo ran a business with. By the time she took a pregnancy test, it was too late to do anything about it. And Teo was happy. He wanted to be a dad, knew what he wanted to name his son, liked to imagine all the things they would do together. They lay close beside each other, making plans.

'I'm not going to be like my dad,' Teo promised. 'And you're the polar opposite of my evil bitch mother. We're going to be the best parents in the world. Or the hottest, definitely the hottest.'

Do you want me to contact any family members?' the chaplain asked. 'Your parents, perhaps? Or Dogge's paternal grandparents?'

'No, thank you,' said Jill. 'That won't be necessary.'

She had only visited Teo's parents three times. The first time was soon after they were married. As they ate breakfast on that first morning, Teo's father went into the guest room where they had slept and found four grams of cocaine in the desk drawer. He threw them out.

Still, during those first years there was money, quite a lot of money. Jill assumed it came from her in-laws. They could travel, more than Jill had travelled in all her life, and they stayed at the kinds of hotels she'd only ever seen in magazines. But the more time that passed, the more sporadic their trips became. Teo made bad deals, he partied, it was expensive to party the way Teo did, and he shopped – clothes, wine, art, there wasn't enough money. The house in Rönnviken was owned by a trust Teo's parents had created. She and Teo weren't allowed to sell it.

'They started that trust so they could control me,' Teo declared. 'My parents hate me. They're punishing me for living a different life from them.'

When his business deals went poorly, his melt-downs became more common and sex increasingly infrequent. He would explode into rages without warning; they came out of nowhere and sucked all the oxygen out of the room. As soon as these rages ended, Teo would forget about them. Jill and Dogge were left behind among the toxic gases his anger pro-duced. The sex got more aggressive, but he had diffi-culty getting hard; she learned to cram it in anyhow and pretend she believed him when he said he had come.

'I hate my life,' he'd said once to Jill, when their relationship was brand-new. 'You're the only thing I love.'

When she met Teo, she thought all her dreams were about to be realized. Those dreams weren't crushed all at once – they rusted away gradually, quietly crumbling, slowly breaking up. By the time they were gone, she no longer remembered what it felt like to have hope. Teo stopped talking about love. He didn't even say he hated his life. There was no need.

The machines Dogge was hooked up to didn't look like the ones she'd seen in movies and on TV, but Jill knew how they would sound when death arrived, the flat line and the protracted beep, like tinnitus.

She waited for that sound. She stared at the machine, at the curve, at the bundle in the bed. Her eyes stung, she glanced down, turned away. But she kept waiting.

Death would free her, just as it had done when it freed her from Teo. When the tone came, there would no longer be anything she had to do, nothing to be held accountable for or take responsibility for. When Dogge died, there would be nothing else for her to screw up.

53

Thanks for being willing to come in again, we appreciate it.'

Svante smelled like mulled wine. 'First, a few words about Dogge. He is in critical but stable condition, whatever that means. They've promised to keep us in the loop. But we're not going to be able to talk to him for a good long time, that much is clear. So we have to find some other way to make progress on Mehdi. Because we are not going to let that bastard run around recruiting new kids into his gang, just so he can waste them later. We're going to put a stop to it. Okay?' As he exhaled he put on a smile so wide Farid thought his face was going to split in two. 'Anyway, I promise you're not going to regret coming in today. Because there may be almost a week left before Christmas Eve, and a ton of crap going on, but I thought I'd hand out the Christmas presents early.'

Farid was sitting beside Lotta, who was dressed for the day in an extra-tight T-shirt that said FEMI-NIST across her breasts.

Is that a warning? Farid thought. Or handling instructions? And why is the text in that particular location? Is it a test?

'Sebastian?' Svante swept a hand towards the forensic coordinator as though he were a ringmaster and Sebastian the lion tamer. 'The stage is all yours!'

'We have two fantastic pieces of news. I'll start with the one from Holland.' Sebastian's cheeks were pink; he kept his eyes on his paper. 'The technicians are certain. As certain as technicians can be. We can report that the traces of DNA, the so-called mixed DNA found on one of the cartridges we picked up at the scene of the murder, came from Mehdi. We got the results from our colleagues in Amsterdam just an hour ago.' He exhaled and gave a big smile.

'The chief there is a good friend of mine,' Svante said, pleased. 'I spoke to him when we sent the stuff down. We were at a conference in Brussels together earlier this year and I dropped him a line to make him see we needed answers fast. He assured me that they'd put our sample at the top of the pile. But I didn't think we'd get it back this fast. I would have guessed around Midsummer.'

'But that's not all.' Sebastian looked around the room. 'The techs from the chicken factory analyzed the four bullets they found up there. And

I don't want to beat around the proverbial bush, so...um...well...'

Obviously, Farid thought, *you can't just spit it out.*

'The first piece of good news is that they found cartridges up at the factory of the exact same type and model as the ones used in the murder. Same manufacturer, even. They've compared them with the bullets we pulled out of the tree up by the playground and the ones found inside Billy. The degree of certainty that they were fired by the same weapon is between +3 and +4. +4 for the ones we found in the tree, and +3 for the ones from Billy. Because the ones in Billy were...not in the same condition, you might say. In any case, that's a really high likelihood. +4 is the highest. When I talked to them on the phone, they just said flat out that yeah, these bullets were fired by the same weapon. So that's...you know, a win.'

Bengt clapped his hands together.

Svante let out a deep sigh. He almost looked moved.

'In addition,' he said, 'and this is almost hard to believe. I can hardly remember the last time I got so much good news at once in an investigation. Because our very own fave feminist has good news too.' He stopped for a dramatic pause. 'Li—I mean Lotta! Lotta on Feminist Troublemaker Street, would you tell us what you've been up to this weekend?'

'Sure,' she said slowly.

Farid looked at her in surprise. She looked cheerful. He'd never seen her acting cheerful before. Lotta went on.

'I spent some time on the phones. And I started with the burner Dogge used to text Billy to ask him to come to the playground.' She cleared her throat. 'The same burner he called 112 on, and the same one he used to call Billy a whole lot, without getting an answer. So this is also the same phone he used, right before he texted Billy, to talk to someone else. We know the number he called goes to another unregistered pay-as-you-go phone.'

Everyone nodded.

'But we want to be able to link it to Mehdi,' Lotta went on. 'So I did a few different things. First I managed to find out which Pressbyrån sold the SIM card. Since the phone companies keep track of which sales outlets they sell their SIM cards to, that wasn't all that difficult. But identifying exactly when a specific card is sold isn't quite as simple, because the sales outlet doesn't have to notify the phone company about any of that. In this case we got lucky, because the SIM card was delivered to the Pressbyrån in question on November ninth, and the number Dogge called from his burner was activated on November eleventh. That means it was purchased sometime between these two dates. And Pressbyrån gave us information about all the credit card purchases made during that period for amounts that equalled or exceeded the cost of the SIM card. There were quite a few.'

Lotta took a breath and brought up a long list of numbers on the projector screen.

'But we got a hit when we requested the cardholders. Mehdi Ahmad made a purchase on the morning of November eleventh, with his personal debit card.' She pointed at a row that was also circled. 'According to the cash register statement, he paid for four items. A can of *snus*, a pack of gum, a Coke and a SIM card.'

'But that's not all.' Svante nodded happily. 'Go on, by all means, go on.'

Lotta brought up a new list.

'We also checked Mehdi's social phone, obviously. His official one. Where has it been? And where has it been in relation to the prepaid SIM card?' She stood up, went to the screen, and ran her finger down the rows. 'Mehdi's social phone and the anonymous phone connected to the same mast – that is, they were in the same place – on more than sixty occasions in the three weeks between the activation of the phone number and the murder.' She stopped her finger on one line. 'For instance, on the night between December sixth and seventh.'

'Damn, Lotta,' Sebastian said, with admiration. Now his cheeks were bright red. He looked like he'd love to get her alone in the room.

'You get it,' said Svante. 'Not only can we link Mehdi to the cartridges that were used during the murder. Thanks to the debit card payment, we can also link him to the prepaid phone Dogge called right before the murder. But we need more! Was he talking

441

to Mehdi? Well, thank Christ, he was. Why else would Mehdi's private phone be in the same place as the phone Dogge called? Shit's finally moving now, it's finally starting to stink around here.'

'Hell, yes!' Sebastian said.

'And, listen,' Svante turned to Farid. 'You interrogated Leila Khalid yesterday, right? How did it go? If she were to decide to tell us something we can use, I think we could put this case to bed. And if we can get baby brother to talk about their target practice up at the chicken factory, we can show that the murder weapon is Mehdi's. Then we could have a very Merry Christmas. Tell us, Farid. We're all ears.'

Farid cleared his throat.

'Unfortunately,' he said, and gulped, 'there was no interrogation. She never showed up. I think she was stressed out by what happened to Dogge. I'll try again in a few days.'

'You do that,' said Svante. 'And focus on that Tusse in the meantime. If he's scared, you just tell him we can get Mehdi off the streets if he helps us. What do you think about bringing up witness protection with them? They tell us about Mehdi and we get them out of Våringe? It really shouldn't be impossible to make that happen. Who the hell wants to stay in Våringe these days? Not the Khalid-Alis, that's for sure. Talk to our friends at Victim Assistance, tell them we've got some witnesses we need to protect. I'll ask the family liaison to arrange a meeting, that can hardly hurt. Make them understand that we'll do anything to help them feel safe. We need them, Farid, and we need you to get them to cooperate. That's why you're here. And now we've paved the way for you. All you need to do is get them to talk. Okay? Do you think you can manage that?'

54

The driveway of Farid's two-storey, yellow-brick house was white with new-fallen snow, velvety soft. He drove silently up and parked in front of the garage. The house was dark, except for the Christmas stars, one in every window. He left the car outside to keep from waking Natascha; her room was right above the garage.

Nadja and Farid had moved in together two months after they met. They lived in his apartment in Våringe for the first few years; it was a few blocks from the house where he'd grown up and where his parents still lived. Farid had always longed to get away from the leaning high-rises of pale-grey concrete, the glassed-in balconies, the laminate floors, the lights and noise of the highway, the hiss of tyres on asphalt, the sweeping, bright headlights and flickering streetlights, all year-round, every hour of every day. Still, there was a part of him that missed it.

For the first few years after they moved out of Våringe, he'd kept going back to take the dog for a run in the park on Sundays. There were always lots of people there. If the weather was nice, they would be playing football, *brännboll*, and even cricket and boules. A group of older folks tended to gather and bend their bodies in the same kind of yoga positions his wife did a few mornings each time they went on holiday. The dog park was full of off-lead pups, and groups of people would gather on every available grassy surface to have a picnic or listen to the radio or read. There was a lot of litter and the lights seldom worked, but there was no point in replacing the bulbs, because each night they would be broken by those who took over the park after nightfall. But during the day, the park was bright, never dangerous, just full of people Farid knew or recognized.

He went to the kitchen, where he opened the fridge and closed it again. There were two half-empty mugs on the counter. He poured the tea out of them and stuck them in the dishwasher, then started it up. The stairs to the second floor creaked. The door to Ella's room was wide open. The two-foot plastic Christmas tree she'd got last year was decorated and lit. She was asleep, with one leg on top of the covers and her arm thrown over her pillow. When he stroked her forehead, she turned onto her side but didn't wake.

The next room was Felicia's. The only part of her visible was her fringe, and she had a new string of lights on her headboard. Farid turned them off.

The window of the kids' room in their apartment in Våringe had never been totally black, only a deep violet, lit up by the surrounding traffic. Here, the night sky settled over them, dark as the inside of a tin can. Natascha was still afraid of the dark; she preferred to sleep with her bedside lamp on.

But tonight it was off. He sat down on the floor just inside her door and listened to her breathing, just as he'd done when she was a newborn. Natascha was the same age as the boys. If they still lived in Våringe, she probably would have been in Billy's class.

When Farid was fourteen, he'd had issues. In just two months during the second term of Year 9, he had skipped school nine days in a row, got caught shoplifting, tried pot, and got way too drunk at a school dance. When he fainted on the dance floor, the hosts called an ambulance. He was taken to the Maria Clinic, where he got to sober up in a locked room with a mattress on the floor. He'd had to sit on the mattress while they hosed down the floor to clean up after the person who'd been there before him, and when he smelled the odour rising from the floor drain it made him puke so violently that it felt like his throat would start to bleed. His parents came to the station. When his mum tried to hug him, he pushed her off so violently she fell over. At that, his dad grabbed him by the shoulders and shoved him up against the wall until the staff arrived to separate them. His mum cried in the car on the way home, while his dad was angrier than Farid had ever seen him. But he had made it through compulsory school and never tried drugs again, and the next time he got drunk it was his high school graduation. He'd asked himself so many times: What had prompted him to get his act together? He didn't have a good answer.

You moved out of Våringe. You moved your children. You can stop working there too. It's not your responsibility. Someone else can take over.

He stayed on Natascha's floor for almost an hour before getting up and going to his own bed. Nadja was awake when he climbed in. The lights were out, but he could see the shine of her eyes. She didn't say anything, just lifted the blanket for him, let him come into her warmth, put her arms around him.

When she placed her hands on his cheeks, light as a feather, he realized that he was crying. She kissed the tears away and brought his head to her breast. He lay like that for a while, perfectly still.

'I can't,' he whispered after a while. 'I can't handle losing another one. Nothing I do, nothing helps. They just keep dying. And Weed? He's not a bad person, Nadja. He's not the enemy. Why should he...it's not fair. Weed isn't...No matter what I do, the people who are actually guilty go free and the best people are sacrificed.'

'Shhh...' she said, pulling him even closer, rocking him. 'Sleep, honey. Take it one hour at a time. Now it's time to sleep.'

THE BOYS

The day before their very last job, Billy called Dogge. He was never the one to initiate contact anymore, but this time he did. He asked Dogge to come to his house. Dogge hadn't been to Billy's place since Leila had asked him not to come back.

It was just past ten in the morning when he rang the doorbell. It was getting cold out, his bike had slipped on the ice in the tunnel and he had had to walk the last little bit. The front hall looked like it had just been cleaned, almost no shoes or outerwear was there. Leila was at work and Billy's siblings were at school. Isak hadn't lived there in over six months.

Billy was home alone, yet he closed the door after them when they went into his room. The Glock was on the bed, it was the first thing Dogge saw.

'What the hell?'

'Tusse was the one who took the bag from the storage unit.'

'Tusse?'

'Yeah. He saw us go take it to the basement. And when the cops got me he went down to get it. He was afraid they would search there.'

'But...' Dogge was standing with his back to the door, unsure how to continue. 'Why?'

'He gave the bag to Dad.'

'Your dad?'

Billy nodded. He kept talking.

Questions began to pile up in Dogge's mind. They swelled suddenly, festering blisters, as though he had stepped in a thicket of stinging nettles. Yet he didn't give voice to a single one.

Billy told Dogge that he had discussed what to do with his father. Isak had decided that the best plan was to ask the imam for help. Hassan acted as an intermediary, helped them return the weapons to Mehdi without involving the police, and at the same time they set up a payment plan for Billy's disengagement.

'I'm moving away,' Dogge heard Billy say. 'Mum says I can live with my great-uncle. When this is over, I'm out of here. They can't get me if I leave Sweden.'

Billy had spoken to so many people, he had done so much. Made so many decisions. But he hadn't said a word about any of this to Dogge.

Dogge gulped. He swallowed down his tears and he swallowed what he wanted to say, that Billy hadn't told him, that all the while he'd let Dogge believe that the bag was still missing, that he had talked to everyone in his family, to Hassan the imam, about what he could do to get free, but hadn't said a word to Dogge. He couldn't bring himself to look at Billy. So he looked at the Glock.

'Yeah.' Billy smiled faintly and went to the bed. 'Dad bought it off Mehdi. He had to pay extra for it. Dad said it was for him. But then he gave it to me, he wants me to have it for protection. But I don't know, I can't defend myself if I don't have any ammunition. And he didn't buy any of that. I don't know what Dad...I don't think that occurred to him, and now I'm out of here.' Billy looked up and met Dogge's gaze. He looked sad, almost like he was about to cry. 'I don't need it. And Tusse...I don't want Tusse or Dad to have it. I can't take it with me. And I thought maybe you might need it?' His eyes had grown shiny. He cast a pleading look at Dogge. 'I can't...but you and I are like...at least, we were...Shit, know what I'm saying? I know Mehdi might...Once I leave he might...and I don't want you to...'

Dogge gulped.

'I could come with you? When you move. I could come with you.'

Billy wiped his eyes with the back of his hand. He was annoyed, Dogge could tell.

'You're so fucking stupid sometimes. Why do you say such stupid things? Obviously you can't come with me. You can't move to Africa, what would you do there? And besides, I mean, it's not like Mehdi's some big-time gangster. He's a big ugly fish in a tiny fucking pond and he's going to get eaten up, and he knows it, so he's trying to mess with us to show how badass he is. That stuff about the whorehouse in Berlin is just bullshit, basically every word he says is just bullshit. He doesn't know any millionaires or CEOs. If he was rich for real, would we have to steal candy from Weed's Market when he wants to watch a movie with some chick? Mehdi's a poser. He doesn't have any power outside Våringe, zip.'

'Or you could stay?' Dogge scratched the back of his knee as hard as he could, but it was hard to get at the itch through his jeans. 'If you say he's not that . . . and we're going to pay it all off. You can stay.'

'I can't stay, I told you. You have to get it through your head. I have to go.'

'But we were supposed to—'

Billy punched the wall.

'Just shut up. I said I'm going to do that last thing, I fucking promised, stop going on about it.'

'Then where are the grenades? Where did you put them? It's super dangerous just to have them lying around. What if Tusse finds them, what if he does something stupid, where did you put them?'

'I've got them, don't worry.'

'Where, though? Aren't you worried your mum will find them? Or Tusse. What if Tusse finds them, and—'

Billy cut him off, picked up the Glock from the bed, and began to herd him out the door.

'They're not here, okay? They're in a safe place. Goddammit, just quit with all your fucking questions. I'll bring them tomorrow, I swear. We'll meet up just like we planned. You should go home now.'

'Promise?'

'Quit fucking nagging me. Take the Glock. Just take it. I don't want to see it ever again. And go home. Goodbye, Dogge.'

55

Today's lunch was fish and roe with potatoes and wrinkled peas. It said so on the weekly menu Weed had received when he got to jail. He spent twenty minutes pushing the food around on his plate. Then his door opened again. He was offered some marshmallow Christmas sweets from a dish.

'Merry Christmas,' said the guard.

'No thanks,' said Weed.

'We'll be leaving in ten minutes,' said the guard.

'Okay,' said Weed.

The prosecutor wanted to keep him in jail until the preliminary investigation was completed. Weed was under suspicion with probable cause for either attempted murder or grievous bodily harm.

'We can expect you'll remain in custody since the minimum sentence is so long,' Weed's lawyer had said.

'How long is it?' Weed had asked.

'If the prosecutor has his way? At least ten years, but up to life,' said Weed's lawyer. 'But if the boy survives,' he added, hesitantly, 'it might not be so bad.'

The detention hearing was held in a room in the same building as the jail, with just a few seats for spectators. A security guard stood by the door. Weed was wearing his own clothes: a cheap but well-fitting suit, a shirt that one of the jailers had hung on the chair in his cell the day before so it wouldn't get wrinkled, and a narrow tie he wasn't allowed to put on until they were in the lift on their way to the courtroom.

His head spun each time he stood up. The nausea wouldn't go away. It was as though he'd broken something inside his own head, not just in the boy's. When he first stepped into the courtroom, he thought he would faint, but he quickly got hold of himself.

There were more people in attendance than there were seats. Still, he spotted Sara first. She reached for him, even though they were too far apart. She would have to leave before proceedings began, the lawyer had prepared them for this. He had also told them that the store could open again. When Weed last spoke to Sara on the phone, she had asked what this really meant. They didn't have the money to hire enough people to run the whole show, and she wasn't going to be able to manage what needed to be done on her own.

'Every unfamiliar face I see,' she'd said. 'Every stranger could be one of the vultures, one of the people who wants to get under my skin and lay me bare to find out things I would never tell anyone.'

'You don't have to open the store,' Weed had said.

'The people I know,' said Sara, 'our friends, even *they* look at me like they're demanding something. I don't know what they want. I can't give it to them. I never want to go back.'

The judge began to speak once the guards had closed the doors. All the seats were taken, and another dozen people stood along the wall.

'Welcome,' said the judge. 'I'm going to throw you all out in a moment. This will be a private proceeding.'

During the detention hearing, no one called Weed 'Weed'. Here, they used his full name, Shemal Aydin, just as it was written in his Swedish passport, and of course he knew how this sounded. He had taken aim and struck the unarmed Douglas Arnfeldt, aged fourteen, in the head with a baseball bat. No one pointed out the fact that the fourteen-year-old outweighed him by at least twenty pounds and was almost four inches taller.

Weed's lawyer spent four minutes arguing that Weed should be released. He wasn't a flight risk, he had only Swedish citizenship, and his connection to Sweden was significant. Nor should he be kept in custody for reasons relating to the investigation. The technical investigation was already completed, and Weed had accepted the prosecutor's preliminary statement of the criminal act as charged. But the prosecutor ended by reminding the court that there existed sufficient grounds for continued custody. He said so in a voice that sounded tired, almost resigned. The judge just nodded.

Then the judge allowed the spectators to return to the room. While the decision was read, Weed stared at the table in front of him. When it was over, he stood up, turned to the jail guard, and put out his hands so the man could cuff him.

Weed didn't want to go home, he didn't want to see anyone. He just wanted to go back to his cramped cell with its narrow bed and bolted-down furniture.

'I'll be home soon,' he said to Sara as he walked by her. She was crying.

'We have to move,' she said.

We were never supposed to have to flee again, he thought. *Do you remember how I promised you that?* But he didn't remind her.

56

Farid didn't usually attend detention hearings if it wasn't absolutely necessary. But this was no usual detention. What had happened at Weed's Market had become a matter of national urgency. Everyone had an opinion on what had happened, and why, and what should be done about it.

Weed had become a hero. There was a Facebook group called Nobilify Weed Now! that had been started by someone calling himself ProudSwedish-Man. Another group was called Give That *Blatte*-Killer a Medal. They had eighty thousand members combined, and all had apparently failed to realize that the boy who had taken a baseball bat to the head was neither a *blatte* nor dead. Mohammed Karim, a member of parliament from the Moderate Party, had tweeted, 'Finally some effective crime-busting in Våringe. Release that hero now! #supportsudden.'

But there was another side as well. Hitting a child in the head with a baseball bat – what kind of person would do such a thing? If he died, and Weed wasn't charged with murder, would that mean that society had accepted that shoplifting was punishable by death? And in between, the minister of justice had publicly promised another investigation and more resources to get a handle on 'the thugs who have taken over our vulnerable suburbs'.

Farid attended the detention hearing to remind himself that Weed was an acquaintance. That he was a person Farid knew. But when Weed stepped into the courtroom, it took a second for Farid to recognize him. He'd spent three days in jail. He displayed none of the usual hallmarks of the life that typically landed people in jail. No nervous tics or hands that wouldn't stay still in his lap, no pockmarks on his face, no bad teeth. Weed was skinny, freshly shaved, with a recent haircut. Until today, Farid had thought he seemed healthy and fit. Still, it was already clear his life had been taken from him.

When the judge explained that the hearing would take place behind closed doors, all the spectators had to leave the courtroom, including Farid. He thought about talking to Sara, expressing his condolences, perhaps asking how Weed was doing and whether they were getting the help they needed. But even if it wasn't his investigation, it felt like this would be crossing a line he should stay far away from.

And then he spotted Leila.

She was wearing a dark hijab and a heavy coat with a hood, and had taken a seat far from the door, right next to one of the two coffee machines. There were four tables, but she had pulled out one of the chairs and placed it far away, right next to a window. The sun was low, the light fell at an angle through the room, but her face was in shadow. She had a handbag in her lap and was gazing vacantly ahead.

'Leila?' said Farid. He pulled his hands from his pockets and stopped a few yards away from her. When she looked up, she didn't seem surprised – more like she had been waiting for him, in fact.

'Good. You are here. I hoped to meet—' She lost her train of thought. 'Do you know how Dogge is doing?'

'No news. He's alive. That's all I know.' Farid turned around to get a chair; he placed it next to Leila's and sat down.

She nodded absently, as though it hadn't quite sunk in.

'You have children, Farid, don't you?'

'Yes. Three daughters.'

She smiled faintly.

'You lived in Våringe before, but then you moved?'

'Yes.'

'I have been thinking since we last spoke.'

'Okay.'

'You know my husband left Sweden?'

'I heard that.'

'I heard you spoke to our imam.'

He nodded.

'Hassan thinks I should talk to you more. That it is important. Hassan is a good person, Farid. He would talk to you if he could, but he can't. He knows I want to move away from Våringe. That Tusane needs to get away from Våringe. Far away. So I was thinking...'

'Yes?'

'My family liaison, the officer who talks about safety, she explained what you can do for people who help... who are witnesses...'

Leila looked up at Farid. Her dark eyes stared into his.

'And I think maybe we remembered wrong, Tusane and I. What I told you when we spoke. We were upset and a little bit stressed.' She waited, as if to see if he was going to protest. Then she went on. 'But in fact, we can tell you many things. Maybe we could get a coffee, Farid? And talk about what happened? So that I know, when Tusane and I meet with the witness protection group, I need to know. I will meet with them tomorrow, already. It's important, I think. Do you have time for a coffee, Farid?'

He cleared his throat. Weed's case was called over the loudspeakers again – it was time for the judge to deliver his decision. He would have liked to be there, but he didn't need to go back into that room to know that Weed would remain in jail.

'Leila,' he began, tentatively. He took her hand. 'I always have time for you, you know that. But I don't think you should...' He tried to make his voice sound certain, reassuring. 'I'll talk to the witness protection group, I'll explain the situation, you don't have to do that. I'll see what we can accomplish without your having to...without you and Tusse having to think about what...really happened. Besides, maybe Dogge will...he might wake up soon, and then we'll know more about what he'll be able to tell us. We need to listen to that first, don't you think? Before you decide what you want to do.'

'You think we'll get help if we don't help you?'

No.

'I'll explain the situation to my colleagues. How serious it is.'

That's not going to help.

'You think Dogge will tell the truth about what happened?'

No.

'Maybe we can convince him to tell us more about what Mehdi is actually capable of.'

'And that would help us? We would get help?'

No.

'I'm going to do everything in my power, Leila. I promise to do everything I can. But it's important that we don't...'

He trailed off. Leila regarded him for a long time, then stood up. Before she left, she turned to him and said:

'Once you've done all you can. Once you've talked to your colleagues. Once they have explained what you know. What I know. That we will not get help, real help, if we don't testify. Once you have done that, Farid, we'll talk then? I want Mehdi...It's his fault. Both Billy and Dogge. His fault.'

She didn't wait for his response, just headed for the door, with her eyes on the floor and her hood up.

The journalists who had gathered outside the courtroom so they could get photos when Sara came out didn't notice Leila, they moved aside and let her pass without a closer look.

Twelve days ago they had been covering her son's murder. Now they no longer recognized her.

57

If Jill pretended she was watching herself from above, a bird's-eye view, she could clearly see what the police, the chaplain, the hospital staff and the social workers saw. A mother who hadn't protected her child, who hadn't said no, set boundaries, made him do the right thing. She wanted to shout at them, grab them and shake them.

It's not what you think, it's not what it looks like, I did everything, I've done everything to give my son a good life, to help him become a good person I could be proud of, but it didn't work. You wouldn't have managed either. No one could have managed.

She would have liked to shout until they listened. But she said nothing. There was nothing she could do, in the sickroom where Dogge lay, but wait.

When he was a newborn, he screamed so loudly and for so long that he became hoarse. He already

sounded exhausted when he woke her up in the morning, or in the middle of the night, when a second ago
he had been out like a light. He woke up crying and
fell asleep squalling. During those first few months,
his screams seemed to last an eternity. Each time he
started, she thought he would never stop. But just
when she thought, *I'm falling apart, I can't take it anymore*, he would stop, the change as sudden as it was
unexpected. She had held him close to whisper and
sing to him, he was the only person in the world Jill
had ever sung for, and sometimes it even helped. And
although he didn't quiet down, just kept screaming,
it helped her to have something to do. Sing, whisper,
rock, sway. She didn't know all that many lullabies,
just one, really, and she would make up her own words
when she forgot the real ones. It worked anyway. Sing,
whisper, rock, sway. And feed him until he was tired.
When she was still breastfeeding, or when she gave
him the thick baby porridge he drank from a bottle
each evening after dinner, up until the year before he
started school, he grew calm, he would fall asleep to
the rhythm of his own sucking and her hoarse singing.

When Dogge got bigger, he would play with his
hair when he lied. When he got caught in a lie, he
would scratch behind his ear. He wasn't especially
good at telling tall tales, but Jill pretended not to notice. It was easier that way.

She had never asked him how old he was when
he started doing drugs, what he started with, or why.
They didn't talk about that sort of thing. When the

murder of Billy was under investigation, the police told her, although she hadn't asked, that Dogge had apparently begun to smoke marijuana before he was twelve, and that he used both amphetamines and hash regularly.

'Did you know that?' the police wondered.

It's not that simple, she wanted to say. *You don't understand*, she wanted to scream.

When Dogge was twelve, he still wanted to lie next to Teo if he had a nightmare. He had a bright little-boy voice and his favourite food was chicken drumsticks with potato wedges, and Jill let him have lingonberries on the side because he was only a kid, and she didn't think kids should have to pay attention to silly rules about what foods go together.

When he was twelve, he was still a little boy who would text her if he was biking to the skate park. Of course Jill wanted to know that he had made it there safely, but if he forgot, she assumed it was because twelve-year-old boys always forgot the promises they made, and if he came home tired it was because they had played too much *FIFA* and drunk litres of Coke.

How, she wanted to ask the police, *how was I supposed to know they were smoking weed and drinking jungle juice made of wine dregs and vodka Dogge had scrounged from home?*

How-how-how, how was I supposed to guess that? But she didn't say anything. No one was interested in what she had to say, only in telling her what they thought she'd done wrong.

The chaplain had left her alone with Dogge overnight. The staff brought in a bed for her to sleep on. They offered her a sleeping pill, but it didn't help.

The next morning, the chaplain returned. He smelled as strongly of aftershave as he had the night before. When he placed his hand on her shoulder, she pulled away. Then he took half a step back and sat down on a chair by the door. The social worker Jill called Aunt Lavender arrived too, early in the morning, to say that the ruling about state guardianship, which was still in effect, would be lifted that day.

'We are all in agreement,' she said, 'that you should be the one to make all decisions concerning Douglas from now on. The ruling was based on Douglas's behaviour...' Here she stumbled, apparently trying to avoid saying that Dogge wasn't about to run out and kill any more teenagers while he was in a coma. Then she completed her thought: 'We don't consider there to be any reason for the ruling to remain in effect. He is your son.'

Aunt Lavender had just had coffee. It was there on her breath.

Smells often stressed Jill out. From feeling like she smelled like sweat, or had bad breath. From wearing too much perfume, or perfume that gave her a headache, or when other people smelled rank. A whiff of sewage, or even of cooking food, also made her anxious. But when the chaplain told her what had happened to Dogge she didn't get nervous, or even sad. It was like he had pressed a button that turned her off, what little of her was still on.

The only scent she found calming was the way Dogge had smelled as a baby. When he was a newborn, she would burrow her nose into the fold at the base of his neck and inhale as deeply as she could. She would do it when he was asleep on her shoulder and couldn't protest.

'I'll help you,' she had told him on the phone just a few days ago. 'Don't worry, everything will be fine soon.'

That was the sort of thing mothers said to their children.

Mothers were supposed to project confidence and calm. Not act scornful and condescending, like her mother had when Jill had her second abortion, or when she got married and her parents met Teo for the first time.

She wasn't like her mother, she had always been the opposite of her. It was other stuff that made life turn out different than she'd expected. Still, she knew Dogge didn't trust her. She knew he was aware that everything she said was only the dead remnants of the mother she tried to be, like phantom pains from an amputated limb. They had both accepted this, and in different ways they pretended as if it didn't matter.

———

After Billy's murder, no chaplains came, only the police. They drove her and Dogge to the station in different cars, and then they made her wait there for hours. First she was angry, annoyed, pacing around the room and wondering how long she would have to stay. She grew so desperate that she shouted.

'Can someone tell me what's going on? Please and fucking thank you?'

When Aunt Lavender explained what they 'needed to do' it took a few seconds for Jill to orient herself, to wake up properly. She 'suggested' that Jill should live at a women's shelter 'for a little while, while we take a closer look at what happened'. There, she was allowed to sleep alone in a room with two beds. All meals were served in the kitchen. She ate alongside women who made no sense to her. They looked at her as though they wondered who had raped her and why she wasn't black and blue. She didn't return their gazes, and provided only curt and evasive answers to all their questions.

The police had come to the shelter to 'talk' four times. Once, Aunt Lavender came to give her an update on 'how it was going'. The more times the police showed up, the more strangely the other women looked at her. Presumably they thought she had an especially dangerous partner whom it took special resources to investigate. No one knew it was her son they were interested in, that he was the dangerous one.

When Aunt Lavender came to tell her that Dogge had run away, Jill decided to move home again.

'If he shows up, I have to be there.'

Aunt Lavender agreed. Presumably, she believed her. Maybe she even thought Dogge would choose to find his way home. To his mother – that that was where he would go as soon as he had the chance.

The first time Jill had been forced to attend a meeting with the police and social services to discuss Dogge, she had taken a pill beforehand, to calm herself down. But it had made her awfully out of it, and she had had to lie on the sofa for a while before they could leave. When they arrived at the meeting an hour late, her brain was still sluggish. It was so hard to understand what they were saying, what they wanted from her, what they thought she should do.

That time two weeks ago, when she was sitting in the interrogation room and listening to the police tell her about Dogge and Billy, she had taken a few pills as well, but not to prepare herself for what they would say, just her usual ones. These days she took pills every day. She took them to sleep, to be more alert, to keep from feeling sad, exhausted, agitated. There was a pill for every feeling and others for pain, that constant aching. Her body hurt everywhere, every single joint, they collected fluid. Sometimes she thought she had developed rheumatism, or bone metastases. Maybe she had cancer as well? There was a pill to keep from worrying, and she took that one as often as she could.

After the chaplain and Jill had been sitting in silence for a while, a doctor entered the room. She said Dogge would be having another operation, and it would take several hours – Jill could wait at the hospital if she liked.

One hour later, two nurses appeared. They had come to fetch Dogge. The aftershave chaplain offered to take Jill to the cafeteria and make sure she got something to eat. She didn't have the strength to protest. In the hours that followed, she let herself be led around by the chaplain. They took a walk around the streets outside the hospital, he asked her if she needed to go to the bathroom, if she was thirsty, if she wanted a cup of coffee. She nodded along and let him take charge.

The chaplain received a call when the second operation was over, and then he took her to a room they'd never been to before. It looked like a pretty typical office, the doctor was sitting at a desk and there was a chair each for Jill and the chaplain. The doctor had documents on the desk and what looked like X-rays. Jill didn't know if those images were of her son, and she didn't really have the energy to listen to what the doctor was saying, but she could tell by looking at both her and the chaplain that it wasn't good news.

When the conversation was over, they went back to Dogge's room; he was still sedated and hooked up to just as many machines. Even so, he looked different. The bed Jill had slept in the night before was still there.

How long do I have to stay? Jill wondered. But she didn't say anything.

The chaplain had to leave, there was someone else he had to see. He handed her a card, very business-like, as though Jill were the sort of person who would flip through her collection of business cards if she needed to talk to him. Then he left.

She sat down on the chair beside Dogge and watched him for a few minutes, then went to the extra bed. Her body ached from within, like she had the flu, not the same kind of pain as when she gave birth to Dogge. This time, no one would reward her with ten tiny fingers and ten tiny toes. No one would congratulate her for sticking it out, no one would say she had done a good job and bring her freshly made sandwiches on a tray, ask if she wanted sugar in her tea. This time, all she had was pain.

S tarting with the day Teo got sick, Dogge became her responsibility alone. At first she protested.

'I'm on sick leave too. I'm sick. I'm not well. It's not my fault.'

She went to yet another doctor. He prescribed more pills. Sometimes she met up with her friends and tried to explain.

'It's going to be okay,' they said. 'I admire you. You're so incredibly strong, I would never manage.'

Jill didn't even have the strength to protest.

If she spoke to friends about her concern that Dogge was acting strange, they always responded the same way. It was all down to puberty, or because he had an unrequited crush on some classmate. Maybe he was wondering about his sexual identity, or maybe he thought he was fat or ugly or just that something was wrong with him somehow. Did she keep tabs on his social media? No, how could she? Was she sure he wasn't cutting himself or making himself throw up? No. She couldn't spy on him, demand that he show her his naked body, or follow him into the bathroom – it would be wrong. It's important to show respect to your child, and there were a thousand, a million, reasons Dogge was the way he was, and they were all perfectly normal twelve-year-old reasons, and there was no need for concern, and she had convinced herself that he would grow up and be like everyone else when they grow up, but not like Teo.

After Dogge shot Billy, no one reached out, no phone calls, not a single message. No one said she was strong. *I would never manage.*

They had made the bed with fresh sheets while she was out with the chaplain. The sheets had sharp creases from having been folded. Jill lay down on top of them, looked at the pale-blue plastic covers she'd pulled over her shoes before they entered Dogge's room. She didn't want to undress, not even her feet, and it felt weird to get under the sheets fully clothed.

Sometimes, right before she fell asleep, she would remember Dogge's little body in her arms, how he got heavier when he finally calmed down, when all his tense muscles gave way and he drifted off. She remembered his jaws working in his sleep. His hands clasping to her, so strong, fingernails as sharp as puppy teeth, grabbing her necklace and not letting go even after he was asleep; she had to pry his fingers open in order to put him down. His nappy butt, his knuckles and knees with dimples in the baby fat. His wavy, dark-blond hair that she let grow way too long, his fringe falling into his eyes, how he blew out to move it away or stroked it aside and tucked it behind his ear with so much concentration that she laughed every time, even if she was tired.

Just a moment later, she rose from the bed, dropped the chaplain's business card on the floor, turned towards the door, walked out, and went home.

58

Tusse looked out the living room window. He wasn't standing directly in front of it, he wasn't that stupid; he stood alongside and gazed down at the street. It was important not to be seen. And not to let himself be lured into a false sense of security. He was looking for signs. A blinking light on an electric scooter that had just been used. A carelessly parked moped he didn't recognize, or a car – it could be a car too. It would be so easy to find their building. He'd heard about people who just came walking by, did what they were there to do, and strolled off. They weren't scared, he was the only one who was scared. There could always be someone standing down there, waiting. Around the clock. All it would take was for him to go outside, get a little too far away from their guard. And it was easy to be fooled. A text from a girl you liked who suddenly wanted to meet up, or a friend you trusted as if he were your own brother.

Billy had told him about this, he knew all about it, and he still got killed.

Anyone could kill you. And Tusse was in danger, he knew that. Everyone thought he had talked to the police, that this was why they had bodyguards. Even in school he and his siblings had an officer following them almost everywhere. And they guarded Tusse most of all. It was so obvious. He was the one they expected Mehdi might kill, to punish him for talking. Even though he'd hardly said anything – at least not so far. Mum had taken time off work. He couldn't remember that ever happening before. She was never sick, and when she had time off she worked at different jobs than the one she was on holiday from. But now it was happening.

Together they were given a ride to a different police station, not the one in Våringe where they'd met with Farid, but one that looked like a regular office building. There they met a group of police officers whose job it was to protect people who needed protection. They were the ones who did everything that needed doing when you had to become a new person no one could find or recognize.

They explained they could do everything necessary to protect witnesses in a murder trial, for instance. They didn't say this in so many words, but Tusse understood. If he and Mum spoke against Mehdi, they would get to move so far away they would never again have to worry.

In the car on the way there, Mum had told him he was absolutely not allowed to say anything while they were there before they had discussed what to say. She'd said so in her own language, the one he understood but never spoke. It was important, she had declared – it might decide what the rest of their lives would be like. She had friends who had been tricked by the police, friends who told the truth but never got the help they were promised, so it had all been in vain and they would never be able to feel safe again.

So Tusse hadn't said a word, not even about the time Mehdi taught Dogge and Billy to shoot, even though he'd already told Farid about that.

That night, after the meeting, Mum had come in to sit on his bed, the bed that would always be Billy's but where Tusse pretended to sleep now. She said she needed his help, that together the two of them would make sure they could receive the help they needed to move away from Våringe.

'It's the only way,' she said. 'We can't spend our lives living in fear. So we will testify, you and I.'

At first he didn't know how this would work. After all, Mum had already told Farid that what Tusse knew wouldn't help the police. That he knew Mehdi had sold the gun to Dad, and Billy had given it to Dogge. The police would never be able to say that Mehdi had asked Dogge to kill Billy if Billy himself had given Dogge the gun. But then she explained. They were going to make up a story, something that would allow the police to target Mehdi after all. That was how it worked, she said. The help they got from the police would be their payment. But it was also important not to talk to them too soon. First they had to get a good lawyer so the police wouldn't trick them.

'Because we know,' Leila said, and he heard the tears surging up in her throat, 'that it was Mehdi's gun that killed Billy. We know that. If you tell them what you did at the chicken factory, that's good for the police. The only part we'll lie about is how it ended up with Dogge. The police don't need to know that. They only need to know what is necessary to put Mehdi away. Maybe you can say you saw Mehdi give the gun to Dogge. You can say Mehdi told Dogge that he needed it for an important job. That's almost true.'

He peered out at the street. There was a lot of snow this year. He loved snow, all his friends were down on the field building forts out of the snowbanks left by the plough. They were having a snowball fight, but he couldn't take part.

His mother talked about lying as though it were simple. But she only thought that because she never lied. She didn't understand that it takes practice. You have to think about the lie so much that eventually you believe it's true.

So he'd started practising. *Mehdi gave the gun to Dogge at the pizzeria down on the square.* It was a good story, since Tusse had seen Mehdi give other stuff to Billy and Dogge at the pizzeria. He would say he'd been there with them, because they had on occasion let him tag along when they were running errands for Mehdi, so it made sense.

He practised his story in his head, answering questions he thought the police might ask. He practised as though he were studying for a test at school, but even harder.

And he looked out the window, down at the street, looking for any sign, to be sure they weren't waiting down there. It was important not to be seen. And not to let anyone fool him. Because if that happened, you could die.

59

On Saturday morning, the hospital called Jill. They wondered where she was. The doctor wanted to meet with her. There were things to discuss.

'I can't come in today, I'm not feeling well.'

Christmas Eve was just two days away, but they insisted. Jill hung up and turned off the T V. Shouldn't they have other things to worry about; why did they care whether she was sitting there staring at Dogge or not? Didn't they have patients to help, Christmas presents to buy, family gatherings to prepare for? Everyone had family to see over Christmas, everyone except Jill. She hadn't heard from her parents in nine years.

'We can see what you two are doing, we know what you're up to,' her mother had said the last time they met, when she and Jill's father showed up one day out of the blue and rang the doorbell.

Jill had tried to explain that they were overreacting, that Teo was just partying, that they liked to have fun.

'Get help,' her father had shouted. 'Both of you. Or else we will never come back.'

There's no need, Jill had wanted to say. *Just stay away, I don't care.*

After Teo's bankruptcy, almost all of her friends had stopped getting in touch. But after Billy's death, she called her closest friend. The conversation was brief.

'Unfortunately, I don't have time to talk.' Her friend's voice was a hiss, like bug spray. 'I hope you get help.'

An hour after Jill turned off her phone to get some peace and quiet, the chaplain showed up and rang the doorbell. She didn't want to answer it, but he wouldn't stop pressing the button. So she got up and stood in the doorway, her legs planted wide to block him from stepping in. He took her arm and told her they had to go to the hospital, that it was very important, that she had a meeting with Dogge's doctor that she *would want to be there for.*

She no longer had the strength to protest. The chaplain had brought a car.

For a few years there, she had enjoyed being Dogge's mother, starting when he was about three. Back then, she wanted to show him off to the whole world, take him with her everywhere. If they were invited to someone's house, she never wanted to get a babysitter, she thought he should come too. Teo protested, of course. There was no reason for them to torture others by dragging their kid around everywhere, he said. She did as Teo wanted. It was easier that way. But she had been proud of Dogge for quite some time. Even when he started school, although it didn't go so well and maybe he got in a fight or two and had some trouble with his numbers and letters.

'Not everyone has to become a doctor or an engineer,' she said to Teo.

'Probably a good thing he'll never have to work,' Teo replied. 'It'll be enough of a win if they teach him to remember the PIN to his debit card.'

'Dogge gets his temper from his father,' Jill had said once at a parent–teacher conference. But when she saw the teacher's anxious expression she knew she had said the wrong thing. 'They're both at a difficult age,' she tried to joke. No one thought it was funny.

The chaplain drove her all the way to the hospital and dropped her off in the car park, where a nurse met them. She wanted to 'show her the way'. It wasn't like Jill didn't understand what they were doing – they didn't want to risk her slipping away.

The chaplain said she could call anytime, that he was happy to 'support' her. But he took off as soon as she'd stepped out of the car. She remained standing in the waiting room, didn't want to sit, until the doctor, whose name was Nora, had shown her into her office and shaken her hand. Jill accepted a glass of water, but it remained on the doctor's desk, untouched.

The doctor said that Dogge had suffered a very serious brain injury. She had already said so the last time they met, but the expression on her face was different this time. Less tired, more grim. It was hard to know just how debilitated he would be, especially while they kept him under sedation. But they wanted to wake him up soon, and then they would have a better idea.

'We're planning to make a first attempt tomorrow or maybe the next day,' she said. 'If you come by at nine o'clock tomorrow morning, we can talk in more detail about what's going to happen.'

Would he be able to talk? Walk? Move? Would he ever wake up?

The doctor couldn't say. Maybe, maybe not. It was hard to predict anything about how badly injured Douglas was. He was still in a critical condition.

'Very critical,' she said, fixing her eyes on Jill as if it were her fault.

'It's not my fault,' said Jill.

'Of course not,' the doctor replied, her voice becoming a smidgen friendlier. If Douglas survived, well, young people had better prognoses for this type of injury than adults did, and he would receive all the help and assistance that was available to optimize his chances.

What chances? Jill wondered, but she said nothing. *And who*, she wanted to ask, *who's going to help me?*

'I can't,' she said, when the doctor had finished speaking. 'I'm not well. I can't do this. I can't, I need to go home.'

'I understand that this is a lot to take in,' Nora responded. 'It's very unfortunate, what happened to your son. But we'll know more once we've woken him up.'

'What happened to him?' Jill shook her head. 'Why does everyone say that? It wasn't random. He didn't take a meteor to the head, he didn't get accidentally run over by a bus. It wasn't like some rabid dog was lurking in the dark and attacked Dogge out of nowhere. That man took a baseball bat and struck him in the head with it.'

'Yes,' Nora said cautiously. 'I've heard that the police are investigating.'

'Oh yeah? You heard that?' Jill scoffed. 'Did you know he hated Dogge? Did you know he spread lies about Dogge? He wanted to kill him. Why won't anyone say so? People think the man who tried to murder my son is a hero. He's a murderer, but people think he did the right thing. Even the prosecutor doesn't seem to know what he should do. "We may have to reclassify the investigation," did you hear he said that? "It depends on how the case develops." He said so on TV. Merry Christmas. What kind of development is he waiting for, do you think? For Dogge to die? That he'll *happen* to die, or just *happen* to become a vegetable? Either way, Merry Christmas. Merry Christmas and a Happy New Year!'

She got up and asked to borrow money for a taxi.

'I forgot my wallet at home.'

The doctor looked confused. But she opened her wallet and took out a 200-kronor bill. Jill took it from her and walked away. Down in the lobby she bought an evening paper and a pack of cigarettes. Then she went out to sit on a bench by the bus station half a mile from the hospital. She waited there for an hour before walking back to the main entrance.

'I need to find the psychiatric emergency department,' she said. 'Can you please help me get there? And maybe call social services as well? You can give them my name, they know who I am. Someone has to take over custody of my son. There's no one but me, and unfortunately I can't do it. I wish I could, but I can't.'

60

'Douglas? Can you hear me?'

He didn't recognize the voice. But he did hear it. He opened his eyes and tried to make them focus. Why wouldn't he hear her? She was standing so close that he could have touched her, even head-butted her, if his head hadn't felt so heavy. It felt like it weighed more than he could lift. The ceiling light was shining in his eyes, he wanted to close them again, they were also too heavy to keep open. But he forced himself to look at her. He didn't recognize her, had never met her before, he could swear he hadn't.

Am I at the police station? Am I in jail? Did they chain me up somehow? Are they allowed to do that?

She didn't look like a police officer, but that didn't necessarily mean anything. Maybe she was a social worker. She didn't look like a social worker either. Dogge let his eyes fall closed, and rested that way for a moment before opening them again, forcing them to open, it felt like it took several minutes.

The woman was still there, just as close as before. She had dark hair gathered at the back of her neck and the hint of a moustache.

'Good morning, Douglas.'

Her smile was too big to take in, tons of white teeth. Why was she happy? He looked around, it was hard to turn his head. The room was full of people, and he didn't recognize a single one. He tried to ask *Where the hell am I, who the hell are you? What am I doing here?* His voice didn't obey. But she kept talking.

'My name is Nora, and I'm your doctor. You're at the hospital, you have a serious brain injury and we've been keeping you sedated to allow your brain to rest and the swelling to go down. We'll let you go back to sleep again soon, but we wanted to check in on how you're doing.'

At last his voice seemed to work.

'Mum?' he managed to say.

His voice sounded weird. Thicker than usual. His throat hurt. He didn't know why *mum* was the word that came out of his mouth, and he felt his cheeks getting wet; the tears surprised him too. Was he sad? Why?

'Your mother isn't here, she's been admitted to psychiatric care. This has all been pretty hard on her, everything that's happened, but she's getting the help she needs, don't worry, I'm sure she'll be feeling well enough to come see you soon. She'll be happy to hear that you were awake and asking for her.'

'Mum,' he said again, just as unexpectedly.

It was like he had forgotten all the other words.

'Don't worry about her. She's getting the help she needs, Dogge.'

The doctor's smile faded a bit. She looked at another woman who was standing beside her, muttered something Dogge couldn't hear.

'Mu—' He cut himself off. What was with him? *A fucking parrot?*

He closed his mouth again. He didn't want to talk about Mum, he wanted to know what had happened.

'Wha?' he managed to say. The doctor turned to him again.

'You received a blow to the head. The police have asked me not to talk about it with you yet, because they'd like to hear from you first, find out what you remember.'

Dogge concentrated. *What I remember? Remember?* He closed his eyes. The memories swirled like a kaleidoscope in his brain.

Shit, are we gonna party, man! He was driving a car and the Italian was beside him. They were blasting music. The music Mehdi's friend made, with tens of thousands of plays on Spotify, that the kids in Rönnviken danced to without actually getting what it was about; only Dogge understood, he wasn't like the rest of them.

The images danced in his mind. Billy laughing, his mouth open, throwing his head back. Then they were in an apartment. There was Mehdi, looking at him, straight at him, without averting his eyes. It looked like he was going to stand up and come over and give him a hug. Say something about how fucking awesome he was, *You're my* abri.

Lightning in his head. *If this is a dream*, Dogge thought, *it's not like any dreams I've had before.* He was at Weed's Market. The Italian was walking ahead of him, pulling stuff off the shelves, Dogge wanted to laugh, wanted to but couldn't, *What a hell of a party.* He wanted to get away. Wake up. Make these images stop. A man picked up a baseball bat. Was it Mehdi? Was Mehdi holding a baseball bat, was he going to hit him with it?

He forced himself to open his eyes, get rid of the images, and focus on the woman standing next to his bed. *Her name is Nora and she's my doctor.* The woman was talking again, but not to him. More people had come into the room, they seemed stressed.

All the words in the room flowed into each other, blending into an unrecognizable jumble, transforming into noise, a sound file playing backward. He tried to shake his head to get someone's attention.

Maybe, if he thought out exactly what he wanted to say and then concentrated really hard, maybe he would be able to speak. But then he couldn't figure out how he should begin. What he should ask first. Something was making a noise, it reminded him of an alarm clock. Lights were blinking. Even more people came into the room.

Dogge closed his eyes again. The images came back. But this time it wasn't a dream. *Weed*, he thought. *Weed hit me in the head with a baseball bat. He tried to kill me.*

Some fluid gushed into his mouth and he wanted to clear his throat, cough, or maybe puke. It felt like he was falling, in freefall. Suddenly there was another voice. It seemed to come from far away.

'We need help here. Quick.'

The woman's voice came closer to his face again. She sounded worried now, placed a hand on his forehead, and only then did he realize that his whole head was shaking.

'Douglas, we're going to have to sedate you again. You're having a seizure because there's still some swelling in your brain that needs to go down before we can take you off all these machines. We also need to find out what's—'

Dogge felt her lifting his arm, but then he didn't feel anything. The pain wasn't his. He was back on the playground. Billy sat with his back to him, swinging, higher and higher, it was dark but the light from the streetlamps showed how the snow was falling diagonally to the ground, he laughed, laughed and laughed, it never stopped. All he could hear were the machines keeping him chained to this bed. Sweeping sounds.

Swish, swoosh, swish, swoosh.

'Now you're going to sleep for a while, Dogge.'

The doctor's voice disappeared. Another voice came in its place. Was it his mum? Was it Dad?

'It's going to be okay, Dogge, don't worry, you'll be okay.'

He closed his eyes. Closed and closed them.

Billy raised the baseball bat high over his head. He laughed until he couldn't breathe, and aimed, and swung. *Swish.*

Billy had a dimple in one cheek, sometimes Dogge used to get the urge to press his finger into it, but he never had. What was he laughing at? The dimple was deeper than ever before. *Swoosh.* He struck Dogge in the back of the head. Dogge heard the crunch, but he felt nothing.

Billy turned around to walk away from him. The baseball bat was gone now. The back of Billy's head was gone too, it was totally open. He was lying down, his belly in the snow, the flakes still falling at an angle, over him, each snowflake perfectly unique, the blood surrounded him, a dark, shiny sea.

They dove. Dad first, then Dogge. Deep into the black seawater, they swam, Dad first, Dogge after. Then Dad was gone. Dogge was back at the playground, back with death. It was snowing, harder and harder.

One flake at a time, Billy's pulse disappeared. Dogge tried to run away, he didn't want to watch Billy die, he didn't want Billy to see him. He wanted to get away, find his dad. But he couldn't, his legs were too heavy, his head was too heavy, he couldn't lift anything, he couldn't move.

Swish. Swoosh. Swish. Swoosh.

Someone was singing. Was it Dad? Dogge couldn't remember Dad ever singing. It wasn't a language he knew. But the melody, it settled around him, it warmed him, everything had grown cold, everything except the voice. *Lorî, lorî.*

'I'm freezing,' he wanted to say, whisper, but he couldn't. His voice didn't belong to him anymore. Only the song was left, but it was soon replaced by loud, piercing noises and needles in his body. His panic was naked and cruel and sharp, until it too vanished into the darkness.

———

The sea roared inside his body, outer space filled his heart. The melody followed him, it stayed inside him when someone else – was it Mum? It didn't smell like Mum – but someone else touched his body with gentle, strong hands and carried him, lifted him and placed him somewhere else. Somewhere where Billy still existed. Billy ran, and Dogge ran after him. Soon they would fly, up, away, home.

Then his legs stopped carrying him forward. In the night, he flew. Higher and higher.

He wanted to shout, but no words would come. Language, pain and shame were gone. He felt nothing, nothing, and then he fell – off to nowhere.

61

First came the darkness. Leila had called him. He didn't know who had told her, but she was crying.

'This has to end,' she whispered. 'This can't go on.'

'I'm about to walk into a meeting,' he had replied. 'We can talk later.'

Nadja wasn't angry when Farid explained why he couldn't come to her parents' house to decorate the Christmas tree like they usually did. She understood.

It was Sunday, the day before Christmas Eve, and Svante couldn't meet until that evening. But no one on the investigative team protested. Everyone would come to the station. No one suggested a virtual meeting.

They didn't have a moment of silence – that would have felt strange. But it was hard to think of anything to say. Even Svante was frugal with his words. He let Lotta summarize the situation. She was wearing a dress, it was dark grey, and she had a run in her tights. Farid had imagined she might have been on the way to a Christmas dinner with family. Or maybe she was coming from a Christmas lunch.

The prosecutor was cautiously optimistic, according to Lotta. The evidence was promising, he had high hopes of being able to bring charges. There was really only one thing missing.

'Witness protection is talking to them,' Svante tried. 'I don't know how it's going, but naturally it would be best if one of us, someone they trust, could be there during the conversations.'

He didn't look at Farid, but everyone knew he was the one Svante was addressing.

'I'll call her,' said Farid. That was all he could say before his voice wouldn't hold.

This has to end.

When he parked the car in front of the house and stepped into the hall, he saw Nadja in the kitchen with a mug of tea on the table in front of her, one of the many mugs she filled, warmed her hands on, and then left undrunk. She must have left her parents' place earlier than planned. She looked at him. The only light came from the Advent candelabras. He walked in without taking off his coat or shoes, just sat down across from her and crumpled. He didn't cry; he was too exhausted for that. For a while they just sat.

'It wasn't supposed to be like this,' he said at last. 'I knew it wouldn't be easy, I knew I would find it challenging. But it was never supposed to be impossible.'

She took his hand. It was warm and slightly damp. He went on.

'Did you know that in Finland you have to take an oath when you start working as a police officer, you have to swear that you will be just and respect everyone's human rights and be helpful and dependable and—' he took a deep breath. 'But they never tell you how far you should go to save lives. How far you should go for justice. True justice. No one ever talks about that. But we are taught that respect for the legal system is so important that sometimes it has to mean that the guilty go free. Still, I wonder...how can it be just for two children to die, and the only person who has to answer for his actions is Weed? We let him down, over and over. He asked us for help, over and over and over.'

He pulled his hand back, placed it over his eyes, and whispered. 'Leila's going to lie for us, give us a false statement because she knows it's the only way Mehdi will face any consequences, and it's the only way for us to help her. She's under police protection now, but that's only for a week or two, then it can be taken away. There are no resources, there is no money in the budget. If she goes into witness protection, though, we can move her out of Våringe, and she'll get lifelong assistance. But if I tell anyone what I know, what she and Tusse told me, that the gun came from Isak and that Billy, not Mehdi, must have given it to Dogge, that won't happen. She won't get any help, and she might even face charges for trying to accuse an innocent man of murder. Filing a false report can bring up to two years in prison. Would it be just to put Leila in prison? Sometimes I think that's all we're missing in this fucking mess.'

Nadja took his hands again. She forced him to look her in the eye. For a moment, Farid felt her betrayal washing over him. *Don't tell me it would be wrong not to say anything, to help Leila. I already know it's wrong. I don't want this*, he wanted to say. He wanted to shout it. *But what can I do? What choice do I have?*

Then she began to speak. Her voice was steady and forthright, with not a shred of sentimentality. It was the voice she used when they were planning the logistics around the kids' activities, or when they discussed how to refinance their mortgage.

'Can you give me Leila's phone number? We have to be very careful that this doesn't reach a deadlock. And before we do anything else, I'm going to make sure she gets in touch with one of my friends. She's a lawyer and has worked with lots of witnesses in sensitive trials. She knows what it takes to get an agreement in place so the police can't pull out if Leila's testimony isn't sufficient, or if...if there should turn out to be other...issues. And also—'

Nadja stood up, poured the rest of her tea into the sink, and reached out for Farid. 'Also I think it's best if I'm the one to talk to her, and not you. What you need to do is consider whether you really want to keep doing this work. You're not well, Farid, it's taking too much of a toll on you. Your children need you, I need you, and you need to get away, far away, from Våringe, and come back to your family.'

62

They came in the middle of the night. A woman and a man, they were cops, but neither was in uniform. Leila and the kids had four hours to pack. They would be moving to temporary housing, a furnished apartment in a city hundreds of miles away; they weren't allowed to know which city.

'It's best if we tell you as little as possible,' they said.

'We'll explain everything later,' they said. 'You have to be able to carry whatever you bring on your own. We'll try to send your larger items to you once you've gotten settled. Where we're going now, it's not where you'll stay, we'll figure that out together at a later date.'

Aisha cried the whole time. Rawdah was silent and angry. Leila filled her bag with photographs.

When he thought no one was looking, Tusse pulled Billy's favourite shirt from one of the boxes where Leila had put his things. He snuck into his room, folded it carefully, and shoved it into the outer pocket of his bag. Leila came in as he was about to stuff the last bit of sleeve in. She was holding Tusse's blankie in her hand. She sat down next to him on the bed and pulled him close. She put the blankie in his lap.

'I don't know where we're going,' she said softly. And in a whisper, in her own language, she told him about the night she had fled with her parents. Tusse had heard it before, the story of how Grandpa had drawn straws to see which country they would go to, how they were a people who had always wandered, and how it wasn't important where they lived, the only thing that mattered was that they got to be to-gether. It had always been a funny story, the straw that caused Leila to end up first in Finland, then in Sweden. But now they weren't laughing.

'We can't draw straws this time, though. I don't even know if we'll get to have a say in where to go. But I know we're going away. We're about to start our journey toward a new future, and even if we don't know, yet, what it's going to be like, and even if it all feels very tough right now, we will remem-ber this night as something good.' She breathed into Tusse's hair. He leaned into her chest and closed his hand around the blankie.

'We may be leaving our home, but Billy will al-ways be with us. I can pack lots of his clothes, if you want me to, we can take a bag with everything you want, but you don't need them to have your brother with you. He won't vanish. I'll always be his mother, you'll always be his brother, I promise you that. Not even death is powerful enough to change that.'

The policewoman took their computers, tablets and phones, even the ones they had just got back from the investigators. They received new ones in exchange.

'Don't turn them on until we've arrived. Our IT department has deleted all your social media accounts and you may not start new ones until you've got settled at your new address, and it's going to be a while, maybe a few months.'

She also took all their debit and charge cards. Leila was given an envelope of cash and two temporary charge cards.

'We have purchased groceries for you, it's all there in the apartment where you'll be staying. There's also a TV there, and some games you can use. You can't go online, but that's only for a little while, until we're finished with your investigation.'

Aisha cried even harder. Rawdah looked like she wanted to punch the policewoman, or maybe Leila. Tusse swallowed all his feelings.

Leila looked calm. She handed the policewoman a cool bag.

'I've prepared some food I want to take along, the things we usually eat on Christmas Eve. That is okay?'

The policewoman hesitated, but only for a second. Then she gave a curt nod. Her colleague carried the bag down to the car, a perfectly ordinary Volvo estate, which was parked next to a police car.

The back seat was too crowded; Tusse got in the police car instead. They switched cars in a garage a few miles away, into a dark-blue van with tinted windows. There were six spots in the back, three on each side, facing each other. Leila sat in one of the seats closest to the front, and leaned her head against the cold window. Tusse sat across from her. Rawdah took the middle seat, next to her mother, and pressed herself close. Leila put her arm around her. Aisha sat on the same side as Tusse, but left the middle seat empty; she turned her back on her brother, but Tusse stretched his arm as far as it would go to reach her. He poked at her leg until she gave him her hand, even as she continued to stare out the side window.

With the Christmas night outside, they left Våringe and drove four hours due north without speaking. There was Christmas music on the radio. One by one they fell asleep, Rawdah first, even before they left the garage. Tusse was next, and Aisha soon followed suit. Only Leila stayed awake. Rawdah lay in her lap with her feet on the seat. Leila placed her hand on her daughter's head, which rested on her belly, against the scar from her second childbirth. Her body would always bear the proof that he had existed. As long as she was alive, he was there as well.

She looked at her sleeping children as they drove into a village. There was a church in it; the early morning Christmas service had just begun. A woman stood at the open church door, welcoming the visitors. The snow sent sparks into the darkness. There were spruce boughs on the ground. The light streaming from the space behind the woman was a warm yellow. On the radio, Birgit Nilsson sang 'Silent Night'.

It wasn't Leila's god they were celebrating, but he was here as well. He held his hand over them, he knew where they were going.

SIX MONTHS LATER

63

By the time the trial was held for case B 1632, the
prosecution versus Mehdi Ahmad, it was early
summer in Rönnviken. The days were growing
longer and longer, the birch trees shimmered with the
most delicate green leaves, and the sea was a brighter
blue than it had been just a week earlier. The national
romantic style had been characteristic of Rönnviken
ever since the city was founded in 1893. Rönnviken
district court was no exception. It wasn't the oldest
courthouse in the country, but it might have been the
loveliest.

It was just after nine in the morning when Farid
locked his bike to the wrought-iron rack along the
western side of the courthouse. With his helmet
clamped under his arm, he went to the kiosk across
the square to get a large coffee to go, and then he
got out his key card, entered the building through the

staff entrance, and headed for the courtroom. The trial wouldn't begin until ten, but he planned to sit in the prosecutor's office behind the room and run through a few things before the day's proceedings.

The night before, he'd had the briefest of meetings with Leila and Tusse at the hotel where they were staying. Tusse was extremely tired; Leila seemed a bit annoyed.

'We know what we have to say. It's not something we would forget,' she said.

When Tusse went to the bathroom, he asked if they were doing okay.

'I don't want to know where you live,' he reminded her.

Leila's smile was so faint that he almost missed it. Of course she knew the rules. She couldn't say anything about their new life, not even to him.

'School was hard, first,' she said. 'Especially for Tusse. I think he blames himself. Because the girls really did not want to move. But it is better now. It's a good school, I think. Many teachers, and they don't seem exhausted. And many checks. Many, many checks. It's like an airport, getting into that school.'

Farid tried to picture it, the life they lived now. He knew a few things, or could make some educated guesses. BOPS, the unit that was in charge of victims of crimes and their personal safety, had called him in to a meeting between Christmas and New Year to discuss the need for protection. He had attended virtually. Leila and the kids weren't there, but their new lawyer, Evin Can, one of his wife's best friends from law school, explained in a voice that didn't quite match her tiny body that she demanded the family be relocated to the United States. Land of the free and home of the brave.

One of the BOPS officials had laughed out loud at that. But Can just raised one eyebrow the slightest bit. She had a lot of experience representing clients who needed witness protection. She might have been Sweden's foremost expert in that arena. It would not be possible to place a family with Leila's appearance and background in the Nordic countries, she declared. And hardly even in Europe. An English-speaking country would be preferable because that would make it easier for the family to adapt to their new life. And everyone in the Khalid-Ali family spoke English – very well, in fact.

Evin Can had also said the forbidden part, since someone had to point it out.

'They come from a clan society. It doesn't matter what new names you give them. You could call them Olsson if you like, but it won't help. All Leila has to do is step into a mosque to be identified. Not to mention what would happen if you sent them to a small town in Norway, or maybe Finland. Not even someone who's colour-blind would have trouble no-ticing them. It would take under an hour to track them down.'

The official became visibly irritated. It would obviously be impossible, he said. The biometrics would mess things up, and besides, such agreements were incredibly unusual.

'The United States has enough criminals already,' he blurted, 'they'll hardly want to accept more.'

Before Evin Can could speak, Farid cleared his throat and reminded the room that no one who would be assigned a new identity in the Khalid-Ali family was a criminal, nor had any of them, as far as he knew, ever visited the United States, so there were no biometrics connected to their old identities. At this, the other BOPS official nodded.

'We can work this out,' he mumbled. 'We're all on the same side here.'

After the meeting, Farid wrote a statement.

'This family remains under considerable threat. The murder of their son is a direct consequence of the family's having dismissed Mehdi Ahmad's attempts at extortion. Leila Khalid and Tusane Ali have stated that they are willing to testify about this before the court.'

He knew the end by heart.

'Since the murder of Billy Ali, Mehdi Ahmad's network has strengthened considerably. Accordingly, the investigative team takes the firm view that this family must receive new identities and placement outside Sweden. All available measures must be taken to minimize the risk that the family will face further deadly violence.'

Once he'd sent the report, he wrote another email. This one went to HR. He gave his notice. Svante called him an hour later and convinced him to take sick leave instead.

The hotel room where he'd met with Leila and Tusse was crowded. There were many things he wanted to ask. Have the kids forgotten their old friends? Have you told your sister where you live? Do you wake up at night and wonder where you are? *Do you still use the names you gave your children when no one can hear?*

He said none of this. He wanted her to say they lived in a city no one ever sang about, wrote about in books, or could see in movies. In a place where they didn't attract stares but were welcomed. That Leila could wear her hijab without anyone hissing *terrorist* after her. That she had found a good job where people appreciated her, that the kids were happier than ever. But he didn't ask.

There is no fleeing from grief.

But once Tusse appeared to have dozed off, fully dressed on the hotel bed, he heard himself:

'Do you regret it?' But he didn't let Leila answer. Instead, he said, so fast that he stumbled over his words, that he had changed jobs, that he was on loan from his new job for this trial. 'I was on sick leave for three months, and now I only work part-time, and not in Våringe anymore.'

His colleagues couldn't wrap their minds around
it. He had offers from every department, from Major
Crimes to NOA, the national operations unit. Yet he
had elected to take a temporary position with the National Council for Crime Prevention. He would be
working as an expert in an inquiry on petty crime.
They would be presenting a plan of action in the autumn. Farid had asked if they couldn't hand in this
list right away; he didn't need more than an hour to
make it. His new boss had responded with a polite,
restrained chuckle and then said they needed to conduct at least a hundred interviews with crime victims – would Farid like to help?

'If we'd helped Weed when he asked for it,
Dogge would probably be alive today. If we want to
make sure it's possible to live a good and safe life in
Våringe, we have to start there, with the graffiti and
vandalism, shoplifting and petty theft.'

This was how he tried to explain it to his colleagues. But Leila didn't need help to understand
exactly what it would take. She asked about Weed.
What had happened to him? She knew he had been
sentenced to prison, did Farid know more? He did.
Sara and the kids had moved to Umeå; Weed was
placed at a facility not far from there.

Many people felt the sentence was too harsh,
even though he'd been given a relatively short time in
prison. Nadja had been incredibly upset; she considered it a failure of the judicial system that he hadn't
been acquitted. But Farid had heard that Weed was

refusing to appeal. Farid had also heard that he had been placed under heightened surveillance in prison. There was still a high risk that he would harm himself, even today. But Leila didn't ask how Weed was feeling, so Farid didn't mention it.

At a quarter to ten, he entered the courtroom. Courtroom 1, where the trial of Mehdi Ahmad would take place, was the only one equipped with the level of security measures needed for today's proceedings. At the entrance stood a metal detector; there was only one more of them in the whole building, by the bag X-ray in the lobby.

This room had a high ceiling, mahogany benches, and velvet chairs for the judges. A huge painting by Gustaf Cederström portraying the parliament of 1720 hung on one wall. In the foreground was the speaker of the nobility estate, Arvid Horn, with his curly, shoulder-length grey hair and mink-trimmed scarlet cape. In his hand he held the newly ratified constitution. Just behind him, and partially hidden, sat King Fredrik I on his tarnished throne, staring down at his lap.

The part of the room where the judge and trial participants would sit was separated from the gallery by a transparent wall of bulletproof glass. The speakers that made it possible for the onlookers to hear what was said on the other side were mounted near the ceiling.

There were no windows to allow a view into the courtroom, but from the foyer you could see the square through tall transom windows. Currently in progress outside was the traditional National Day market; some of the dealers there were wearing costumes: freshly ironed kerchiefs, ruffled aprons, and clunky wooden clogs painted with *kurbits* patterns. The coffee kiosk had set out a few chairs and a small table on the pavement, even though it didn't have a permit for outdoor seating. No one was too picky about that kind of thing in Rönnviken; no one would make a fuss if you parked facing the wrong direction or built your boathouse a few yards too close to the beach. The important thing was that the citizens got on well and didn't bother each other if they didn't have to.

Leila entered the room at four minutes to ten. Tusse wouldn't be testifying until later, so she was accompanied only by her lawyer and a man from witness protection. Her back straight, she walked all the way up to the plaintiff's table. In the first row of the gallery sat three men of around twenty-five, all with thick necks; they sat with their legs spread and arms crossed. Farid didn't recognize them, but they had to be new friends of Mehdi's.

When Mehdi stepped into the courtroom, wearing his green jail clothes, Leila lifted her head and looked straight at him. He didn't look back. Once his handcuffs were off and he was in his seat, the chief judge turned on her microphone and leaned forward.

'I would like to welcome you all to the district court,' she said. 'My name is Ulrika Bonde, and I will be in charge of today's proceedings.'

64

our days of trial later, Ulrika Bonde struck her gavel on the table in front of her and declared the proceedings finished.

'The defendant will remain in custody. The verdict will be read on Wednesday of next week.'

Then she gathered her things and left the room. She and the lay judges had had a brief consultation and decided that they would meet on Monday to review the verdict. But there would be no need for lengthy discussions; they were generally in agreement already.

Back inside her office she kicked off her shoes, took off her jacket, and sat at her desk. It was nearly six in the evening; the closing arguments had gone long – the defence lawyer was a young rising talent, full of indignation and lofty ideals.

The chief judge's husband and youngest daughter had already headed out to the countryside. She had texted them during a break to say that she would try to make it out tomorrow. This wasn't a complicated case. If she started tonight, she could finish writing her opinion after deliberations with the lay judges on Monday.

A trial in a criminal case always generally followed the same trajectory, and there was some comfort to be found in that. In cases like this one, when Ulrika had to work in the secure courtroom and with heavy media scrutiny, with all the searches and attention that involved, she sometimes still felt nervous at first. But the nervousness always dissipated as soon as she was able to get started. The routines, the rules of procedure – there were no choices to be made, no words to get hung up on. She was a priest reading a service word for word; her congregation knew exactly when to speak and when to remain silent.

The mother of the murdered boy had attended all week. She had remained calm and collected, even when delivering her own account, telling the court what she knew about her son's life and the threats her family had experienced from the defendant, especially after her son had joined the council's disengagement programme.

Only once did she fall apart, when her youngest son was testifying. When the little boy, whose voice hadn't even broken yet, told the court that the defendant had given what was assumed to be the murder weapon to the boy who had carried out the murder, the plaintiff had squeezed her fists so hard Ulrika could see her knuckles go white. She became even more agitated when it was the defence lawyer's turn to ask questions. But he kept his time brief, and when it seemed that the boy might start to cry he quickly ended his examination.

Ulrika herself had found it difficult to keep her emotions in check. It was heartbreaking to see the little brother of the murdered boy, so nervous but still brave enough to testify in court, not to mention in such close proximity to the defendant and with the defendant's friends lined up in the first row.

His testimony had been recorded. That bright voice, his words so clear and well stated.

'"This is for you," Mehdi told Dogge. I was there when he said it because sometimes I went with Billy when he met up with Mehdi. And I was there that time. The day he gave him the pistol. "It's for you," Mehdi said, "and you're going to use it when I tell you to, or else I'll shoot you." He said so, Mehdi did. To Dogge. When he gave him the Glock. I know it was a Glock because Billy told me later. It's a really nice pistol and everyone wants one.'

In a secular society, the courts, not the church, are in charge of delivering justice. Ulrika thought about this often. When public debate was at its storm-iest, she was one of the few people in her position to admit that she could sympathize with the desire for revenge. Retribution had always been a crucial component of the justice system. She had written an article about it, one that had been published in the legal journal *Juridisk Tidskrift*, and she had received some reactions, not entirely encouraging ones, from colleagues she otherwise respected. But she stood by her views.

'It's clear,' she said to her husband, Robert, 'that people will take the law into their own hands if they can't trust the police and the courts. It's important to demonstrate that we're here for them.'

The evidence in the Mehdi Ahmad case was compelling. To be sure, there was no murder weapon, and the two strongest witnesses were related to the victim. But the chain of evidence was strong. The defendant's DNA on the bullets, the technical investigation of the physical evidence found at the chicken factory, the images indicating a serious threat, and the shooter, now deceased, who had, in his first interrogation, named the defendant as instigator. You could hardly ask for more. All she had left to do was decide how to formulate the opinion, and perhaps they would still have to discuss, if only for the sake of appearances, whether Mehdi Ahmad should receive life in prison or a time-limited sentence.

On her desk was a photograph of her three children. In this photo, Matilda was six and had braids and a gap in her upper teeth, and was holding her youngest sister Isabelle in her lap. Isabelle wasn't even a year old yet. The frame was silver, and Oscar was standing beside Matilda with his mouth ringed in chocolate and a crease between his eyebrows. He had been an anxious child. Worried about the way the world was going even before he started school. Ulrika ran her index finger over the photo and opened her desk drawer. There lay her watch, necklace, earrings, bracelet and wedding rings. She put them on, along with the reading glasses she always kept next to her computer. Her vision had begun to deteriorate just after she turned forty; the first time she went to the optician he had thought her worsening eyes were a result of a pregnancy, but that wasn't the case. That had been over ten years ago, and her older kids had moved out by now.

Matilda was a law student in Uppsala, just as Ulrika had been once upon a time, and Oscar was travelling around Asia for eight months with a group of environmental activists whose focus was educating farmers in small-scale sustainable agriculture. It was extremely unclear what Oscar's contributions to these educational efforts might be. Beyond the sad sprouts he had failed to make grow in the kitchen window, Ulrika had never seen him cultivate anything. But he was planning to begin an environmental studies programme in Lund in the autumn. She was glad he'd finally found something meaningful to do; he'd always had such trouble focusing. He started at least two new activities at the beginning of every term. By spring term, he'd have given them up. But he didn't seem to get tired of being environmentally engaged. 'So far,' as her husband cynically added each time she said so.

Only their fourteen-year-old daughter Isabelle was still at home in their turn-of-the-century villa in Rönnviken. Isabelle, with the temper and singing voice she didn't want to acknowledge. She found maths easy but Swedish hard, and wanted to get a tattoo of a sunflower on her wrist.

Ulrika Bonde had had an aquarium when she was little. She'd bought it with her own money, to the extent that the amount deposited into her bank account each month, without her having to do anything in return, could be considered hers. She kept the aquarium in her room; the humming of the little contraption that oxygenated the water sounded like a dishwasher. She had named one of the fish Algvar. Algvar ate the grime that collected on the inside of the aquarium walls, he pressed his open mouth against the thin green layer of algae and sucked it up, silently, one narrow strip at a time. 'I've turned into such a bureaucrat,' Ulrika liked to say. 'Practical, flying under the radar, taking care of crap, my own and others', without complaint.'

How could anyone make any sense of Mehdi Ahmad's actions? Surely not even a priest could explain how anyone could order the murder of a child? The evil, the injustice, then a psalm and God's blessing, please return the hymnal after the service is over, you can send any amount to the collection by electronic transfer.

A *life sentence is the only option*, she thought, turning on her computer. She felt satisfied, almost eager, as she faced her work. It wasn't always an easy job. But sometimes, justice really did prevail.

THE BOYS

Billy and Dogge's final task for Mehdi was simple. All they had to do was go to a building in Öster-malm and throw two hand grenades though a first-floor window. They had been given everything they needed. The address, and the grenades, which were no larger or heavier than a couple of oranges. They wouldn't enter the building, just toss the stuff inside.

Dogge waited by the entrance to the underground. The time Mehdi had told them, the time at which they should throw the grenades, came and went.

One hour later, Billy still hadn't shown up. Dogge called, but there was no answer. He stood in the ice-cold rain, he sat down on a bench, it was wet.

That's where he was sitting when Blue-Boy called.

'Billy isn't here,' said Dogge. 'He didn't come, I tried calling. I can't do it, I don't have the stuff, it won't work, I've called him a thousand times.'

Blue-Boy's voice was calm. At first it sounded like he was talking about the day's lunch specials, fish or meat, vegetarian or vegan. He spoke so softly that Dogge couldn't hear everything he said. But he was too afraid to ask him to repeat himself, and Blue-Boy's voice slowly grew louder. Then he got angry. He was shouting.

'You fucking idiot. How could you be so stupid? How is it possible to fuck up such a simple job?'

He tried to explain. Blue-Boy had to understand.

'I will throw the grenades, I can do it later, but I don't have them. Billy's got them. I'll go get them, and then I'll do it.'

Blue-Boy ignored him.

'It's too late. The guy we wanted taken care of is gone now. Mehdi...' he gave a deep sigh. 'Mehdi's not happy, not happy at all. Look...a little shit like you isn't hard to kill, but I'm going to take my time. You can live without testicles for days. But sooner or later I suppose you'll bleed out.'

Dogge was sobbing uncontrollably now.

'Billy won't answer when I call, I don't know what to do – what should I do?'

'Don't act dumber than you are. Start by tracking down Billy and the stuff.'

Dogge texted Billy, he knew they were never supposed to text, but he had no choice. It wasn't a long message, but he wrote that Billy had to come to the playground, he had to bring the grenades, or else Mehdi would come to his house. He didn't use Mehdi's name, but Billy would understand and it would scare him.

As he waited, he took two tramadol. It was Jill's, he had snuck them one at a time so she wouldn't notice, and he'd saved them for this grenade job. One of them was meant for Billy, but now he didn't need it and Dogge didn't have anything else to take, he had to make his heart stop pounding, he had to stay calm, he had to explain to Billy what he'd done, how serious it was.

Billy was trembling when he showed up.

'I'm cold as shit,' he said. But it wasn't the cold. He tried to laugh, but he wasn't happy.

Dogge had tucked the Glock into his waistband; his shirt was baggy and his coat hid the bulge. Billy's eyes danced around the playground, he turned around more than once, but he hardly looked at Dogge.

You're afraid there might be someone else here, Dogge thought. *But you're not afraid of me.*

'I couldn't come, couldn't get away. You get it, you know how she is.'

As they reached the swings, Billy seemed more exhilarated, less anxious. His words were coming faster. He was spouting stories about school, it was chaos, lots of fights, there was some new guy, Dogge had met him a few times, he had spit in one of the teachers' faces.

'What a pussy, right?' Billy said. 'Just headbutt him if he messes with you, I told him. Spitting is only for if you've got AIDS, do you have AIDS? That's when you spit, get 'em in the eye.'

He laughed again, but he still sounded nervous. Then he sat down on a swing. He pumped his legs into the air. The faint lights made all the edges fuzzy. Dogge looked up at the sky. It had started snowing. Billy shouted from the swing, suddenly happy.

'For real, Dogge. Why did you want me to come? You have to get it through your head that, like...this is history for me, you have to know by now that I wasn't going to do that. I gave *you* the Glock, I told you I was getting out, I'm leaving any day now, you had to know I wasn't going to risk all that just because Mehdi wanted help messing up some stupid guy's apartment.'

Slowly, slowly the first flakes floated to the ground. Dogge watched them fall. He reached out and caught a few, and they melted in his palm. Then he went up to the swing and grabbed the tyre, using his whole body to force it to a stop.

'What did you do with the grenades?' He had to struggle to keep his voice from cracking, to keep from crying. 'What the fuck did you do with them? If you weren't going to do it, why didn't you give them to me? So I could do it? Why don't you give a shit—' His voice betrayed him; he had to stop talking.

Billy slid down and sat in the tyre. His legs brushed Dogge's. He leaned forward and took Dogge by the shoulders. His voice was serious now.

'I'm sorry, Dogge,' he said. 'I'm sorry I – but I panicked. I mean, look. When I left the pizzeria with those damn things in my bag, he stuck them in there just like that, right in my bag. But, like, what the fuck? Those things are so dangerous. One of my mum's cousins has no hands and like no goddamn legs because he picked up a grenade one day when he was playing, there's tons of unsecured grenades in the fields down there, left over from the civil war, and he was only like eight or nine when it happened, and I've seen him when we FaceTime with Mum's family, and, I mean, he looks like a fucking grilled turkey, it's so sick. What would you do if you lost both your hands? So I panicked, you have no idea, I went up to the bridge and dumped them in the bay on my way home. I've never been so freaked out in my life, I thought I was going to shit myself, but I just took them out of my bag and hurled them as far as I could and they didn't float. Look, I wasn't thinking, it wasn't like I planned it, this is what I'm going to do, but you have to understand, I couldn't keep them in my bag, I couldn't fucking take them home, like, keep them under my bed, that would have been nuts. Anything could have happened.'

'You threw them away?'

'Yeah.' Billy sounded annoyed now, tired of talking. 'I'll explain to Mehdi, I swear.'

'You threw them away?'

'Chill out. I'll call him. I'll just tell Mum she's gotta pay, I promise. Or, maybe Dad. He can talk to Mehdi. But I'm getting out of here, you get it, tell me you understand, brother.'

Dogge let go of the swing and backed away from Billy. His mouth was dry.

'But I'm not getting out of here. I will still be here. What am I supposed to do? What did you expect me to do? Maybe your fucking dad will make a deal with Mehdi, but my dad can't, did you ever think of that?'

Billy looked away. He put down his feet and backed up, his butt on the swing.

'Well, you'll figure it out. You can say it was my fault.'

When he'd backed up as far as he could, he hopped onto the tyre again, stuck out his legs, and let the swing carry him.

Dogge started to walk off, heading for the path that led up to his house. He slipped. The rain that had fallen earlier in the day had made the ground damp, and now it was freezing. When he came up behind Billy, he heard him laugh.

'And you'll have money soon, right? Once your grandparents sell the house, you'll have tons of dough. I mean, your family is filthy rich, you can tell by looking at that house. It's one thing that your dad had...' Billy hesitated. 'That he had a lot of, like, bad luck, but now he's dead. They can't just drop you, you're family. Tell them that, they have to see. Family takes care of each other. Then you can pay Mehdi, then you can go wherever you want. You and your mum can move to Majorca, she likes Spain, right?'

Dogge stopped. *Family*, he thought. His head was spinning. There was thunder in his ears. Images of everything Billy took for granted, that Dogge had never even come close to having, flashed through his mind. Billy's sister Aisha, shrieking with laughter as she nabbed Billy's freshly made sandwich, ran into the bathroom, and ate it up as Billy tried to get in. Rawdah, falling asleep with her head in Billy's lap when they watched a movie. Tusse, who always wanted to be close to Billy, even when Billy didn't want him to. Who would sit there in the room with them as they played video games for hours on end and wouldn't even ask if he could have a turn. Billy's mum, who, whenever she got close enough, bent down and pulled him close, pressed her lips to his forehead, cheek, hand. She always knew whether he had showered or changed clothes, what he had and had not eaten, she hugged him even though he didn't want her to, she scolded him, but she never looked at him with disgust, not even when he had done the worst things. Billy had the siblings Dogge never had. The mother he should have had. Billy got to go away, leave Våringe and stay with a relative he'd never met, he would be allowed to live there, just because they were related and relatives take care of each other when times are tough.

'I don't have any family,' he said softly, and turned around. Billy didn't hear him, he just kept swinging in the fuzzy light of the streetlamps.

Dogge raised the pistol, he had loaded it before leaving home, with the bullets he had secretly kept from the day Mehdi taught them to shoot. That had been a good day, a day when he felt strong. Him and Billy, friends forever.

When the swing fell back, and Billy's back and head were at the closest point, he pulled the trigger – twice in quick succession.

'You should have shown up.'

He was still whispering. Billy never listened; if he ever had listened, he had stopped long ago.

'You promised me we would do it, you told me you would. Why didn't you show up?'

As Billy fell off the swing and landed on the ground with a dull thud, Dogge squeezed his eyes shut and fired again, into the night. The whining sound ended with a crack of the whip as the bullets hit the trees.

Only when the gun clicked did he open his eyes again. His hand was buzzing like a limb that's gone to sleep, as if the pistol had been electrified.

I don't have any family. I only have you.

The snow was falling, just as slowly but heavier now, as Dogge began to run.

Far, far away, as fast as he could.

Acknowledgements

Chief Inspector Gunnar Appelgren, for letting me ask a thousand questions at all hours of the day, and for taking the time to read and comment on the manuscript and to help me with the police investigation and understanding how gangs work.

Lillian Aune, Tony Silvernäs and Stefan Antonsen at the Bärby state youth home for allowing me to come for a visit, and for so generously sharing your experiences.

Anders Dereborg, chief judge at Attunda district court, for taking the time to answer my questions over the phone when I was in lockdown in Brussels. Attorney Evin Cetin for detailed discussions about witness protection, Rojda Sekersöz for the beautiful lullaby, Suad Ali (my gifted author colleague) for guiding me when I was naming some of my characters, and my friend Christoffer Carlsson, criminologist and outstanding author, for help making contacts both under- and aboveground.

And deepest thanks to my publisher, Åsa Selling; my agent, Astri von Arbin Ahlander; and my editor, Katarina Ehnmark Lundquist. You read the many thousands of pages that I'm now using to light fires in the tile oven, yet you never gave up hope that I would find my way to the boys' story.

Thanks as well to my dearest friends Mari Eberstein and Måns Hirschfeldt, for reading, sharing opinions, and always seeing what I have missed or ignored.

And to Christophe, Elsa, Nora and Bea. All of the stories I tell are for you.

—Malin Persson Giolito